3

HUMOUR
IN THE WORKS
OF MARCEL PROUST

MAYA SLATER

OXFORD UNIVERSITY PRESS

1979

Oxford University Press, Walton Street, Oxford OX2 6DP

OXFORD LONDON GLASGOW
NEW YORK TORONTO MELBOURNE WELLINGTON
KUALA LUMPUR SINGAPORE JAKARTA HONG KONG TOKYO
DELHI BOMBAY CALCUTTA MADRAS KARACHI
IBADAN NAIROBI DAR ES SALAAM CAPE TOWN

Published in the United States by
Oxford University Press, New York

British Library Cataloguing in Publication Data

Slater, Maya
    Humour in the works of Proust. — (Oxford
    modern languages and literature monographs).
    1. Proust, Marcel — Humor, satire, etc.
    I. Title   II. Series
    843'.9'12   PQ2631.R63Z/   79-40596
    ISBN 0-19-815534-4

Set by Hope Services, Abingdon
and printed in Great Britain by
Billing & Son Ltd.,
Guildford, Worcester and London

ACKNOWLEDGEMENTS

I am grateful to Professor J. M. Cocking and the late Professor S. Ullmann for their valuable comments on the thesis on which this book is based; to Mrs. E. Thornton for typing the original manuscript; and above all to the late Dr. R. A. Sayce for his patient help and unfailing encouragement when I was preparing my thesis. My husband's advice and support have been indispensable throughout the process of composition.

CONTENTS

ABBREVIATIONS OF PROUST'S WORKS

ALR   *A la Recherche du temps perdu*, ed. Pierre Clarac and André
Ferré, 3 vols., Paris, 1954.
When quoting from *ALR*, only the individual title followed by
the volume number is given.

CS I	*Du Côté de chez Swann* (*Combray*)
S I	*Un Amour de Swann*
NPN I	*Noms de Pays: le nom*
JF I	*A l'Ombre des jeunes filles en fleurs*
NPP I	*Noms de Pays: le pays*
CG II	*Le Côté de Guermantes*
SG II	*Sodome et Gomorrhe*
P III	*La Prisonnière*
F III	*La Fugitive*
TR III	*Le Temps retrouvé*

PJ	*Les Plaisirs et les jours*
JS	*Jean Santeuil*
C	*Chroniques*
CSB	*Contre Sainte-Beuve*
PM	*Pastiches et Mélanges*
Corr. gén.	*Correspondance générale*

INTRODUCTION

'La gaîté est un élément fondamental de toute chose' wrote Proust in *JS*. He was using the word *gaîté* in a very wide sense, implying that this stimulus to laughter is present not only in moments of light-hearted merriment, but also, as a latent emotion, at times that we would think of as anything but 'merry'. In this book, 'humour' will serve a similar function. It will be used, for want of a better generic term, to include all the elements that are often subdivided into 'wit', 'irony', 'sarcasm', 'satire', 'farce', 'flippancy', and so on.

Laughter, which to Proust underlies everything, is the unifying feature that links all the types of humour considered in this book. This fact creates its own problems. Any attempt to analyse laughter as the common element in humour is doomed to disappointment (D. H. Monro, in *Argument of Laughter*, points out that 'laughter is one of the unsolved problems of philosophy'). One obvious difficulty that bedevils any attempt to explain humour through laughter is that laughter can be provoked in a context that is anything but humorous. We may laugh with relief, satisfaction, pleasure, or as a reaction against fear, grief, or anger. Proust is hinting at this paradox when he describes the conversation of the melancholy poetess, Mme Gaspard de Réveillon (a character based on Anna de Noailles) as 'd'une gaîté continue'. He implies that laughter and tears are so closely linked that it is impossible to separate them.

A further problem which interferes with our analysis is that laughter is subjective. We are all familiar with the exchange: 'I don't think that's funny.' 'Well, I do.' Proust himself often makes this point. True, when studying humour as opposed to laughter we are not concentrating on a response to a situation but on the inherent nature of the situation. By analysing the common features of humorous situations, philosophers have striven for centuries to find an undetected objective definition of humour, a definitive theory to explain every instance of it.

In their search for an objective definition of humour, philosophers seem to me to suffer from three main drawbacks. First, their formula becomes too general. Some of the features singled out would apply just as well to tragedy. Secondly, they still fail to account for all cases. Thirdly, even if their formula applies, it is not necessarily the most illuminating one for all cases, and it seems perverse to insist on applying it universally. These deficiencies dog the main theories of humour, including the one that I prefer and that I have loosely applied throughout this book.

The first of my criticisms, that of the too-general formula, might be levied against some important observations, which must be made all the same. To begin with, humour is essentially concerned with the human element. Animals and inanimate objects are not funny unless they remind one of human beings. This fact seems important for the understanding of humour. When we think of many of the things we regard as funny—indecency, pretension, small misfortunes, veiled insults, clumsiness—we realize that this emphasis on the human element is also characteristic of tragedy.

Again, humour is almost always concerned with the relationship between two things, between the customary and the unusual, between the permissible and the illicit, between reality and pretence. This fact will form the basis of the incongruity theory that I will discuss later. But this preoccupation with relationships is as characteristic of poetic imagery as it is of humour. This will emerge clearly in the chapter on Imagery, where this point will be discussed at some length.

My second objection was that many so-called characteristics of humour are not applicable to all cases. This is certainly true of several important features. Brevity and conciseness, for example, often seem essential to humour. Freud, in *Wit and its Relation to the Unconscious* made this claim, using the term 'economy'. Proust, as we shall see, can be devastatingly compressed when he is being funny. This fact may perhaps seem surprising to those familiar with the length and elaboration of the normal Proustian idiom. But we cannot pretend that Proust's humour invariably demonstrates Freud's 'economy'. Sometimes his humorous effects can be lengthy and elaborate.

This would invalidate another would-be universal trait, spontaneity, although it often seems to be essential to humour. Certainly Proust's characters may claim that they are being spontaneous when they are trying to be witty. Probably true wit has at least to give the illusion of spontaneity; but wit is only part of humour.

What, then, are the principal theories of humour? The oldest seems to be the degradation theory, already found in Aristotle. He and his successor in this field, Hobbes, claim that the observer of humour must feel superior to the protagonist. More modern theorists like Ludovici and Bain detect a note of condescension, a feeling of degradation, in all humour. And indeed it is certainly true that humorous writers tend to laugh at rather than with their characters, to mock at their absurdity rather than sharing a joke with them on equal terms. I shall have occasion to point this out repeatedly in connection with Proust.

Before discussing this theory, however, it must be said that it fails to account for all aspects of humour. In particular, it cannot explain wit, the sort of humour that makes one admire the humorist's cleverness even as one laughs. Neither does it allow for irrational merriment at nonsense.

Despite these shortcomings, the degradation theory is central to an understanding of Proust's humour. Proust the humorist is a devastatingly critical observer of humanity, whose humour is almost invariably aimed at degrading his characters. Often he goes further and implicitly attacks his characters' real-life prototypes. There is no separate chapter on satire in this book, simply because ridicule is used so regularly to expose the folly of Proust's contemporaries that one could not possibly consider any aspect of humour in his writing without assuming that a satirical element may be involved. Even purely verbal wit can conceal a biting attack. He seems at times to confirm the theory of James Feibleman (*In Praise of Comedy*) that all humour is satire, 'the world as it is contrasted with the world as it ought to be'.

The degradation theory applied to Proust gives us an interesting insight into the extraordinary subtlety of his humour. He uses superiority as a double-edged weapon. He often shows us a superior observer laughing at a hapless victim. Then he suddenly turns the tables and shows us how ridiculous it is that the observer should consider himself superior. The reader assumes he is exempt from this treatment. But even he does not emerge unscathed from a reading of Proust. He is shown how unfounded his smug assumptions were. He will join in the callous mockery of M. Verdurin, failing completely to realize that he is misjudging a fine artistic mind. Proust maliciously leads him up the garden path and then, in the Goncourt pastiche, confronts him with his own error.

On the whole, though, Proust's humour is so complex and subtle that it cannot be fully explained by a degradation theory which postulates a superior observer and inferior protagonists. Where degradation is involved in his writing, it is not always clear who is degraded. He is suspicious of the smug superiority implicit in the degradation of others; indeed, he mocks at all superiority, even, as we shall see, at his own seemingly impregnable pre-eminence as author, incorporating sly digs at himself and at his protagonist, the Narrator, both of whom are far from being the purely superior observers of Aristotle or Hobbes.

Bergson's theory of humour, in his *Le Rire*, is a variation on the degradation theme. To put it briefly, he argues that humour consists in mockery at the expense of something which lacks the elasticity and versatility to adapt to its situation. This lack of adaptability is what he calls 'mécanisme'. Bergson and Proust have several times been compared. And certainly there are numerous examples of Bergsonian rigidity or 'mécanisme' in Proust.

An interesting question that arises in connection with Bergson is the emotional position of the observer. Bergson sees him as essentially detached, uninvolved. Proust, however, as he laughs, often introduces at the same time an element of sympathy or concern for his victims, or at least an awareness of how painful their predicament must be. Indeed, much of his humour is so painful that one can scarcely bear to laugh: sometimes because we are simultaneously put in the position of the observer or the aggressor and the victim; at other times, more subtly, because the humour and the pathos are integral and interdependent.

Bergson goes on to take this theory a step further, and claims that one cannot laugh at oneself. This naturally follows from his belief in detachment, but is perhaps refuted by Proust through the character of the Narrator of *ALR*. This character is intensely self-absorbed. If Bergson were right, he would be incapable of standing back and viewing himself in a ridiculous light. But he does just this, and frequently too. Bergson might have objected that this was not a true case of self-mockery, but that the author was mocking at a chracter he had created. But the Narrator is so excessively realistic that one cannot sensibly postulate that his self-mockery is really something else. Proust combines it with serious treatment of this character, with skilful inter-weaving of past and present personality, and with emotionally charged situations, to create some of his most subtle humorous effects. The case of the Narrator in fact makes one more inclined to agree with William McDougall (*The Theory of Laughter*) that humour is intrinsically a painful subject.

Bergson's 'mécanisme' will also be found in other aspects of humour than the humour of character. Devices like repetition, artificial co-incidence, stylistic quirks like alliteration, clichés in speech, are all artificial, unreal patterns rigidly superimposed on the much more flex-ible pattern of real life and which appear ridiculous as a result. We will see these elements in play when I come to consider style.

I now come to the incongruity theory, the one that I feel is applic-able to most cases, if taken in its widest sense. Almost all examples of humour seem to involve, somewhere, the juxtaposition of two things which do not strictly go together. The nature of this juxtaposition is very variable. Often it is a departure from the norm, as L. W. Kline maintains in *The Psychology of Humour*. The incongruity would then lie in the contrast between what usually happens and what has happened in this case. An example in Proust is when a hostess politely invites a guest to sit down. But the chair she indicates is already occupied. This type of incongruity is closely related to satire. If one contrasts stock stitutions or attitudes with unexpected ones, an underlying criticism of the stock situation may well be suggested.

Where character humour is concerned, incongruity may often reside in the contrast between hypocrisy and sincerity. This is one of Proust's chief satirical preoccupations. He repeatedly emphasizes the contrast between ostensible and real feelings and attitudes, to the detriment of either or both. When his characters mouth conventional condolences with expressions of blithe indifference, it is not clear whether he most deplores the artificiality of the verbal formulae or the indifference of his speakers.

L. W. Kline sees humour as a release from inhibition, which one could view as another form of incongruity—the disparity between the habitual restraints of life and the uninhibited nature of laughter. Incongruity is also the means towards this feeling of freedom—departures from the norm cause an uninhibited response.

The norm, however, persists as an underlying idea. Departures into the realm of pure fantasy, with no connection with the real world, are not funny. There has to be the feeling that the ordinary world has been dislocated, 'smashed out of shape and as it ought not to be', to quote Stephen Leacock (*Humour: its Theory and Technique*).

These reflections on incongruity present a view of humour that is by no means incompatible with the degradation theory. Implicit in this approach is the assumption that the reader is superior, able to pick out the absurd incongruity that may well pass unnoticed by the characters.

But incongruity does not always involve this superior, critical approach. There is a distinct pleasure in linking disparates for the sake of the exercise. When Proust compares a professor to a rose, we laugh because of the ingenuity of finding links between these two seemingly unrelated objects (the old man's wrinkled pink face might not be unlike the crumpled petals of a pink flower). We need not seek for an underlying criticism either of the professor or the rose. This type of incongruity accounts for the linking of disparates that makes us gasp with admiration, the juggling with words, images, and ideas that is a characteristic feature of Proust's humour. We will see examples of it when we come to consider surrealism in imagery.

Poetic comparisons may well be built around the juxtaposition of unlike things. But their task is to prove that unlike things are really alike. A humorous comparison, on the other hand, juxtaposes unlike things to throw the dissimilarity between them into relief. To illustrate this point from Proust with a poetic and a humorous comparison between a young girl and a flower, there is his poetic comparison between a pink hawthorn and a girl dressed up for the *mois de Marie*. The juxtaposition might seem far-fetched; but he carefully introduces it by means of repeated references to the religious and feminine quality of the flowers, until when the young girl in pink finally materializes she seems eminently appropriate. When, on the other hand, he makes a humorous comparison between lilac flowers and young girls, he singles out the fact that lilac hangs from trees, which is clearly totally inappropriate to young girls. And in this case we laugh.

The complex interplay between what the reader knows is appropriate and what he knows is out of place presupposes a rigorous set of unwritten rules or conventions. The effect would be lost if the reader did not immediately realize when such conventions were flouted. When Bloch tells the Narrator that his memories of their recent schooldays together moved him to such a pitch that he wept all night, the reader knows that it is not done to give way to violent emotional outbursts unless under extreme provocation, and laughs at Bloch.

This reliance on accepted convention explains in part the topical character of much humour. The author draws widely on the attitudes of his contemporaries, expecting his readers to know these attitudes as well as he does himself. In the case of Proust, writing more than half a century ago, this fact becomes apparent when we can see him trying to evoke a response that is no longer appropriate. His anti-Semitic jokes, for example, seem painful to a post-Second World War reader. The snobbery of some of his social climbers has lost its bite in a more egalitarian age. But usually his jokes survive because he tends to provide built-in incongruity so that we are able to laugh at least at some of the would-be humorous features. Legrandin's snobbery may seem intrinsically less ridiculous than it might have to Proust's contemporaries; but the incongruity between his ostensible unworldliness and lurking sycophancy still arouses our merriment.

The features singled out here give us some guidelines in our attempt to define humour. One could continue this discussion indefinitely, since the subject is not only elusive but enormous. As Proust says, 'une personne fine [. . .] voit partout du comique'.

To some extent, the emphasis of this book is on the fact that Proust relies for humour not only on large-scale effects, but also on the finest details both of style and of subject-matter. With this in mind, I have concentrated not only on the more conventional subjects for such a study, but also on the most detailed aspect of Proust's writing, that is his style, which I have followed with a description of his broader stylistic effects in a chapter on 'structure'. Imagery is discussed next, as it draws on both style and subject-matter, followed by different aspects of subject-matter itself: character portrayal, and after it the portrayal of one unique and vital character, the Narrator of *ALR*. This character deserves a chapter to himself, since the difference between him and the author is used to provide some of the most unusual humour in the novel. Finally, some of the main subjects that preoccupy Proust are discussed inasmuch as they provide humour. In the Conclusion, general trends in Proust's humour are discussed. In each chapter, except for Chapter 5 (Author and Narrator), I have tried to refer not only to *ALR* but also, where necessary, to Proust's other works. However, the bulk of the material must of necessity come from Proust's masterpiece, and the earlier works in particular are often mentioned to show how they fall short of *ALR*.

In view of the vast masses of material at the disposal of the student of Proust, I have as a rule limited my examples to his work alone. I have also tried to avoid complicating the issue by introducing theories about the nature of humour into the main body of the text. Wherever possible, I have allowed Proust to speak for himself.[1]

---

[1] In this respect I differ from other writers on Proust's humour. For a discussion of their work see my Bibliography.

I
STYLE

Le style n'est nullement un enjolivement comme croient certaines personnes, ce n'est même pas une question de technique, c'est—comme la
couleur chez les peintres—une qualité de vision, la révélation de
l'univers particulier que chacun de nous voit, et que ne voient pas les
autres. (*CSB* p. 559, interview with E.-J. Bois)

Proust considered style to be of paramount importance. It is at the
same time the means whereby the writer's vision is transmitted and the
vision itself. Proust expresses the same idea several times, approaching
the central point from different angles. In one key passage he maintains
that the writer's task is not that of inventor but of translator:

Le devoir et la tâche d'un écrivain sont ceux d'un traducteur. (*TR*
III 890)

The writer must aim for the right word and construction to render his
own thought, just as the translator does for the thoughts of others.
This view leads to a dual standpoint. On the one hand, Proust is imbued
with an almost mystical reverence for style, the writer's one means of
expressing his innermost being. But at the same time, he is rigorously
firm about the actual language used: the ideal style is a combination of
individuality and correctness. In a letter to Mme Straus, he writes:

Chaque écrivain est obligé de se faire sa langue, comme chaque violon-
iste est obligé de faire son 'son' [. . .] Je ne veux pas dire que j'aime les
écrivains originaux qui écrivent mal. Je préfère—et c'est peut-être une
faiblesse—ceux qui écrivent bien. Mais ils ne commencent à écrire bien
qu'à condition d'être originaux, de faire eux-mêmes leur langue. (*Corr.
gén*. VI 93)

Proust's preoccupation with style grew as he matured as a writer. There
are increasing numbers of references to the subject in his letters. His
preface to Paul Morand's *Tendres Stocks* (1921) takes the form of
a discussion on the styles of different writers. The final part of *ALR*
is the richest in discussion of style.

Not only did Proust think style important, he also revelled in it. At
the level of the single word, we see this in the meticulous choice of
adjectives to convey associations. The word 'Parme'

m'apparaissant compacte, lisse, mauve et doux, si on me parlait d'une
maison quelconque de Parme dans laquelle je serais reçu, on me causait
le plaisir de penser que j'habiterais une demeure lisse, compacte, mauve
et douce [. . .] (*NPN* I 388)

And his enjoyment of style also shows in the careful, loving construction of the long, elaborate sentences that are so characteristic of his
writing.

Most critics place a proper emphasis on Proust's style; but relatively
few have seen that humour must be one of its essential features. When
Proust plays with words, he wants not only to describe things, but also
to examine the words themselves. He isolates words or juxtaposes them
with others to produce not only new meanings but also new understanding of the atmosphere of the words. If the atmosphere and meaning
seem accurately expressed through the words, as in the 'Parme'
example, the effect will be poetic. If there is incongruity between the
meaning and the words, the effect will be humorous. This incongruity,
which is a regular feature of Proust's style, tends to be overlooked by
critics in favour of the more poetic element.

A humorous style, then, is principally concerned with the relationship between words and meaning. This might not seem to be invariably
the case: certain words or groups of words are strikingly incongruous
enough in themselves to make the reader laugh. Quite apart from their
contexts words like 'turlututu', 'taratata' or 'patatipatali', all of which
Proust uses, themselves contain a monotonous repetition of sounds
such as one does not expect to find in adult speech. But even in these
straightforward examples, the meaning of the words and their atmosphere underlies our seemingly simple response to their sound. We react
not so much because the words sound silly as because they are imbued
with the aura of the nursery. There are many French words that sound
equally silly in their repetition of vowels, but which do not make one
laugh because their meaning is perfectly serious: *avatar*, *cuscute*, and
so on. In discussing style, therefore, we must always remain aware of
the duality between the words themselves and their content.

Before embarking on a detailed discussion of style, it is worth illustrating the varied effects that can be produced by changing the relationship between words and context, to show how the context enhances
the humorous potential of a word, and how the words do the same for
the context.

Single words can be made to seem amusing almost purely through
their context. A word like *ostrogoth* is not itself funny. But clearly,

in its monotonous vowel-repetition, it has humorous potential. Proust makes Albertine use it in the question she asks when she sees Bloch: 'Comment s'appelle-t-il, cet ostrogoth-là?' (*JF* I 880). By making a young lady use the word to describe a young gentleman on a fashionable sea-front, and by combining it with a colloquial style of speech, Proust sets the word in an absurd context. But although the incongruity is as much one of setting as of vocabulary, it is the word that stands out as humorous.

More often, however, the opposite bias is found, and the style serves to enhance the effect of an amusing context. For instance, Mme Verdurin is so horrified at hearing the name of La Trémoïlle pronounced in her presence that she freezes like a statue. Proust uses stylistic tricks to enhance the absurdity of this reaction:

son front bombé n'était plus qu'une belle étude de ronde bosse où le nom de ces La Trémoïlle chez qui était toujours fourré Swann, n'avait du pénétrer. (*S* I 258)

The resounding nasalized 'o' sound suggest the rounded head of the statue in their roundness of shape and sound. The use of words, too, contributes to the humour of the sentence: the word *fourré* seems much too colloquial for the rest of the passage until we realize that we are here acquainted with what Mme Verdurin is actually thinking, through indirect speech, so that the rather undignified word is at once incongruous and appropriate.

Elsewhere the style does more: it provides the humour in a passage which might otherwise not be amusing. During the course of a serious description of Mme Swann's clothes, we have the following passage:

dans la toilette de Mme Swann, ces souvenirs incertains de gilets, ou de boucles, parfois une tendance aussitôt réprimée au 'saute en barque' et jusqu'à une allusion vague au 'suivez-moi jeune homme', faisaient circuler sous la forme concrète la ressemblance inachevée d'autres plus anciennes [. . .] (*JF* I 619)

Here the humour rests on the purely stylistic device of placing the technical names for types of clothing in an ambiguous position, so that not only their technical meanings but also their vivid original meanings, which for Proust's readers would have been obscured through constant repetition, are brought into play. Odette not only wears tops reminiscent of those known as 'sautes en barque', but she also appears to repress an urge to jump into a boat; not only does she favour curls rather like the ones known as 'suivez-moi jeune homme', but she seems to cast a vaguely come-hither eye at young men, which is inappropriate in view of her present status, but at the same time provides an impertinent allusion to her past career as a *cocotte*.

Sometimes these effects can be exceedingly subtle, hinted at in a single word. M. de Charlus angrily speaks 'd'une voix claquante'. (*CG* II 560.) He seems almost to strike at his interlocutor with his voice. Mme Blatin is 'harnachée d'une toilette' (*NPN* I 397). Her appearance clearly reminds the Narrator of a horse.

Elsewhere, Proust may use style as the serious element in a humorous context. The style then provides a contrast which brings out the potential absurdity of the context. This is a device very frequently used by Proust. For instance, he describes a public lavatory in serious, poetic language, which would leave one perfectly straight-faced if it were an Egyptian mausoleum that were being described; he talks of

la porte hypogéenne de ces cubes de pierre où les hommes sont accroupis comme des sphinx [. . .] (*JF* I 493)

In the discussion of style which follows, the distinction between words, content, and context illustrated by these examples will always be implicit, as an essential vehicle for providing the incongruity which forms·the basis of humorous style.

Most critics who devote some space to Proust's style concentrate on the salient features—the long, rhythmic sentences, the imagery, the balance of ideas. These elements will be discussed; but in an attempt to get to the root of Proust's style I have gone into them in some detail. Proust's eye for stylistic detail is excessively sharp. He even criticizes the use of an unnecessary *en* in an article by Jacques-Émile Blanche (*Corr. gén.* III 126). It seems only appropriate, then, to go into small stylistic details: the extent of Proust's skill can be measured by the way he manages to extract humour from simple words.

I am therefore beginning the discussion of his style with the smallest unit, the individual word, and working up through groups of words and phrases to whole sentences. The larger units of paragraphs and episodes will be discussed in the chapter on structure which follows.

Vocabulary

Proust's awareness of the comic potential of words is revealed above all in the number of ways in which he uses them. He himself sometimes goes into the implications of words in great detail. For instance, he describes at length the reason for Françoise's use of the slang phrase 'et patatipatali et patatipatala', borrowed from her daughter, explaining that she so admires her daughter that she assumes that all her turns of speech, however vulgar, must be admirable, and imitates them (*TR* III 749). We can distinguish between two levels of humour in this example. First, Proust is laughing at the words themselves, at their sound, at their lack of proper meaning, at their childishness. Secondly, he is laughing at the character of the speaker, and at her inordinate desire to emulate people she admires, which makes her lose her judgement. We shall see in the chapter on character that most of Proust's humorous vocabulary is found in recorded speech, and is used to make points about character of the type described here.

But the 'patatipatali' example also illustrates another feature of Proust's humorous use of vocabulary: his intense interest in every facet of a word. He is so aware of the implications of words that he often evolves complex attitudes towards them and their users. His opinion of this sort of baby talk actually evolves as he matures as a writer. In *JS* he clearly considers the use of such onomatopoeic, childish words to be a despicable characteristic. He tells us as much:

'Bravo le tourlourou!' s'écria M. Duroc. A ces mots, Jean ressentit un malaise inexprimable, suivi d'un bien-être délicieux. M. Duroc avait beau être tout ce qu'il était, savoir tout ce qu'il savait, il avait dit cela et Jean ne l'aurait pas dit, ni un être vraiment intelligent. (*JS* p. 442)

In *ALR*, Proust is never as crudely explicit about his attitude. Either he appears to sympathize with the speaker, as in the Françoise example, or he leaves his characters to condemn themselves out of their own mouths simply by their choice of vocabulary. But his implicit attitude remains the same, as can be seen by his choice of characters who use such words: Cottard, Bloch *père*, Mme Bontemps, Brichot.

A different type of humorous word depends for effect not on its sound but on its etymological origins. Proust's characters often combine elements from various words to form new ones: the combinations are often unusual, and sometimes appear to be actual coinages. Proust's attitude to this more learned, skilful use of unorthodox vocabulary is on the whole more lenient. Occasionally we even find a coinage or an unusual hybrid word which seems to be used simply because Proust thinks it witty, and not because its use makes the speaker seem ridiculous. Here again, Proust's attitude has evolved, but in the opposite direction. In *CSB* the Narrator's mother, whom he admires, refers to him as *crétinos* (p. 124 of the Le Fallois edition). Proust's early correspondence abounds in coinages and in words which seem to be part of the special vocabulary of himself and his friends and family. They are used because he (and presumably the recipients of his letters) finds them amusing (the best examples are found in his letters to Reynaldo Hahn, in which we find whole passages of invented words which are often very funny. Here, for example, we have *rébulé* for *réveillé* (p. 84), *moschancetés* (p. 127), and *fastiné*, probably *fasciné* and *fatigué* (p. 232). There are also incomprehensible words such as *guerchtnibels* (p. 187)). But by the time he was writing *ALR*, Proust confined himself almost entirely to using coinages and unusual forms of existing words as a means of casting ridicule on the characters in the novel. It had come to represent a pedantic type of humour, such as makes the speaker appear absurdly pompous. In particular, such words are regularly put into the mouth of Brichot. He calls a man with extreme political opinions a *jusquauboutiste* (*TR* III 728). Here the rather learned suffix *-iste*, which one expects to refer to people with serious preoccupations (*philatéliste, oculiste* and so on), is combined with the very ordinary and colloquial *jusqu'au bout* to make a spuriously scholarly term. Elsewhere, Brichot refers to practical jokes as *pures pantalonnades* (*P* III 202) and describes a character in Molière's *Le Malade imaginaire* as *M. Purgon* [. . .] *de moliéresque mémoire* (*SG* II 891). Most of these words are not actually coinages, but are amusing because they are rare, and much too pompous for ordinary speech.

Brichot is, of course, trying to be funny here, though his heavy humour falls flat. Elsewhere, manipulation of words can be perfectly serious on the part of the speaker. Proust is equally scornful of people who try to compress words, to produce new forms of existing words in order to express themselves more clearly. Here the effect is involuntarily ridiculous, rather than involuntarily unfunny as in the case of Brichot. A good example is the tendency to make verbs out of nouns, which tends to produce a pompous, pseudo-technical impression. In Proust's day as nowadays this tendency was marked, particularly in newspapers. It seems to have attracted Proust's attention chiefly at the end of *ALR*, when he was describing the First World War. This is not surprising, since he must have read the papers with particular attentiveness at this time. At one stage, Proust makes Saint-Loup describe the political situation. He says:

Il aurait fallu [. . .] européaniser la Turquie au lieu de monténégriser la France [. . .] Pourquoi ne pas faire des concessions plus larges à l'Italie par la peur de déchristianiser la France? (*TR* III 761)

The humour rests largely on the contrast between what the speaker intends and what he achieves. Saint-Loup no doubt wishes to express himself as concisely as possible by substituting single words for cumbersome phrases; but the words he uses are themselves so clumsy that they jar far more than a phrase would have done.

Humour derived from single words is closely associated with humour in character portrayal. It is easy to see why. The words are rarely intrinsically funny, but are placed in a context that makes them so. Who placed them there? Did he intend them to be funny? Does one admire him for his wit, or mock at its failure? Considerations like these will be implicit in the humour. It is significant that most of the examples given occur when Proust's characters are speaking.

With groups of words a different type of humour prevails. Here Proust tends to address the reader directly. He gives free rein to his fondness for dense effects when juxtaposing words. For instance, he says of M. de Charlus:

Il avait pris l'habitude de crier très fort en parlant [. . .] Sur les boulevards cette harangue était [. . .] une marque de mépris à l'égard des passants, pour qui il ne baissait pas plus la voix qu'il n'eût dévié de son chemin. *Mais elle y détonnait, y étonnait* [. . .] (*TR* III 799)

In this example the humour is provided by the reiteration of the same sounds so close together in the words *y détonnait, y étonnait*, the meaning being quite unremarkable. It is moreover plain that the sentence has been juggled with here, since the construction is unusual: a transitive and an intransitive verb are juxtaposed as if they were exactly equivalent. A more ordinary construction might have been *elle y détonnait en étonnant les passants* where the humorous sound repetition is absent.

If the words juxtaposed have a particularly rich sound or meaning or both, the resulting phrase is amusing largely because of its density. An instance is Proust's description of the Courvoisiers inviting *laiderons calamiteux* to meet the Princesse Mathilde (*CG* II 469), largely effective because of the elaborateness of the expression (though the fact that it is ugliness that is being described also contributes to the humour).

On a larger scale, many of Proust's sentences consist of similar dense groups of striking words. For instance, he writes:

Les chaises désertées par l'assemblée imposante mais frileuse des institutrices étaient vides. (*NPN* I 397)

It is absurd to use such long words to describe mere governesses, or such pompous terms in a sentence whose subject is empty chairs. Furthermore, the vocabulary contains a contradiction: the governesses are self-important and dignified (*assemblée imposante*), but at the same time pathetic and vulnerable (*frileuse*). Again, the sentence ends on a note of bathos; the structure emphasizes the contrast between the former dignity of the inhabited chairs and their present pointless emptiness.

Elsewhere, the vocabulary simply emphasizes the meaning: but this emphasis may be so strong that the sentence seems overloaded. One may see a slight absurdity in the solemn intensity with which Proust describes the outside of Gilberte's house. The Narrator is not as yet privileged to call on the Swanns. He visits the outside of their house, which is steeped in significance; even the concierge knows that he is

de ceux à qui une indignité originelle interdirait toujours de pénétrer dans la vie mystérieuse qu'il était chargé de garder. (*NPN* I 417)

Here the juxtaposed *indignité originelle interdirait* form an overpowering, forbidding trio, which suggest the exaggerated importance attached by the Narrator to anything connected with Gilberte.

Another technique much favoured by Proust is to juxtapose words that are so different in meaning that they make each other stand out by contrast. Here Proust often achieves a feeling of paradox. There is a genuine paradox in his description of Docteur Percepied. He talks of the Doctor as having a 'réputation inébranlable et imméritée de bourru bienfaisant' (*CS* I 147). Here *inébranlable* and *imméritée* clash; an unshakeable reputation stands firm, and one feels that it should be standing on a foundation of reality; but Proust tells us that it is completely undeserved. There is a further clash between *bourru* and *bienfaisant*, since the former has pejorative, the latter estimable overtones. The symmetry of sound in the two pairs wittily contrasts with the clash in their meanings.

Elsewhere, the impression of paradox is a spurious one. For instance we are told that Swann was very fond of gingerbread and

en consommait beaucoup, souffrant d'un eczéma ethnique et de la constipation des Prophètes. (*NPN* I 402)

The meaning is enhanced by the deceptively authoritative juxtaposition of two unusual words beginning with the same letter in *eczéma ethnique*, which seem at first sight to have a meaningful connection. And always Proust will increase his effects by attention to small details like alliteration, apparent in the above example, more striking when he tells us how the Narrator's grandfather, introduced to his seemingly

Gentile friends, worms their Jewish origins out of them: and Proust makes the grandfather seem far more cunning by consistently using sly sibilants:

si c'était le patient lui-même déjà arrivé qu'il avait forcé à son insu, par un interrogatoire dissimulé, à confesser ses origines [. . .] (*CS* I 91)

A different technique is to build up patterns of ideas with words. By balancing the different components, and fitting them into neat shapes, he produces sentences whose sheer virtuosity makes one smile. Usually, the neat shape of the sentence will be contrasted with an element of falseness or incongruity in the meaning, so that the humour is enhanced by the contrast between the perfect form and the flawed content. For instance, he can use the same part of speech to describe incompatible elements, so that one begins by assuming that their meaning too is equated. An example is the sentence:

la princesse d'Épinay [. . .] *s'extasiait sur son chapeau, son ombrelle, son esprit.* (*CG* II 463–4)

Here, by attributing exactly the same importance in the sentence to the three objects of the verb, Proust establishes a spurious link between them. We are expecting the third object of the verb to be another article of apparel, and automatically equate the wit with the hat and umbrella. In another example of zeugma, the servants at Combray stand at the gate

à regarder tomber la poussière et l'émotion qu'avaient soulevées les soldats. (*CS* I 89)

Finally, we find Proust becoming excited, almost carried away, by words. He enjoys cascading them forth, and laughs himself, partly through amusement, partly through exhilaration. Albertine's famous description of ice-cream contains several such deluges of words, and, although the Narrator says 'Je trouvais que c'était un peu trop bien dit', he admires her, and makes her laugh

et ici le rire profond éclata, soit de satisfaction de si bien parler, soit par moquerie d'elle-même [. . .] (*P* III 130)

Elsewhere the opposite is achieved, and we laugh when he deliberately seeks an effect of monotony, and repeats the same words over and over again. This usually occurs in conversation, and indicates a highly excited state on the part of the speaker. In the case of the Narrator's 'Zut, zut, zut, zut' on seeing a beautiful landscape (*CS* I 155), Proust is making the point that language can be completely inadequate to express emotions. Elsewhere, a character may be unable to use varied speech because he is paralysed by excitement or rage. Morel shouts at his fiancée:

'Voulez-vous sortir, grand pied de grue, grand pied de grue, grand pied
de grue [. . .] Je vous ai dit de sortir, grand pied de grue, grand pied de
grue' [. . .] (*P* III 164)

These repetitions are so automatically ridiculous that one cannot help
but be amused at Morel, or at the young Jean Santeuil's real rage and
anguish when it is expressed in a series of repetitions:

—Je ne la verrai plus, s'écria Jean, je ne la verrai plus? Canailles que
vous êtes tous, je ne la verrai plus, je ne la verrai plus? (*JS* 224)

Proust eliminates such monotonous reiteration in emotionally charged
situations in *ALR*, except when the protagonists are being laughed at.
For the inability to express oneself when one's feelings are strong contains a built-in incongruity between the feelings and their expression
that is bound to seem ridiculous. This is another respect in which he has
evolved between *JS* and *ALR*.

Playing with Logic

Proust frequently makes the reader laugh by calling his attention to an
idea that is so common as to be taken absolutely for granted, and showing that there is no need to accept it. For instance, when in a restaurant
someone makes a comment on the fog,

La justesse de cette pensée frappa le patron parce qu'il l'avait déjà
entendu exprimer plusieurs fois ce soir. (*CG* II 406)

Why, indeed, should one assume that ideas are striking because they are
new and not because they are repeated?

Another example is the reaction of Tante Léonie, when told she will
live to be a hundred:

Je ne demande pas à aller à cent ans, répondait ma tante, qui préférait
ne pas voir assigner à ses jours un terme précis. (*CS* I 70)

One laughs here because of the complex interplay of conventional and
personal interpretations of an accepted phrase. She ought to be
meaning that she does not want to live so long; but at the same time it
is true that most people, like her, do not enjoy the idea that any
specific date is set aside for their death. Most people would be capable
of exactly the same sort of hypocrisy.

Conversely, the author may be more honest than the character, and
may deflate his pretensions with a comment which completely destroys
them. Of Octave it is said that:

il ne pouvait jamais 'rester sans rien faire', quoiqu'il ne fît d'ailleurs
jamais rien. (*JF* I 879)

and of the Directeur of the hotel at Balbec that he uses 'expressions
choisies mais à contresens' (*JF* I 663). In both cases, the second half
of the sentence demolishes the first. A more subtle example is his reference to 'de jolies veuves qui n'avaient peut-être jamais été mariées'
(*CS* I 75). Here Proust implies that he doubts the ladies' right to the
title of widow even as he courteously bestows it upon them.

Proust can use his ruthless logic to point out the looseness of
meaning in accepted language. Sometimes he chooses to ignore the
idiomatic use of a word or phrase and takes it literally. Thus Mme
de Cambremer-Legrandin invites the Narrator to dinner, and adds:

'Vous *retrouverez* le comte de Crisenoy' que je n'avais nullement
perdu, pour la raison que je ne le connaissais pas. (*SG* II 822)

The Narrator is, of course, quite right. Mme de Cambremer's banal
formula, which is meant to be flattering in that it implies that *of course*
he must know her distinguished friend, is in fact inaccurate and hence
ridiculous. The ridicule is greatly increased, however, by the fact that it
is such a trivial speech formula that is being taken literally in this rigorously pedantic way.

Conversely, Proust can be deliberately illogical, as in this description
of the *côté de Méséglise*:

Comme la promenade du côté de Méséglise était la moins longue des
deux [. . .] et qu'à cause de cela on la réservait pour les temps incertains, le climat du côté de Méséglise était assez pluvieux. (*CS* I 150)

This statement seems doubly absurd because it is couched in the form of
a logical syllogism: the first two clauses provide the conditions for the
'logical consequence' which is contained in the third clause. The
absurdity of the final clause is emphasized by the verb *était*. Had Proust
written *semblait*, the sentence would have been much less amusing. The
effect here is further complicated by there being a certain logic in this
very illogicality. If the child Narrator went towards Méséglise only on
doubtful days, it is perfectly natural that he should think of the place
as lying beneath a dull, rainy sky.

Elsewhere, a word is used both idiomatically and literally in a
sentence. For example, Mme de Villeparisis is described in an archaic
idiom as being very intelligent: 'elle tenait *un bureau d'esprit*'. The
Narrator comments:

Quant à moi, sans bien me représenter ce 'bureau d'esprit', je n'aurais
pas été très étonné de trouver la vieille dame de Balbec installée devant

un 'bureau' ce qui, du reste, arriva. (*CG* II 150)

One expects one of Proust's usual jokes at the expense of the pompous idiom, which he would tend to take literally in order to show how it didn't really make sense. He satisfies our expectation when he says that he wouldn't be surprised if he found her at a *bureau*. But then this is exactly what happens, much to the astonishment of the would-be sceptical reader.

Again, Proust uses idioms taken literally to comment on the actual plot of the novel. He describes the progress of the Narrator's one-sided love-affair with Mme de Guermantes as follows:

A ma demande d'aller voir les Elstir de Mme de Guermantes, Saint-Loup m'avait dit: 'Je réponds pour elle.' Et malheureusement, en effet, pour elle ce n'était que lui qui avait répondu. (*CG* II 141)

Here the words of the polite formula are used rather like an ambiguous prophecy: they come true, but not in the sense that it was assumed they had when first they were spoken.

Elsewhere, Proust ironically says the opposite of what he means, as when he describes a trivial event as *quelque événement d'importance* (*CS* I 54). Or again, he describes the obvious as if it were highly special and unusual:

La figure de Traves était la figure d'un homme et sa conversation exprimant par un enchaînement logique des mots, des idées, était aussi d'un homme et en cela avait quelque chose de raisonnable, de commun à tout le monde. (*JS* p. 478)

Here he isolates and comments on characteristics that are so obvious that they deserve no comment whatsoever.

At times, playing with logic seems so important to Proust that it takes first place even when he is analysing very serious subjects. Thus he talks of

ces jaloux qui permettent qu'on les trompe, mais sous leur toit et même sous leurs yeux, c'est-à-dire qu'on ne les trompe pas. (*P* III 278)

This contradiction is a false one, for it equates the two different meanings of the word *tromper*: 'to be unfaithful' and 'to deceive'. Clearly here Proust is subordinating psychological accuracy to stylistic conceit.

In playing with logic in these ways, Proust reveals a special type of humorous awareness. He produces these epigrammatic twists with a flourish. Often the humour is totally irrelevant to the characters involved, a direct comment from author to reader. Proust may be reluctant to pun directly, but here he is quite willing to dazzle the reader with his wit. Where these polished epigrams are used to comment on character, their compression makes them devastating. In the comment on Octave, Proust shows us that this character's whole life is based on a contradiction. This sort of character-sketch is highly economical, and contrasts with the lengthy character-analysis that one habitually associates with Proust.

Juxtapositions

To Proust, comparing two things was one of the writer's main concerns. The nature and extent of his comparisons will be discussed in a later chapter. Here we are concerned with the techniques for comparing things. There are two principal ways of formulating comparisons: either one produces a perfectly balanced parallel or one weights one of the elements at the expense of the other.

If the elements in a comparison are basically incompatible, then an effect of humorous incongruity will be achieved if the sentence is perfectly balanced, as in the following example:

je ne fis qu'un bond jusqu'à la maison, cinglé que j'étais par ces mots magiques qui avaient remplacé dans ma pensée 'pâleur janséniste' et 'mythe solaire': 'Les dames ne seront pas reçues à l'orchestre en chapeau, les portes seront fermées à deux heures.' (*JF* I 445)

At times Proust takes this technique to considerable lengths. For instance, this is how he describes Tante Léonie's bedside table:

D'un côté de son lit était [. . .] une table qui tenait à la fois de l'officine et du maître-autel, où, au-dessous d'une statuette de la Vierge et d'une bouteille de Vichy-Célestins, on trouvait des livres de messe et des ordonnances de médicaments, tout ce qu'il fallait pour suivre de son lit les offices et son régime, pour ne manquer l'heure ni de la pepsine, ni des vêpres. (*CS* I 52)

Here every reference to religion is perfectly balanced with a mention of medicine. The effect is very subtle. First, we are struck by the absurdity of placing such different subjects on a par. Secondly, we are told something about Tante Léonie's attitude: Proust equates religion and medicine because to her they are equally important. Finally, in the process of balancing the two, Proust hints at several comparisons of a different order. A statue of the Virgin is juxtaposed with, and hence, by implication, compared to a bottle, which does indeed have roughly the same shape as an upright figure. The prayer-books and the medical prescriptions are juxtaposed to give the impression of a confused heap of papers. This impression strengthens the feeling that Tante Léonie does not clearly distinguish in importance between her faith and her health.

Elsewhere, Proust has unbalanced comparisons, and produces incongruity by overweighting a trivial element. He describes and juxtaposes Mme Verdurin's eating a croissant with her feelings at learning of the sinking of the *Lusitania*:

Elle reprit son premier croissant le matin où les journaux narraient le naufrage du *Lusitania*. Tout en trempant le croissant dans le café au lait, et donnant des pichenettes à son journal pour qu'il pût se tenir grand ouvert sans qu'elle eût besoin de détourner son autre main des trempettes, elle disait: 'Quelle horreur! Cela dépasse en horreur les plus affreuses tragédies.' (*TR* III 772–3)

Here the two subjects are fairly straightforwardly juxtaposed in the introductory sentence. But in the next sentence, Proust places great emphasis on the smallest detail of Mme Verdurin's breakfast: how she holds the newspaper or dips her croissant in the coffee. It is not until the reader sees her comfortably ensconced, with everything just right, that he is allowed to have her verdict on the tragedy, stated far more concisely than the description of her breakfasting. In this way, Proust indicates the character's attitude to the subject-matter. Mme Verdurin's technique of holding the newspaper is described in detail because it is very important to her that she should be comfortable in bed, and, being a selfish person, she will make sure of her comforts before she even bothers to think of the disaster. It also indicates her hypocrisy, since her actions are selfish, but what she says, even though it is to herself, is conventional and insincere.

Conversely, Proust sometimes places the stress on the more important element in a comparison, and then adds a brief reference to a more trivial subject, which may produce a passing touch of humour in a basically serious passage. There may be a juxtaposition of this kind, perhaps even an unconscious one, in the perfectly serious description of the windows of Saint-Hilaire at Combray:

l'un était rempli dans toute sa grandeur par un seul personnage pareil à un Roi de jeu de cartes, qui vivait là-haut, sous un dais architectural, entre ciel et terre (et dans le reflet oblique et bleu duquel, parfois les jours de semaine, à midi, quand il n'y a pas d'office [. . .] on voyait s'agenouiller un instant Mme Sazerat, posant sur le prie-Dieu voisin un paquet tout ficelé de petits fours qu'elle venait de prendre chez le pâtissier d'en face et qu'elle allait rapporter pour le déjeuner). (*CS* I 59–60)

The effect of the comparison is to degrade the stained-glass windows, but also to ennoble the *petits-fours*, which become imbued with the beauty of their surroundings. The link between banality and beauty is important in Proust, and will be discussed later.

Climax and Anticlimax

It is curiously difficult to isolate an example of a true humorous climax in Proust. Something which we have been waiting for since the beginning of a passage finally occurs, but the climax is at the same time ludicrously disappointing. For instance, Saint-Loup and the Narrator are sitting on the beach, and

nous entendîmes d'une tente de toile contre laquelle nous étions, sortir des imprécations contre le fourmillement d'Israélites qui infestait Balbec. 'On ne peut faire deux pas sans en rencontrer, disait la voix. Je ne suis pas par principe irréductiblement hostile à la nationalité juive, mais ici il y a pléthore. On n'entend que: "Dis donc, Apraham, chai fu Chakop". On se croirait rue d'Aboukir.' L'homme qui tonnait ainsi contre Israël sortit enfin de la tente, nous levâmes les yeux sur cet antisémite. C'était mon camarade Bloch. (*JF* I 738)

There is a considerable build-up of tension here. The speaker gradually becomes more of a person. At first, his presence is indicated merely through *des imprécations*. Then we learn he has a *voix*, and a vivid way of talking (incidentally very like Bloch's, so that had it not seemed so unlikely, the reader might have guessed early on that it was he). He then becomes a person, *l'homme qui tonnait ainsi*, and finally his whole attitude is put into a nutshell: he is *cet antisémite*. This final remark makes it the more shocking when we discover that it is a Jew speaking. But at the same time, the shock has an element of the bathetic about it. In the first place, instead of a violent *antisémite*, all we have is the rather despicable Bloch, merely a *camarade*, not a man powerful enough to *tonner contre* anything with much success. In the second place, to have a Jew expressing anti-Semitic feelings is not a true climax. Instead of a building up to a final crescendo, the passage concludes with a twist.

A truer climax, but one which also contains an element of bathos, is found in the initial description of Odette's attitude towards Mme Verdurin and the *petit clan*. When we first meet her, Odette is *une femme presque du demi-monde*; almost Mme Verdurin's only other female *fidèle* is a woman *laquelle devait avoir tiré le cordon*. Proust explains that Mme Verdurin has indoctrinated these two women to despise the leaders of the aristocracy, with the result that

si on leur avait offert de les faire inviter chez ces [. . .] grandes dames, l'ancienne concierge et la cocotte eussent dédaigneusement refusé. (*S* I 189)

Here there is a true climax in the culmination of Mme Verdurin's process of indoctrination, in the imagined confrontation of the *fidèles* with the aristocrats, ending, as one is expecting, with a triumph for Mme Verdurin. But at the same time, one is brought down with a bump at the realization of how impossible this imaginary triumph would be. Proust has glossed over the true status of Odette and her fellow *fidèle*; but when they are confronted with the aristocrats, he bluntly makes it plain that one is an *ancienne concierge*, the other a *cocotte*: the sort of people that would, in the normal course of events, never have any social contact with the leading ladies of the aristocracy.

It would seem, perhaps, that bathos is more appropriate to humour than true climax. There are in fact numerous examples of bathos in Proust. Sometimes the bathos can be one of style rather than content, as in Proust's description of the historical significance of Bloch's appearance, which concludes:

Il n'est pas, d'une façon plus générale, jusqu'à la nullité des propos tenus par les personnes au milieu desquelles nous vivons qui ne nous donne l'impression du surnaturel, dans notre pauvre monde de tous les jours où même un homme de génie de qui nous attendons, rassemblés comme autour d'une table tournante, le secret de l'infini, prononce seulement ces paroles—les mêmes qui venaient de sortir des lèvres de Bloch—: 'Qu'on fasse attention à mon chapeau haute forme.' (*CG* II 191–2)

In this sentence, Proust prepares us from the beginning for a bathetic anticlimax to Bloch's interesting appearance, by telling us that what he says will be trivial. But while preparing us, he succeeds in building up a serious atmosphere which collapses when Bloch's actual words, the climax of the long build-up, are spoken.

A different way of producing a bathetic effect is to make the reader expect something, and then give him something completely different. Proust makes frequent use of this device. He describes how the Narrator's family are nervous of interrupting their servants during their long lunch-hour; but finally they begin ringing the bell:

quand les coups commençaient à se répéter et à devenir plus insistants, nos domestiques se mettaient à y prendre garde et, estimant qu'ils n'avaient plus beaucoup de temps devant eux et que la reprise du travail était proche, à un tintement de la sonnette un peu plus sonore que les autres, ils poussaient un soupir et, prenant leur parti, le valet de pied descendait fumer une cigarette devant la porte, Françoise, après quelques réflexions sur nous, telles que 'ils ont sûrement la bougeotte', montait ranger ses affaires dans son sixième, et le maître d'hôtel ayant été chercher du papier à lettres dans ma chambre, expédiait rapidement sa correspondance privée. (*CG* II 27–8)

The first half of this sentence works up to a climax, to which the syntax contributes a great deal. Proust prolongs the temporal clause with which he begins the sentence so that the reader is full of expectancy by the time the main clause appears. The main clause is given added prominence by the fact that it is introduced by a series of introductory phrases which make one aware that it is coming: *se mettaient à y prendre garde, prenant leur parti* and so on. This elaborate introduction can, it seems, lead to only one conclusion, the servants will reluctantly return to work. Proust prolongs the illusion as long as possible: in the sentence *le valet de pied descendait* the reader still believes he is going to work, so that the second half of this sentence, in which the contrary conclusion is finally reached, strikes us with the full force of the unexpected. It is interesting that Proust does not stop there. He can no longer rely for his humorous effect on the surprising fact that the servants are not doing what is expected of them. And therefore the actions of the other two servants are amusing in themselves, quite apart from the bathetic effect described above. Françoise both has her cake and eats it: she has the satisfaction of being rude about the Narrator's family while at the same time disobeying them. The *maître d'hôtel* is amusing because of the extent to which he takes his theft of the Narrator's writing paper for granted; and Proust, incidentally, emphasizes this by describing the theft in a subordinate phrase, so that it appears to be a trivial means towards the important end of writing his own letters.

The most frequent technique for producing unexpected effects is, however, to stop at the climax of the sentence, to drop the unexpected like a stone and leave it to sink without keeping the subject afloat by means of added points. For example, the Narrator opens *Le Figaro*, to which he has submitted an article:

J'ouvris le journal. Tiens, justement un article sur le même sujet que moi! Non, mais c'est trop fort, juste les mêmes mots . . . Je protesterai . . . mais encore les mêmes mots, ma signature . . . c'est mon article. (*CSB*, Le Fallois ed. p. 95)

Proust produces similar effects even in serious, poetic passages. For example, at the end of a serious description of rain falling, he adds a humorous touch:

Mais nous ressortions de notri abri, car les gouttes se plaisent aux feuillages, et la terre était déjà presque séchée que plus d'une s'attardait à jouer sur les nervures d'une feuille, et, suspendue à la pointe, reposée, brillant au soleil, tout d'un coup se laissait glisser de toute la hauteur de la branche et nous tombait sur le nez. (*CS* I 150)

In this example, the effect of the end of the whole sentence is a complex one. In the last few words of the sentence, Proust destroys the poetic effect of his description by indicating another aspect of the rain: not only is it beautiful to look at, but it makes you wet. The mood of exalted contemplation is immediately dispelled, and one is left imagining how annoyed the Narrator and his family must be at the raindrops landing on their noses. Many of Proust's most poetic, serious descriptions contain little pinpricks of humour which momentarily deflate the tone and destroy the build-up.

Parts of Speech and Syntax

In the selection which follows, I cannot do more than indicate the scope of Proust's use of syntax and of parts of speech to create humour. The examples given, starting with small grammatical details and moving on to syntax proper, are chosen from thousands available. Indeed, every humorous passage in Proust will be enhanced by the sort of devices mentioned here.

First, the substitution of a singular for a plural can be used to good effect. In a conversation between the Princesse des Laumes and M. de Froberville, we have the following exchange:

—Ah! princesse, vous n'êtes pas Guermantes pour des prunes. Le possédez-vous assez, l'esprit des Guermantes!
—Mais on dit toujours l'esprit *des* Guermantes, je n'ai jamais pu comprendre pourquoi. Vous en connaissez *d'autres* qui en aient, ajouta-t-elle dans un éclat de rire [. . .] (*S* I 339–40)[1]

Here, the witticism depends on the questioning of the use of the plural, and the impertinent suggestion that the singular would be better.

Using pronouns of the wrong person is often enough to produce

---

[1] Proust himself makes a similar joke in a letter to Mme Straus: '—J'ai reçu de Corby cette lettre (il me demande *quelle* Mme Straus! il y en a donc d'autres!)' (*Corr. gén.* VI 145).

humour. The sculptor Ski makes himself seem ridiculously affected by talking of himself in the third person:

'oui, parce que Ski aime les arts, parce qu'il modèle la glaise, on croit qu'il n'est pas pratique [. . .]' (SG II 874)

Curiously enough, however, addressing an interlocutor in the third person is rarely mocked at in Proust. This is partly because the servants normally address their superiors in the third person, so that there seems little point in singling this custom out unless it is abused, as for instance in Aimé's letter:

'Monsieur,

'Monsieur voudra bien me pardonner si je n'ai pas plus tôt écrit à Monsieur' [. . .] (F III 515)

Elsewhere, Proust makes his most moving characters in their most intimate moments address each other in this way. The Narrator's grandmother, for instance, expresses her tenderness for her *petite souris* in the third person (*JF* I 669). The device is, however, potentially absurd because it is one used by adults when talking to small children; even in serious instances of it, therefore, we may smile at its babyish overtones.

Using the wrong gender is also an intrinsically humorous device. The French language lends itself to subtle manipulations of gender. M. de Charlus is not being inaccurate when he refers to a tram-driver as *quelque curieuse petite personne* (*SG* II 610). Indeed, he later refers to la petite personne, dont nous ne parlons au féminin que pour suivre la règle.

Nevertheless, the fact remains that the phrases *petite personne*, *jeune personne*, *une beauté*, used to describe this tram-driver, are, by accepted usage if not by rule, confined to descriptions of females: M. de Charlus's use of them here is an impudent indication of his homosexual outlook.

The tense of the verbs Proust uses can also contribute to the humour if there is an incompatibility between the tense and the meaning. For example, when we first meet the Verdurins we are told that their *soirées* are essentially spontaneous in character:

Les Verdurin n'invitaient pas à diner: on avait chez eux 'son couvert mis'. Pour la soirée, il n'y avait pas de programme.

Proust then proceeds to imply that this is not true by describing these 'impromptu' soirées in the continuous past tense, implying that what is described occurred habitually, so that there *was* in fact a programme:

Si le pianiste voulait jouer la chevauchée de la *Walkyrie* ou le prélude de *Tristram*, Mme Verdurin protestait, non que cette musique lui déplût, mais au contraire parce qu'elle lui causait trop d'impression. (*S* I 189)

In general, Proust places considerable emphasis on verbs. He draws our attention to Flaubert's use of active verbs for inanimate objects to make his descriptions more vivid and interesting (*CSB*, 'A Propos du "style" de Flaubert' p. 589). He himself often uses the same technique, for instance in describing the hotel room at Doncières:

la draperie fit entrer un silence sur lequel je me sentis comme une sorte d'enivrante royauté; une cheminée de marbre; [. . .] me faisait du feu, et un petit fauteuil bas sur pieds m'aida à me chauffer [. . .] (*CG* II 83)

The humour here lies in the unusual idea, conveyed entirely through the verbs, of someone being literally waited on by furniture.

Elsewhere, Proust uses the opposite of Flaubert's technique, and has passive or inanimate verbs to describe animate objects and people. For instance, Mme Verdurin several times becomes as rigid and as motionless as a marble bust, simply in order to avoid hearing something disagreeable. At one stage this image is much enhanced by her speech being described using verbs which might indeed have been applied to talking marble:

Mais le marbre finit par s'animer et fit entendre qu'il fallait ne pas être dégoûté pour aller chez ces gens-là, car la femme était toujours ivre et le mari si ignorant qu'il disait collidor pour corridor (*S* I 259)

Here the first verb *finit par s'animer* suggests the effort that has gone into bringing the marble to life. It also enables Mme Verdurin to speak without turning back into a flesh-and-blood woman: she is still marble, but talking marble now. The second verb *fit entendre* manages to make sounds come from the statue without describing any movement or even volition on its part: one might have used the expression for chimes coming from a clock.

The actual clauses of a sentence have considerable humorous potential. In particular, Proust puts the subordinate clause to good use. The implication is normally that its contents are in some way less important than the main clause of the sentence. If the opposite is true, the effect can be very amusing. An example is the mad rush of the gardener's daughter to see the soldiers pass:

Quelquefois j'étais tiré de ma lecture, dès le milieu de l'après-midi, par la fille du jardinier, qui courait comme une folle, renversant sur son

passage un oranger, se coupant un doigt, se cassant une dent et criant:
'Les voilà, les voilà!' (*CS* I 88)

Here, the main clause merely tells us that the Narrator was disturbed by the girl while he was reading. All the violent events that follow seem to be less important to him than the initial disturbance.

A particular type of subordinate clause or phrase can make its own specific contribution to the humour. For instance, Proust may use a concessive clause or phrase where no concession should be implied in the meaning. Bloch goes towards Rachel to congratulate her on a poetry recital,

passant sinon sur le corps du moins sur les pieds de ses voisins. (*TR* III 1001)

The concessive phrase serves two purposes here. Ostensibly, it makes a ludicrous point in Bloch's favour: although he did tread on his neighbours' toes, things are not as bad as they might have been, since he didn't tread on their bodies. At the same time, the concessive phrase enables the reader to visualize the latter as a possibility: although Proust specifically states that Bloch did *not* walk over people's bodies, the image of him doing so is suggested. A further element of humour is provided by the fact that the phrase *passer sur le corps* is a military one meaning to trample over or ride down: the military connotations are absurdly unsuitable in the context of a poetry recital, with all their overtones of physical violence and brutality.

Many other syntactical forms are used humorously. Interrogation can produce various effects. It is rather a brusque form that can break the continuity of the atmosphere. Cottard exclaims in the middle of a *soirée*: '*Où ça, un baron? Où ça, un baron?*' (*SG* II 912), and the explosiveness of his question cuts across the polite atmosphere. Cottard's questions recur throughout the novel as instances of his lack of social know-how (see, for instance, *S* I 202, 216).

A different type of interrogative is the rhetorical question. This again is potentially a humorous form: it seems absurd to ask a question when you don't expect an answer. Again, it is a device closely associated with rhetoric, and hence with a pompous tone of speech. Proust relies on these two underlying features in examples such as the following:

on chercha en vain le philosophe norvégien. Une colique l'avait-elle saisi? Avait-il eu peur de manquer le train? Un aéroplane était-il venu le chercher? [. . .] Toujours est-il qu'il avait disparu sans qu'on eût eu le temps de s'en apercevoir, comme un dieu. (*SG* II 975–6)

There is considerable incongruity between the triviality of the event and the pompous thoroughness of the theorization about it, and also beween the different hypotheses produced as explanations. By couching these incompatible elements in the same syntactical form, Proust suggests that he sees no difference between them, as well as producing an atmosphere of measured pomposity that is appropriate to some, inappropriate to other elements.

An equally pompous syntactical form is the invocation, a device which normally occurs during conversations. Sometimes the invocation can be perfectly acceptable in itself, but can appear ridiculous because of the circumstances. For instance, Françoise says:

Ah! Combray, quand est-ce que je te reverrai, pauvre terre! (*CG* II 18)

a phrase which would provoke no amusement if it formed part of a classical tragedy, but which seems a little incongruous when put into the mouth of an old cook, sitting digesting a large lunch in the company of a valet.

Elsewhere, an exhortation can itself contain incongruous elements. Thus Brichot, when told by Cottard not to mention something to Mme Verdurin, replies:

—Soyez sans crainte, ô Cottard, vous avez affaire à un sage, comme dit Théocrite. (*SG* II 901)

The pompous exhortation is reminiscent of and alludes to classical literary style; Cottard's pedestrian name is eminently inappropriate in such a context.

Interjections have a slightly different effect. They tend to produce an atmosphere of heightened excitement, which can appear inappropriate in the context. Cottard's interjection seems far too violent for a trivial situation:

'Cré nom, s'écria le docteur, ma femme a oublié de faire changer les boutons de mon gilet blanc'. (*SG* II 893)

Syntax in a broader sense also contributes to the humour of style. At times the construction of a sentence can seem amusing not so much because specific devices are used as because the form of the sentence echoes the meaning. A disorganized sentence is used to describe a confused situation. For instance, Proust describes the Narrator's first morning at Balbec as follows:

Mais le lendemain matin!— après qu'un domestique fut venu m'éveiller et m'apporter de l'eau chaude, et pendant que je faisais ma toilette et essayais vainement de trouver les affaires dont j'avais besoin dans ma

malle d'où je ne tirais, pêle-mêle, que celles qui ne pouvaient me servir
à rien, quelle joie, pensant déjà au plaisir du déjeuner et de la promenade, de voir dans la fenêtre et dans toutes les vitrines des bibliothèques,
comme dans les hublots d'une cabine de navire, la mer nue, sans
ombrages [. . .] (*JF* I 672)

Here the feeling of rather aimless excitement and the disorientation of
one's first awakening in a new setting is echoed by the awkwardness of
the sentence. In particular, by means of rather jerky phrases, we are
given an impressionistic description of the Narrator searching through
his suitcase for clothes, pulling out first one thing then another. When
he suddenly exclaims 'quelle joie' we assume that he has found the
garment he has been looking for. We continue to think this during the
interpolation about his anticipation of breakfast, and become mystified
when we realize that his joy is in fact caused by something he can see
in all the windows. We do not realize until we have been kept in
suspense for several phrases that this is the sea.

Elsewhere, a sentence may be mystifying without necessarily
echoing the meaning. An example mentioned earlier is a description of
what the Narrator sees on a walk:

Si je levais la tête, je voyais quelquefois des jeunes filles aux fenêtres,
mais même en plein air et à la hauteur d'un petit étage, çà et là, souples
et légères, dans leur fraîche toilette mauve, suspendues dans les feuillages, de jeunes touffes de lilas se laissaient balancer par la brise sans
s'occuper du passant qui levait les yeux jusqu'à leur entresol de verdure.
(*CG* II 157)

Here the actual comparison between lilac and young women is not
particularly unexpected. The reader is already accustomed to Proust's
comparing flowers to girls, and indeed, lilac has previously been compared to a group of young houris (*CS* I 135). But Proust has made the
transition between talking of girls to talking of lilac without one realizing it; thus when one reads that what one thinks are young ladies are
suspendues dans les feuillages, one has a picture of girls hanging from
trees, which comes into perspective in the next clause when one realizes
that he is talking of flowers. The mystification is in itself amusing; but
the sudden explanation of the mystery makes the whole sentence funny
because the reader has been obliged to perform mental acrobatics which
lead to what he finally sees is a perfectly reasonable conclusion.

Taken as a whole, one of the most striking features of Proust's humorous style is its repeated use to make a critical comment or create a

derogatory attitude in the reader. In description he subtly criticizes his subject-matter by making us see its ridiculous side. He consistently deflates subjects that we would expect to take very seriously: a poetic description of rain-wet leaves or the tragic sinking of a great ship. Sometimes he seems to be parodying his own style, when a lyrical description suddenly dissolves into ridicule.

With characters' speech, the overall effect, too, is disparaging. We are given the spurious impression, by *ALR* at least, that Proust is allowing his characters to speak for themselves; if they say ridiculous things it is their fault, not Proust's. But we must remember that it is Proust who has created them, selected the words they speak, omitted almost every stylistic feature we might have admired or twisted it to produce effects the speaker never intended.

The initial impression given by the humorous element in Proust's style is the opposite of poetic: here his sharp, observant eye, his awareness of detail are paramount. But Proust's humorous style also gives us an insight into his style as a whole. If we examine any passage, however serious, in the same sort of detail, looking for the effect of syntax, sentence-structure, even of single words, we can see the same lucid attention to detail, the same sharp awareness of tiny effects, that we have witnessed here.

A final point worth noting is that most of the examples used here are taken from *ALR*, and not from Proust's earlier works. This is because the humorous element in Proust's style was far less developed in his earlier works. Apart from the *pastiches*, there is hardly any stylistic humour in *PJ*: in *JS* and *CSB*, as has been shown with reference to a few examples, the humour is far less skilful than in later versions of similar episodes. The obvious conclusion is that Proust's sense of humorous style developed later than many of his other qualities. Indeed, as Mr Michihiko Suzuki shows, many of the humorous elements in *ALR* itself were actually written in at quite a late stage in the composition of the novel (*Bulletin*, 1961, pp. 387-91). Mr Suzuki puts forward the theory that humour requires detachment on the part of the author, and that the younger Proust was too involved with the people and the subjects he was describing to be able to see the funny side very clearly. And it is certainly true that many of the examples quoted in this chapter show careful, lengthy exploration of comic possibilities. Proust strikes one as a craftsman of humour: he is doing the job properly, unhampered by considerations of haste or by the desire not to offend people. Such writing probably emerged from the later part of his life, when he lived for his novel alone, not from his earlier, more hurried and active existence.

II
NARRATIVE TECHNIQUES AND STRUCTURE

Any joke-teller knows that the effect of a joke depends almost more on how it is told than on its content. Proust himself shows us Saniette making exquisitely delicate jokes which fall flat simply because his narrative technique is not arresting enough to make his audience want to listen.

Not only actual jokes, but humour in general benefits from skilful techniques of narration, and Proust's narrative is frequently manipulated to produce particular effects. Here we are limited to discussing the techniques that actually produce humour. These vary from devices of capital importance, such as the division of 'je' into Protagonist and Narrator, to the finer details of the construction of a particular episode.

After a general assessment of the importance of structure in Proust's humour, we must take a detailed look at his use of various types of humorous device. The material has been divided into two sections which represent two distinct categories. First, Proust uses various techniques for presenting his material in a humorous light. How he describes an effect clearly determines the humorous impact. Secondly, what he describes must be considered, for there are many examples of the inclusion of potentially amusing elements, such as coincidence, far-fetched links between people, exaggeration and repetition.

Finally, the relationship of the comic element to the rest of the narrative must be considered. How are the comic scenes introduced? How does the humorous element combine with the serious in the narrative? These questions will form the conclusion of this discussion.

General Considerations

'L'échafaudage fait partie de l'œuvre, la vision de Proust a créé sa propre technique', writes Louis Bolle.[1] The individuality of the structure of *ALR* has escaped nobody. But B. G. Rogers has shown that

---

[1]*Les Lettres et l'absolu*, Geneva 1959.

many of Proust's basic narrative techniques were already present in *PJ*, although others did not evolve till *ALR*.[1] Rogers singles out two basic trends in Proust's early writing:

the one consisting of reflexions, aphorisms and general conclusions in the manner of La Bruyère [. . .] the other comprising all the traditional preoccupations of the novelist, with conventional attitudes and techniques which place the ordering of a fictional story about comment and observations. (pp. 10–11)

Of these trends, the first is very important for humour, for it involves detachment on the part of the author, and detachment is a frequent element in humour.

In *PJ*, Proust was already using the rudiments of the techniques that produce the humour in *ALR*. The detachment which enables him to generalize wittily and to produce humorous anecdotes and reflections is already present as whimsical asides to the reader:

Il y a, paraît-il, dans la province, des boutiquières dont la cervelle enferme comme une cage étroite des désirs de chic ardents comme des fauves. (*JS* p. 44)

or as comparisons which show an early awareness of the humorous potential of imagery:

La malveillance de chacun d'eux exagérait d'ailleurs bien contre son gré l'importance de l'autre, comme si l'on eût affronté le chef des scélérats au roi des imbéciles. (p. 97)

At the same time, Proust has passages in which the sustained humour is reminiscent of the great comic scenes in *ALR*. 'Un dîner en ville', in particular, contains the mixture of close observation and implied judgement that one later associates with Proust's humorous character portrayals. The description of a fringe member of the aristocracy contains these lines:

Portant toujours les mêmes raisins, sa coiffure était invariable comme ses principes. Ses yeux pétillaient de bêtise. Sa figure souriante était noble, sa mimique excessive et insignifiante. (p. 99)

Compared to Proust's mature writing, there is perhaps more comment and less observation here; but the difference is one of degree rather than of kind. And, indeed, Proust will remember this passage when he describes the headdress of Mme de Cambremer (*S* I 328).

In *JS*, Proust's first full-length work of fiction, there are several points to be noted. First, Proust already seems to have adopted the technique he uses in *ALR*. He tends to describe particular episodes

---

[1] *Proust's Narrative Techniques*, Geneva 1965.

with an overall humorous or serious tone. The introduction to *JS* is generally lighthearted. We have the naïve admiration of the two young devotees of C., C's relationships with the local people and so on. In fact, the introduction seems inappropriate to the novel, which takes itself much more seriously. In the novel itself, the Mme Cresmeyer episode strikes one as amusing on the whole, while Jean's vocation and the problems surrounding it do not. This technique reappears in *ALR*. We remember the first meeting between M. de Charlus and the Verdurins as amusing, the Narrator's journey to Venice as serious. But both in *JS* and in *ALR*, the overall atmosphere does not prevent Proust from adding the odd inappropriate touch, serious references to the genius of C. in the introduction to *JS*, humorous conversations between the Narrator and his mother on the way home from Venice.

Another way in which Proust has evolved between *PJ* and *JS* is in his ability to reproduce humorous dialogue. In *PJ* the characters hardly speak, and never say anything witty or ridiculous. By *JS*, we have the absurd conversation of Rustinlor, an older prototype of Bloch, or of M. Duroc, a younger version of M. de Norpois.

But the greatest difference between *ALR* and the earlier fiction is that the later novel is conceived as a whole, while *JS* seems to represent a groping search for a suitable form. The sense of purpose behind the structure of the whole of *ALR* is bound to affect the humour. Often, the humour is vital to the structure as a whole, as will be shown with reference to the *coup de théâtre* at the end of the novel. Elsewhere, the humour serves to build up suspense (for instance in the increasing references to M. de Charlus's homosexuality, which the Narrator naïvely fails to understand), to increase the poignancy of a tragic moment (M. de Charlus is ridiculed just when Morel rejects him), to provide relief from tension like the Porter scene in *Macbeth* (M. de Guermantes is brought in while the grandmother is dying) or to provide a clash between atmospheres which make both stand out sharply (the grandmother's stroke occurs after a comic scene). Elsewhere, humour is used as the best way of making a point about a character or driving home a general reflection. Only rarely does it seem gratuitous or superfluous, involving anecdotal episodes or characters who appear only once or twice. The fact that humour is closely interwoven into the structure, not superimposed on it, has several effects. First, the humour is more complex. To put Cottard next to Odette is to juxtapose a cartoon to a Botticelli; but Cottard is not simply a caricature, he is a *fidèle*, a doctor, a husband and a friend. Secondly, the way is open for sudden changes of standpoints in which a serious episode is 'unmasked' and shown to be comic, or vice versa. Proust may seem deeply involved with the subject-matter, only to stand back from it suddenly to make a humorous generalization. Conversely, he may seem to take out a quizzing-glass in the middle of a serious passage, and observe his material with a close, impertinent scrutiny. Finally, the humour itself is taken more seriously, since we become aware that it may be used to make a serious point later on.

Techniques of Presentation

'Toutes les scènes que je vous raconte, je les ai vécues', wrote Proust (*JS* 490). Any narrative based on reality consists in origin of an innumerable series of details, from which, as Tristram Shandy found to his cost, the writer has to select the relevant ones. The straightforward way of telling the story is to choose these facts and present them in order of occurrence. This is clearly the simplest device the writer has at his command, since he need not alter the actual material. But although it is simple, it provides Proust with scope for creating a variety of humorous effects.

For Proust does not always select the most obvious elements for his narrative. He elaborates at length on a minor, barely relevant point, perhaps creating a momentary impression of woolly-mindedness. Conversely, he can make the narrative seem neater, more logical and self-contained than it could ever really be. Most important, he can eliminate large sections of narrative, linking widely disparate elements.

First, we have the rambling, lengthy technique, giving the impression that Proust has included far more detail than is strictly necessary. The effect is often remarkable simply because of the skill involved in bringing the reader back to the point through a maze of indirectly relevant or seemingly irrelevant allusions. For instance, Proust tells us at one stage that Françoise's vocabulary has altered for the worse, and then goes back on his tracks to give a copious and seemingly meandering account of the process (*P* III 154-5). Proust begins by telling us that Françoise's daughter has had a bad influence on her vocabulary. He then shows us the two women standing in the Narrator's room conversing privately in *patois*; then their righteous indignation at his actually beginning to understand their secret language, their subsequent renunciation of *patois* and their conservations in increasingly bastardized

French bring one progressively back to the beginning, and Proust repeats his original point. But there are also hypotheses about the meaning of the *patois* word *m'esasperate*, the inevitability of any curious listener's learning a foreign language that is frequently spoken in his hearing, and Françoise's scorn for the Narrator's attempts to speak *patois*: these are all incidental details. Nevertheless, they are so cleverly incorporated into the narrative that one smiles at the sheer skill of the performance. From digression to digression, one is brought back to the point of departure without realizing one was getting there: Proust has achieved a *tour de force* comparable to that of the Narrator's father when he brought the whole family, completely lost, face to face with their own garden gate (*CS* I 115).

Conversely, Proust may present his material neatly, concisely, and shortly. Brevity, the soul of wit, is an almost essential feature of humorous anecdote, unless, as in shaggy-dog stories, one is deliberately using lengthy narrative for a particular purpose. Sometimes it actually provides the humour, when the subject-matter deserves much more elaborate treatment, so that there is an incongruity between the elaborate subject and the cursory way in which it is expressed. Proust describes a complex situation in a few words, as if that was all there was to it. Of M. Bontemps's marriage he says:

Sa femme d'ailleurs l'avait épousé envers et contre tous parce que c'était un 'être de charme'. Il avait, ce qui peut suffire à constituer un ensemble rare et délicat, une barbe blonde et soyeuse, de jolis traits, une voix nasale, l'haleine forte et un œil de verre. (*JF* I 512)

Clearly the whole process of Mme Bontemps's falling in love with this attractive but unprepossessing suitor is a much more complex one than these two sentences allow. It is certainly not this list of superficial attributes that caused her to marry him for love. Again, M. Bontemps's salient features, though they are all relevant, do not fit together comfortably in a list, since some are attractive, some not. The compression also makes this list of characteristics amusing in another way: one is told what people find attractive in M. Bontemps; there is no room to tell one why. The reasons for liking a fair, silky beard are obvious; the reasons for feeling attracted by a glass eye are highly obscure. Had Proust gone on to explain, as he does with M. Bonami in *JS*, that a physical disability gives a man a distinctive personality and a distinguished air, the humour would have been of a different order. One would have been amused by the preferences of women, and not by the narrative technique.

Brevity and length can be combined to create a contrast. Swann's love for Odette is described from Swann's point of view, with a wealth of poignant detail. The description is suddenly interrupted to give M. Verdurin's view summed up in a single sentence: 'Je crois que ça chauffe' (*S* I 226). M. Verdurin's statement is amusing in itself as an expression of a pedestrian and irreverent attitude to romance. But the greater part of the humour lies in the contrast between Swann's painstaking analysis of every aspect of his love and M. Verdurin's crude and summary attitude towards it. This contrast is brought out through the difference in the methods used to describe the two attitudes. And as well as making a humorous point, Proust is here demonstrating the loneliness of the individual, whose opinions and feelings are not echoed by those around him.

The sequence of events in a narrative passage need not be treated in a homogeneous way. Certain events can be examined at length, others briefly sketched in. If the content is at odds with the technique, a humorous effect may be achieved. Proust may discuss a relatively minor element in considerable detail, and merely mention a much more important point. An example is the account of the Narrator's brief passion for Gisèle. They meet, and the Narrator, dazzled by her golden hair and blue eyes, falls in love with her immediately. He remembers having seen her before, and decides that she must be as attracted to him as he is to her. His interest in her is evident enough to make Albertine jealous, with reason, since he decides to accompany Gisèle to Paris. She is due to leave that evening, and he makes elaborate plans to meet her on the train. During the journey to the station he imagines what his meeting with her will be like. At this point, Proust suddenly breaks off the narrative, and takes it up at a later point in the story:

Quelques jours plus tard, malgré le peu d'empressement qu'Albertine avait mis à nous présenter, je connaissais toute la petite bande du premier jour, restée au complet à Balbec (sauf Gisèle, qu'à cause d'un arrêt prolongé devant la barrière de la gare, et un changement dans l'horaire, je n'avais pu rejoindre au train, parti cinq minutes avant mon arrivée, et à laquelle d'ailleurs je ne pensais plus) et en plus deux ou trois de leurs amies qu'à ma demande elles me firent connaître. (*JF* I 890–1)

Here the narrative technique has produced a humorous effect. Proust has told us the outcome of the story briefly and in parentheses, as if it were an incidental point not worth mentioning, contrasting the elaborate build-up with an understressed climax. The story in itself, if told straightforwardly, would not have seemed particularly amusing: on other serious occasions the Narrator falls briefly in love with a girl whom he forgets afterwards (cf. the Mme de Stermaria episode, *CG* II 383–95, and his brief interest in a young *crémière*, *P* III 139–44).

Finally, whole sections of narrative can be omitted. Talking of Flaubert, Proust writes:

A mon avis la chose la plus belle de *l'Éducation Sentimentale*, ce n'est pas une phrase, mais un blanc. (*CSB*, 'A Propos du "style" de Flaubert' p. 595)

Proust, like Flaubert, compresses his narrative in places, eliminating intermediate elements and juxtaposing things which in reality should be separated. This technique can often bring out a humorous connection between the juxtaposed passages which might otherwise be lost in the intervening material. Such effects are achieved on all sorts of scales. On a small scale, a few intermediate words may seem to be omitted. For instance, we have the following passage, in which Cottard is horribly rude to his wife:

Mais son sourire devint vite triste, car le professeur, qui savait que sa femme cherchait à lui plaire et tremblait de n'y pas réussir, venait de lui crier: 'Regarde-toi dans la glace, tu es rouge comme si tu avais une éruption d'acné, tu as l'air d'une vieille paysanne.'
—Vous savez, il est charmant, dit Mme Verdurin, il a un joli côté de bonhomie narquoise. (*SG* II 962)

Apart from the grotesque rudeness of Cottard, and the falseness of Mme Verdurin's opinion of him, there is no transition between the insult and ludicrously inappropriate compliment paid to the insulter. Normally, one would expect a little more introduction to Mme Verdurin's remark: we are not told whom she is addressing and do not even know that it is she who is speaking until the impact of her remark has had its effect.

This technique of juxtaposition can also be used on a larger scale. For instance, the fact that people's opinions can change and that the same characteristics can be admired at one stage, ridiculed at another, is put into a nutshell by the close juxtaposition of people's ideas at different times. Such ideas may have taken years to evolve; but the process in the novel takes just one page: at one stage Swann is admired; later he is despised:

'Il n'est pas régulièrement beau, si vous voulez, mais il est chic: ce toupet, ce monocle, ce sourire!' (*S* I 319–20)
and later

'Il n'est pas positivement laid si vous voulez, mais il est ridicule; ce monocle, ce toupet, ce sourire!' (p. 320)

The effect of this juxtaposition of contradictory opinions is much increased by almost exactly the same words being used to make Swann seem praiseworthy or contemptible. This technique helps to make a whimsical implied comment on the fickleness of human judgements and the shallow grounds on which they are based.

On a still larger scale we find the same technique. The contrast between the youthful aristocrats and their final travesty, 'disguised' as old people, is given its full impact because the twenty years it takes them to age are skimmed over almost without a mention: we know that the Narrator has retired from the world, and, like him, we fail to notice the passing of time during those twenty years. Without this technique, the humorous contrast between youth and old age, as well as the serious reflections involved, would be blurred. (See *TR* III 920 ff.)

The next technique to be discussed involves more manipulation of material, although still on a fairly simple level. This is the alteration of the normal order of presentation.

In this respect, the writer is usually at an advantage: he knows what the end of his story is going to be. This gives him enough control over his material to produce relevant facts not when they might logically be expected but when they are likely to make the most impact. Proust often manipulates the order of his narrative for humorous purposes. He may withhold an essential fact till late in the narrative, so that it retrospectively colours all that came before it. He can use this technique in three basic ways. First, he can hint at the future revelation, causing the reader to feel mystified and expectant until the truth is finally revealed. Secondly, he can leave the reader blissfully unaware that anything is wrong until the truth suddenly dawns. Thirdly, the reader may be in the know, and it may be the characters that are unaware of an essential fact. I shall consider these three techniques in turn, naming them respectively *Anticipation*, *Surprise*, and *Dramatic Irony*. Discussion of Proust's use of these three devices will be followed by that of two others: the narrative can be allowed to emerge in fragments, each one contributing to the gradual building-up of an effect. Secondly, and conversely, the effect can be made before it is allowed to build up, by means of a preliminary generalization. These two devices are also used by Proust for humour.

Anticipation. First, let us consider the situation in which the reader is aware that something is about to be revealed to him, but not sure what. We have already seen this technique used on a small scale in the last chapter, when the Narrator and Saint-Loup anxiously waited for an anti-Semite to come out of a tent, only to find that it was Bloch. A similar technique can be found on a much larger scale. For example, Legrandin visits the salon of Mme de Villeparisis. Earlier that day, the Narrator meets Legrandin in the street, and the latter says to him:

Pendant que vous irez à quelque *five o'clock*, votre vieil ami sera plus heureux que vous, car seul dans un faubourg, il regardera monter dans le ciel violet la lune rose. (*CG* II 154)

This remark provides a preliminary to the mystification of the reader which is to take place later that afternoon. Apart from being ridiculously affected in themselves, Legrandin's remarks lead one to assume that he disapproves of social life. When we later learn that Mme de Villeparisis is constantly besieged by an importunate visitor we are anxious to learn who he is; but it never crosses our minds that it might be Legrandin. Mme de Villeparisis is finally obliged to receive the visitor:

Le visiteur importun entra, marchant droit vers Mme de Villeparisis d'un air ingénu et fervent, c'était Legrandin. (*CG* II 200)

Here the narrative technique cannot be distinguished from the humorous content. But the build-up of suspense does strengthen the impact, and because the effect is amusing in any case, the shock makes the humour seem more vivid.

Surprise. The humour in a situation can be brought out after it seems fully revealed to the reader if some unexpected factor is added which will retrospectively colour the whole situation. This is a device frequently used by Proust in *ALR*, so frequently that it might seem to imply a comment on the fact that things turn out so differently from one's expectations that one cannot rely on observation to reveal the truth. It can make a serious impression, but more often the effect is humorous, since the reader feels he has been led up the garden path.

The technique can be used within a particular episode. Mme Cresmeyer receives a telegram, which, she assumes, is about her dying aunt's condition. As she is giving the most important dinner-party of her career that evening, she decides not to open the telegram; for the news of her aunt's death would oblige her to cancel the party. One laughs at the attitude of Mme Cresmeyer, who prefers a shallow worldly triumph to a matter of life and death, and forgets the affair. But the whole situation is changed when she opens the telegram after the party. It does not contain the announcement of her aunt's death, but a re-quest from a general, the flower of her acquaintance, to be invited to dinner that evening. She had been longing to invite him, and through her own callousness had prevented herself from fulfilling her worldly ambitions to the full (*JS* pp. 792-5).

This technique is also found on a much larger scale, interspersed with other elements in the narrative, and taking a considerable time to evolve. It is for instance possible to overlook the hidden significance behind the Narrator's remarks about M. de Charlus:

Pensant que cela pouvait produire une impression très favorable sur Mme de Villeparisis que je fusse lié avec un neveu qu'elle prisait si fort: 'Il m'a demandé de revenir avec lui, répondis-je avec joie. J'en suis enchanté. Du reste nous sommes plus amis que vous ne croyez, Madame, et je suis décidé à tout pour que nous le soyons davantage.' (*CG* II 284)

It is not until some four hundred pages later that we learn why Mme de Villeparisis was upset by the Narrator's unconsciously ambiguous remarks: M. de Charlus is a homosexual, so that the Narrator appears to be hinting at an illicit relationship with him. These hints may well fail to amuse at a first reading.

Another simpler example is the series of references to asparagus at Combray. We gradually become accustomed to the idea that one particular summer, Françoise often serves them. Tante Léonie says to her:

—Vous qui, cette année, nous mettez des asperges à toutes les sauces [. . .] (*CS* I 55)

And later there is a long description of the beauties of asparagus, to-gether with the spectacle of the kitchen girl gloomily preparing them:

La pauvre charité de Giotto, comme l'appelait Swann, chargée par Françoise de les 'plumer', les avait près d'elle dans une corbeille, son air était douloureux, comme si elle ressentait tous les malheurs de la terre. (*CS* I 121)

This melancholy does not seem particularly odd to the reader—the kitchen-maid is a poor creature who has only just been delivered of an illegitimate child, and her general mood seems to be one of gloom. But later a revelation is made which changes the meaning of these passages. We learn that:

Françoise trouvait pour servir sa volonté permanente de rendre la maison intenable à tout domestique, des ruses si savantes et si impitoyables que, bien des années plus tard, nous apprîmes que si cet été-là nous avions mangé presque tous les jours des asperges, c'était parce que leur odeur donnait à la pauvre fille de cuisine chargée de les éplucher des crises d'asthme d'une telle violence qu'elle fut obligée de finir par s'en aller. (*CS* I 124)

This passage retrospectively casts light on the two former ones, on the deception beneath the apparent ordinariness of the Charité occupation. The devilish subtlety of Françoise's plan constrasts humorously with its banality. The episode has the same quality as a detective story: a seemingly innocent character is suddenly revealed to have been the criminal all along; but here the effect is even more devastating, for not only were we unaware of the identity of the criminal, we did not even know that the crime existed.

Dramatic Irony Proust frequently uses dramatic irony to create humour. He lets the reader in on a secret. We may or may not then witness the discovery of the secret by the characters. The humour in such situations can be contained in the ignorance of the character before the discovery, or in the shock of the discovery and his response to it, or in both elements put together. A good example of this sort of situation is the Legrandin passage, the earlier part of which has already been mentioned: Legrandin, having professed to despise society, emerges as an eager, importunate hanger-on of Mme de Villeparisis. He does not know that, as he slavishly grovels before her, he is being watched by the Narrator:

—Je vous remercie beaucoup de me recevoir, Madame, dit-il en insistant sur le mot 'beaucoup': c'est un plaisir tout à fait rare et subtile que vous faites à un vieux solitaire, je vous assure que sa répercussion . . .
   Il s'arrêta net en m'apercevant. (*CG* II 200)

There are two distinct stages here: first, Legrandin reveals his hypocrisy, little knowing that he is betraying the truth to the Narrator. Secondly, we have his sudden discovery of the Narrator's presence, and we can imagine the feelings of humiliation expressed by his eloquent silence. Later, Proust adds a different type of dramatic irony. Legrandin, unacquainted with a vital fact, betrays himself. He will never know that he has done so, so that the dramatic irony is forever to be concealed from him. He proceeds to tell the Narrator his reasons for coming to Mme de Villeparisis's salon, thereby attempting to justify his evident hypocrisy:

—Naturellement, quand on me persécute vingt fois de suite pour me faire venir quelque part, continua-t-il à voix basse, quoique j'aie bien droit à ma liberté, je ne peux pourtant pas agir comme un rustre. (p. 204)

He is not to know that, before he ever came in, Mme de Villeparisis had been complaining that he ceaselessly disturbed her with his importunities.

Such unconscious self-betrayal is frequently used by Proust: M. de Charlus expresses disapproval of homosexuals, thinking that he is taking his listeners in: Mme Lawrence, the snobbish mistress of a M. de Ribeaumont, expresses disapproval of snobbery and loose morals, and mentions M. de Ribeaumont as one of her husband's best friends, trying to divert suspicion by talking freely of the very things she should be inhibited about.

The dramatic irony in all these examples is so closely dependent on the personalities involved that the rightful place of dramatic irony might seem to be a chapter on character. Dramatic irony cannot be amusing unless the 'victim' is guilty of some sort of falsehood. When we are anxiously awaiting Morel's rupture with the unknowing M. de Charlus, our sympathy for M. de Charlus is heartfelt because his passion is sincere (*P* III 278 ff.); but when Legrandin discovers that he has exposed his hypocrisy, we laugh at him because he deserved to be discomfited. But though acute observation of character forms the basic content of dramatic irony, the actual technique seemed worthy of separate consideration.

Generalization Preceding Specific Illustrations   This technique is again closely interwoven with humour of character, for the humorous instances of its use occur in character portrayals or accounts of human behaviour. The normal way of getting to know a character, the way one real person usually gets to know another, is by meeting him. One gradually builds up an opinion about him, based on his behaviour on various occasions. Proust sometimes reverses this normal process, summarizing the character's salient features before he actually appears on the scene. This technique tends to give a humorous bias from the first. One knows exactly how a character is going to evolve; and sure enough, he neatly fits himself into his pre-ordained niche.

Introducing a character in this way will affect his subsequent development. Cottard's behaviour is described in general terms (*S* I 200–1) before he has done more than make the briefest of appearances;

from the first, he is a puppet-figure. M. de Charlus, on the other hand, is gradually revealed to us through the eyes of the Narrator, who first sees him as a mysterious stranger (*JF* I 751), and then gets to know him little by little. The initial introduction of M. de Charlus leaves him in possession of all his initiative, so that there is scope for treating him seriously or humorously as the case may be. Cottard is forced from the beginning into his role of caricature.

This technique can produce elaborate, sustained effects. The generalization can include a number of features, all of which will be neatly exemplified later. For instance, M. Vinteuil and his daughter are initially described in general terms:

M. Vinteuil, très sévère pour le 'genre déplorable des jeunes gens négligés, dans les idées de l'époque actuelle' [. . .] Sa seule passion était pour sa fille, et celle-ci, qui avait l'air d'un garçon, paraissait si robuste qu'on ne pouvait s'empêcher de sourire en voyant les précautions que son père prenait pour elle, ayant toujours des châles supplémentaires à lui jeter sur les épaules. Ma grand'mère faisait remarquer quelle expression douce, délicate, presque timide passait souvent dans les regards de cette enfant si rude, dont le visage était semé de taches de son. Quand elle venait de prononcer une parole, elle l'entendait avec l'esprit de ceux à qui elle l'avait dite, s'alarmait des malentendus possibles, et on voyait s'éclairer, se découper comme par transparence, sous la figure hommasse du 'bon diable', les traits plus fins d'une jeune fille éplorée. (*CS* I 112–13)

Later we see the Vinteuils in action. They are ostensibly responding to a specific situation. But unknown to themselves, they are also tidily fitting in with their preordained pattern of behaviour:

Nous causions un moment avec M. Vinteuil devant le porche en sortant de l'église. Il intervenait entre les gamins qui se chamaillaient sur la place, prenait la défense des petits, faisait des sermons aux grands. Si sa fille nous disait de sa grosse voix combien elle avait été contente de nous voir, aussitôt il semblait qu'en elle-même une soeur plus sensible rougissait de ce propos de bon garçon étourdi qui avait pu nous faire croire qu'elle sollicitait d'être invitée chez nous. Son père lui jetait un manteau sur les épaules, ils montaient dans un petit buggy qu'elle conduisait elle-même et tous deux retournaient à Montjouvain. (*CS* I 114)

The deliberateness of the technique is illustrated by the fact that virtually every element that Proust mentioned as true of the Vinteuils in general is brought out the first time we see them together. Proust has listed their characteristics, and insists on bringing in the whole contents of the list when we meet them. The neatness of the procedure is itself amusing: the reader, having recognized instances of all the other characteristics mentioned in the first passage, will find even the shawl mentioned in the second.

Fragmentation of Narrative   The writer need not produce his narrative consecutively; he can allow his story to emerge in fragments, interweaving it into the rest of the narrative. This technique can make the humour more vigorous, since each fresh fragment of narrative has its own independent impact, and is not merely a continuation of the story.

At times this fragmentary narrative is used to make subtle humorous points. An example is the confrontation of Bloch and the Narrator's father, in which their incompatibility is revealed by their respective attitudes to the weather:

Il avait commencé par agacer mon père qui, le voyant mouillé, lui avait dit avec intérêt:
—Mais, monsieur Bloch, quel temps fait-il donc? est-ce qu'il a plu? je n'y comprends rien, le baromètre était excellent.
Il n'en avait tiré que cette réponse:
—Monsieur, je ne puis absolument vous dire s'il a plu. Je vis si résolument en dehors des contingences physiques que mes sens ne prennent pas la peine de me les notifier.
—Mais, mon pauvre fils, il est idiot ton ami, m'avait dit mon père quand Bloch fut parti. Comment! il ne peut même pas me dire le temps qu'il fait! Mais il n'y a rien de plus intéressant! C'est un imbécile. (*CS* I 92)

One seems to be laughing at Bloch, not at the Narrator's father. But the latter, who appears perfectly reasonable here, is actually rather ridiculous if one remembers earlier references to his fondness for meteorology. We have seen him inspecting the barometer, to his wife's admiration:

Mon père haussait les épaules et il examinait le baromètre, car il aimait la météorologie, pendant que ma mère, évitant de faire du bruit pour ne pas le troubler, le regardait avec un respect attendri, mais pas trop fixement pour ne pas chercher à percer le mystère de ses supériorités. (*CS* I 11)

His interest in meteorology is perhaps as great as Bloch's indifference to the subject; so that the meeting between the two is an absurd clash of two contradictory and abnormal attitudes.

In this example much of the humour rests on a subtle link between the two passages, the second being more amusing if one remembers the first. Elsewhere, the opposite effect occurs, when the earlier passage can be appreciated retrospectively: this sort of effect has already been discussed under the heading 'surprise'.

By fragmenting the narrative in this way, Proust can make us accept humour of a much more outrageous kind than we could have tolerated in a continuous narrative. For instance, Mme de Guermantes completely contradicts a previous statement. She claims at first that she loathes Empire furniture:

je ne connais rien de plus pompier, de plus bourgeois que cet horrible style, avec ces commodes qui ont des têtes de cygnes comme des baignoires. (*S* I 338)

In the later episode, we are reminded of the Duchess's former dislike of the furniture, but in a much attenuated form:

la duchesse, à qui Swann et M. de Charlus [. . .] avaient à grand'peine fini par faire aimer le style Empire, s'écria:

—Madame, sincèrement, je ne peux pas vous dire à quel point vous trouverez cela beau! J'avoue que le style Empire m'a toujours impressionnée. (*CG* II 519)

The violence of the Duchess's previous statement, if juxtaposed with her later ones, would have seemed so far-fetched as to be incredible.

Anecdotes Proust by no means confines himself to one thread of narrative at a time. Self-contained thumbnail sketches of quirks of human behaviour or of amusing occurrences are frequently included. I shall call these anecdotes, and consider how they contribute, as narrative tools, to the contexts in which they lie. Their scope and elasticity is striking: they can range from being purely self-contained to extending their influence through a whole episode, or through the life of a character.

They may be used to illustrate a point. For example, Proust tells us that

les [. . .] amours les plus effectifs [. . .] peuvent non seulement se former mais subsister autour de bien peu de chose. (*JF* I 858)

and illustrates this with a very funny, but touching anecdote about an old drawing-master, heartbroken at the death of his mistress, the mother of his child, although he admits 'Je ne l'ai jamais vue qu'en chapeau' (p. 859).

Elsewhere, an anecdote is brought in fortuitously, without appearing to contribute to the narrative. The madam of a brothel is shown, in the intervals of discussing the morals of various aristocrats, parlant à un gros monsieur qui venait chez elle boire sans arrêter du champagne avec des jeunes gens, parce que, déjà très gros, il voulait devenir assez obèse pour être certain de ne pas être 'pris' si jamais il y avait une guerre (*F* III 662)

This anecdote was not included because of its particular relevance. Indeed, it reappears elsewhere, in a completely different context (*TR* III 835).

Anecdotes may also reveal truths about characters. In *JS*, we are introduced to the Vicomte de Lomperolles. We are told that he hates young men, and a quirk of his is related:

il avait quarante perruques très légèrement plus longues les unes que les autres. Quand il était arrivé à la plus longue, il mettait sans transition la plus courte pour faire croire qu'il se faisait couper les cheveux. (*JS* 677)

This anecdote is striking enough to make us remember M. de Lomperolles. And this is vital, for at the end of *JS* we suddenly learn that he was a homosexual and killed himself because of this. The shock effect of this revelation depends entirely on one remembering the character well enough to be surprised. There has been another brief reference to his hatred of effeminate young men (p. 676), but what has really fixed him in our minds is his extraordinary wigs; and retrospectively this seems so abnormally vain that we realize that the key to his character must have been his homosexuality.

Content of Narrative

So far, we have discussed narrative techniques with little reference to content. We must now consider the alterations that Proust makes in his material. The writer of fiction need not confine himself to realistic material, for his work does not have to create the impression of having been really and truly lived. There is nothing to prevent Proust from manipulating not only the order and the scope of his narrative, but also its content, by means of novelist's tricks which make the novel more striking, richer, more coherent or more meaningful.

The devices I shall discuss are: coincidence, links between characters, complication, exaggeration, and repetition.

Coincidence. and Links   Coincidence is basically an artificial device, such as one would find in a formal comedy. It tends to impose a graceful symmetry on the narrative, and to make the humour seem patterned rather than realistic.

Proust uses coincidence in this formal way. The Narrator is waiting for the Swanns. But every time the door opens and he gets to his feet, he finds himself confronted with a servant:

Je m'étais assis, mais je me levais précipitamment en entendant ouvrir la porte; ce n'était qu'un second valet de pied, puis un troisième [. . .] Un nouveau bruit de pas retentissait, je ne me levais pas, ce devait être encore un valet de pied, c'était M. Swann. (*JF* I 527)

The repeated coincidence produces a miniature dance-pattern, with the Narrator rising and sitting at intervals. Another feature is the diappointment and embarrassment of the Narrator, which is inescapable however he might vary his behaviour to try and avoid it.

Such purely artificial coincidence is rare. Since Proust is, ostensibly at least, a realistic writer, he incorporates coincidence in a much more informal way. For instance, Bloch and *L'historien de la Fronde* are admiring Mme de Villeparisis's flower-paintings:

Bloch voulut faire un geste pour exprimer son admiration, mais d'un coup de coude il renversa le vase où était la branche et toute l'eau se répandit sur le tapis.
—Vous avez vraiment des doigts de fée, dit à la marquise l'historien qui, me tournant le dos à ce moment-là, ne s'était pas aperçu de la maladresse de Bloch. (*CG* II 215).

This coincidence, though unlikely, is not impossible.

A similar device is to create unexpected links between characters, places, habits, morals and so on. This technique produces a pleasing effect of interweaving which prevents Proust's writing from seeming too diffuse. More important, it is deliberately used in *ALR* to illustrate the effects wrought by time on different elements in the characters. Such instances will be mentioned as they arise.

Often, the links seem amusing because they are far-fetched, although (like some of the coincidences already mentioned) Proust usually points out that though far-fetched they are not impossible. It is amazing to find in Saint-Loup's beloved mistress the cheap little prostitute Rachel *quand du Seigneur*; and to have to search the polished French features of Jacques du Rozier for the Jewish face of Bloch. But it is only too comprehensible how both these changes came about; these links are entertaining without being unnatural.

At the same time, such links almost always have a much deeper significance than their mere entertainment value. One may smile ironically when Jupien's little niece marries a Cambremer; but a serious point is being made: the classes parade their uniqueness and exclusiveness; but invaders can frequently enter the sanctuary of the aristocracy. Similar links are made when find Odette as the mistress of M. de Guermantes while Mme Verdurin has become the Princesse de Guermantes, and Oriane is a neglected outsider. And when it comes to the emotions, all classes are equal. M. de Charlus receives letters from valets, and writes passionately to Aimé. The Narrator himself frequently falls in love with shopgirls or country girls, and Swann eagerly pursues his friends' cooks.

Other links, equally significant, can have a cumulative effect. This is particularly the case with the Sodomites and Gomorrhans. First one character then another and another is brought in, usually with the same effect of humorous shock. Again, a serious point is illustrated by this building-up of links, though the links may be individually amusing. Proust is always aware of the human jungle beneath the veneer of society. He insistently makes the leaders of society, the Duc and Duchesse de Guermantes, show themselves unable to cope with, or even care about, truly grave human problems. As more and more characters, people the reader knows, reveal hidden depths of perversion, we become increasingly aware that there are sinister levels in every human being. Proust is very insistent on this point, and spares hardly any of the characters. Thus Bloch is allowed to insinuate that the Narrator's own great-aunt led a loose life in her youth (*CS* I 93), or that Odette, even after she has become the elegant Mme Swann, is still willing to be seduced by an unknown man in a train. Ostensibly amusing links between characters can contribute to the structure of a meaningful and sinister edifice.

A different type of link occurs at the end of *ALR* when each character is given his aged counterpart. The whole novel has worked up to the point at which all the characters' lives are over: it is only when time has been lost that the Narrator can set out in search of it. At the same time, on a more technical level, the impact of the final parade of ancients has been carefully prepared. We have seen the ageing process in almost nobody (the main exception being M. de Charlus, who throughout has appeared pathetically vulnerable since he ages far more visibly than everyone else). To achieve this effect, Proust has to explain the fact that the Narrator was completely oblivious of the passing of time. Rather artifically, he puts the Narrator into a *maison de santé* for years; the Narrator feels just the same when he emerges as he did when he went in, and we too forget that he must in fact be older. As a result, when we suddenly burst in upon the now aged characters, the shock is immense. In most cases, we are reminded of the previous appearance of the various individuals. Their transformation is described as though they ought still to be young, so that the change seems even more abrupt. Fezensac has put something on his face to make it suddenly harden; M. d'Argencourt has put on an extraordinarily white beard; and under these disguises, the Narrator is anxiously searching for the characters he knew before, and lamenting their unattractive disguises. Of Fezensac's wrinkled face he says:

cela le vieillissait tellement qu'on n'aurait plus dit du tout un jeune homme. (*TR* III 921)

Proust is here manipulating the content of the novel to bring the contrast between the aged and the young characters out at one specific moment: the individual links are used to create a series of amusing variations on a theme, a final set-piece that is striking enough in its impact to serve as a climax to the whole novel.

Exaggeration: The Farcical Element   Exaggeration or overcomplication of the content is another device that produces a theatrical effect, this time one of farce. In a characteristic farcical situation there is so much going on that both audience and characters are bewildered. Proust produces a variety of effects springing from this device. An example is a conversation between the Narrator and Mme de Cambremer:

si, pour causer avec elle, j'employais les expressions de Legrandin, par une suggestion inverse elle me répondait dans le dialecte de Robert, qu'elle ne savait pas emprunté à Rachel [. . .] (*SG* II 819–20)

This lack of spontaneity immediately makes both speakers appear artificial. Again, their efforts to please are doomed to failure. Mme de Cambremer-Legrandin is ashamed of her brother (*SG* II 807), and the last thing to make her feel at ease is to talk like him. The Narrator despises Saint-Loup's turns of phrase, learnt from a former prostitute, and so will not be inclined to respect someone who imitates them. Both speakers achieve the opposite of the intended effect.

Over-elaborate situations are more amusing if they come into conflict with real emotions. For example, the Narrator is trying to carry on a serious telephone conversation with Françoise about Albertine. However, he cannot speak to her directly, but has to do so through the intermediary of the operator:

'Elle n'était pas fâchée? Ah! pardon! Demandez à cette dame si cette demoiselle n'était pas fâchée? . . . —Cette dame me dit de vous dire que non, pas du tout [. . .]' (*P* III, 155–6)

Again, Proust can produce a perfectly plausible situation, then proceed to manipulate it as it develops. Sometimes this manipulation strikes one as exceedingly artificial. He can build up a situation to a climax and then give it a bathetic twist so that the whole build-up is destroyed. This frequently happens on all sorts of scales. An example is the episode in which the Narrator makes elaborate efforts to engineer a situation such that Elstir will introduce him to Albertine and her friends. The whole episode culminates in the desired situation occurring—but then Elstir does not bother to make the introduction (*JF* I 852–6).

Proust can produce even more complex manipulations of situation. He reverses a situation, putting it right again afterwards. The Narrator begs M. de Norpois to mention his name in the presence of Odette; but M. de Norpois, simply because he realizes that the Narrator is desperate to meet her, refrains from doing so, leaving the Narrator desolate. But then Bloch tries insincerely to achieve the same effect as the Narrator: he too is anxious to meet Odette, and pretends to Cottard that he knows one of her best friends:

il avait entendu dire que Mme Swann m'aimait beaucoup, par une personne avec qui il avait dîné la veille et qui elle-même était très liée avec Mme Swann [. . .] (*JF* I 502)

Bloch's efforts, like the Narrator's, are utterly selfish. But, fortunately, he accidentally triggers off a selfish reaction in Cottard, who,

ayant induit de ce qu'il avait entendu dire à Bloch qu'elle me connaissait beaucoup et m'appréciait, pensa que, quand il la verrait, dire que j'étais un charmant garçon avec lequel il était lié ne pourrait en rien être utile pour moi et serait flatteur pour lui [. . .] (p. 503)

The very characteristic which defeated the Narrator's attempts with M. de Norpois causes him to succeed without trying in the end. Here again, Proust has introduced an element of plausibility, and made a serious point, namely that every man is out for himself. At the same time, he has produced an amusingly complex situation.

Another technique Proust uses is slapstick; this is where he comes closest to actual farce, combining exaggerated physical activity, mischief and disregard for discomfort and even death. For instance, the writer C. is kindly treated by a lighthouse keeper and his wife; but then we are told:

Quelquefois [. . .] la femme courait dans les chemins pour ramener ses oies, que l'aboiement du chien avait fait envoler jusqu'à la mer, où souvent l'une se noyait, car elles nageaient fort mal. Une fois, mon ami et moi, espionnant d'un rocher le travail de C., nous le vîmes après s'être assuré que le gardien du phare et sa femme ne pouvaient le voir, s'amuser à faire sauver les oies jusqu'à la mer. Quand la femme revint et ne trouvant pas ses oies se mit à crier, C. eut l'air de ne s'apercevoir que seulement alors qu'elles n'étaient pas devant la maison. (*JS* 186–7)

This scene could be performed on the stage, with the two young men hiding, watching C's action and his artificial air of innocence when the result of his mischief is discovered, which effectively prevents the woman's shrieks from moving the audience to anything but laughter, although some of her geese may be drowned.

Again, we laugh at the irritation of the Narrator when, for instance, he begs the lift-boy again and again to close the door, since he has a private and urgent matter to communicate to him:

Avant de lui faire mes recommandations, je vis qu'il avait laissé la porte ouverte; je le lui fis remarquer, j'avais peur qu'on ne nous entendît; il condescendit à mon désir et revint ayant diminué l'ouverture. 'C'est pour vous faire plaisir. Mais il n'y a plus personne à l'étage que nous deux.' Aussitôt, j'entendis passer une, puis deux, puis trois personnes. Cela m'agaçait à cause de l'indiscrétion possible, mais surtout parce que je voyais que cela ne l'étonnait nullement et que c'était un va-et-vient normal. 'Oui, c'est la femme de chambre d'à côté qui va chercher ses affaires. Oh! c'est sans importance, c'est le sommelier qui remonte ses clefs. Non, non, ce n'est rien, vous pouvez parler, c'est mon collègue qui va prendre son service.' Et comme les raisons que tous les gens avaient de passer ne diminuaient pas mon ennui qu'ils pussent m'entendre, sur mon ordre formel, il alla, non pas fermer la porte, ce qui était au-dessus des forces de ce cycliste qui désirait une 'moto', mais la pousser un peu plus. 'Comme ça nous sommes bien tranquilles.' Nous l'étions tellement qu'une Américaine entra et se retira en s'excusant de s'être trompée de chambre. 'Vous allez me ramener cette jeune fille, lui dis-je, après avoir fait claquer moi-même la porte de toutes mes forces (ce qui amena un autre chasseur s'assurer qu'il n'y avait pas de fenêtre ouverte). (*SG* II 792–3)

The exaggerated harping on the theme of the open door, with constant unwanted interruptions which utterly belie the lift-boy's assurances that it is perfectly all right, the physical violence of the Narrator, which produces just the opposite of the desired effect, the false logic, the sudden popping of an American head through the door, and the underlying feeling of mounting, frustrated tension in the Narrator, all make the scene worthy of inclusion in a Feydeau farce.

Repetition   Humorous repetition again involves manipulating the content of the narrative, multiplying humorous effects so as to increase them, or serious points to make them amusing. It is one of the most effective devices of the writer of comedy. One need only look at any play of Molière's to see how frequently the device is used. There seem to be two main reasons for employing repetition. First, it can produce an effect of symmetry, a spurious tidiness which in itself tends to appear ridiculous and which enhances such humour as may already be present. In Molière's *L'Avare* the miser's daughter curtsies to her father as she brutally refuses to marry the suitor he has chosen for her; the comic effect is much increased when the miser returns the curtsey with a bow as he equally brutally insists that she do as she is told:

Élise   (Elle fait une révérence) Je ne veux point me marier, mon
            père, s'il vous plaît.
Harpagon (Il contrefait sa révérence) Et moi, ma petite fille, ma mie,
            je veux que vous vous mariiez, s'il vous plaît.

Secondly, repetition can be used simply to insist on a point until it becomes ridiculous through sheer reiteration. L'Avare's 'sans dot' (the reason he reiterates for his refusal to allow his daughter to marry the man she loves) is a case in point.

Proust, like Molière, produces effects both of straightforward humorous symmetry and of humorous exaggeration by means of his use of repetition; however, as it is novels he is writing, he does not have to confine himself to crude effects such as will be immediately obvious to the audience, but has scope for much more subtle manipulation of repetition.

An example of a straightforward symmetrical effect is that of the tomato-faced twins. Not content with showing us a boy who has a face like a tomato (in itself an amusing picture) Proust doubles the impact by giving him an identical twin. But here, as in most of Proust's repetitions, there is a deviation from perfect symmetry which contributes to the subtlety of the humorous effect. The two tomato-faced twins differ markedly in their amatory preferences:

La tomate n° 2 se plaisait avec frénésie à faire exclusivement les délices des dames, la tomate n° 1 ne détestait pas condescendre aux goûts de certains messieurs. (*SG* II 854)

And this leads to humorously complicated misunderstandings. There are also episodes in which repetition has the second effect suggested: sheer reiteration makes a ridiculous impression. For example, we have the tendency of the Narrator's grandfather to hum songs which have some relevance to the situation, background or attitude of people he meets. At first this trait seems simply to be an amiable eccentricity; but the skill with which the grandfather succeeds in finding an appropriate hum arouses our amusement and admiration, quite apart from our response to each individual episode.

Sometimes, Proust's use of repetition is much more subtle, and he takes full advantage of the enormous scope provided by his long novel. Situations are repeated without much apparent connection between the two instances: instead of creating a cumulative humorous effect, each instance is independently amusing.

But almost invariably there does seem to be an important underlying connection between humorous episodes referred to at a great distance from each other. Cottard makes the same impression on different people who meet him for the first time at a dinner-party. When Swann first meets Cottard, he is shocked by his knowing looks:

Il n'eut un moment de froideur qu'avec le docteur Cottard: en le voyant lui cligner de l'œil et lui sourire d'un air ambigu avant qu'ils se fussent encore parlé (mimique que Cottard appelait 'laisser venir'), Swann crut que le docteur le connaissait sans doute pour s'être trouvé avec lui en quelque lieu de plaisir [. . .] (*S* I 202)

And the same thing happens much later to M. de Charlus when he too meets Cottard for the first time:

Cottard, qui était assis à côté de M. de Charlus, le regardait sous son lorgnon, pour faire connaissance, et rompre la glace, avec des clignements beaucoup plus insistants qu'ils n'eussent été jadis, et non coupés de timidités. [. . .] Le baron, qui voyait facilement partout des pareils à lui, ne douta pas que Cottard n'en fût un et ne lui fît de l'œil. (*SG* II 919)

Cottard has not changed, only grown more insistent, in the many years that separate these two episodes. But the repetition, if one isolates and examines it, also provides a cynical comment on Cottard's interlocutors. For the striking fact about these two episodes is that they reveal how much their emotional tendencies dominate both Swann and Charlus. Swann, the inveterate womanizer, immediately assumes that it is to this that Cottard is alluding. M. de Charlus, the homosexual, interprets Cottard's look as referring to his perversion. Proust constantly stresses the fact that one's taste in love colours one's whole outlook. And here, by means of a humorous example, he is illustrating this fact.

At other times a repetition might serve to explain or illustrate an idea that is difficult to grasp. An example of this is the use of the same tricks of speech by both Cottard and 'M. Tiche' (Elstir), which are stylistically humorous, but used structurally to make a serious point. Cottard tends to underline his naïve and banal remarks by the expression *n'est-ce pas?*

'Sarah Bernhardt, c'est bien la Voix d'Or, n'est-ce pas? On écrit souvent aussi qu'elle brûle les planches. C'est une expression bizarre, n'est-ce pas?' (*S* I 201)

Here the inelegant repetition of the phrase makes Cottard's speech seem clumsy. 'M. Tiche' uses the same ridiculous phrase in describing Vinteuil's Sonata:

'Ah! c'est tout à fait une très grande machine, n'est-ce pas? Ce n'est pas, si vous voulez, la chose "cher" et "public", n'est-ce pas?' (*S* I 212)

Here the repetition is not clumsy and naïve but affected. Later, when the reader meets the real Elstir, he finds it very difficult to associate this genius with the ridiculous painter of Mme Verdurin's salon. But the fact that 'M. Tiche' had adopted the same clumsy speaking habits as Cottard's might perhaps help to explain this transformation. In his desire to fit in with the *petit clan*, Elstir had gone so far as to adopt the method of speaking of some of its members. Later, when he becomes the true Elstir, he loses all these tics: by extension, one can assume that he had adopted the ideas of the *petit clan* and later dropped those too. A humorous illustration of a serious fact has again been given.

A different point is implied when both Albertine and the Guermantes use the same phrase. The two episodes occur within a fairly short space of each other. We are told of Albertine that

elle prenait déjà des façons de femme de son milieu et de son rang en disant [. . .] si on s'amusait à des imitations: 'Le plus drôle, quand vous la contrefaites, c'est que vous lui ressemblez.' (*CG* II 355)

Curiously, exactly the same phrase is shown to be characteristic of the truly aristocratic Guermantes, as opposed to the rather inferior Courvoisiers:

les Guermantes un peu cultivés s'écriaient: 'Dieu qu'Oriane est drolatique! Le plus fort c'est que pendant qu'elle l'imite, elle lui ressemble! . . .' (*CG* II 461)

It seems inconceivable that the very features that characterize the cream of the aristocracy should also epitomize the bourgeoisie, unless we assume that the repetition provides a cynical comment on both classes: despite the elaborate attention they pay to class distinctions, there is very little intrinsic difference between them.

The Introduction of Comic Scenes

Proust, like a great comic playwright, has his important comic scenes, constructed as individual entities, as well as being linked to the rest of the novel. Often he sets the scene for his comic action. He may introduce these scenes gradually and carefully. The Verdurins's dinner-party at La Raspelière is provided with its own prologue in the train and carriage journey the guests have to take to get there (*SG* II 866-99). The journey contains the basic humorous elements of the dinner-party proper, since most of the *fidèles* are present, being their usual selves. But at the same time there is an atmosphere of increasing expectancy: the Narrator is anxious not to miss Cottard, who is to help him on his journey; the *fidèles* are in full evening dress and 'pétillaient déjà de la causerie prochaine' (p. 866), and so on. Each member of the *petit clan* is filled with such an air of expectation that he seems important to the other passengers on the train:

Le Futur vers lequel il se dirigeait le désignait à la personne assise sur la banquette d'en face, laquelle se disait: 'Ce doit être quelqu'un' [. . .] (p. 868)

Moreover, a more concrete reason for feeling tense with anticipation is provided for the *fidèles*: Mme Verdurin's favourite pianist has just died: will they be able to get through the evening without upsetting her? How will she have taken the dreadful news? the actual arrival at La Raspelière and the dinner-party will provide the climax of the journey and of the scene, and the solution of this problem; the reader, as well as the guests, arrives in a party mood, in a flutter of agreeable anticipation mingled with tension.

Elsewhere Proust separates the comic scenes from the rest of the narrative by placing them after an episode without much action, so that the impact of the scene is strengthened. For example, the Narrator's visit to Odette's *jardin d'hiver* forms an episode in itself. It is separated from accounts of previous visits to Odette by a long and anguished description of the Narrator's misery at his rupture with Gilberte (*JF* I 585-91). Proust then introduces us to Odette's surroundings as if they were completely new. The Narrator sets out to visit her, *déjà dans la nuit*, as if going off into the unknown. The district in which the Swanns live is *considéré* [. . .] *comme éloigné*; the darkness and loneliness of Paris is stressed. Everything is motionless. When a carriage moves, the visitor is surprised, since everything appeared to be under the influence of a mysterious enchantment; but even the sound of the horses hooves is meaningful:

les roues caoutchoutées donnaient au pas des chevaux un fond de silence sur lequel il se détachait plus distinct et plus explicite. (*JF* I 592)

Proust goes on to describe in further detail what one sees, still from outside. One cannot see much as the window is too high up; but one can make out a profusion of plants: this leads Proust to compare the *jardin d'hiver* to a miniature indoor garden. Hitherto, he has stressed the enchanted emptiness of the scene; now for the first time, he introduces people:

Enfin, au fond de ce jardin d'hiver, [. . .] le passant, se hissant sur ses pointes, apercevait généralement un homme en redingote, un gardénia ou un œillet à la boutonnière, debout devant une femme assise, tous deux vagues [. . .] (*JF* I 593)

Significantly, the people are motionless and almost invisible. Only the most basic details of their appearance are described. Suddenly, at this stage, we are properly introduced into the salon: the mention of the samovar leads Proust to comment on what Odette thinks of it. She is shown offering tea to the man standing before her, who bows gravely. The dimly-perceived figures at the back of the salon have come to life. Proust introduces us to the characters there and allows the comic scene, consisting in outrageous remarks from Mme Cottard, Mme Bontemps etc., to proceed.

Although the introductory passages to this scene are not in themselves humorous, it is important to see how carefully such introductions are built up, and also to notice how the seriousness of the introduction influences the humour of the subsequent scene. The preliminary description has served to create a mysterious and beautiful atmosphere, which persists however ridiculous the remarks made in the salon may be. It is significant that although Odette's salon is intellectually inferior to Mme Verdurin's it does not appear as ridiculous as the latter's. I think this is simply because in Mme Verdurin's, the comments of the *fidèles* are not so carefully placed in a beautiful setting.

Elsewhere, Proust tells a comic story as a separate entity, giving it its own beginning, middle and end. One could appreciate the humour of the story if it were lifted bodily from the context. For instance, there is a self-contained humorous episode in which Tante Léonie unknowingly reveals a dream she has had to the Narrator. The story is contained within one single, not over-long paragraph (*CS* I 109–10). It is worth examining the episode to show how Proust builds up humorous narrative on a small scale.

The story begins with a brief description of Tante Léonie's normal quiet way of life ('son "petit train-train" '). Then we are told of an event which upset this way of life, namely the delivery of the kitchen maid's child, which bothers Tante Léonie for two reasons: first, the girl's screams disturb her, and secondly, her maid Françoise is too busy to attend to her properly. Tante Léonie's egoism is amusing in itself, and prepares us for the outcome of the anecdote, which is to be a demonstration of colossal selfishness. But so far, the events related are scarcely more than an introduction, told in an impersonal style. At this point, the hero himself appears, to see if his aunt needs anything, and from now on the events are told in a vivid, first person narrative. The Narrator enters Tante Léonie's apartments. Tension is built up by a detailed description of Tante Léonie's snores: the Narrator is nervous so that the sounds affect him very strongly. At this point we come to the climax of the episode, Tante Léonie's awakening, which is told in sentences which get shorter and more dramatic until we finally see her face:

la musique du ronflement s'interrompit une seconde et reprit un ton plus bas, puis elle s'éveilla et tourna à demi son visage que je pus voir alors; il exprimait une sorte de terreur [. . .]

Our curiosity as to the reason for these violent feelings is immediately satisfied when we learn that Tante Léonie has been having a nightmare, and sympathize with Tante Léonie's relief when she realizes it was only a dream. At this point, her feelings are described with unctuous emotion:

un sourire de joie, de pieuse reconnaissance envers Dieu qui permet que la vie soit moins cruelle que les rêves, éclaira faiblement son visage [. . .]

Now, suddenly, Proust twists the situation by explaining what it was Tante Léonie had actually dreamt:

'Voilà-t-il pas que je rêvais que mon pauvre Octave était ressuscité et qu'il voulait me faire faire une promenade tous les jours!'

The pious sentiments, in which we have been vicariously participating, have been caused by her relief because her husband is not alive. Proust has tricked us into sympathizing with something that we ought to have been condemning. This is the humorous point of the story. Proust neatly finishes off the episode in a single sentence. Tante Léonie, who had suddenly come to life in this paragraph, sinks back into oblivion and sleep; there is a 'happy ever after' ending in which the Narrator tells us that:

je sortis à pas de loup de la chambre sans qu'elle ni personne eût jamais appris ce que j'avais entendu.

Although this story has its roots firmly embedded in the novel as a whole (we depend on the rest of the novel for our understanding of the delivery of the kitchen-maid, of Tante Léonie's relationship with Françoise and so on), it also forms a complete story in its own right. The impact of the humorous twist at the end, when Tante Léonie's selfishness emerges, is very strong. A longer build-up might have increased our feelings of suspense, but could not perhaps have focused our attention so closely as does this compressed narrative, in which every word is important.

All these humorous episodes depend for their impact on their context. Proust is here manipulating the reader, making him see the funny side of an occasion which at another time might have seemed perfectly serious.

The Serious and the Humorous in Narrative

We must next consider the juxtaposition of the serious and the humorous on a smaller scale: within a particular episode. First, the transition between humorous and serious narrative can be very sudden. A serious situation can suddenly, momentarily, seem amusing. In the middle of a serious discussion about Jean's lack of will-power in *JS* the following exchange occurs:

'Cette force dont l'absence est un terrible écueil, dit Mme Santeuil, c'est la volonté.—Pas de volonté, mauvaise affaire, répondit M. Santeuil en éloignant vivement du feu ses chaussettes qui commençaient à brûler.' (*JS* pp. 232–3)

After this mention of M. Santeuil's burning socks, the narrative continues on its original, serious level. We have been briefly transported to a mundane plane of narrative in the middle of a serious one.

Again, a serious situation can suddenly change into an absurd one (Mme de Cambremer-Legrandin rushes forward to rescue a candlestick from the top of the piano during a recital (*S* I 336)). Or an amusing situation can suddenly become serious: the Narrator witnesses an absurd scene between a lavatory attendant and her clients as he waits for his grandmother; but when she emerges, he sees at once that she has had a stroke (*CG* II 309–12).

Finally, within a short space, Proust can shift repeatedly from serious to humorous and back again, just as one's mood can change. There is, after all, no intrinsic reason for the two elements to be confined each to its own context. A good example of the freedom with which Proust intermingles the serious and the humorous in his narrative is the basically serious description of the meeting of the Narrator and his grandmother with the Princesse de Luxembourg, which contains numerous incidental amusing references, as the Princesse, for some reason, treats them like friendly animals in a zoo (*JF* I 699–700).

Elsewhere, the humorous element can stand out by contrast to the rest of the context, and seem twice as funny. An example is Jean's anguished hesitation outside a brothel. He finally steels himself to ring the bell, and hears from within a vulgar voice exclaim: 'Ah bien! voilà quelqu'un de pressé, par exemple.' (*JS* p. 241)

Conversely, humorous elements can be affected by the general atmosphere, so that a serious, strange or painful prevailing mood prevents potentially humorous elements from having their normal effect. A good example is the scene in which the Narrator discovers that M. de Charlus and Jupien are homosexuals. The emotional content of this scene is so great that the humorous element seems strange rather than funny. Proust explains that

Cette scène n'était pas [. . .] positivement comique, elle était empreinte d'une étrangeté, ou si l'on veut d'un naturel, dont la beauté allait croissant. (*SG* II 605)

And this strange beauty persists, despite Proust's constant insistence on the absurd elements in the scene, which, indeed, contains some of the most deliberately humorous writing in Proust.[1]

Proust creates a feeling of continuity in the novel by treating all these scenes of sexual discovery in exactly the same way. There are two other such scenes: the one between Mlle Vinteuil and her friend in which the Narrator learns about sadism, and the flagellation of M. de Charlus, in which he learns about masochism.

In each case, one is given a vague warning that the revelation is

---

[1] For instance, there is the sustained comparison between M. de Charlus and a bumble-bee (p. 606) which is amusing on all sorts of levels.

coming; then, in the middle of some innocent occupation, the Narrator stumbles on some private activity. After the initial revelation, the scenes grow in excitement until they reach a climax. The shape of these scenes invariably determines our response to the humorous element they contain. Thus one fails to laugh at the irony of Mlle Vinteuil's perverted friend making cynical remarks in order to be kind (*CS* I 161), or at M. de Charlus's ludicrous disappointment on finding that his torturers are actually quite nice young men (*TR* III 827).

Conversely, the humour in a passage may be so far-fetched that it needs an elaborate build-up to make it credible. An example is the scene in which the Narrator visits M. de Charlus in his *hôtel*. The passage reads like a fairy tale. The Narrator is magically transported into M. de Charlus's antechamber, and ushered into his presence as though he were a king (*CG* II 552). This elaborate setting of the scene is distasteful to the Narrator, who comments:

Cette mise en scène autour de M. de Charlus me paraissait empreinte de beaucoup moins de grandeur que la simplicité de son frère [. . .] (p. 553)

But it is useful in that it takes us out of our normal mood in preparation for the extraordinary behaviour of the baron, who begins by remaining as still as a statue, breaks into scatological invective, and at a moment of reconciliation seems to summon out of the air the strains of Beethoven's pastoral symphony.

The Narrator is slowly brought back to normal during the ride home. Finally, we come back to the beginning with a reminiscence of the fascinating things that were in the Narrator's mind when he was driving *to* M. de Charlus:

j'allai sonner à ma porte, sans avoir plus pensé que j'avais à faire à M. de Charlus [. . .] des récits tout à l'heure si obsédants, mais que son accueil inattendu et foudroyant avait fait s'envoler bien loin de moi (p. 565).

The magical and elaborate effect is achieved partly by M. de Charlus's machinations, partly through Proust's treatment of the scene. The Narrator's burning desire to talk is forgotten. Proust contributes the magical 'transformation scene' effect by means of which the Narrator suddenly finds himself standing in the antechamber. M. de Charlus's contribution is the absurdly elaborate preparation surrounding the visit, aimed at investing himself with kingly grandeur.

This build-up not only contributes to the humorous effect but is essential if the episode is to be convincing, for, as has already been said,

M. de Charlus's behaviour is so odd that one can accept it only if one has been stripped of one's customary attitudes and opinions. It is not surprising that in this scene the Narrator, too, is shown to be completely different from his usual self. He, too, loses his self-control and behaves with extraordinary brutality, the only occasion in the book on which he actually resorts to such a degree of physical violence.

This combination of the magical and the absurd produces a comparable duality of humour. The reader is amused at the violence of M. de Charlus, at his brutal invective, at the incomprehensible shifting of mood; but his laughter is puzzled laughter. Part of the humour of this scene will not be apparent till later, when the reader realizes that M. de Charlus is a homosexual, and retrospectively views his grotesque behaviour as an attempt to seduce the Narrator, who, like the reader, has not the slightest glimmering of the truth.

Finally, let us return to the idea that humour in narrative is much more a matter of treatment than of content. In different places Proust uses exactly the same subject-matter to create a serious or a humorous effect. When we first hear Mme de Monteriender say that she admires the performers of a duet:

'C'est prodigieux, je n'ai jamais rien vu d'aussi fort . . .' Mais un scrupule d'exactitude lui faisant corriger cette première assertion, elle ajouta cette réserve: 'rien d'aussi fort . . . depuis les tables tournantes!' (S I 353)

her remark seems ludicrously naïve; but later Swann is suffering agonies because Odette has confessed to having had affairs with women:

Involontairement Swann pensa à ce mot qu'il avait entendu chez Mme de Saint-Euverte: 'C'est ce que j'ai vu de plus fort depuis les tables tournantes.' Cette souffrance qu'il ressentait ne ressemblait à rien de ce qu'il avait cru. (S I 363)

Another example is an episode illustrating the ignorance of Albertine:

'—Ah! vous avez été en Hollande, vous connaissez les Ver Meer?' demanda impérieusement Mme de Cambremer et du ton dont elle aurait dit: 'Vous connaissez les Guermantes?', car le snobisme en changeant d'objet ne change pas d'accent. Albertine répondit non: elle croyait que c'étaient des gens vivants. (SG II 814)

This exchange shows up both the snobbery of Mme de Cambremer-Legrandin and the ignorance of Albertine. But a serious version of the same episode occurs when a similar ignorance is attributed to Odette:

'Vous allez vous moquer de moi, ce peintre qui vous empêche de me voir (elle voulait parler de Ver Meer), je n'avais jamais entendu parler de lui; vit-il encore?' (*S* I 198)

The variation in tone between the two remarks is interesting. Albertine's *faux pas* forms the culminating point of a ridiculously snobbish conversation; Odette's admission is a touching expression of her feelings of inadequacy and of inferiority to Swann.

In general, humour can be interwoven with serious elements without being affected by them or influencing them (the Princesse de Luxembourg episode); it can stand out in contrast to a serious description (M. Verdurin's comment on Swann's love): it can alter according to the mood of the passage (the sexual revelations). Curiously, humour does not always win over the serious side: the humorous passages in the description of the grandmother's death do not make the whole episode amusing. This is because these very funny touches are so different from their context that it seems inappropriate to dwell on them. Elsewhere if the humour is appropriate to the context (as in the visit to M. de Charlus) it may well colour our view of the whole scene.

In combining the serious and the humorous in narrative, Proust is not an innovator, but a disciple of writers like Balzac, Flaubert, and Dickens, all of whom he admired. Where he is unique is in the delicacy of touch, the fleeting smile, the wry note that imperceptibly and momentarily alters the mood. Another exceptional feature is the variety of tone, ranging from delicate pastel touches to strong, vivid comedy. Looking back over this section, we can see variety not only in the *way* Proust passes from seriousness to laughter but also in the *kind* of laughter he elicits from us. A crude snigger is the appropriate response to the prostitute in *JS*, a bewildered smile to the antics of M. de Charlus. It is important to consider what kind of laughter is being elicited when we look at the effect of the humour in an episode. Proust can be subtly manipulative: he makes us laugh scornfully at Mme de Monteriender's inane remark on table-turning, then shows that there is a great deal of truth in it. He has subtly criticized our readiness to scorn what we have not fully understood.

III
IMAGERY

Till now, we have been considering Proust at his most craftsmanlike, looking at his techniques for building up humour. We must now move on to another aspect of his work, one which may not seem obviously connected with humour: his imagery.

There is no need to insist on the importance of imagery in Proust's theory of the novel. Every student of Proust is familiar with statements like:

je crois que la métaphore seule peut donner une sorte d'éternité au style. ('A Propos du "style" de Flaubert', *CSB* p. 586)

or

la vérité ne commencera qu'au moment où l'écrivain prendra deux objets différents, posera leur rapport [. . .] et les enfermera dans les anneaux nécessaires d'un beau style. (*TR* III 889)

But Proust uses this, the most distinctive feature of his style, to produce humour as well as truth or beauty; here, we will be concerned with the ways in which he does so.

In this chapter, 'imagery' will be taken in its widest sense to refer to any comparison, hinted at in a single word or expanded over several pages. The long description of the *baignoire* of the Princesse de Guermantes as an underwater cavern (*CG* II 41-4) counts as an image; so does this:

Mme Verdurin s'assit à part, les hémisphères de son front blanc et légèrement rosé magnifiquement bombés. (*P* III 248)

where *hémisphères* and *bombés* are enough to imply a comparison of Mme Verdurin's brow with a globe.

All Proust's humorous comparisons rely on one factor, the interplay between the appropriate and the inappropriate. They have to be appropriate to some extent, otherwise there would seem to be no point in them. If a motor-car were compared to a palm-tree, the effect would be mystifying, not amusing. Proust does frequently indulge in seemingly inappropriate comparisons, but takes care to explain enough to justify their existence. He oddly compares Gilberte's signature to a monkey's tail, but shows us that this comparison can be both of visual and of evolutionary significance (*F* III 587). Similar justifications are provided to account for his comparing *l'esprit des Guermantes* to biscuits (*CG* II 458), or the smell of a roast chicken to virtues (*CS* I 121), all of which might at first seem far-fetched.

More frequently, there is an obvious justification for including an image which yet comprises an element of the inappropriate. For instance, Cottard's change of personality is compared to turning a garment inside-out (*JF* I 434). On reflection, one can see that this can be apposite since the way we behave in the latter half of our lives is sometimes the reverse of our earlier behaviour, as Proust points out. But at the same time it seems inappropriate to compare a complex personality change, involving a living being, with such a trivial action.

Most of Proust's humorous images fit into this second category of comparisons which, though ostensibly appropriate, contain an element of incongruity. We will therefore have to examine the different types of incongruity involved. Before doing so, however, we must consider another essential factor, the implications inherent in an image. Each element in a comparison has its own individual implications, its own particular atmosphere. It may touch the element with which it is being compared at some points, but at others it is completely independent. Compare the moon to a cheese: though their shapes and colour seem roughly similar, there are a thousand differences between them, differences of size, dignity, durability, availability and so on. Proust is well aware that the elements of a comparison have different implications and uses this consistently to create humorous effects. Very often, indeed, there is no humour in the direct or actual comparison, but only in the implications. For instance, the Princesse de Guermantes

disait: 'Mes petits Cobourg' comme elle eût dit: 'Mes petits chiens'. (*SG* II 659)

Here the actual comparison is between the possessive attitude of the Princess and the tone of voice she uses in both cases. But the effect is produced by the implied parallel between the Cobourgs (*Altesses* of royal blood), and little dogs.

The above example illustrates another important point: by mentioning similarities between two things, one tends to suggest differences. One would never think of the differences between the moon and cheese or between *Altesses* and little dogs if a parallel had not been drawn between them. Proust frequently compares two things which, though similar in some respects, are very different in others. This technique is in itself sufficient to create an impression of incongruity and hence of humour.

The following discussion of Proust's humorous comparisons will necessarily involve analysing the inappropriate element and the implications behind the images. With these factors in mind, I shall consider the different sorts of subjects that are compared with each other, that is to say, Proust's use of the animate and inanimate, of different types of people or groups, and of ideas. I shall then discuss, briefly, the use of the senses to produce humour in comparisons. Finally, I shall consider some of the techniques which, though they do not provide it, often serve to alter the effect and hence modify the humour in a comparison.

Lower Forms of Life

In humorous comparisons involving living creatures other than human beings, people almost always have some part to play in the proceedings. Comparing one animal or insect to another is not in itself potentially humorous, whereas comparing an animal to a human being almost always is. Animals endowed with amusing personalities, from Musset's *merle blanc* to Mickey Mouse, tend to have many human characteristics. This fact gives strong support to the theory that humour is essentially a human preoccupation. In all the comparisons discussed in this section, human beings will be involved, at least by implication.

The most obvious way of using lower forms of life in comparisons is to compare the baseness of the animal with the dignity of the human being, to the detriment of the latter. Proust very often makes use of this technique. In his book, *The Imagery of Proust*, Victor E. Graham has picked out dozens of belittling images of this kind, all of which are more or less amusing. In particular, he points out that 'the world of society' is most often the subject of animal comparisons. Graham's theory is that 'intelligence alone sets man apart from animals', and that high society is particularly susceptible to comparison with animals because 'here one might say the intelligence is least in evidence.' But from the point of view of humour at least, there is a much more important factor involved. Aristocrats are supposed to be the cream of society: therefore they will suffer much more than lower ranks of men from a comparison with a lower form of life. Thus M. de Charlus, though highly intelligent, is effectively ridiculed by being compared to a bumble bee in a passage already mentioned (*SG* II 606). In such comparisons, an element of social criticism is commonly present.

Almost always, comparisons between human beings and animals or insects have some degree of visual relevance as well as the basic degradation of the human being to the level of an animal. Sometimes this visual element can be convincing. The striking description of Mme Verdurin as a drunken bird (*S* I 205) is a case in point, as is the comparison of old men to seals:

car devant les vieilles gens qui écoutent, nous sommes souvent comme devant ces phoques à tête blanche, à petits yeux usés, en cage, dont nous ne connaissons pas les habitudes et dont nous nous demandons s'ils dorment quand ils sont immobiles [. . .] (*JS* p. 620)

Here, there is an element of degradation in the process of reducing dignified old men to the level of caged animals. But there is also a strong physical resemblance between the white-headed, rheumy-eyed, mustachioed old seals and their human equivalents. This resemblance enables one to appreciate more fully the point of the comparison. If old men look so like seals, why should they not be equally enigmatic?

At times, though this rare, the visual implications seem more relevant than the human–animal comparison. For instance, the lift-boy is described as a squirrel:

un personnage encore inconnu de moi, qu'on appelait 'lift' [. . .] se mit à descendre vers moi avec l'agilité d'un écureuil domestique, industrieux et captif. (*JF* I 665)

The visual resemblance between a lift running up and down with its human passenger and the clockwork effect of a squirrel's swift rush up and down is the most striking feature here. There is also a belittling element in the comparison, for the lift-boy's industry is reduced to the level of a tame squirrel's; but this is not the most noticeable element.

Often, there is more disparity than resemblance between the visual elements in a comparison, and this disparity is enough to make the comparison humorous. To compare a person to something very small for instance is potentially amusing. Human beings are frequently compared to insects, arachnids, and other small living things. As the visual element is implausible, it is usually the behaviour of a person that is compared to that of an insect. Françoise's cunning at tormenting all other servants is compared to the skill with which a particular type of wasp paralyses its prey (*CS* I 123-4). Mme Cottard's industry at spreading social news is compared to that of a bee (*JF* I 516). In such cases Proust takes care to minimize the physical resemblance. He preserves many of Mme Cottard's human characteristics:

Mme Swann [. . .] savait le nombre énorme de calices bourgeois que pouvait, quand elle était armée de l'aigrette et du porte-cartes, visiter en un seul après-midi cette active ouvrière.

By arming the bee with an aigrette and visiting cards, he makes us visualize a tiny Mme Cottard buzzing from flower to flower.

If a human being is compared to a disproportionately large animal, the effect is a shade less bizarre. Again, these comparisons tend not to be directly visual but to provide an explanation of a phenomenon. Describing deformed women in their old age, he writes:

elles n'avaient même pas l'air d'avoir vieilli. La vieillesse est quelque chose d'humain; elles étaient des monstres, et elles ne semblaient pas avoir plus 'changé' que des baleines. (*TR* III 945)

The ostensible point here, that grotesque-looking women show their age as little as do non-human things such as whales, is a perfectly acceptable one. It could have been exemplified in a hundred other ways, by comparing them to stone, for instance. But the visual element is essential to the humour. One laughs at the brief glimpse of the huge, grey monsters, which, if the point is stretched to its limit, could for a second be said to resemble monstrous old women. In this case, then, the visual element can be accepted, albeit fleetingly.

In these examples, the comparisons are ostensibly related to behaviour, but have unspoken visual overtones which give pungency to the whole, and also have their own separate impact. Elsewhere the opposite effect is achieved. An image purports to be visually significant, but its unspoken behavioural implications add to the point, and can, indeed, be much more important than the visual one. For instance, when Bloch finally succeeds in penetrating into the closed world of the Guermantes, Proust comments: 'Bloch était entré en sautant comme une hyène' (*TR* III 966). There seems to be little visual importance in this image. One is surely not meant to imagine Bloch on all fours. The point is provided by the implications. Hyenas are by reputation base scavengers, that feed on the carrion left by nobler animals. So Bloch battens on the post-war remnants of the noble Guermantes salon.

These comparisons are chiefly concerned with the human element in the image. Men and women are compared to giraffes, wasps, whales, swallows and so on, with the result that the human beings appear less than purely human. This effect is paramount in almost all the animal and insect images of this kind.

Finally, Proust's animal–human comparisons often take on the form of crowd-scenes, in which each human being becomes an animal. The humour in the description of the aristocrats as various types of fish

(for instance in the *baignoire* of the Princesse de Guermantes) is largely
due to the amazing ingenuity with which Proust accumulates the
parallels.

The Inanimate and People

Let us next consider comparisons between inanimate objects and
people. The effect here tends to be slightly different from that of comparisons involving people and animals, which have a degrading, belittling effect on the human beings involved. This deterioration is by
no means essential to the inanimate comparisons. The impression given
is more one of unnaturalness—there is something odd in comparing a
man to a geometrical solid or a woman to a talking statue (*JF* I 478-9,
S I 258-9). This feeling of inappropriateness will be at the root of the
humour in most of the comparisons which follow.

Despite the importance of this unnatural element, the belittling tendency that is so vital to Proust's portrayal of human beings can also
appear in comparisons with the inanimate. The particular object
involved is the deciding factor here, for inanimate objects, unlike
animals, do not necessarily have an element of the inferior to them.
To many people, even a noble animal, a horse or an eagle, is inferior
to man. But inanimate objects such as the sun, the earth, the sea and
so on can seem far nobler and more meaningful. If one is looking for a
belittling comparison involving the inanimate, the object has to be a
trivial one.

Perhaps the most obviously disparaging type of comparison is
between a human being and something that is both trivial and man-
made. Proust compares Mme de Cambremer-Legrandin to a honey-cake:
je pouvais, dans la chaleur de cette belle fin d'après-midi, butiner à
mon gré dans le gros gâteau de miel que Mme de Cambremer était si
rarement et qui remplaça les petits fours que je n'eus pas l'idée d'offrir.
(*SG* II 811)

Although the reason for the comparison is that Mme de Cambremer-
Legrandin is behaving very sweetly to the Narrator because he is an
intimate friend of the Guermantes, the actual comparison is a very
direct and concrete one. The idea of Mme de Cambremer as a cake is
real enough to be juxtaposed to actual cakes, the ones the Narrator
forgot to offer. This example also has an element of strangeness which
gives the humour a particular flavour: one is aware of the oddness of

comparing someone to a cake, and the curious atmosphere is enhanced by considerable juggling with size. Mme de Cambremer-Legrandin may be compared to an ephemeral object; but at the same time she has been turned into something so enormous that the Narrator is the size of a bee by comparison to the cake she has become, since he can *butiner* in it. This manipulation of size is a constant feature of comparisons involving the inanimate. Old ladies are indirectly compared to scaffolding (*JS* 774); or they can be like the tiny manikins which appear or disappear from a barometer according to the weather (*JS* 341). This manipulation of size does not in itself provide the humour; but it captures the reader's attention and strengthens his reaction to the comparison as a whole. This element of strangeness prevents even such belittling comparisons as the honey-cake one from seeming too degrading.

The most striking feature of these comparisons is their visual impact. With considerable ingenuity, Proust finds resemblances between the most unexpected elements. For instance, there are frequent comparisons between people and objects which Proust makes us realize are similar in shape. Old men are compared to dolls (*TR* III 924), and valets to milk-cans (*S* I 325). But these images are taken far beyond their initial visual expression, and Proust leads us to think of wider parallels. Take for instance the comparison between servants lining the stairs of a grand house and milk-cans before each door on a squalid staircase. The reader initially pictures both the subjects and recognizes the similarity between the liveried, motionless dignity of the servants and the shiny immobility of the milk-cans, which, with their cylindrical bodies and narrow necks, are not unlike a crude, limbless caricature of the human form. But the implications of the comparison go much further. The servants represent the grandeur of the house whose steps they line: they are said to be 'représentant le service intérieur'. The milk-cans to which they are compared are visible only because their owners are too poor to live in a house that has a back staircase. Hence they are a symbol of the poverty of the people on the staircase. Thus the comparison is ironic, since by ascribing the same function and the same physical attributes to valets and milk-cans, Proust implies that there is an intrinsic similarity between them. The comparison becomes humiliating to the valets, human beings likened to objects, and also to their masters, owners of valets likened to owners of milk-cans.

So far the emphasis has been on comparisons which illustrate the human element in the comparison by likening it to something inanimate.

Elsewhere the opposite effect can also be achieved. In such cases the humour seems more gratuitous: it produces an isolated effect, and does not contribute to one's picture either of a particular element or a general one. This is partly because the home truths that Proust wishes us to remember are usually concerned with human beings. When Proust compares servants to milk-cans, he is making a general point about their status, which will help to build up the whole picture of the servant–master relationship in *ALR*, by providing a fresh instance of its false-ness and pretension. But when Proust compares a church to a novice he tells us nothing about churches in general. The comparison goes on as follows:

son clocher, en se préparant à la nuit, semblait avoir cette bonne volonté dont font montre les novices pour se faire accepter de leurs camarades, mais ne parvenait pas par son petit air brave à arracher un sourire d'encouragement aux vieux arbres qui continuaient à se plaindre éternellement de leurs douleurs aux pommiers [. . .] (*JS* p. 513)

The reader, attuned to the human element in comparisons, will con-centrate more on the picture of the novice than on the principal element, that is to say the steeple. At the same time, one smiles because Proust has turned the normal comparison inside out.

Also inherent in this comparison is a slight feeling of impertinence: it seems degrading to compare a steeple to a mere novice of the religion to which the church is a monument. At times Proust goes even further, for instance when he confronts the sun with a human being and makes the human being seem the larger and more powerful of the two. This implied comparison occurs several times in Proust. In *CSB* the Narrator expresses his power over the sun:

[. . .] pour m'asseoir sur le siège sans être dérangé par le soleil qui le chauffait, je lui dis: 'Ote-toi de là, mon petit, que je m'y mette'. (*CSB*, Le Fallois ed. p. 65)

M. de Guermantes later says the same thing (*CSB*, Le Fallois ed. p. 231).

In these comparisons with the inanimate, Proust achieves highly original effects, stretching our credulity to its limits. We are here laugh-ing in part through surprise, an important aspect of Proust's humour.

People

When Proust makes comparisons between people, he is not simply being funny. We are here faced with some of Proust's most pointed, biting criticism of his times and his contemporaries. Indeed, humorous comparison between people almost always turns out to be satirical. This is because such comparisons invariably contain an element of the inappropriate. Where two people are compared inappropriately, this usually means that one of them would find the comparison belittling and degrading: consider the feelings of an aristocrat who found out that he had been compared to a dustman. The aristocrat becomes a 'victim', made to seem ridiculous, forced into a confrontation of which he would strongly disapprove. It is the fact that he would disapprove that provides the satire, mockery of his aristocratic snobbery and also of the social set-up that makes it impossible to equate two fellow-men.

Most frequently, then, Proust compares two people in a way which, by implication, degrades one of them. The simplest means of achieving this is to compare a person with someone of much lower status. Proust often adds to the subtlety of such comparisons by allowing the social satire to slip in by implication. Rarely is it the ostensible point. Most often, in fact, the apparent comparison is between the physical appearances of members of different classes.

There are many comparisons between aristocrats and plebeians, and almost all of them refer to the appearance of the aristocrats. Thus we have a well-born couple,

le baron et la baronne de Norpois, habillés toujours en noir, la femme en loueuse de chaises et le mari en croque-mort, qui sortaient plusieurs fois par jour pour aller à l'église. (*CG* II 32)

Seemingly, the comparisons are made simply in order to help us to visualize these characters. Moreover, they are in some ways appropriate, since the Baron and Baronne are regular church-goers, and they are compared to people who earn their living from the Church. The humour emerges only when one thinks of the difference between the two classes: the *loueuse de chaises* and the *croque-mort* are vulgar, rather macabre figures, probably dirty and illiterate to boot. And the Baron and Baronne would certainly be highly insulted at Proust's comparison.

Comparisons like these provide obvious instances of social criticism. Others are more subtle, though no less biting. One curious technique is to belittle a character by comparing him to someone far greater and better than he is. Here the 'victim' would be delighted at the comparison, and his delight, like his potential disgust in the previous example, is used to make an implied criticism of his standards and his inflated idea of his own value. Proust repeatedly compares members of the

bourgeoisie, particularly women, to kings, Louis XIV (*CS* I 118), the
Kings of Orient (*JS* p. 734) or the kings at the Field of the Cloth of
Gold (*NPN* I 399). Proust can take these comparisons to ludicrous
lengths. In describing Mme Verdurin's futile attempts to keep her
fidèles when they are determined to go elsewhere, Proust writes:

Et c'était en vain que Mme Verdurin leur disait alors, comme l'impéra-
trice romaine, qu'elle était le seul général à qui dût obéir sa légion,
comme le Christ ou le Kaiser, que celui qui aimait son père et sa mère
autant qu'elle et n'était pas prêt à les quitter pour la suivre n'était pas
digne d'elle, elle, seul remède et seule volupté. (*SG* II 877)

The most inappropriate comparison, between Mme Verdurin and
Christ, is underlined by her use of Christ's actual words.

Such an approach does not invariably have a satirical aim. Some
comparisons between people result in a different type of humour,
bizarre and fantastic. They may also contain an element of social
criticism, but their prime effect is to give us a momentary glimpse of
the subject in an unexpected guise. It is often the shock of this glimpse
that makes us smile.

This is often the case when an ordinary, civilized Parisian is
compared to an evil, wild character, often from the past. For example,
Mme Verdurin

éprouvait la colère d'un grand inquisiteur qui ne parvient pas à extirper
l'hérésie [. . .] (*S* I 259)

The atmosphere of sinister power and cruelty associated with a grand
inquisitor seems astonishing in comparison with Mme Verdurin, who is
here expressing childish petulance. The comparison is not altogether
inappropriate, however. Mme Verdurin is capable of savage cruelty
when given the chance: witness her treatment of Saniette.

Again, a character can be compared with someone much more
violent and wild than he. Mme de Cambremer-Legrandin in her
enthusiasm over Debussy's *Pelléas* is compared to a savage:

s'approchant de moi avec les gestes d'une femme sauvage qui aurait
voulu me faire des agaceries, s'aidant des doigts pour piquer les notes
imaginaires, elle se mit à fredonner quelque chose que je supposai
être pour elle les adieux de Pelléas [. . .] (*SG* II 814)

Here the humour depends not only on the contrast between Mme
de Cambremer and a savage, but also on a trick on the part of the
author. He has momentarily abandoned the tacit conventions of
civilized life, and is looking at Mme de Cambremer with the eyes of an
explorer in a new land. It is plain that this technique can produce

humour in all sorts of situations. Voltaire made frequent use of it, describing things that we take for granted as though seeing them for the first time, and thereby bringing out their inherent absurdity.

Conversely, a character can be compared with another who is far more formal and artificial than he. Like many of the previous examples, this technique frequently involves a comment on behaviour: a character is reacting formally where he should be being sincere. This element usually provides much of the humour. For instance, if one lady in a salon inquires after a sick friend,

Aussitôt, comme dans un ballet, toutes les femmes, même celles qui ne savaient pas de qui il s'agissait, prenaient un air triste [. . .] (*JS* p. 661)

Here one laughs at the contrast between the formality of their response, preordained according to the code of manners just as a ballet is choreographed in advance, and the pretence they make of serious concern; and also at the visual picture of the corps de ballet, with its exaggerated, stylized gestures identically reproduced by each individual dancer. A further contrast between the grace and beauty of ballet and the shallowness of society women may contribute to the humour. There are many comparisons of this kind, between dancers or, more frequently, actors, and socialites (see *P* III 236 where the *fidèles* are compared to a troupe of actors, *CG* II 446 where the Guermantes are compared to a *corps de ballet* and so on).

The humour of an inappropriate comparison can be enhanced when the characters' emotions are brought into play. Emotion can often seem excessively funny if it is exaggerated or inappropriate: witness Alceste's extreme rages in Molière's *Le Misanthrope*. When Legrandin is forced to admit that he is not acquainted with the Guermantes, he is compared to a martyr:

le regard restait douloureux, comme celui d'un beau martyr dont le corps est hérissé de flèches: 'Non, je ne les connais pas', dit-il [. . .] (*CS* I 127)

Such a trivial cause of dissatisfaction is not worthy of being compared to martyrdom; but in this case the exaggeration is not superimposed on the situation by Proust, but inherent in Legrandin's own passionately snobbish personality.

Proust sometimes builds up a series of comparisons to create a cumulative effect, as for example in the series of comparisons involving a change of sex. Apart from the description of Jupien as a *grande coquette trahie*, we have Saint-Loup as a fairy:

comme une fée hargneuse dépouille sa première apparence et se pare
de grâces enchanteresses, je vis cet être dédaigneux devenir le plus
aimable, le plus prévenant jeune homme que j'eusse jamais rencontré.
(*JF* I 732)

Aimé smiles with

le même sourire orgueilleusement modeste et savamment discret de
maîtresse de maison qui sait se retirer à propos. (*JF* I 695)

There is also the startling comparison between M. de Charlus in his
grief at being deserted by Morel and a nymph pursued by Pan (*P* III
318). It is significant that in all the examples quoted here the subject
has homosexual leanings. This gives an underlying truth to the superficially ridiculous picture of a male character, with whose appearance
we have become familiar, suddenly turning into a female version of
himself. Elsewhere, this element of truth seems more important than
the initial absurdity of the concept. For instance, in comparing M.
de Charlus to a woman, Proust points out that it is only too apposite to
draw such parallels:

je comprenais maintenant pourquoi tout à l'heure, quand je l'avais
vu sortir de chez Mme de Villeparisis, j'avais pu trouver que M.
de Charlus avait l'air d'une femme: c'en était une! (*SG* II 614)

And M. de Charlus, indeed, is the person most frequently compared to
a woman in Proust. He is indirectly compared to a pregnant woman
(*SG* II 613), he looks like Mme de Marsantes when he comes into a
room (*SG* II 908). When he expresses his preference for *la fraisette* he
talks like *une douce et souriante dame* (*SG* II 967). In all these
examples there is an element of humour, combined with serious
examination of a curious phenomenon.

Non-Visual Comparisons

Most of Proust's imagery is visual. However, he was keenly aware of all
the senses. He frequently makes comparisons of smells, of tastes, of
sound and of sensation; also he combines the different senses in his
images. However, there are few humorous images involving senses other
than visual and auditory ones. A rare example involving the sense of
smell is the comparison between the effect of asparagus on one's urine
and a play by Shakespeare:

toute la nuit qui suivait un dîner où j'en avais mangé, elles jouaient,
dans leurs farces poétiques et grossières comme une féerie de Shakespeare, à changer mon pot de chambre en un vase de parfum. (*CS* I 121)

Taste is indirectly involved in the comparison between the professional secret of Françoise's good cooking which remains as mysterious as the elegance of a great lady or the art of a great singer (*JF* I 485).

There are, however, many auditory images that make one laugh. In particular, Proust had a good ear for different voices or tones of voice, and frequently uses comparisons to get these across to the reader. Thus M. de Bréauté's voice is several times described as harsh and grating. When the Narrator is despairing of ever being introduced to the Princesse de Guermantes,

le mot 'bonsoir' fut susurré à mon oreille par M. de Bréauté, non comme le son ferrailleux et ébréché d'un couteau qu'on repasse pour l'aiguiser, encore moins comme le cri du marcassin dévastateur des terres cultivées, mais comme la voix d'un sauveur possible. (*SG* II 654)

Incidentally, this comparison is interestingly put. We are told that the voice is *not* like a knife being sharpened nor a boar; but we are clearly meant to infer the contrary. Apart from this the actual elements of the comparison are amusing. Both the knife and the boar are unattractive and violent, apart from the unpleasant noises they make. This contrasts with the polite 'bonsoir' actually pronounced by M. de Bréauté. Later, Proust repeats one of the objects of the comparison, and talks of

M. de Bréauté [. . .] dont la voix de couteau qu'on est en train de re-passer fit entendre quelques sons vagues et rouillés. (*P* III 42)

Here, again, there is the same contrast between the sound and the polite formulas the speaker is uttering. In this case we infer from the context that M. de Bréauté's inarticulate murmurs are made 'par politesse pour Mme de Guermantes'.

Though he repeats the same image when describing the same voice, there is immense variety in the humorous images used to describe different people's voices. The voice can be likened to something enormous and exaggeratedly loud. One of the most famous examples is the vast rumbling laugh of Grand Duke Wladimir (*SG* II 657–8). Proust is vague about the actual nature of this noise. At first it seems to be a roll of drums; later it has become thunder. All that we can be sure of is the extraordinary loudness of the sounds, which are funny just because they are far too loud to be credible. Proust is here using the same technique as Rabelais, who is vague about the size of his giants, making it impossible for the reader to limit their dimensions by visualizing them too precisely.

Other voices are too pretty to be taken seriously. For instance, Ski's laugh is compared to a peal of bells, emphasizing the obvious affectation and pretentiousness of his whole personality:

Ski [. . .] se mit à rire [. . .] Ski prenait d'abord un air fin, puis laissait échapper comme malgré lui un seul son de rire, comme un premier appel de cloches, suivi d'un silence où le regard fin semblait examiner à bon escient la drôlerie de ce qu'on disait, puis une seconde cloche de rire s'ébranlait, et c'était bientôt un hilare angélus. (*P* III 289 footnote)

Apart from the dissection of Ski's affectation provided by the close analysis of his laugh, the actual sound is suggested: it is one of those laughs on a scale of clearly distinct, musical notes, which cannot ever be sincere. The fact that the laugh is unnatural though attractive makes it seem ridiculous: its beauty does nothing to counteract its affectation. The general atmosphere is enhanced by the elaborate analysis and the precious words *escient* and *hilare*. Elsewhere, Proust takes this musical artificiality of the voice still further and compares it to music or musical instruments of different kinds, with considerable humorous results.

Techniques

Proust's imagery is particularly interesting from the point of view of technique, since it provides us with an opportunity of stressing the scope and variety of Proust's humorous effects. The most basic point has already been made, namely that a humorous image can be suggested through the use of a single word, or can be elaborated on at considerable length. If the image is too inappropriate to seem anyting but farfetched on close inspection, it is alluded to briefly in passing. If, on the other hand, the comparison is relevant on all sorts of levels, Proust dwells on it; and even if he leaves the reader to draw his own inferences, he at least ensures that the reader is likely to do so by making him take time over the image. The first type, in which a single word is enough to suggest an image, is comparatively rare. There are occasions like that in which, when the visitors' bell had rung, 'on envoyait en éclaireur ma grand'mère' (*CS* I 14). But even here, the far-fetched idea of the Narrator's family sending out a scout in the shape of an old lady is taken up in a later paragraph. Indeed, exaggerated, far-fetched effects are an essential part of humour; and Proust often makes one laugh simply by elaborating on a seemingly unlikely comparison. For instance, there is a comparison very similar to the one between the grandmother and scout, but which produces more humour simply because it is longer:

Le cœur battait un peu plus vite à la princesse d'Épinay qui recevait dans son grand salon du rez-de-chaussée, quand elle apercevait de loin, telles les premières lueurs d'un inoffensif incendie ou les 'reconnaissances' d'une invasion non espérée, traversant lentement la cour, d'une démarche oblique, la duchesse coiffée d'un ravissant chapeau et inclinant une ombrelle d'où pleuvait une odeur d'été. 'Tiens, Oriane', disait-elle comme un 'garde-à-vous' qui cherchait à avertir ses visiteuses avec prudence, et pour qu'on eût le temps de sortir en ordre, qu'on évacuât les salons sans panique. (*CG* II 462)

Proust has here introduced amusing sidelines: the comparison involves not only Mme d'Épinay but also Mme de Guermantes and the other guests. It is inappropriate to call a fire 'inoffensive' and to compare a mere human being to a conflagration or an invasion. And yet both a fire and an invasion make people flee before them; and Mme de Guermantes too empties the Princesse d'Épinay's salon of its guests. The description of the salon being 'evacuated' adds further humour: the near-panic of a crowd menaced by fire or invasion can be compared to the polish of the aristocrats politely taking their leave.

On the whole, Proust is fonder of exploring the possibilities of his humorous comparisons than of slipping them in as mere asides. This tendency is in character with his writing as a whole, which is remarkable for its close analysis of things that we tend to take for granted. As well as this, lengthy treatment in general may be an important feature of humorous technique, since, as has already been said, it can produce a feeling of humorous exaggeration and overstatement which in itself may be enough to make one laugh. Length can produce impressions of pomposity, monotony, lack of moderation, and general lack of contact with the audience or reader which can be manipulated to good humorous effect.

There is another way in which a writer can expand his comparisons. Instead of analysing them at length when they first occur, he can repeat them, adding fresh nuances with every reiteration. This Proust is extremely apt to do. Further, he builds up his humorous comparisons into groups. For instance, he epitomizes the role in life of various classes by comparing it to the part played in nature by certain plants. It is only too appropriate to compare a motionless footman to an exotic plant: both are equally decorative and fundamentally useless; both are rather delicate: the footman may lose his job at any time and disappear, just as the plant may wither and die (see *JF* I 706-7, 723). The aristocrats, who have their roots in the ancient soil of France, more

frequently tend to be compared to trees. This is in itself an amusing
means of rendering the dignity and the old-fashioned character of the
people involved. It also gives Proust scope for variations on the theme.
For instance, Mme de Guermantes's bow is like a shrub bending:

Elle [. . .] déplia et tendit la tige de son bras, pencha en avant son corps
qui se redressa rapidement en arrière comme un arbuste qu'on a couché
et qui, laissé libre, revient à sa position naturelle. (*CG* II 254–5)

The extent to which Mme de Guermantes is transformed into a shrub
is as amusing as the idea behind the comparison. Not only is her basic
shape that of a shrub but her arms are branches, and she even moves
like a tree. Moreover, the slight insolence of her bow is implied in the
image, for she makes one feel that it is unnatural for her to be bowing,
just as it is unnatural for a tree or shrub to be bent double. Again,
ageing aristocrats after the war are like

ces arbres dont l'automne, en variant leurs couleurs, semble changer
l'essence. (*TR* III 937)

Proust has again fitted the image to the subject; aristocrats are trees,
so it is only fitting that old aristocrats should be trees in autumn.

This technique of studying a particular image from all sides is a
standard procedure in humorous writing. An obvious example is La
Fontaine's habit of comparing particular animals to particular human
beings, and continuing the analogy throughout a poem. Proust, writing
at length, clearly has great scope for using this technique. One might
add that serious comparisons gain a humorous undertone if considered
as part of a group. For instance, Odette is several times compared to a
flower, and in old age, to *une rose stérilisée* (*TR* III 950). If one
remembers the series of plant images, this parallel seems only too
appropriate: whereas aristocrats have good solid roots, *cocottes* such as
Odette are essentially frivolous and live only for the present, like
flowers.

Conversely, a serious point can be suggested by placing a particular
comparison within a specific group of humorous images. For example,
by frequent repetition of the comparison, Proust leads us to think of
ageing society women as associated with priests (we will see shortly that
society itself is repeatedly associated with religion). The dowager Mme
de Cambremer is hung about with little bags, which are described as
'les ornements de sa tournée pastorale et de son sacerdoce mondain'
(*SG* II 808); or Mme de Lambresac is described as 'un prélat un peu
ramolli' (*SG* II 681). These comparisions are individually amusing; but
it is significant that the only male who is consistently described as an

ecclesiastic is M. de Charlus, who, with his *paupières d'ecclésiastique*
(*P* III 290) is endowed with *l'onction d'un ecclésiastique en train de
dire son chapelet* (*SG* II 1037). If one remembers on what occasions
this comparison has been used, it becomes plain that M. de Charlus is
being treated exactly like an ageing society woman: so that these individually amusing images provide a further allusion to his homosexuality.

Again, a group of comparisons can colour the rest of the text so that
an allusion to the same subject, whether or not it be couched in the
form of a comparison, can be affected by the previous images. A good
example is M. de Palancy. He figures prominently in the comparisons
between the aristocrats and fish which frequently recur in *ALR*. First,
in the long description of the monocles at Mme de Saint-Euverte's,
M. de Palancy is particularly striking:

M. de Palancy qui, avec sa grosse tête de carpe aux yeux ronds, se
déplaçait lentement au milieu des fêtes en desserrant d'instant en
instant ses mandibules comme pour chercher son orientation, avait l'air
de transporter seulement avec lui un fragment accidentel, et peut-être
purement symbolique, du vitrage de son aquarium [. . .] (*S* I 327)

This description is amusing both because of the impertinence of
comparing a nobleman to a fish, and because of the skill with which the
monocle is translated into a fishy context. Later, in the Princesse de
Guermantes's *baignoire,* he is described in very similar, equally striking
terms:

Le marquis de Palancy, le cou tendu, la figure oblique, son gros œil
rond collé contre le verre du monocle, se déplaçait lentement dans
l'ombre transparente et paraissait ne pas plus voir le public de
l'orchestre qu'un poisson qui passe, ignorant de la foule des visiteurs
curieux, derrière la cloison vitrée d'un aquarium. (*CG* II 43)

The cumulative effect of these two descriptions is sufficient to make
the appearance of M. de Palancy memorable to the reader, largely
because of the reiterated fish image. When he is next referred to, the
reader is likely to remember him as the carp-man, so that the reference
will appear ridiculous, in part at least, because it is mentally juxtaposed to the earlier descriptions: the Duchesse de Guermantes enters
the *baignoire* of the Princesse de Guermantes, and preserving the
underwater imagery that has been prevalent during the whole scene,
Proust writes:

Elle alla droit vers sa cousine [. . .] et, se retournant vers les monstres
marins et sacrés flottant au fond de l'antre, fit à ces demi-dieux du

Jockey-Club—qui à ce moment-là, et particulièrement M. de Palancy, furent les hommes que j'aurais le plus aimé être—un bonjour familier de vieille amie [. . .] (*CG* II 53)

Here, the humour is contained almost more in one's remembrance of M. de Palancy's round, fishlike eyes and rhythmically moving jaws than in the actual imagery of the *monstres sacrés* (which in itself, of course, adds to the effect, since it seems absurd that a young man should long to be a marine monster, however sacred). Proust is using imagery here to produce a contrast between the prestige of a character and his ridiculous appearance, a contrast which he frequently makes.

Again, within these families of humorous comparisons, Proust can produce witty details, which depend on the existence of the groups for their effect, but which are individually amusing, always provided they are noticed. For instance, within the large group of comparisons between aristocrats and animals or fish which has already been mentioned, there are actual family resemblances. M. de Guermantes and M. de Charlus, who are brothers, are the only two aristocrats to be compared to sharks. M. de Guermantes has

une main à demi dépliée flottant, comme l'aileron d'un requin, à côté de sa poitrine [. . .] (*CG* II 224)

M. de Charlus, trailing some ruffian in his wake, is

toujours escorté quoique à quelque distance, comme le requin par son pilote [. . .] (*P* III 204)

In both cases, the description refers to the way the brothers move, not to their appearance; but at the same time, the shark's pointed snout and streamlined head is not unlike the typical Guermantes head, which, in other animal parallels, is compared to an eagle's or vulture's (see *CG* II 62, 53).

It is, however, unlikely that the reader, unless he is isolating the images in Proust for some particular purpose, will notice such details as the family resemblance between the shark-Guermantes. In fact, Proust's manipulation of humorous imagery is extraordinarily subtle, so much so that many of the effects will almost certainly be lost on most people reading him for the first time. Moreover, they argue enormous awareness on the part of the author: I do not consider that any of the more subtle points I have picked out are accidental. On a larger scale, we find that Proust uses humorous imagery to give a particular flavour to specific sections or episodes of his novel. Most of the comparisons between M. de Charlus and a woman or a priest occur in *SG*. Although M. de Charlus frequently appears in the other books, this side

of his character is elsewhere given far less importance. The view of
M. de Charlus as a woman is thus particularly appropriate to the title
of *SG*. It is as though the Narrator's eyes, once opened to M. de
Charlus's homosexuality, were repeatedly struck by fresh instances of
it. At the same time, there is the occasional image elsewhere which does
link up with the *SG* ones; thus we do not feel that M. de Charlus has
become a completely different person for the duration of *SG*, since we
have, albeit occasionally, seen him compared to a woman elsewhere
(for instance in *JF* I 764 and *P* III 318).

This use of humorous imagery as one of the threads that links up the
different elements in *ALR* cannot be too strongly emphasized. It is by
such threads, not by the conventional threads of plot, chronology and
so on, that Proust's novel is given its internal cohesion.

A further point emphasizes the complexity of Proust's use of
imagery. He is not often content to reiterate the same image in a particular context, but develops and transforms his images as they recur.
Several of the humorous comparisons in *ALR* have prototypes in *JS*
or other earlier works. In almost every case, Proust has developed the
later image much further in the direction suggested by its humorous
potential. It is worth giving an example. The vivid *ALR* comparison
between Françoise and Michelangelo seems to stem from an earlier
parallel in *JS*, where he talks of:

Félicie dont les mains grossières comme celles de certains sculpteurs
et de certains pianistes composaient pour lui, avec des retouches si
délicates, un ouvrage d'un fini merveilleux. (*JS* pp. 337–8)

The somewhat banal contrast between the roughness of the hands
which produce a culinary as well as a sculptural masterpiece is vastly
expanded in the *ALR* version. Far from being uncertain as to whether
the cook is to be compared to a sculptor or a pianist, Proust has turned
her into a particular sculptor, 'le Michel-Ange de notre cuisine' (*JF* I
458), an epithet that is amusing in itself. Apart from stressing this
parallel by referring to her cooking as 'composer [. . .] dans l'effer-
vescence de la création' (p. 445), Proust has extended the image to the
very limits of its relevance to provide many incongruous yet apposite
parallels between the old peasant woman and the rugged, tortured
genius. Like Michelangelo, she chooses her materials herself, which
seems appropriate since she takes her cooking so seriously, but inappropriate because instead of choosing marble, she is picking out
calves' feet and steaks. At the same time, there is a physical resemblance even here, since her beef jelly is 'pareil à des blocs de quartz

transparent' (p. 458), while her York ham is 'comme du marbre rose' (p. 445). This visual parallel implies visual incongruities: one imagines Françoise choosing huge pieces of meat the size of marble slabs; one pictures her, conversely, as a giant, casually arranging vast blocks of quartz on a monstrous platter, and so on. Again, Françoise's exhaustion during the process of creation is compared to that of Michelangelo when he was working on the Medici Tombs: which seems appropriate until we mentally juxtapose the relevant works, the masterly but sombre sculpture and the beef jelly. There seems no need to go further into the *ALR* image (though there is scope for longer discussion) to show how much more the humorous potential has here been realized than in its earlier counterpart.

There is not sufficient space here to analyse the numerous similar instances, such as the 'adieu aux aubépines' (*CS* I 145) which is clearly based on and has evolved from an earlier passage in *CSB* (Le Fallois ed. pp. 292-5) and the earlier, more banal version of the witty description of the hotel room at Doncières, in which the furniture is compared to various living things, published in *Textes retrouvés* ('Une Chambre d'hôtel', p. 22, cf. *CG* II 82-4).

Elsewhere, Proust completely alters the implications of his own earlier imagery. In *ALR* he seems to be mocking at his own early tendency towards preciosity when he puts into the mouth of the ridiculous Legrandin exactly the sort of image he would himself have used earlier: Legrandin's remark:

'Et ce petit nuage rose, n'a-t-il pas aussi un teint de fleur, d'œillet ou d'hydrangea?' (*CS* I 130)

is very like the description of clouds in *PJ*, though the actual imagery is different:

Légers comme de claires couronnes flétries et persistants comme des regrets, de petits nuages bleus et roses flottaient à l'horizon. (*JS*, p. 19, 'Mort de Baldassare Silvande')

Finally there is the very important question of the way an image is developed within a particular work. It is too simple to maintain that Proust does not do more than make straightforward comparisons, or even reiterate images to produce a composite picture. He will often manipulate imagery to produce a feeling of considerable progression. For instance, he may introduce an image only after a careful and subtle process of preparation, so that it can be slanted towards specific effects, as well as being interesting in its own right. If a single striking parallel is aimed at, the comparison may well be included without any preparation. But if Proust is intending that a particular object should seem irresistibly to suggest a comparison, then he tends to introduce the comparison gradually, so that it will appear almost inevitable. For instance when one thinks of M. de Guermantes's cousins Walpurge and Dorothée, one remembers them as female mountaineers. This parallel has in fact been progressively introduced. Proust begins by referring to a different aristocratic lady and pointing out how odd it is that she should carry a stick:

La première de ces dames [. . .] tenait à la main une canne. Je craignis d'abord qu'elle ne fût blessée ou infirme. Elle était au contraire fort alerte. (*CG* II 574–5)

Walpurge and Dorothée then come in as 'deux autres dames porteuses de cannes' (p. 575). Thus at their very first appearance, their sticks are singled out as being their most striking feature, the first thing to be mentioned. We are already interested and mystified by the fact that these old ladies carry sticks, since they have no need of them. Having made us aware of the sticks, Proust begins to introduce the alpinist comparison. The sticks make it seem as if they have had a long and arduous climb; so Proust exaggerates the height of their actual climb to their nearby *hôtel*:

Aussi, bien que descendues des hauteurs de l'hôtel de Bréquigny pour voir la duchesse [. . .] ne resterent-elles pas longtemps, et, munies de leur bâton d'alpiniste, Walpurge et Dorothée (tels étaient les prénoms des deux sœurs) reprirent la route escarpée de leur faîte. (p. 575)

One smiles here at the use of *hauteurs*, *escarpée*, *faîte*, which are completely inappropriate to a walk through Paris, but which fit in with the *bâton d'alpiniste*. The Alpinist flavour is enhanced by Proust's choosing this moment to introduce the sisters' Germanic names. Proust places further emphasis on the sticks by indulging in more or less frivolous speculations as to the real reason for their carrying them (they walk through Paris as if through the grounds of their own domain, armed with a stick because of some old fracture; they are rheumatic; they have been reaching for fruit from their trees, and are visiting the Duchess on the way home from their orchards, pp. 575–6). Next time the two old ladies appear, Proust launches straight into the comparison, and since the reader cannot have failed to notice it last time, he is able to accept it without trouble:

M. de Guermantes [. . .] se heurta devant sa porte, sévèrement gardée par elles, aux deux dames à la canne qui n'avaient pas craint de descendre nuitamment de leur cime afin d'empêcher un scandale [. . .]

par ces maudites montagnardes, il était averti de la mort de M. d'Osmond [. . .] Et sans plus s'occuper des deux parentes qui, munies de leurs alpenstocks, allaient faire l'ascension dans la nuit, il se précipita aux nouvelles [. . .] (*SG* II 725)

Here the transformation is complete: the ladies are mountaineers, their sticks alpenstocks. Had this transformation not been previously prepared, it might well have seemed too far-fetched to be acceptable; and by preparing it gradually, rather than all at once, Proust has prevented the process from seeming too elaborate and cumbersome. There is another extremely important function of such images. By including them at relevant places in the text, Proust links up disparate situations. The first mention of Walpurge and Dorothée occurs just as the Guermantes are about to go out to dinner. The discovery of M. de Charlus's vice follows this episode; then we have a party at the Princesse de Guermantes's *hôtel*, which actually takes place on the same evening as the dinner-party. Following this, the Duke and Duchess are to go to a fancy-dress ball; and it is at this stage that the two old ladies reappear. By continuing the same humorous image, Proust establishes a link between the two halves of the evening. Thus here, as in the comparisons between M. de Charlus and an ecclesiastic mentioned earlier, humorous imagery is being used to give continuity to the structure, and to establish a link between otherwise unconnected elements.

Elsewhere, instead of gradually unfolding one image, Proust allows the image to evolve, to suggest further images, which, in turn, bring others to mind. A good example is the imagery applied to Mme Blatin. We know very little about the appearance of *la vieille lectrice des Débats* (*NPN* I 405) until Swann, in accordance with his favourite habit, compares her to a painting:

Quelle horreur! Elle n'a pour elle que de ressembler tellement à Savonarole. C'est exactement le portrait de Savonarole par Fra Bartolomeo (*JF* I 535).

This comparison is funny and at the same time distinctive. Anyone who has seen the portrait will remember the idiosyncratic ugliness of Savonarola, and it is quite easy to imagine an old woman who looks rather like him. The incongruity comes when one thinks of the burning zeal of the monk and compares it with the dull-witted, vulgar frivolity of Mme Blatin. Swann then embroiders on the theme of Mme Blatin's appearance. He asks Odette:

—Quoi, vous croyez qu'elle a un derrière bleu ciel comme les singes?

Ostensibly, this is simply a piece of irreverence, and will serve to introduce the anecdote of Mme Blatin at the zoo which is to be discussed later. But the comparison is particularly amusing because it suggests various possibilities. First, there is an implied insult not only to Mme Blatin but to Savonarola in comparing her (presumably) to a mandrill. Secondly, a mandrill is not unlike a grotesque caricature of Savonarola with its heavy brows, small, close-set dark eyes, and long, slightly curved nose. Thus while we laugh at the impossibility of any woman's having 'un derrière bleu ciel', we may also smile at the fact that this most preposterous of comparisons has a grain of visual truth behind it. Swann goes on to tell an anecdote about Mme Blatin's experiences at the zoo which involves another implied comparison. Mme Blatin addresses a Senegalese as 'négro'. He replies: 'Moi négro . . . mais toi, chameau!' Here again the comparison is not apparently visually relevant. The point, of course, is that it is degrading and insulting to any Frenchwoman to call her a *chameau*. But, again, there is an element of similarity between the portrait of Savonarola and the long, buff nose, the curling underlip and the supercilious expression of a camel. So that the insolent animal comparisons applied to Mme Blatin may seem doubly insolent in that they are not without some relevance to her appearance.

The effectiveness of juxtaposing the three apparently unrelated comparisons described here suggests another point: the context is of vital importance to the image in many cases. There are numerous images in Proust which would be perfectly acceptable as serious comparisons, but which seem absurd simply because of the context. For example, there is a description of Mme de Lambresac's smile:

Mais ce sourire, au lieu de se préciser en une affirmation active, en un langage muet mais clair, se noyait presque aussitôt en une sorte d'extase idéale qui ne distinguait rien, tandis que la tête s'inclinait en un geste de bénédiction [. . .] (*SG* II 681)

There may be a faint tinge of impertinence in the close and somewhat clinical observation of this smile; but if the smile of a venerable mystic were being described, the passage could be taken perfectly seriously. What makes us laugh is that the smile is on the face of an aristocratic lady at a party. Again, when Mme de Villeparisis is taking leave of an importunate guest,

La marquise fit le léger mouvement de lèvres d'une mourante qui voudrait ouvrir la bouche, mais dont le regard ne reconnaît plus. (*CG* II 249)

This comparison would not strike one as amusing in the least if the Marquise were very ill.

Thus there are two fundamentally distinct categories of comparison: the intrinsically funny ones and the ones that depend on their context for their effect.

It has been possible to do little more than simply suggest the complexity and variety of Proust's humorous imagery. The richness of this aspect is striking to the student of Proust's humour in general. One begins to wonder whether there is a particular link between imagery and humour that makes it such a valuable source for humorous effects. Proust himself, when he wrote that 'les poètes feraient mieux d'écrire des histoires comiques' (*JS* p. 524), may have meant that one of the poet's essential gifts, that of making vivid comparisons, could serve equally well in a humorous context; and this is also implicit in his description of the brilliant poetess Mme Gaspard de Réveillon:

sa conversation était d'une gaîté continue, elle faisait rire perpétuellement par des rapprochements comiques [. . .] (*JS* p. 522)

It is just because she is a poetess that she can make these humorous comparisons, since imagery is one of the most essential elements in poetry. But one of the most striking features of any comparison, as has already been pointed out, is that it contains both relevant and incongruous elements. A perfectly serious, poetic comparison can, by the merest twist, turn into a humorous one, because the humorous potential is already there. For instance, Proust adds a humorous touch to a poetic comparison between wild roses and peasant girls:

Combien naïves et paysannes en comparaison [avec les aubépines] sembleraient les églantines qui, dans quelques semaines, monteraient elles aussi on plein soleil le même chemin rustique, en la soie unie de leur corsage rougissant qu'un souffle défait! (*CS* I 138)

the blushing bashfulness of the girls is the humorous element. Visually it is relevant, since the roses are blush-pink; but the emotional implications, which are not relevant, have been singled out for comment: this is what makes one smile. He could similarly have added a humorous touch to the famous comparison between the pink hawthorn and a young girl in her Sunday best (*CS* I 139–40), and to many of the other serious and beautiful comparisons in his work. In short, imagery, which is so essential to Proust's writing, lends itself almost by definition to humorous treatment. Far from being two distinct and bewildering facets of a dual personality, Proust's poetic gifts and his humour are closely, almost inextricably, intertwined.

Fantasy

There is a very important category of images in Proust that has not yet been singled out for comment: the extraordinary images which make one pause in bewilderment before one can laugh at them. In the examples already discussed the imagery combines the incongruous and the congruous; the parallel is relevant on many levels apart from the one singled out by the author. Now we come to something completely different: comparisons between elements that are so unlike that it is a brilliant feat to have succeeded in drawing any parallel at all. Proust is not in such cases writing like a surrealist. Surrealists tend to juxtapose elements which have no point of contact in order to puzzle and even to distress the public; but Proust always gives a reason for his oddest images, always ensures that they are, to some extent at least, relevant. The effect on the reader is more that of Corneille's *L'Illusion comique*: we are tricked into seeing things in what we later discover is a false light, and laugh at the skill of the writer in achieving this effect as well as at the intrinsic humour of the text.

Perhaps the most interesting question to be asked about the element of fantasy in Proust's comparisons is how he achieves this effect of almost complete incompatibility between the two elements in the image. The basic technique is to select elements which are at the opposite end of the scale from each other, but which meet at one single point. Thus something visible will be compared to something invisible, something enormous to something minute, something animate to something inanimate. Added to this, Proust manipulates the relationship between the two elements: for instance, in his inability to assimilate his surroundings at his new flat, the Narrator is like a boa constrictor having to swallow the furniture:

pareil à un boa qui vient d'avaler un bœuf, je me sentais péniblement bossué par un long bahut [. . .] (*CG* II 10)

The normal relationship between a human being and a room is that the human being, smaller and less solid than his surroundings, 'fits in' with them. But in describing the painful feelings of the Narrator, Proust has reversed this relationship, and it is the room that literally fits inside the human being. Or, conversely, when the Narrator first arrives at Balbec and feels suspicious and uneasy in his new surroundings, Proust reverses the relationship so that it is the furniture that is suspicious of the human being, not the human being of the furniture:

ma chambre de Balbec [. . .] était pleine de choses qui ne me connaissaient pas, me rendirent le coup d'œil méfiant que je leur jetai et, sans tenir aucun compte de mon existence, témoignèrent que je dérangeais le train-train de la leur. (*JF* I 666)

These two examples provide a clear illustration of the effect of almost total incongruity which is yet highly relevant in one respect. Here, the odd imagery renders very vividly the real and recognizable feelings of the Narrator.

In the discussion which follows, I shall isolate the different elements that are manipulated to produce fantasy, and consider them in turn. I shall use the word 'imagery' in a slightly looser sense than in the previous sections, to include pictures which are not compared directly with something else, but whose effect depends on an implied comparison between their extravagance and a real or normal version of the situation.

The most frequently manipulated element in such comparisons is size. Proust is constantly making people look like giants or insects beside the object of the comparison. We have already had occasion to mention the comparisons between Mme Cottard and a bee, between Françoise's meat and blocks of marble and so on. A particularly fantastic dimension is added to these jugglings with size when the comparison involves a contrast between the animate and the inanimate as well. A good example is the description of the head of Saint-Loup:

Sous la peau fine, la construction hardie, l'architecture féodale apparaissaient. Sa tête faisait penser à ces tours d'antique donjon dont les créneaux inutilisés restent visibles, mais qu'on a aménagées intérieurement en bibliothèque. (*JF* I 819)

Not only has Saint-Loup's head been magnified many thousands of times, but it has turned into a building. The learning he so eagerly pursues is symbolically rendered as books inside the tower, and the aristocratic bone-structure has been turned into stone in the shape of crenellations and battlements. This comparison, far-fetched as it may seem, is yet a fairly reasonable one since so many features of the original have been preserved. A more extreme case is the description of the Duc and Duchesse de Guermantes, in which he acts as a foil to her wit:

vous êtes toujours dans les extrêmes, Oriane, dit M. de Guermantes reprenant son role de falaise qui, en s'opposant à la vague, la force à lancer plus haut son panache d'écume. (*CG* II 510–11)

Here both protagonists have lost their human features as well as vastly increasing in size. The whole comparison is rather far-fetched, relying perhaps on a verbal source, *panache*, a word that can be used either for foam or for wit. Another, and even more monstrous example of this technique is the comparison between M. de Cambremer's eye and the sky:

l'effet de ce rire était de ramener un peu de pupille sur le blanc, sans cela complet, de l'œil. Ainsi une éclaircie met un peu de bleu dans un ciel ouaté de nuages. (*SG* II 978; see also 913)

This comparison is even more far-fetched than the last because the point of it is visual. Whereas the cliff/wave analogy applies, ostensibly at least, to the behaviour alone of the Guermantes, we are here required to visualize an eye, forgetting the relative sizes of eye and sky, and to consider only the relative proportions of blue and white in each. This is an impossible effort to make, so that the comparison is bound to jar: and the combination of relevance and utter preposterousness is extremely amusing.

Elsewhere, Proust can take a banal, hackneyed image and, by manipulating the size and degree of animation, turn it into something extraordinary. For instance, he takes the old joke of people growing to look like something else, usually their dogs (or dogs like their owners) and makes of it something new:

Certains [. . .] avaient fini par ressembler à leur quartier, portaient sur eux comme le reflet de la rue de l'Arcade, de l'avenue du Bois, de la rue de l'Elysée. (*TR* III 951)

To imply a physical resemblance between a human being and a street is impossibly far-fetched: presumably, Proust is implying that they look like the typical inhabitants of their particular district. But the reader, accustomed to the concept of people looking like some element that they are constantly in contact with, may well accept the comparison initially, until further thought makes it seem too puzzling. Conversely, Proust can produce what is ostensibly a perfectly relevant comparison, but in which the conflict between the relevant and the far-fetched appears when the implications are considered. When Bloch has succeeded in hiding his Jewish origins by means of *un chic anglais*,

grâce à la coiffure, à la suppression des moustaches, à l'élégance du type, à la volonté, ce nez juif disparaissait comme semble presque droite une bosse bien arrangée. (*TR* III 953)

The actual comparison between the skilful suppression of an undesirable physical feature by the subject and object is perfectly straightforward. But there is also a visual element. A hooked nose and a hump clearly have some visual affinities. But the resemblance between them is immediately combated by the dissimilarities: the hump is far bigger, is behind instead of in front and so on. One is left not quite knowing what to do with the visual pictures that the image has evoked.

It is curious that the humorous images in which the subject is bigger than the object are far rare in Proust. There are a few examples, such as the comparison between Mme Bontemps and a chicken coming out of an egg (*TR* III 729), but this is funny largely because of the inappropriateness of comparing a dignified, self-important lady with a newly-hatched chicken. The reason for the scarcity of images of compression may be that something too big is intrinsically more ridiculous than something too small. A giant is coarse, lumbering, and clumsy, hence ridiculous. A dwarf is neat, enigmatic, and rather pitiful: one may feel rather guilty at laughing at him. Also, distinctions in the size of small things quickly become uninteresting: the difference between relative sizes of a fly and a lizard seems insignificant. There is far more scope for enlarging things; and, as has been shown, very different effects can be achieved by juggling with size, comparing, say, a nose to a hump and an eye to the sky.

Weight as well as size is used by Proust in extravagant images. Here, as in the wit/water parallel quoted earlier, dual meanings in the words used to describe a perfectly ordinary image seem to be at the root of the comparisons. For instance, at one stage M. de Guermantes is described in terms of his wealth:

On aurait dit que la notion omniprésente en tous ses membres de ses grandes richesses, comme si elles avaient été fondues au creuset en un seul lingot humain, donnait une densité extraordinaire à cet homme qui valait si cher. Au moment où je lui dis au revoir, il se leva poliment de son siège et je sentis la masse inerte et compacte de trente millions que la vieille éducation française faisait mouvoir, soulevait, et qui se tenait debout devant moi. (*CG* II 284)

This comparison derives its effect mainly from the various clichés of mass that are applied to wealth. One might for instance talk of *une solide fortune*, or *la masse de ses richesses*. Proust is taking an idiom literally and showing how absurd it really is. A similar effect is achieved when he says of Bloch that he

supportait comme au fond des mers les incalculables pressions que faisaient peser sur lui non seulement les chrétiens de la surface, mais les couches superposées des castes juives supérieures à la sienne [. . .] (*JF* I 744)

where the source of the comparison may well be the habit of talking of the *pression* or *contrainte* of social circumstances. This example is considerably enriched by the geological element in the imagery, Bloch being squeezed slowly by the superior strata of society.

Elsewhere, an image can consist in the confrontation of singular and plural. Here, the effect is produced by a completely artificial process of juxtaposing two elements that would normally be scattered. Compare for instance the perfectly acceptable speculations of the Narrator as to the different appearances of Albertine or Gilberte on different days with the compressed account of his vision of the *petite crémière*: when the latter meets him for the first time, he writes

Elle prenait un air tout penaud de n'avoir plus (au lieu des dix, des vingt, que je me rappelais tour à tour sans pouvoir fixer mon souvenir) qu'un seul nez, plus rond que je ne l'avais cru, qui donnait une idée de bêtise et avait en tout cas perdu le pouvoir de se multiplier. (*P* III 143)

It is not funny to imagine that the *crémière*'s nose looks different every time he sees it; but it is funny to recall all these differences and apply them to the nose at one and the same time, so that she appears to have several noses on her face at once.

Indeed, it may well be that we remember the number of very striking serious references to this multiplicity of appearance in the loved one, and laugh at the *crémière*'s noses in part at least because they provide a parody of the Narrator's attitude to the women he really loves.

There are other instances of this manipulation and convergence of juxtapositions to provide an impression of spurious multiplicity. If the original point is a humorous one, the effect will be considerably increased by this technique. For instance, at one stage M. de Charlus's voice is compared to a girlish one, which makes him appear slightly ridiculous in the first place. But not content with this parallel, Proust multiplies the effect, and makes his voice that of a whole bevy of girls:

sa voix elle-même, pareille à certaines voix de contralto en qui on n'a pas assez cultivé le médium et dont le chant semble le duo alterné d'un jeune homme et d'une femme, se posait, au moment où il exprimait ces pensées si délicates, sur des notes hautes, prenait une douceur imprévue et semblait contenir des chœurs de fiancées, de sœurs, qui répandaient leur tendresse. (*JF* I 764)

The converse of this effect can also be used to produce humour, where a collection of different people are fused into one. Thus the *fille de cuisine* is 'élevée à la hauteur d'une institution', as Cottard might have said, when she is described as being one and the same person as the years go by;

La fille de cuisine était une personne morale, une institution permanente à qui des attributions invariables assuraient une sorte de continuité
et d'identité, à travers la succession des formes passagères en lesquelles
elle s'incarnait, car nous n'eûmes jamais la même deux ans de suite.
(*CS* I 80)

Here, however, the situation is basically less amusing; it is not surprising
that the *filles de cuisine* behave in exactly the same way, since they all
have exactly the same job to do. To make us laugh, Proust has to manipulate the sentence structure, leading one on to the bald statement of
fact at the end, which provides an amusing constrast to the rather
grandiose abstract theorizing of the earlier part of the sentence.

In all the examples mentioned so far the actual material of the
imagery is perfectly acceptable; it is the relationship between the
elements that is odd. Elsewhere, Proust can use intrinsically very odd
material in imagery. For instance, Mme de Guermantes tells the
Narrator that Bergotte did not address a single word to M. de Cobourg

en signalant ce trait curieux comme elle aurait raconté qu'un Chinois
se serait mouché avec du papier. (*CG* II 212)

To a generation as yet unused to paper tissues, this must have seemed an
anthropological curiosity, quite apart from its use in a comparison.

Another technique is to juxtapose images, so that one is aware of the
relationship between the different objects of the comparison as well as
between the subject and each individual object. There are many such
images. A good example is the Narrator's first meeting with Bergotte
(*JF* I 547-8). The striking factor in this meeting is that the Narrator,
totally unprepared for a perfectly ordinary-looking man, is deeply disappointed. Proust renders this disappointment by means of juxtaposed
images, in which the numerous and different ways in which he had
thought of Bergotte are brought in, and juxtaposed both with each
other and with Bergotte as he really is:

Mme Swann [. . .] prononça le nom du doux Chantre aux cheveux
blancs. Ce nom de Bergotte me fit tressauter comme le bruit d'un
revolver qu'on aurait déchargé sur moi [. . .]; devant moi, comme ces
prestidigitateurs qu'on aperçoit intacts et en redingote dans la poussière
d'un coup de feu d'où s'envole une colombe, mon salut m'était rendu
par un homme jeune, rude, petit, râblé et myope, à nez rouge en forme
de coquille de colimaçon et à barbiche noire.

The shock of hearing the name, which Proust compares to a pistol-shot,
leads him on to the next image, of the conjurer. By linking the two
images, Proust makes it seem extraordinary and magical that Bergotte

should be standing there, actually intact, whereas, of course, there is
nothing odd about it in reality. The pistol-shot also symbolizes the
death of the old vision of Bergotte as the *doux chantre aux cheveux
blancs*, who is as if by magic transformed into this young, ordinary
man, while the white dove (often used for the soul and things spiritual)
seems to be the old, pure, imaginary Bergotte disappearing, although at
the same time it is merely part of the conjurer's act. Not content with
this complex series of interrelated images, Proust goes on to introduce
further comparisons:

J'étais mortellement triste, car ce qui venait d'être réduit en poudre,
ce n'était pas seulement le langoureux vieillard, dont il ne restait plus
rien, c'était aussi la beauté d'une œuvre immense que j'avais pu loger
dans l'organisme défaillant et sacré que j'avais, comme un temple, con-
struit expressément pour elle, mais à laquelle aucune place n'était ré-
servée dans le corps trapu, rempli de vaisseaux, d'os, de ganglions, du
petit homme à nez camus et à barbiche noire qui était devant moi.

Here we have the further idea of the dust already referred to being all
that is left of the old Bergotte, and the contrast between the sacred
temple and the stocky little man who has to contain it within himself.
Finally, Proust goes on to explain that he had built up a picture of
Bergotte drop by drop, like a stalactite, which refused to be linked with
the real man's nose and beard. Basically, the 'effect of the passage
depends on the interrelation of beautiful, noble imagery (relating to the
doux chantre) and the vulgar, petty, ordinary picture of the real
Bergotte. This happens on all sorts of different scales. The snail (his
nose) is juxtaposed to a dove, an ugly, rather sordid human body to a
temple, a little red nose to a transparent stalactite. At the same time,
one thinks of Bergotte throughout as a conjurer, so that the contrast
between the temple and the human being is more violent. The exceedingly elaborate effect of the whole (and the image is further extended
later when his voice is first heard) is justified by the fact that Proust has
told us from the beginning that he is talking about a conjuring trick, a
sleight of hand.

It is clearly impossible to go into the numerous instances of multiple
imagery of this type in Proust. It is worth looking at the digesting
family in *JS* (p. 289), who are compared to hares, into whose furry
paws are placed cigars and liqueurs, as an earlier version of the
technique.

Perhaps the most truly 'surrealist' images in Proust occur during the
dream sequences: though here, simply by making it plain that they are

dream images, Proust does give them a *raison d'être*. They are not completely gratuitous, they are illustrations of the meaningless quality of
dreams. Some of the dream pictures are odd without being amusing. One
wonders why Swann is two people at once, one of whom is himself,
another a young man in a fez; but one does not necessarily laugh (*S* I
378-9). On the other hand, if there is a strong contrast between the
dream picture and reality, the effect is likely to be amusing. For
instance, one laughs at the vain Mme Verdurin's moustaches in the same
dream; or, in another dream, one laughs at her buying a bunch of
violets that cost five thousand million francs, since we know that she
is rather mean (*SG* II 986).

In conclusion, it may be suggested that this element of fantasy represents what may be the most advanced element of Proust's imagery.
It is certainly the case that in the earlier works there are no real
examples of complete fantasy. In general, Proust's interest in imagery
seems to have evolved with experience. The number of images in *ALR*
is many times greater than that of the images in the earlier works.

Another feature of Proust's humorous images is that they are rarely
included for their own sakes alone. They are most often used in
character portrayals. Here they serve two purposes: they bring life to
a character, drawing attention to both physical and mental attributes,
a squinting eye or a snobbish nature. They also help to build up the
overall impression of a character, pinpointing his most fundamental
characteristics. A case in point is the use of female images applied to
M. de Charlus, which draws attention to his homosexuality.

Such effects tend to be very subtle, for one of the most striking
features of Proust's humorous comparisons is that the humour is more
often implied than stated. The overall impression is one of malicious
insinuation rather than straightforward merriment. This lends a
spurious atmosphere of delicacy to what can at times be crude,
impertinent observation.

It is a curious fact that the bulk of Proust's humorous comparisons
are aimed at deflating the people concerned. He here reveals a strongly
critical attitude towards his fellow-men. This disparaging approach will
be seen to be an essential feature of his humorous portrayal of character.

IV

CHARACTERS

Character and Caricature

Proust's humorous characters are of two types. First, we have those
that are taken seriously on the whole, but are from time to time portrayed in a humorous light. Most of Proust's important characters are
treated in this way: Jean Santeuil pastes his moustache to his cheeks,
the child Narrator envies Swann his baldness. This treatment is essential
to realistic portrayal, since no real person goes through life without
sometimes appearing ridiculous. It also adds to the interest of the
characters, making them seem many-sided.

The opposite effect is achieved when a character is presented as a
figure of fun, ridiculous from the first. Such characters are potentially
one-sided, since they produce but one reaction in the reader—laughter—
and often do so through a single humorous characteristic. One tends to
laugh at Cottard for his crude lack of *savoir-vivre*, Brichot for his
pedantry and so on. These characters can fairly be called caricatures,
the essence of caricature being such distortion. The word, from Italian
caricare, 'to load', implies the stressing of one feature in a character
at the expense of other, probably equally important, elements.
Characters such as Cottard automatically evoke a particular response in
the reader, which rarely changes. Paradoxically, then, humour in
character-portrayal can produce an effect either of variety or of same-
ness.

But though the above distinction should be borne in mind, it cannot
be taken too far. For Proust is much too subtle a writer to be content
with a crude, one-sided caricature, except where minor characters are
concerned. Buffeteur remains a brutish lout (*JS* pp. 259–60), and the
Directeur of the hotel at Balbec regularly produces malapropisms. But
even seemingly obvious caricatures such as Mme Blatin change in the
eyes of the reader; and some characters start off seriously and become
distorted (Legrandin), or *vice versa* (Elstir). These processes will be
discussed later. Here it must be pointed out that it was vital to Proust
that his characters should both change themselves, and also reveal traits

whose existence we had never suspected, though they had been present
from the start. By such means he illustrates two of his chief preoccupations. One is the impossibility of pinning down psychological reality:
just as one thinks one has got to the truth, everything seems to change.
This point recurs again and again in *ALR*, with reference to relationships between people (particularly love), and to individual personalities.
And humour, by presenting the facts in a different light from the
serious, is clearly an important technique to use here. The second preoccupation is closely related to the first. Proust called *ALR* 'la psychologie dans le temps' (*Textes retrouvés*, interview on *Swann* with E.-J.
Bois, p. 217), and explained that

Tels personnages se révéleront plus tard différents de ce qu'ils sont dans
le volume actuel, différents de ce qu'on les croira, ainsi qu'il arrive bien
souvent dans la vie, du reste.

It is essential to Proust's purpose that characters who appear serious
should later seem amusing, and *vice versa*. On the whole, then, it seems
that true caricatures do not fit in with Proust's aims as well as characters who have a humorous element in them.

However, there are considerable differences in degree. Some
characters are almost always taken seriously, or, if they are mocked at,
the seriousness to some extent permeates the humour. Others are so
consistently mocked at that one is incredulous if they are ever taken
seriously. The difference between the two types shines out if they are
juxtaposed. Gilberte talking to Mme Blatin is reminiscent of Tenniel's
illustrations to *Alice in Wonderland*, in which the realistic Alice stands
next to the caricatured Duchess. Often such juxtapositions have their
own humorous effect: the presence of the critical Swann provides an
unspoken scathing comment on everything that goes on at the Verdurins', and reminds the reader that judged by other standards the *petit
clan* is ridiculous.

Bearing in mind the distinction between character and caricature,
various features of Proust's humorous treatment of characters must be
discussed. It is impossible to be comprehensive, since every character
is treated differently. I shall consider in turn five main aspects: first,
the different ways of looking at a character; secondly, character
development; thirdly, intrinsic qualities of character; fourthly, speech,
the characters' chief means of self-expression; and fifthly, the sense of
humour of the characters.

Standpoints

1) *Individuals*   It is impossible to do more than roughly indicate the immense variety of approaches Proust uses in creating humour in character. His standpoint will vary from character to character, from moment to moment. On the most basic level, he sometimes adopts an omniscient, superior attitude towards his characters, at other times treats them as if he is not quite sure what they are going to do next. For instance, he goes into Mme Verdurin's motives for repeating a phrase about the portrait 'M. Tiche' is painting of Cottard:

—Vous savez que ce que je veux surtout avoir, c'est son sourire: ce que je vous ai demandé, c'est le portrait de son sourire.' Et comme cette expression lui sembla remarquable, elle la répéta très haut pour être sûre que plusieurs invités l'eussent entendue, et même, sous un prétexte vague, en fit d'abord rapprocher quelques-uns. (*S* I 203)

Proust is here transgressing the rules of first-person narration: strictly speaking, his Narrator has no right to this insight into the mind of another character. On other occasions, the Narrator hypothesizes about motives as though he did not know what they really were, witness M. de Norpois's putative motives for keeping still when he talks. By pretending to be uncertain of the truth, Proust can include amusingly disparate motives (here, M. de Norpois may be trying to gain the upper hand through his calmness, or to look like a Greek statue, *JF* I 452–3). On the whole, it is more characteristic of the 'X-Ray' technique of observation which Proust, through the Narrator, applies to his characters, that he should be able to see through their surface hypocrisy to the true motives underneath. This merciless insight creates the impression that the author, and reader, are superior to the character who is made so transparent.

As a result of this superiority, Proust usually appears to be laughing not with but at his characters. The combination of mockery with sympathy or respect is rare in Proust, confined to very few characters like the Narrator's grandmother, with her understandable desire to cultivate the body by exposing it to fresh air, the mind by steeping it in culture (*CS* I 10–11, 39–41 etc.). Usually, even the best of intentions are somehow twisted to the detriment of the characters. For instance, Mme de Cambremer's genuine affection for a friend is ridiculous because she is a figure of fun.

The techniques to be discussed, then, are almost all ways of belittling a character, rendering him ridiculous in the reader's eyes. One of the most effective techniques is to subject a character to detailed scrutiny. If the Narrator really admires or is emotionally involved with a character, he is unable to describe him in great detail: the character seems too complex, too changeable to fit into neat patterns, and the writer has too much respect for him to subject him to a humiliatingly close inspection, as though he were a specimen under a microscope. The most detailed descriptions are almost always of characters whom Proust can portray without emotion, looking down on them as he makes them ridiculous. For example, Mme de Guermantes, when she is old and no longer much respected by the Narrator, is described as follows:

Dans les joues restées si semblables pourtant de la duchesse de Guermantes et pourtant composites maintenant comme un nougat, je distinguai une trace de vert-de-gris, un petit morceau rose de coquillage concassé, une grosseur difficile à définir, plus petite qu'une boule de gui et moins transparente qu'une perle de verre. (*TR* III 937)

This is not ostensibly a humorous description, but the subject is degraded: she is seen in public, at an elegant *matinée*, but is described in such detail that it seems as if the author has been peering at her through a magnifying glass in front of all the other guests.

Elsewhere, a few key features, or even a single characteristic, physical, mental, or behavioural, are singled out and scrutinized with the same impertinent intensity. When this happens, the character becomes a caricature. The vividness of Proust's caricatures depends on the fact that as well as being exaggeratedly emphatic, they are also simplified. For the overloading of one feature in a fictional character must mean the neglect of others; it would be beyond the scope of any novelist to overstress every feature in a character. Hence one-sidedness of character-portrayal is an essential feature of caricature. The reader's attention is focused on salient features, just as the beholder's is drawn to the enormous nose or bulldog jowls of a political figure in a cartoon.

An example of insistence on one or two physical features is the portrayal of the 'Marquise' who looks after the public lavatory in the Champs Elysées. She is described as a 'vieille dame à joues plâtrées et à perruque rousse' (*JF* I 492). The outlines of her appearance are suggested by pinpointing a few key features. A further technique is to repeat the same description with slight modifications or enlargements at different points in the book. The 'Marquise' is later described as follows:

Au contrôle, comme dans ces cirques forains où le clown, prêt à entrer en scène et tout enfariné, reçoit lui-même à la porte le prix des places, la 'marquise', percevant les entrées, était toujours là avec son museau énorme et irrégulier enduit de plâtre grossier, et son petit bonnet de fleurs rouges et de dentelle noire surmontant sa perruque rousse. (*CG* II 309)

The basic elements of the caricature remain the same, with the addition of the incongruously frivolous little hat. But Proust has expanded on the overall ugliness of the 'marquise' by the use of disrespectful or pejorative words ('museau' and 'grossier'), and has suggested an impertinent comparison between her and a clown.

This technique can result in the stressed features becoming the symbol of the character's identity (as the politician in a cartoon is not only ridiculed for, but also recognized by, his nose, pipe, etc.). M. de Palancy never appears without his monocle being described (see *S* I 327, *CG* II 43). If the stressed feature is essentially unimportant, this emphasis on it is in itself ridiculous. Mme Blatin, for example, is permanently linked in the reader's mind with the newspaper she always peruses (*NPN* I 397, etc.).

These extraneous features which are adopted as a symbol of the character to whom they belong can also consist of physical or mental peculiarities and even characteristic sounds. In this respect, the author has an advantage over the cartoonist; for he has at his disposal more than the visual element (we will later come across peculiarities of speech and behaviour that make caricatures of the Directeur and Cottard). Proust can also create more complicated symbols. For instance, he endows the Prince de Borodino with a resemblance to both Napoleon I and Napoleon III. Here the effect of the comparison rests largely on the ludicrous combination of the two Emperors' physiognomies and the inappropriate contexts in which these physiognomies appear (*CG* II 131).

The stylized character portrayals which result from such one-sided caricatures affect the humour involved. Caricatures cannot be realistic and stylized at the same time, so the reader is unlikely to identify with them, and will feel little if any sympathy for them. There is no reason to feel sorry for them: they are not like real people. Laughter at the expense of caricatures can often be very cruel. In his description of the 'Marquise', the author has stripped his victim of all the attempts she must have made to disguise her age and ugliness (putting on a wig, painting her face). He mercilessly exposes her in the crudest of lights. And because she is not a realistic character but a caricature, the reader has no compunction at joining in the laughter.

Other characters are given their own brand of humorous description without being turned into caricatures. The main difference here is in the degree of importance attributed to the particular characteristic. Odette's tendency to use English expressions is as absurd as Mme Blatin's fondness for *Les Débats*; but she has so many other characteristics that we do not remember her exclusively as the character who constantly says 'darling', 'Christmas', or 'home'. The young Gilberte, too, has a characteristic, childish way of lisping (*JF* I 511–12). Mme de Villeparisis dresses like 'une vieille concierge' (*S* I 244), and her shabby appearance is mentioned at intervals throughout *ALR* (see *JF* I 678, *F* III 630). But these characters mean so much to the reader that these particular foibles merely become part of the information, serious or otherwise, that one has about them, rather than being the symbol of their personalities.

It is, however, interesting that these humorous characteristics, like those of true caricatures, tend to be mentioned repeatedly, so that one comes to expect them and to associate them with the people to whom they apply. Odette's English expressions, for instance, reappear regularly throughout the book.

2) *Groups*   Proust's personages have an identity not only as individuals but also frequently as members of a group which itself is endowed with a collective identity. Sometimes this identity does not depend on actual physical association; members of the aristocracy, for instance, have both individual characteristics and the common characteristics of their rank, irrespective of whether they actually frequent each other's company. Saint-Loup and Mme de Guermantes may be very different as people; but their way of acknowledging an introduction is very similar. Much of the humour in Proust's character portrayals, either in fact (where groups are portrayed) or by implication (where individuals who typify a group are described), concerns collective rather than individual personalities.

There are obvious advantages in portraying groups. Uncomplicated humour is easier to create with groups, which do not have to be studied in depth; common characteristics tend to be straightforward and simple, since they have to suit the disparate individuals that make up the group. As a result, the humour in such portrayals tends to be crude rather than complex. Compare for instance the unsubtle admiration of aristocratic groups for Mme de Guermantes (*CG* II 441 ff.) with the complicated attitude of an individual, Mme de Gallardon (she has evolved an elaborate behaviour-pattern to enable her to reconcile two incompatible facts: she is a Guermantes and is kept at a distance by Mme de Guermantes. She succeeds by pretending that she is so ultra-Guermantes that it would be degrading for her to have anything to do with the less conventional members of her family. The most curious thing about this pretence is that she firmly believes it herself: *S* I 329).

As a rule, humour is applied to groups with the straightforward result of multiplying the effect. Simple comic effects are much funnier if many people are involved (in *Love's Labour's Lost* not one but four characters abjure the female sex, and then fall involuntarily in love).

Multiplication of all sorts of effects is achieved by Proust. He shows up the absurdities of snobbery by describing each individual variation on the theme. He multiplies sadistic humour. The scenes in which Saniette is tortured by M. Verdurin are lent a certain grim humour by the presence of the whole pack of *fidèles* howling at his heels:

–Qu'est-ce que vous voulez dire? hurla M. Verdurin tandis que les invités s'empressaient, prêts, comme des lions, à dévorer l'homme terrassé. (*P* III 265 footnote)

If group members are individually portrayed, the multiplication of humour is different: instead of allowing the collective humour to strike with its full impact, Proust gradually builds a composite picture by referring first to one member, then later to another. The discovery of the group character may take some time. The Narrator himself makes such discoveries, for instance when he recognizes the individual behaviour of the Princesse de Luxembourg and the Princesse de Parme as typical of the class they belong to:

Alors je compris tout, la dame présente [la Princesse de Parme] n'avait rien de commun avec Mme de Luxembourg, mais [. . .] je discernai l'espèce de la bête. C'était une Altesse. (*CG* II 425)

The portrayal of groups and their members also gives scope for a more ironic type of humour, directed at the blindness of those characters who think that they are original and individual without realizing that they cannot be those things simply because they are a group. Proust produces instances of mass 'originality' which turns out to be a new conventionality. The *petit clan* refuses to dress for dinner, thus establishing a protocol as rigid as that of more conventional groups who insist on dinner-dress (*S* I 189).

The essence of the 'group character' makes it suitable as a medium for creating ironic effects. All groups have one characteristic in common which colours the behaviour of their members and lays them open to mockery. It is the desire of each member of the group to do the same as the others. Proust mocks even the Narrator when he slavishly imitates everything that Gilberte and her parents do. He also shows us that people are not ashamed of behaving ridiculously as long as others are doing the same. Indeed, people may deliberately choose to be ridiculous rather than left out. Even group leaders like Mme de Guermantes are not free from this tendency. For example, at a musical *soirée*, she is impressed by the way Mme de Cambremer nods her head to the music, and copies her:

elle battait pendant un instant la mesure, mais, pour ne pas abdiquer son indépendance, à contretemps. (*S* I 331)

She herself believes that as a group leader she is independent of lesser members of the group; but her behaviour is merely an overcomplicated variation on the group theme.

Even if a group was originally formed for some other reason than interdependence for its own sake, it is this aspect of the group that finally seems to unite the members. Many of Proust's groups are originally formed because the members have something in common. They share the same social status (the *gratin*), or occupation (the servants). But once the group exists it is the interdependence of the members that keeps it together, and that provides one of the chief sources of group humour.

Various techniques are used to portray these groups. Large groups tend to become featureless. The individual members lose their identity and manifest only the characteristics common to the group. This is the easiest method of delineating a group without muddling the reader, and it enables Proust to portray amusing group characteristics that would be implausible in individuals, such as the credulous devotion of the *fidèles* to Mme Verdurin or the *gratin*'s slavish adulation of Mme de Guermantes.

The individual personalities of group-members may seem less important than their group character even to the other members of the group, to whom, after all, they ought to seem like real people. M. and Mme Verdurin, for example, are interested in the members of their *petit clan* only as long as they contribute to the collective personality of the group. If they leave or die, the *patron* and *patronne* become indifferent.

At other times, the opposite occurs: the characters in the group are endowed with such strong personalities that it is impossible to put them together in one room without hopelessly muddling the reader. Proust occasionally does this, creating humour from the complicatedness of what is going on. An example is a conversation between several members of the *petit clan*, who, temporarily assuming strong per-sonalities, talk about their respective interests (*SG* II 964–5). Again, the independent actions of individuals may seem absurd in conjunction with the actions of the rest of the group. An example is the scene in which three journalists ignore the slap that Saint-Loup gives a fourth. Independently, each journalist, in accordance with the general way of behaving of his group, decides that he had better keep out of trouble by pretending that he had noticed nothing. If one journalist only had been present and had reacted in the same way, the reader would have felt slightly disgusted at his cowardliness and not in the least amused. As there are three, each one really knowing what has happened and pre-tending that he has not noticed, the effect is of three grotesque varia-tions on a theme:

Quant à ses amis, l'un avait aussitôt détourné la tête en regardant avec attention du côté des coulisses quelqu'un qui évidemment ne s'y trouvait pas; le second fit semblant qu'un grain de poussière lui était entré dans l'œil et se mit à pincer sa paupière en faisant des grimaces de souffrance; pour la troisième, il s'était élancé en s'écriant:
—Mon Dieu, je crois qu'on va lever le rideau, nous n'aurons pas nos places. (*CG* II 181)

With larger groups, Proust may make many of the members retain their individuality. He does this in various ways. Sometimes the group scenes are subdivided. The salon scenes usually consist of groups within groups. At the *soirée* given by the Princesse de Guermantes, the Narrator spends his time talking to a series of small groups, or even to single characters; and the individual eccentricities of those characters are set against a moving background of guests who are not described in any detail but serve to create the impression of a large gathering.

At times the group may be too small to include a crowd of feature-less characters as a background, yet too large for all the characters to retain their individuality without the situation becoming confused. In such cases, Proust may make the reader concentrate first on one then on another character, while the rest temporarily fade into the back-ground. This technique is repeatedly used for describing large dinner-parties. The impression given, however, is one of artificiality. If one hears only a few characters talking at a time, it seems as if all the others are simply sitting round in silence listening to the talker; whereas the essence of the impression given by a real dinner-party is of different conversations going on at the same time. But this very artificiality can contribute to the humour in a passage, as at the Verdurins' dinner-party when Mme Cottard suddenly begins to speak (*S* I 256-7). Her ex-aggeratedly detailed speech on a frivolous topic undeserving of lengthy treatment, is combined with what seems like an equally exaggerated degree of respectful silence on the part of the others.

None of these techniques is restricted to a single group, and no one group is described by means of a single technique. Proust varies the standpoints from which he views the groups, thereby preventing them from seeming static. He also frequently describes the evolution of groups in time. Even their most fundamental standards can change. The situation may then appear ridiculous: the group has rejected the very things it stood for. Yet, unaware of its own inconsistency, it con-tinues to exist, and, outwardly at least, seems little different from its earlier self. For example, the *gratin* was essentially exclusive and beyond the reach of the bourgeoisie. But at the end of *ALR* we find members of this very bourgeoisie taking over the leadership of the *gratin* and becoming just as snobbish about others of their kind who have not yet 'arrived' (*TR* III 726).

A variation on this technique is to juxtapose one group with another. Here attitudes seem over-simplified and aimed at ego-boosting: the *petit clan* refers to alien groups as *les ennuyeux*. The most subtle means of creating humour through such comparisons is to make one group parody another.

Such parodies can be sustained and complex. For example, Proust's servants always try to behave in a correct, even aristocratic way; but all they achieve is a pitiful approximation of the desired effect. They attempt to use correct language, but constantly spoil the effect by mis-pronouncing words: Françoise's young *valet de pied*, trying to sound elegant, says to her: 'Voyons, Madame, encore un peu de raisin; il est esquis' (*CG* II 17). The lift-boy at Balbec thinks he knows all about the local aristocrats, the Cambremers, but unfortunately calls them 'Camembert' (*SG* II 825 etc.). This distorted view of noble life may induce in a reader a suggestion of scepticism as to the true worthiness of the way of life that the servants parody. If the mere fact that a few letters in a name are distorted can make it ridiculous, is it intrinsically so grandiose? But Proust is more subtle than this. He makes the reader familiar with the fact that mispronunciation is essentially ridiculous and associated with servants. The servant classes consistently mis-pronounce words. Then suddenly we find not only the servant class but also the upper classes doing it. And, in fact, it transpires that the smartest way to talk, the way that only the very cream of the *gratin* can talk, is like a peasant. The acknowledged leader of the *gratin*, the Duchesse de Guermantes, achieves unparalleled elegance because she does not care about speaking with an elegant accent; she says things like 'Moi, je suis *eun* bête, je parle comme une paysanne' (*P* III 43), and though clearly nobody believes that she is like a real peasant, the terms in which she makes her claim to simplicity are significant: the servants' ambition is to be like the *gratin*, while the *gratin* thinks it smart to be a little like the servants.

At the same time, the intrinsic similarities between the two classes are constantly in evidence. Almost all the characteristic absurdities of the servants turn out to be characteristic of aristocrats too. The servants are naïvely credulous. Françoise believes in the infallible cures advertised in newspapers (*CG* II 65-6). But aristocrats can be equally credulous and, what is more, they share with the servants the tendency to go on believing something no matter how often they are told it is not true. Mme de Varambon insists that the Narrator is the nephew of some admiral he has never met, despite all his protestations (*CG* II 498-9). The upper classes are obsessed with matters of protocol; but so are the servants. Françoise wants to go back to Balbec to say goodbye to the hotel *gouvernante*, to whom she had rudely omitted to pay her respects (*P* III 16). The servants imitate those members of a high-ranking group whom they admire. But so do the aristocrats. Both the servants and the aristocrats share an overweening interest in the leaders of the *gratin*, the Duc and Duchesse de Guermantes. Of Françoise it is said that the Guermantes 'étaient sa constante préoccupation' (*CG* II 16), and the Princesse de Parme is described as imitating Mme de Guermantes's way of dressing, repeating the same witticisms and serving the same cakes (*CG* II 457). The similarity between the servants and the aristocrats, when the latter claim to be on a much higher plane than the former, is telling. So is the fact that both groups take their individuality so seriously when their behaviour is so much less exclusive than they imagine. Proust hints at the similarity between the two groups by means of an image which at different times he applies to both classes. Both are compared to early Christians officiating at a service. During the lunch of the Narrator's family servants,

Françoise, qui était à la fois, comme dans l'église primitive, le célébrant et l'un des fidèles, se servait un dernier verre de vin [. . .] (*CG* II 17)

Of the guests of the Guermantes, Proust says·

Ils se réunissaient là en effet, comme les premiers chrétiens, non pour partager une nourriture matérielle, d'ailleurs exquise, mais dans une sorte de Cène sociale. (*CG* II 512)

Both regard their occupations as sacred, and both believe that they are the chosen members of an important and select group. But since these groups can be described in terms of the same image in both cases, there is less difference between them than they think.

The relationship between the group and the individual outsider provides a further source of humour. The contrast between the isolation of the individual and the clannishness of the group is in itself ironical, since the group is made up of a number of individuals like the isolated one. Almost invariably the individual who has dealings with the group comes to long to be one of its members. This gives rise to ridiculous episodes in which the individual loses all dignity by |desperately trying to behave in a way which he thinks will be acceptable to the group (witness the *historien de la Fronde*'s behaviour at Mme de Villeparisis's salon: *CG* II 231). The individual cannot understand what the basic attributes of the group are, and imagines that the most ridiculous things are the key to its identity. The Narrator thinks that if Françoise wore a hat like Gilberte's governess, he would be accepted by the Swanns (*CS* I 411). Through the humour here, Proust is making an implied point about the structure of society.

If a whole group mocks at an individual, the effect is magnified, just as, to use an example mentioned by Proust, an old gentleman falling over is much more ridiculous if he does so in a public place (*CG* II 141). Hence not only the reactions of the individual to the group but also the attitude of the group to the individual can contribute to the humour in the relationship between the two.

Development

The next question to be discussed is that of Proust's 'psychologie dans le temps'. It is necessary for the writer of any long novel, particularly a novel in which the effect of time on personality is an essential feature, to make his characters evolve as time goes on. Proust avoids possible monotony by making the reader uncertain of what his characters are going to do next, while at the same time illustrating the psychological point that one is virtually a different person at different moments in one's life.

This sort of treatment has considerable relevance to the subject of humour, which often relies on surprise and shock to make its effect. Indeed, the concept of a *coup de théâtre* is potentially amusing, and plays an important part in farce. Where characters are concerned, the effect can be one of sudden shock, as at the discovery of Jupien's niece's aristocratic marriage, or of gradual build-up, as with the slow accumulation of facts contributing towards the realization that Legrandin is a snob.

The way the character is introduced when he first appears will affect the reader's opinion of him later. Occasionally, Proust singles out the comic qualities that are henceforward to characterize a person: Bloch's ridiculous language, his over-emotional attitude and his malice are indicated from the first (*CS* I 90-2). Often, however, the introduction is deliberately misleading. Legrandin, for instance, is introduced as a violent opponent of the aristocracy,

allant jusqu'à reprocher à la Révolution de ne les avoir pas tous guillotinés. (*CS* I 68)

This introduction enables Proust to hoodwink the reader as to the real key to Legrandin's personality, and to make the discovery of his snobbery into an exciting event.

Another technique is to introduce a character through an incidental quality, which at the time seems to be the most important thing about him. M. de Charlus, for instance, is given two separate introductions to the Narrator (since he has had time to forget the first meeting by the time the second occurs). When he first sees him at Tansonville, the Narrator is struck by the intensity of his gaze (*CS* I 141); later, at Balbec, this intensity produces a ludicrous impression, and M. de Charlus's behaviour makes the Narrator think he must be a madman, a spy, or

un escroc d'hôtel qui, nous ayant peut-être remarqués les jours précédents, ma grand'mère et moi, et préparant quelque mauvais coup, venait de s'apercevoir que je l'avais surpris pendant qu'il m'épiait [. . .] (*JF* I 752)

Later, we discover that M. de Charlus, far from being a swindler, is an excessively elegant nobleman, so that the initial impression seems to have been utterly false; but when we discover his secret shady life, we realize that there was some truth in the seemingly inappropriate introduction.

After the initial introduction, then, Proust often changes what seems to be the truth about a character, or presents him from a completely different angle. It is interesting to compare Elstir with his ridiculous earlier self, 'M. Tiche', but difficult to find any point of similarity: one can only assume that he has completely changed from a comic figure to a serious, admirable painter. While some characters undergo a single transformation of this type, others are subjected to a bewildering series of changes. Perhaps the most striking example is M. de Charlus. On a large scale, he changes from a proud aristocrat to a vicious, degraded pervert, and thence to a touchingly courteous white-haired old gentleman.[1] On a smaller scale, his different moods and attitudes affect him so much that we seem to be looking at a different person almost with every description of him. Physically, his appearance at one moment may contradict his looks at another. Sometimes he looks like a farcical figure:

M. de Charlus avait placé verticalement sur sa bouche ses mains gantées de blanc, et arrondi prudemment son regard désignateur comme s'il craignait d'être entendu et même vu des maîtres de maison. (*P* III 268)

Sometimes he appears handsome in the most inappropriate of contexts: in the middle of a ludicrously hysterical scene with the Narrator, he is described as 'Apollon vieilli' (*CG* II 555). Or again he can look ridiculously ugly. At one stage Jupien amorously gazes at

la figure du baron, grasse et congestionnée sous les cheveux gris. (*SG* II 610)

Nevertheless, the reader is not at any point upset by the extraordinary differences between M. de Charlus's various physiognomies. M. de Charlus is such a changeable character, so erratic in his behaviour, that the changes in his face seem to contribute to, rather than detracting from, an understanding of him.

At other times a similar effect of variety is achieved by changing the context in which a character appears. Thus a further variation on the Charlus theme is obtained by his suddenly being observed in public, as if by a stranger:

les promenades de M. de Charlus [. . .] se bornaient [. . .] plus souvent à un déjeuner ou à un dîner dans un restaurant de la côte, où M. de Charlus passait pour un vieux domestique ruiné et Morel, qui avait mission de payer les notes, pour un gentilhomme trop bon. (*SG* II 1006)

There is an element of irony in this introduction of a new perspective.

---

[1] It is interesting to note that Proust regarded the humour in his treatment of M. de Charlus as rescuing the character from seeming vicious and shocking. He says that there is 'aucun détail . . . choquant', or that if there is, a potentially shocking passage will be 'sauvé par le comique'. (Letter to Eugène Fasquelle, Oct. 1912, *Choix de Lettres* p. 183.)

The reader suddenly realizes that the character with whom he has been so deeply involved, and whose self-confidence is such that it carries the reader with him is nothing more than a pathetic, rather undignified-looking old man. The addition of touches like this to the portrayal of a humorous character lends it scope and perspective.

Not all character studies present such a broad picture: many of Proust's caricatures are simply vehicles for displaying humorous personality traits. Proust is not interested in presenting them as people. But the importance of character development to Proust is clearly illustrated by the fact that he manages to produce a development even in these potentially most static characters. In caricature, where the basic traits have been singled out from the beginning, one would expect little if any variation on the basic theme. But Proust avoids the danger of monotony. Sometimes he describes certain characteristics of a particular person at one stage and then, without again referring to these, amplifies the description by later adding other traits, gradually building up a complete picture by means of repeated incomplete descriptions. When we first meet the Directeur of the hotel at Balbec, certain elements are brought to our notice:

le directeur, sorte de poussah à la figure et à la voix pleines de cicatrices (qu'avaient laissées l'extirpation sur l'une, de nombreux boutons, sur l'autre, des divers accents dus à des origines lointaines) [. . .] (*JF* I 662)

The next time the Directeur is described, Proust makes no attempt to remind us of this parallel between his complexion and his voice, but gives a new description which is amusing in itself:

il arpentait les corridors, vêtu d'une redingote neuve, si soigné par le coiffeur que sa figure fade avait l'air de consister en un mélange où pour une partie de chair il y en aurait eu trois de cosmétique, changeant sans cesse de cravates [. . .] (*JF* I 951)

The inaesthetic contrast between the Directeur's elegant garb and caked face will seem much stronger if the reader recalls the earlier description of his skin.

Another technique of description, particularly important where caricatures are involved, is to place the character in a sufficient variety of interesting situations to compensate for his potentially static quality. A good example is that of Cottard. Before he enters into the action of *ALR*, his distorted character is described in detail. We learn that his most striking characteristic is the lack of the basic instinct which tells people how to behave. Because of this deficiency, we are told, Cottard is desperately anxious to pick up clues from others as to how he should react; but he is unable to interpret those clues, and can only take the things that people say at their face value. He is at his most vulnerable when jokes are told, for jokers often do not say what they mean. When we first meet Cottard he has found a temporary shield against the exposure of his weakness in the shape of a *sourire conditionnel et provisoire* which can be interpreted as worldly-wise if a joke is made or as sympathetic if remarks are serious. Meanwhile, we are told, he has (as is his custom) taken at its face value the advice of *une mère prévoyante*, and is learning up witticisms, puns, idioms and so on so as not to be caught off his guard (*S* I 200). Already Cottard's way of dealing with his social problem seems ludicrously crude. The very fact that the problem exists for him at all is ridiculous, as most normal people are able to take for granted the social behaviour of others without having to study it systematically. But at the same time, Cottard is potentially a boring character. One can see that most of the humour in his portrayal is going to consist in the exposure of his weakness in various social contexts. But one cannot see how Proust will achieve any unexpected variations on this theme. Yet after a few demonstrations of Cottard's ridiculous behaviour (*S* I 201, 289 etc.), Proust, by means of a brilliant trick, suddenly places him in a completely new perspective. We know that Cottard believes what he is told; what will happen if he is told that in future he must adopt an impassive attitude which implies disbelief of what he is told? Logically, he should obey his new instructions and without fundamentally changing he should outwardly become a completely different person. This is just what happens:

Quel ami charitable lui conseilla l'air glacial? L'importance de sa situation lui rendit plus aisé de la prendre. (*JF* I 434)

The very idea of completely changing one's character is in itself ridiculous. When this character-change is so complete (Proust calls it 'un véritable vêtement retourné') it is ludicrous. The whole idea that now Cottard has found an answer to all his social problems simply by adopting another crude technique, but this time a more successful one, makes him seem ridiculously unsubtle.

Proust now examines this new Cottard. He points out that Cottard's new severity is not natural to him, but, characteristically, another learnt lesson:

Il tâchait de se rappeler s'il avait pensé à prendre un masque froid, comme on cherche une glace pour regarder si on n'a pas oublié de nouer sa cravate. (*JF* I 498)

Together with his increasing fame as a doctor, the success of his new image gives Cottard the confidence he lacked when we first met him. And this new-found confidence brings about a further change in his character. He ceases to assume that his inability to understand subtleties of social behaviour is a failure in himself. Instead, he confidently assumes that anything he doesn't understand is meaningless, and becomes brash and overbearing towards the very people towards whom he used to be timid.

But although he gains in confidence, he does not gain in insight. He continues to take things at their face value. When M. de Charlus, with polite irony, tells him that he is honoured to travel in the same compartment as him, Cottard assumes that he is being completely sincere (*SG* II 1040). In his exaggerated new smugness, he even arouses his long-dormant critical faculty, with grotesque results. Instead of questioning others to find out what he ought to believe about philosophy, he decides for himself:

—Qu'est-ce qu'il y a dans cette philosophie? peu de chose en somme. (*SG* II 1051)

Thus, by gradual degrees, and because of the same distortion in his character, Cottard has changed from an anxious young man, completely incapable of dealing with other people, to a self-satisfied, successful doctor, ready to believe that others find him intelligent and even attractive (he is sure that M. de Charlus is longing to seduce him). When last we see him, he is smugly pretentious, laying down the law about the 'manque de psychologie' of the Germans (*TR* III 778). And all these changes are the natural outcome of his personality when we first saw him. Proust has manipulated a potentially static character to provide a great deal of entertainment and variety.

In general, character development is extremely important in Proust. It is one of the factors that not only multiply the humorous effect but also replace the more conventional types of development in the novel. Proust does not keep us in suspense by means of an exciting plot, and, indeed, often deliberately rejects potentially dramatic intrigues, as has been seen in the chapter on Structure. But he does rely on the changing personalities of his characters to keep the reader's interest, as well as illustrating the changes wrought by Time.

Intrinsic Qualities of Character

Proust's humour, like Molière's, frequently involves an implied 'serious criticism of human vices. Proust's chief target is the selfishness of humanity. A vast majority of his characters care for others only as an audience to show off to or impress. Their lack of real concern for their fellow-men is barbaric. Together with this deep-rooted selfishness, there is a slavish adherence to the rules of the social game, an adherence that is as passionate as it is pointless and that helps to conceal the egoism of the individual behind a façade of carefully-ordered civilization. There are few really anti-social characters. Those that pretend to be, such as Legrandin or Rustinlor, turn out to be hypocrites who have selected ostensible indifference as a means of worming their way into society. Those that wish to rise above their fellows can only envisage the process in terms of society as it stands. Mme de Cambremer-Legrandin's ambition is limited to the desire to be able to speak familiarly of those who are at present her social superiors. The basic picture, then, is a hypocritical one: the characters are indifferent to others yet play along with them and obey the rules.

For while indifferent to others' misfortunes, Proust's characters are not indifferent to others' opinions. On the contrary, they passionately desire recognition and admiration. They become highly emotional, even hysterical. Mme Cresmeyer is so anxious about her dinner-party that she has to take to her bed.

Proust derives considerable humour from such emotions. Unbridled feelings can often appear ridiculous, and Proust's world is one of violent, often disagreeable passions. The characters often dislike each other, and this can be very funny. They have their own individual ways of expressing dislike. Rachel vindictively destroys theatrical rivals who happen to have antagonized her (*CG* II 173, *TR* III 1014–15). M. de Charlus is content to comment on his victims in their presence, so rudely that the Narrator is amazed that they are not utterly confounded (*SG* II 700–1).

Other characters lose their tempers with each other. In Proust's earlier writings he does not seem to have been so keenly aware of the potential humour underlying violent demonstrations of anger; but in *ALR* the rule seems to hold that anger becomes ridiculous as soon as it becomes uncontrollable. Even if the situation is basically serious, the moments of anger tend to emerge as humorous. When Saint-Loup slaps a journalist, his love for Rachel is making him desperately unhappy, almost a tragic figure. But the delivery of the slap and the response it receives are ridiculous.

Proust seems to think of uncontrollable impulses to be cruel as potentially less ridiculous than ungovernable rage. If a character seems helpless in the grip of instincts that he knows to be cruel, he appears pathetic. There may be a bitter irony inherent in the contrast between his real self and the vicious deeds he cannot help doing (Mlle Vinteuil desecrates her father's memory with sadistic delight only because she is basically virtuous). But on the whole Proust observes conscious but uncontrollable cruelty with compassion.

On the other hand, there often seems to be remarkably little sympathy for the victims of cruelty. Proust repeatedly makes the characters amuse themselves by hurting others, and expects the reader to laugh heartlessly at the expense of the victims. The *maître d'hôtel* makes us laugh by horrifying Françoise with tales of German atrocities (*TR* III 843).

Proust is also keenly interested in the ridiculous aspects of vindictiveness and resentment. Françoise is constantly revealing resentment of the Narrator by needling him (in these situations, the reader laughs as much at the Narrator's helpless rage as at the cunning with which Françoise baits him).

Jealousy, which involves great anguish in Proust, would not at first sight seem potentially ridiculous. But Proust mocks at the possessive person who will go to ludicrous lengths to gain control over the object of his affections or interest. Mme Verdurin's possessiveness of her *fidèles* also involves, by implication, jealousy of the outsiders who take her favourites away from her. Thus she prevents her *fidèles* even from seeing their own families:

La tante du pianiste exigeait qu'il vînt dîner ce jour-là en famille chez sa mère à elle:
—Vous croyez qu'elle en mourrait, votre mère, s'écria durement Mme Verdurin, si vous ne dîniez pas avec elle le jour de l'an, comme en *province*! (*S* I 190)

This situation is not unlike manifestations of the Narrator's or Swann's jealousy, except that Mme Verdurin has less excuse than they have for being emotionally involved, and yet is even more demanding. Here the difference between serious and comic jealousy is not one of kind but of treatment.

The quality of a character's emotions largely depends on his intelligence. Proust from the first mocks at stupidity, which can make every act seem ridiculous. In *PJ*, he writes of a character:

elle prétendit à l'intelligence, lut beaucoup, devint pédante et fut [. . .] intellectuelle [. . .] avec des maladresses ridicules. (*JS* p. 38).

The reader must assume that this woman is ridiculous because the author has told him so. In his later writings, Proust is more likely to imply that his characters are stupid by describing their behaviour than baldly to say that they are. Already in *JS* he describes Buffeteur as:

ce gros garçon qui se mouvait à travers l'année d'une place de dernier à l'autre, sans perfectionnement, sans erreur, sans hésitation avec l'invariabilité brute d'une loi de la nature. (*JS* pp. 259–60)

He makes no direct reference to Buffeteur's stupidity, but builds an amusing conceit out of the fact that he is always bottom of the class. This is so inevitable (because Buffeteur is so stupid, of course), that it has become a law of nature.

In general, Proust writes from the point of view of someone more intelligent, more sensitive, more aware of the implications of a situation, than his characters. In *JS*, he constantly insists on the fact that Jean is more intelligent than almost every person he meets (see *JS* 238 etc.). In *ALR* he tends to imply that the Narrator is the most intelligent person by making him realize the absurdities of the others. It is by being more aware than the others that he succeeds in depicting their failings with such humour.

However, Proust also points out that it is always easier to detect faults in others than in oneself, and ridicules this weakness. At one stage he mockingly comments on the blindness of people:

vivant béatement au milieu d'une collection de photographies qu'ils avaient tirées d'eux-mêmes tandis qu'alentour grimaçaient d'effroyables images, habituellement invisibles pour eux-mêmes, mais qui les plongeraient dans la stupeur si un hasard les leur montrait en leur disant: 'C'est vous.' (*CG* II 272–3)

Naturally, the implication is that the writer or Narrator will be able to see the defects of characters other than himself more easily than he sees his own: thus in the eyes of the reader he will seem more intelligent than his characters.

But intelligence is not enough to prevent a character from seeming absurd. For intelligence can be placed at the service of questionable desires: an intelligent character achieving an ambition may be ridiculous simply because the ambition itself is ridiculous. The Swanns show great ingenuity in making sure that Mme Verdurin will hear of their social successes, by telegram if necessary (*JF* I 513).

Again, intelligence may well be vitiated by insensitivity or blindness to the real feelings of others. Scarcely any of Proust's characters are free from this taint. Even the Narrator is constantly alternating between exaggerated suspicion of Albertine and tragic unawareness of her true feelings.

If the situation is intrinsically trivial, this insensitivity can be light-heartedly amusing. For example, Odette at one stage gossips to the Narrator in English about the people sitting close to them in a café: she fails to notice that the only person in the café who does not understand every word she is saying is her interlocutor (*JF* I 544). Elsewhere it can seem more painful, when, for example, a character fails to realize that he is hurting others by his remarks. The tactless Bloch is one of the chief offenders in this respect.

Inconsistency, too, is a feature even of Proust's most intelligent characters. It is extremely funny to watch Mme de Cambremer-Legrandin changing her mind about different musicians just because she hears they have become fashionable; there is even a kind of grim humour in the inconsistencies in Albertine's explanations of her actions, though the realization that she is lying is painful to the Narrator. It is not that Albertine is stupid; but she is not as aware as the Narrator of the significance of every word she is saying.

Not content with mocking at one emotion, Proust can also laugh at a clash between the feelings of different characters. When the Curé of Combray visits Tante Léonie, there is a clash between his keenness to inform and edify and her fear of boredom. Indeed, boring characters have long been the stock-in-trade of the comic writer (the Pedant is a traditional figure of fun in Italian and French theatre). It is worth looking at Proust's treatment of his boring Curé. It is clear that his character cannot really be boring, otherwise the reader would not be amused, but bored, at reading about him. Proust must make him seem, but not be, dull. He achieves this effect by means of a simple trick: he makes the Curé's tediousness apparent not through what he says but through the response of his listeners. Tante Léonie dreads his visits because:

Le curé [. . .] habitué à donner aux visiteurs de marque des renseigne-ments sur l'église [. . .] la fatiguait par des explications infinies et d'ailleurs toujours les mêmes. Mais quand elle arrivait ainsi juste en même temps que celle d'Eulalie, sa visite devenait franchement dés-agréable à ma tante. (*CS* I 103)

Proust has here made it clear that one is expected to find the Curé tedious. At the same time, he has pointed out that this tediousness does not reside so much in what he says as in the fact that he says the same thing every time he appears. The reader will only witness one of these appearances. This is enough to enable one to imagine how unspeakably boring it would be to hear the Curé repeat himself, but not enough to bore one. Ironically, the very fact that the Curé is so practised at delivering his speech about the church makes that speech, if heard only once, seem coherent and clear, rather than monotonous.

Not only the fact of the listeners' boredom, but also their patience at enduring it can seem amusing. Proust frequently mocks at the *Faubourg* for suffering agonies of boredom simply in order to do as others do. Concerts and play-readings are attended by ignoramuses who have to pretend that they enjoyed every moment, although they do not know one musician or poet from another. Whatever the reason, when a victim is trapped in a boring situation, we laugh at his anguish as he writhes, helpless in the toils of tedium.

Other frustrating situations are used by Proust for humour, but as they usually involve the Narrator, they will be discussed in the next chapter.

Apprehension, too, is frequently made to seem funny by Proust. Often the cause of the apprehension can be ridiculous in itself; and its manifestations are exaggerated to emphasize the absurdity. An example is the farcical behaviour of Cottard when he is about to serve as a witness to M. de Charlus's duel:

Cottard arriva enfin, quoique mis très en retard, car, ravi de servir de témoin mais plus ému encore, il avait été obligé de s'arrêter à tous les cafés ou fermes de la route, en demandant qu'on voulût bien lui indiquer 'le no. 100' ou 'le petit endroit'. (*SG* II 1071)

Many of the emotions used by Proust for the purposes of humour and described here also appear as serious emotions in his works. Jealousy, affection, apprehension, frustration and so on are all treated seriously. Other emotions, such as boredom and rage, seem, by *ALR* at least, to have been considered as intrinsically comic emotions. This difference means that in the humorous use of potentially serious emotions Proust must rely mostly on tricks of treatment to create humorous effects; but when he is describing a basically ridiculous emotion he can simply state what is happening and leave the humour to the subject-matter. He rarely does this, however. He is so interested in enriching his comic effects that even when an emotion is amusing in itself, he treats it with humour.

We must next consider emotions which are in themselves admirable, and which are made to seem humorous exclusively through treatment. Naturally, mocking at emotions which the reader would normally admire presents problems. The author must make his characters deserve to be mocked at despite their admirable emotions. There are two ways of achieving this effect. Either the author makes the character ridiculous in other ways, so that a disrespectful light is cast on his emotions as well; or the author subtly points out that it is not a sincerely admirable emotion that is involved, but an approximation or imitation of it.

The first of these techniques is found in Proust's treatment of affection. When, for example, a character is in love, the love can be ridiculous simply by the character's being inaesthetic. This technique is frequently used when M. de Charlus's love for Morel is described.

The second technique, of showing up ostensibly good emotions as being in fact corrupt, is used chiefly when another type of affection is being described: the desire to make others happy, at one's own expense if necessary. This emotion is regularly exploited by hypocrites. Proust is constantly exposing consideration for others as self-centred. To Proust, the hypocrisy at the root of society often consists in a pretence of consideration for the feelings, welfare, or desires of others which is contrasted with complete egoism within the hypocrite. On the rate occasions when this pretence is dropped, the humour often resides in the fact that the hypocrite continues to play the old game, even though he knows it is no longer relevant. M. de Guermantes, when he is told by Swann that the latter is at death's door, realizes that he has not much hope of concealing the fact that he does not really care (*CG* II 595). He nevertheless comes out with banal phrases of encouragement, and provides a devastating example of the selfishness of humanity.

Speech

We have considered the various ways in which Proust describes the appearance and feelings of his characters. It is worth devoting a separate section to their speech, which is particularly illuminating since it can be viewed from outside while at the same time expressing the character's own opinions.

The speech of Proust's characters is particularly successful because it has an authentic ring. Proust's powers of observation and of memory enabled him to reproduce conversations that he had actually heard. Mme de Varambon's conversation is closely based on that of a real person at Princesse Mathilde's *salon* (see his article on the subject, *CSB* 447–8). Many of Mme de Guermantes's remarks were really made by Proust's friend Mme Straus. But Proust does more to make characters' speech funny than simply reporting remarks he has heard. He manipulates speech to make personalities appear amusing. There are three principal ways in which he does this: first, he uses speech to reveal a character's ignorance or stupidity; secondly, he uncovers disparities between the real and the ostensible purpose of spoken words; thirdly, he makes speech betray feelings, characteristics or situations which the speaker would prefer to conceal. These three categories will underlie the discussion which follows.

(i) *Mistakes in Speech*   One of the simplest ways of creating humour in speech is to cause the characters to make mistakes. Just as Proust is aware that one looks silly if one turns up to a dinner-party in the wrong clothes, so he mocks at characters whose ignorance or pretension lead them to neglect the rules of correct speech.

In such cases the humour will be partly due to the speaker's ignorance, partly to the intrinsic humour of the incorrect forms used. Perhaps the most consistently ungrammatical speaker is Françoise. Proust often points out that the effect is not funny but picturesque, archaic, and beautiful; but even in this beauty there is an element of the undignified. Françoise's attempts at respectability cannot be taken seriously when she is saying things like 'plutôt que non pas aller' (*CG* II 24), or 'je vas seulement voir si mon feu ne s'éteint pas' (*CS* I 56).

Usually Proust inserts these inaccuracies slyly into a conversation or speech, so that their impact is increased by their unexpectedness. Elsewhere he draws our attention to them by pointing out that they are habitual mistakes:

elle tenait [. . .] à ce que l'on sût que nous avions 'd'argent' (car elle ignorait l'usage de ce que Saint-Loup appelait les articles partitifs et disait 'avoir d'argent', 'apporter d'eau'). (*CG* II 21)

He may also subject them to a detailed analysis (see *P* III 190 and *TR* III 749 for two examples).[1]

A modification of this type of humour often occurs when the character is made to realize how ridiculous his own speech is, either at the time or later. Thus Bloch, who attempts to pronounce the English

---

[1] It is interesting to note that the prototypes of Françoise in *JS* talk correctly where Françoise herself would have made picturesque mistakes (see *JS* pp. 206–7). As a result the contrast between Françoise's dignity and unconsciously laughable speech, which provides much of the humour in Proust's portrayal of her, is non-existent in these earlier versions.

word 'lift' with easy casualness, is later discomfited when he finds out that it should really be 'lift' and not 'laïft' as he had thought (*JF* I 738–40).

Usually the character who is trying to impress in this way is vaguely conscious of the fact that he is not really succeeding: Bloch is only too ready to believe that it is he who was wrong about the 'laïft', although accepting this must be painful to him. This fact adds a spice of cruelty to the humour.

At other times the speaker is unaware of the ridiculousness of what he is saying. This can make him doubly ridiculous when he persists in making the same kind of mistake. But one speaker's self-confidence is so colossal that the reader is almost convinced that he had not made a mistake at all. M. de Guermantes misuses words on more than one occasion, and Proust draws the reader's attention to this (see *SG* II 720). But it never occurs either to the other characters or to the Narrator to laugh at him and feel superior to him to the extent that they would if Bloch were to misuse a word. The exalted social status of M. de Guermantes has made him a somewhat awesome figure; though one may disapprove of him or even laugh at him, nothing he does or says can seem as ridiculous as almost anything Bloch does. This example suggests an important point: a ridiculous remark cannot be studied entirely on its own merits, but must be related to what the reader knows of the speaker.

Risible speech may be the result of lack of familiarity with the language. Proust portrays several foreigners in his work, and mocks at their French in different ways. The crudest type of foreigner's French is pidgin French. In *ALR*, Proust has two examples of *petit nègre*. In both the speaker is highly excited, so that contrast is provided between the genuine emotion of the speaker and its ridiculous expression (*CG* II 533–4 and *JF* I 536).

A similar contrast between genuine emotion and inaccurate speech occurs on a much more sophisticated level when the foreigner speaks French well. Here the contrast is given added bite because the speaker may well be unaware of the impression he is making. Mme Sherbatoff might well think that she is speaking perfectly when she says, with genuine admiration:

—Oui, j'aime ce petit celcle intelligent, agléable, pas méchant, tout simple, pas snob et où on a de l'esplit jusqu'au bout des ongles.'(*SG* II 893)

The humour here is provided by means of a malicious trick of Proust's:

he isolates a speech particularity which most people would scarcely notice, and uses ridiculous spelling to reproduce it. The Princess's Russian 'r' is certainly not exactly the same as an 'l', and even Proust does not claim that it is since he simply says that:

le roulement des *r* de l'accent russe, était doucement marmonné au fond de la gorge, comme si c'était non des *r* mais des *l*.

But in this example of her speech, the awkwardness of words like *celcle* makes one laugh because Proust has changed her 'r's into 'l's as if the two were exactly the same sound. The humour is created by Proust and not obvious in the subject-matter.

In such cases, the other characters will be too familiar with the speaker to notice how ridiculous his speech is. But Proust chooses to point out such defects at moments calculated to destroy the speaker's dignity. He describes in Stendhalian terms the machinations of the brilliant Prince Von to have himself made a member of the Académie des Sciences Morales et Politiques. After a long analysis, in which the Prince's cunning, sang-froid and intelligence are stressed, the answer is found to the Prince's problem: a visit to Mme de Villeparisis. And when he makes his visit, in many ways the climax of his career,

en s'inclinant, petit, rouge et ventru, devant Mme de Villeparisis, le Rhingrave lui dit: 'Ponchour, Matame la marquise' avec le même accent qu'un concierge alsacien. (*CG* II 263)

The Prince's accent makes him appear utterly ridiculous by contrast to his earlier dignity. But we must remember that this bathos is a pure invention of Proust's; for the Prince's 'concierge' voice was used throughout the negotiations, and it is Proust's fault if the reader was not told of it before. Proust's mockery here is relatively harmless: he ridicules without criticizing. In general where he uses speech, he tends to be more satirical.

(ii) *Affectation*   Much of the humour in the above examples is due to the incompatibility between the speaker's good faith and the inaccurate way he expresses his beliefs. A different effect is obtained when the speaker is not straightforward. Artificiality in speech is in itself ridiculous: it does not matter what the subject is; as long as the tone of the speaker is insincere, one is disposed to laugh.

This accounts for the humour when a character is making a conscious effort to appear natural and unaffected. Mme de Cambremer-Legrandin speaks to the Narrator with an easy casualness that is obviously premeditated:

'Contente d'avoir passé la soirée avec vous, me dit-elle; amitiés à Saint-Loup, si vous le voyez.' (*SG* II 978)

There is something excruciatingly embarrassing as well as amusing about the way Proust has isolated this self-consciousness and made his character reveal her insincerity without realizing it. Proust emphasizes this aspect by analysing Mme de Cambremer-Legrandin's remark before she actually makes it:

elle employa, en prenant congé de moi, deux de ces abréviations qui [. . .] me semblent encore, même aujourd'hui, avoir, dans leur négligé voulu, dans leur familiarité apprise, quelque chose d'insupportablement pédant. (*SG* II 977–8)

This is ludicrously inappropriate treatment of a phrase which was intended by the speaker to make an easy, natural impression.

Conversely, an attempt on the part of a speaker to be pompous and unnatural can produce the same sort of effect. Attempts to be 'natural' and attempts to be pompous are not all that different, since they have in common the fact that the speaker is not being straightforward. For instance, we are told that M. de Guermantes calls the Bishop of Mâcon 'Monsieur de Mascon', the reason being that 'le duc trouvait cela vieille France' (*CG* II 478).

It seems, then, that the attitude of the speaker, more than his actual words, makes speech seem affected. The speaker tends to be aware that he is trying to make an impression through speech, and this is one of the chief reasons we laugh at him.

Occasionally, however, seemingly affected speech can come naturally to the speaker. This is the case with Brichot. Brichot initially strikes one as an affected speaker, whose pompous, learnedly colloquial language must be directed at impressing his audience. But later one finds that he uses the same sort of language even under the stress of real emotion. When he thinks of Mme Verdurin's sorrow at the death of her friend Dechambre, he exclaims:

—Ah! mille tonnerres de Zeus [. . .] ah! ça a dû être un coup terrible, un ami de vingt-cinq ans! [. . .] Ah! il a pu dire plus justement que ce m'as-tu vu de Néron, qui a trouvé le moyen de rouler la science allemande elle-même: *Qualis artifex pereo*! (*SG* II 896–7)

The context makes it quite clear that Brichot's emotion is absolutely genuine: it would seem then that affected classical allusions and disrespectful references to history are the most natural terms for him to express his feelings. Perhaps what originally started off as an affectation has become second nature to him, but it still seems so unnatural to the reader that one laughs at him as if he were being deliberately artificial.

Another technique of affected speech is to try to shock through forthrightness. Proust often points out the disingenuousness underlying such comments as Tiche's that a painting looks as if it were 'fait [. . .] avec du caca'. Proust tells us that the whole object of the painter's speech was to 'se faire admirer des convives en plaçant un morceau' (S I 254). Again, when Mme de Guermantes or Mme Verdurin say that something is written 'comme par un cochon', they are making the statement not because it is their honest opinion, but because they want to make their listeners sit up. As a result, one laughs partly at the insincerity of their motives, and partly at the gullibility of their audience, who react exactly as they are expected to.

But this self-conscious approach is not essential to affected speech. Saint-Loup, for instance, takes over the speech of others, and repeats what they say as if he were voicing his own ideas. But basically, his attitude is unselfish: he copies others because he believes them to be more worthwhile than he is. Not only is he unselfish, but he seems to be unaware of the fact that he is a plagiarist. Nevertheless, the fact that his speech is not original is sufficient to make it appear affected and hence ridiculous. In imitation of Rachel and her set he says:

'Elle a quelque chose de sidéral et même de vatique [. . .]' (CG II 125)

and the Narrator comments that he uses such language because

il était imbu d'un certain langage qu'on parlait autour de cette femme dans des milieux littéraires. (p. 125)

The Narrator implies that Saint-Loup has assimilated this type of speech to such a degree that he reproduces it unconsciously. This is an example of artificiality by proxy: the speaker is sincere, but the source of the remark probably was not.

Affected speech can vary considerably in scale: it is often suggested by the mispronunciation of a single word. Mme Verdurin calls one of her guests (probably Rachel) a *mugichienne* (TR III 984), thereby revealing her affectation and also making an insulting pun on the words 'mugir' and 'chienne'. Conversely, the affectation of Bloch or M. de Norpois is revealed during the course of long speeches.

Despite their common element of affectation, these examples have little in common. Their variety indicates the extent of Proust's preoccupation with the subject. And indeed, affectation in speech is one of Proust's essential tools for exposing the selfishness of the inhabitants of the human jungle.

(iii) *Miscellaneous Effects*   A few humorous tricks of speech are selected here to emphasize further the enormous scope of Proust's use of humour in speech.

When a speaker is trying to talk persuasively, humour may arise when he is telling untruths. Mme Verdurin tells Brichot that M. de Charlus 'a eu de sales histoires et que la police l'a a l'œil' (*P* III 280). She confirms this by the assertion:

'Mais je vous en réponds! c'est moi qui vous le dis'

and goes on to state that Jupien is an ex-convict who is blackmailing M. de Charlus:

je le sais, vous savez, oui, et de façon positive.

We laugh at Mme Verdurin because of the excessive disparity between the facts and her emphatic assertions (ironically, she turns out to be at least partly right about the 'sales histoires').

Speech can reveal character traits, such as obstinacy, as when the Narrator's *maître d'hôtel* insists on pronouncing *envergure* as *enverjure* in order to assert his independence (*TR* III 842). Lack of originality too, can be revealed, as when Gilberte, talking of the title of Prince des Laumes, says: 'un si joli titre! Un des plus beaux titres français!' and Proust comments that even intelligent people are sometimes guilty of 'un certain ordre de banalités' (*F* III 584). The words spoken are as commonplace as the exchanges after lunch in *JS*, when the characters cannot rouse themselves to produce more than the most ordinary of comments:

Ah! il fait vraiment chaud. Un orage ferait du bien. —Rien que pour venir du pré ici j'étais tout en eau, il m'a fallu changer de chemise. —Si on ouvrait, ferait-il plus frais?—Oh! non, il fait bien plus chaud dehors que dedans etc. (*JS* p. 291)

Here the characters are being far more 'natural' than one expects in a novel: usually, for fear of boring the reader, the author eliminates the sort of remarks that the reader can be expected to hear every day. Here, simply by introducing them at length, he produces an unusual humorous effect.

Occasionally, speech is amusing simply because it is strange. For example, when the Narrator wakes from a dream saying:

—Tu sais bien pourtant que je vivrai toujours près d'elle, cerfs, cerfs, Francis Jammes, fourchette.' (*SG* II 762) the meaningless combination of words may seem funny to the reader.

Another quality of speech is its picturesque, poetic side. Here humour usually lies in the contrast between mundane, domestic subject-matter and poetic expression. Céleste goes into lyrical raptures at the sight of the Narrator throwing aside a half-eaten croissant (*SG* II 847), while Françoise, in a sustained poetic image, contrasts the rustic paradise of Combray with the hell of her life in Paris, her damnation being announced by the bell summoning her to attend the Narrator (*CG* II 17–18).

One of Proust's most interesting effects is to juxtapose characters. The differences and similarities between the various styles of speech are then singled out for mockery.

First, there are characters who use the same speech tricks. These are so little stressed by Proust that in some cases one wonders whether he was conscious of them himself. Nevertheless, these juxtapositions seem to make some comment on both the speakers involved. For example, there is a certain similarity between the language of M. de Norpois and of Bloch. M. de Norpois uses imagery which he thinks is appropriate to a statesman. Bloch uses what he thinks is ironic, poetic imagery. But both share a desire to impress through their poetic language and both are strained and artificial. This similarity is far too slight for the reader to notice it without it being brought to his attention. But when Bloch meets M. de Norpois, we see their two ways of talking juxtaposed. And, to the reader's surprise, M. de Norpois admires Bloch's conversation. The reader is bound to be struck by this, since M. de Norpois might be expected to despise Bloch for his cynical, tasteless remarks. The only explanation for this admiration, and one which M. de Norpois himself suggests, is that Bloch's speech, in some respects at least, is like his own:

Il est assez amusant, avec sa manière de parler un peu vieux jeu [. . .] (*CG* II 243)

says M. de Norpois of Bloch; but elsewhere the identical words are used to describe M. de Norpois himself:

ma mère jugeait M. de Norpois un peu 'vieux jeu', ce qui [. . .] la charmait moins dans le domaine [. . .] des expressions. (*JF* I 437)

The implied irony of the juxtaposition is obvious: there is not such a great difference between the convictions of a reactionary elder statesman and those of a left-wing intellectual as either supposes, since they can express their convictions with a certain degree of similarity.

Social as well as political differences between characters are levelled

by this kind of juxtaposition. For example, the Swanns pronounce
many words in the same way as the Guermantes (*JF* I 511), although
the Guermantes consider Mme Swann too far beneath them to agree to
meet her.

(iv) *Sound*   When Proust comments that

Il y a des moments où, pour peindre complètement quelqu'un, il
faudrait que l'imitation phonétique se joignît à la description [. . .]
(*SG* II 942)

he is referring not only to his characters' speech, but also to the sound
of their voices. Often the sounds that the characters make are so ridiculous in themselves that there is no need for the author to do more
than describe them baldly. The most striking example of this is the way
M. de Charlus pronounces *Monsieur*:

Il sourit avec dédain, fit monter sa voix jusqu'aux plus extrêmes
registres, et là, attaquant avec douceur la note la plus aiguë et la plus
insolente:—Oh! Monsieur, dit-il en revenant avec une extrême lenteur
à une intonation naturelle, et comme s'enchantant, au passage, des
bizarreries de cette gamme descendante [. . .] (*CG* II 556)

One can easily work out from this description exactly what M.
de Charlus's words sounded like. Besides this, the very fact of
combining a detailed, over-charged description of sounds with the
everyday words 'Oh! Monsieur' lends the passage a humorous over-
emphasis.

The characters with memorable voices are few and far between, and
their voices are referred to at intervals throughout *ALR*. So the reader
will tend to remember these voices, which will help bring people to life.
They also help us to understand the characters' personalities. For example, Cottard's voice is symptomatic of his social behaviour as a
whole. Just as he is unable to gauge the appropriate moment for making
a joke, so he cannot modulate his voice to suit the general mood. He is
constantly making his companions jump by uttering unexpected
shouts: when Brichot is in the middle of a learned remark about
medicine,

il ne put achever sa phrase. Le professeur venait de sursauter et de
pousser un hurlement. (*SG* II 891–2)

At first the reader assumes that there is something seriously wrong.
Then he is given the impression that the *fidèles* have gone past their
station:

Nom de d'là, s'écria-t-il en passant enfin au langage articulé, nous avons
passé Maineville (hé! hé!) et même Renneville.

But finally it is made clear that the only thing wrong is that the
Princesse Sherbatoff has got on to the train. Cottard's explosion seems
ridiculously inappropriate in retrospect.

In Brichot's case, description of his voice contributes to the depic-
tion of a character which is the opposite of Cottard's. Whereas
Cottard's voice betrays his lack of *savoir-vivre* and control, Brichot's
is exaggeratedly over-precise and pompous:

Si fait, mon cher hôte, si fait, si fait, reprit-il de sa voix bien timbrée
qui détachait chaque syllabe [. . .] (*S* I 252)

Proust can also use sound to indicate the state of mind of his characters. For example, he often makes it plain from the way he describes a
character's tone of voice that the character is being hypocritical. He
simply has to use the word *factice* for the reader to realize that a whole
speech is hypocritical and therefore ridiculous:

'Mais non, pourquoi? rasseyez-vous donc, je suis charmée de vous
garder encore un peu', disait la princesse d'un air dégagé et à l'aise (pour
faire la grande dame), mais d'une voix devenue factice. (*CG* II 462)

Hypocritical amiability frequently occurs in comedies (witness the
tête-à-tête between Célimène and Arsinoë in *Le Misanthrope*). Proust,
too, realizes the theatrical character of this device, and mentions the
theatre in connection with it. Mme Verdurin, making small talk and
pretending not to notice the arrival of her aristocratic guests, the
Cambremers, is described as talking 'du même ton factice qu'une marquise du Théâtre-Français' (*SG* II 912). Other noises, too, can indicate
hypocrisy. A laugh can make it plain that the character is not amused:

Mme de Guermantes fit avec la gorge ce bruit léger, bref et fort comme
d'un sourire forcé qu'on ravale, et qui était destiné à montrer qu'elle
prenait part, dans la mesure où la parenté l'y obligeait, à l'esprit de son
neveu. (*CG* II 256)

No one except the Narrator notices how ludicrous Mme de Guermantes's laugh is. Proust extends this ironical observation of convention
to other aspects of social life. At one stage he points out the inappropriateness of the tone of a servant's voice:

un maître d'hôtel [. . .] s'inclina [. . .] et annonça la nouvelle: 'Madame
est servie', d'un ton pareil à celui dont il aurait dit: 'Madame se meurt',
mais qui ne jeta aucune tristesse dans l'assemblée [. . .] (*CG* II 434)

Here the spice of the humour lies in the fact that everybody else must
takes these sepulchral tones, with their echo of Bossuet, for granted.

At other times sounds can be combined with situations for humorous
effect. For example, when the Narrator is embarrassed by the loudness

of M. de Charlus's voice when they talk in the street (*TR* III 799), the reader laughs just as much at the discomfiture of the Narrator as at the unsuitability of M. de Charlus's voice. The question of loudness of voice in general interests Proust. At one stage he presents an amusing paradox. Mme de Mortemart, talking to M. de Charlus, adopts a low voice so that Mme de Valcourt will not hear that she is arranging a *soirée*. Mme de Valcourt immediately becomes suspicious because of her air of secrecy. When M. de Charlus replies at the top of his voice, his ordinary tones dispel Mme de Valcourt's suspicions (*P* III 269-70).

It is worth mentioning in connection with Proust's evident interest in the sound of his characters' voices that he himself, from all accounts, was a skilful mimic of others' voices. He is particularly remembered for his imitations of Comte Robert de Montesquiou who was in many respects the prototype of M. de Charlus. From the descriptions of Montesquiou's voice, it would seem that Proust must have taken it over with scarcely any modification for M. de Charlus.

Sense of Humour

When characters are endowed with a sense of humour, the author has the unique opportunity of making the reader laugh with as well as at them. He can also make them seem totally ridiculous if they fail in their attempts to be funny. Speech is, naturally, the only means the author has for allowing the characters to express their sense of humour, for by gesturing they can only indicate it, as Cottard does when he shows his appreciation of a joke by winking (*SG* II 974). And it is in reproducing the characters' actual words that the author can make the best use of the subtle variations in humour between laughing with and laughing at his characters.

How then does he treat his characters' witticisms? If he thinks humorous remarks are amusing enough as they stand, Proust is content simply to record them. An example is M. de Charlus's very witty play on words during the course of a conversation; Morel has taken to writing articles, and M. de Charlus says:

je serais vraiment très content que Charlie ajoute à son violon ce petit brin de plume d'Ingres. (*P* III 221)

But more often, Proust deliberately places his characters' jokes in a favourable context, thereby increasing the effect. For example, Mme de Guermantes makes a skilful play on words:

—Ce pauvre général, il a encore été battu aux élections, dit la princesse
de Parme [. . .]
—Il s'est consolé en voulant faire un nouvel enfant à sa femme.
—Comment! Cette pauvre Mme de Monserfeuil est encore enceinte,
s'écria la princesse.
—Mais parfaitement, répondit la duchesse, c'est le seul *arrondissement*
où le pauvre général n'a jamais échoué. (*CG* II 512)

This punch line is placed at the end not only of a paragraph but of a
whole episode, in a highly conspicuous position. Proust thereby implies
that he thinks that the joke is a good one, since he considers it worthy
to end the whole long description of the Guermantes dinner-party;
and its impact is certainly increased by the striking position it occupies.

There are very few such examples. Almost always Proust adopts a
positively disparaging attitude towards his characters' humour. He may
make a speaker disapprove of his own jokes. It is said of Mme de Guermantes, whose witticisms frequently involve punning, that she

détestait les calembours et n'avait hasardé celui-là ['quand on parle du
Saint-Loup'] qu'en ayant l'air de se moquer d'elle-même. (*CG* II 254)

The general impression that Proust disapproved of punning is reinforced
by a significant fact. Although Proust frequently makes his characters
play with words, he himself is reluctant to do so in narrative passages.
One understands why when one actually comes across one of the rare
examples: they seem ponderously deliberate compared with his normal
lightness of touch. An example is:

chacun déployait sur ses genoux une serviette candide comme la joie
qui brillait dans tous les yeux. (*JS* p. 458)

Indeed, Proust said of himself 'Je n'ai pas l'art du calembour' (in a
letter to Mme Straus, January 1917).

Another reason for condemning witticisms is if they are not spontaneous. The repetition of even an intrinsically amusing joke destroys
its spontaneity and hence its merit. M. de Guermantes, when describing
his wife's 'dernier mot', takes great care to emphasize its spontaneity:

Oriane n'a pu s'empêcher de s'écrier, involontairement, je dois le confesser, elle n'y a pas mis de méchanceté, car c'est venu vite comme
l'éclair: 'Taquin . . . taquin . . . Alors c'est Taquin le Superbe!' (*CG*
II 465)

The Duke's assertion is meant to make his wife seem even wittier
because of her spontaneity. But the way the joke is retold by the Guermantes is not spontaneous. Proust insists on this. He tells us that the
Duchess speaks because 'le moment de donner la réplique à son mari

était venu' and describes the joke-telling technique of the couple as those of a 'femme d'esprit et son imprésario'. He mocks at the Guermantes for telling a carefully prepared joke which claiming for it the virtues of spontaneity.

Repetition of a witticism is occasionally tolerated if it enhances the humorous effect. The Narrator's grandfather makes a reiterated joke of a serious remark originally made by Swann's father: 'Souvent mais peu à la fois, comme le pauvre père Swann' (*CS* I 15), repeating it in amusingly unexpected contexts.

At other times it is not the actual witticism that is deprecated but some incidental fault that is revealed in the speaker. Many witticisms depend for their effect on the fact that they involve malice at others' expense. In Mme de Guermantes's 'arrondissement' joke, for example, the reader laughs as much at the belittling of the poor general as at Mme de Guermantes's witty turn of phrase. The reader may be just as amused by these malicious jokes as by any others; but he may be slightly uncomfortable at the spite with which the speaker destroys his victim's dignity.

It may be through no fault of his own that the speaker is penalized and his humour ruined. Proust often seems deliberately to destroy the intended effect of a witticism by placing it in a context which spoils it. For example, a knowledge of previous events is bound to distort Saint-Loup's witticism when, talking of the *petit clan*, he says:

'La question n'est pas, comme pour Hamlet, d'être ou de ne pas être, mais d'en être ou de ne pas en être. Tu en es, mon oncle Charlus en est. Que veux-tu? moi je n'ai jamais aimé ça, ce n'est pas ma faute.' (*SG* II 1022)

Not long before, the Narrator has witnessed another occasion on which these words were used, by M. Verdurin, referring to a society of unworldly intellectuals:

'Excusez-moi de vous parler de ces riens, commença-t-il, car je suppose bien le peu de cas que vous en faites. Les esprits bourgeois y font attention, mais les autres, les artistes, les gens qui *en sont* vraiment, s'en fichent. Or dès les premiers mots que nous avons échangés, j'ai compris que vous *en étiez*!' M. de Charlus, qui donnait à cette locution un sens fort différent, eut un haut-le-corps. Après les œillades du docteur, l'injurieuse franchise du Patron le suffoquait. 'Ne protestez pas, cher Monsieur, vous *en êtes*, c'est clair comme le jour, reprit M. Verdurin. Remarquez que je ne sais pas si vous exercez un art quelconque, mais ce n'est pas nécessaire. Ce n'est pas toujours suffisant. Dechambre, qui vient de mourir, jouait parfaitment avec le plus robuste mécanisme,

mais *n'en était* pas, on sentait tout de suite qu'il *n'en était* pas. Brichot
n'en est pas. Morel *en est*, ma femme *en est*, je sens que *vous en êtes* . . .
—Qu'alliez-vous me dire?' interrompit M. de Charlus, qui commençait
à être rassuré sur ce que voulait signifier M. Verdurin, mais qui préférait qu'il criât moins haut ces paroles à double sens. (*SG* II 941)

From the moment he reads this passage, the reader is bound to
associate the phrase *en être* with homosexuality, and to remember it
as the vehicle for an amusing *double entendre*. When Saint-Loup uses
the phrase, the reader is incapable of appreciating the wit of his de-
formation of Hamlet's words but instead will laugh at him for his unconscious use of an ambiguous phrase. Thus the effect of his witticism
is twisted through no fault of his own, and the reader is prevented from
laughing with Saint-Loup and made to laugh at him.

The reverse also occurs. A witticism may at first seem funny but its
effect may be perverted by the contexts in which it subsequently reappears. Mme de Guermantes's 'derniers mots', when they are first told,
seem amusing. But later, other members of the *Faubourg* take possession of these jokes and one learns of their fate in phrases like:

le 'mot' se mangeait encore froid le lendemain à déjeuner, entre intimes
qu'on invitait pour cela, et reparaissait sous diverses sauces pendant la
semaine. (*CG* II 466)

These reactions affect one's opinion of the original joke: although one
laughs at its fate, one can no longer admire it for its wit.

At times Proust goes further and obliges the reader to disapprove of
a witticism by stating categorically that it is a failure. Saint-Loup, who
during the war becomes much readier than before to express his ideas in
a witty form, is critically described at this stage as 'le discoureur, le
doctrinaire qui ne cessait de jouer avec les mots' (*TR* III 760-1).
His witticisms are later criticized for their lack of originality, and the
reader cannot admire his puns without feeling that he is not reacting
as the author expects.

Proust's critical approach to his characters' witticisms is in fact a
skilful way of making them seem twice as funny. In almost all the examples quoted here, Proust, by distorting his characters' humour, adds
a new humorous twist to what they have said, so that they are aware
of only part of the impact of their words.

But Proust can be crueller than this. He makes his characters
produce witticisms which are not at all funny in the way the speaker
intends them to be, but which make the reader laugh at him because,
in producing them, he makes himself seem ridiculous.

The crudest way in which a speaker can spoil his own jokes is through bad taste. Cottard is one of the chief offenders in this respect. When this tastelessness is combined with the laborious lack of spontaneity that typifies Cottard's humour, the effect is excruciating. On one occasion, Cottard makes a joke to the Narrator who is ill. Its forced jocularity is in very bad taste, but the effect of its tastelessness is immeasurably increased when we learn that Cottard is in the habit of making this joke on other, equally unsuitable occasions:

je veux bien que vous preniez quelques potages, puis des purées, mais toujours au lait, au lait. Cela vous plaira, puisque l'Espagne est à la mode, ollé ollé! (Ses elèves connaissaient bien ce calembour qu'il faisait à l'hôpital chaque fois qu'il mettait un cardiaque ou un hépatique au régime lacté) [. . .] (*JF* I 498)

The reader is embarrassed by the extent of Cottard's bad taste, which at the same time is so ludicrous that he is obliged to laugh: Proust frequently evokes an embarrassed snigger from the reader. There is one character whose entire conversation consists in tasteless witticisms: Françoise's daughter. The Narrator sharply criticizes her for this by making remarks such as 'ce n'était pas de très bon goût' (*SG* II 728), and repeatedly points out that besides being offensive in herself, she has a bad influence on others, notably Françoise.

But Cottard and Françoise's daughter are not the most obnoxious of characters, for they do not attempt to be anything but amusing. There are characters who use humour as a means for arousing other feelings than amusement in their audience. Humour in speech is frequently used to arouse admiration in the listener. The moment such motives are detected by the Narrator, he becomes completely merciless in exposing them. And if listeners are taken in, they too are criticized.

Attempts are often made to induce listeners to admire the speaker's social position. The *Faubourg* consistently repeat Mme de Guermantes's witticisms; their motive is not a desire to amuse but to impress. Other characters, Brichot in particular, may use humour to make themselves seem attractive or intelligent. In Brichot's opinion, using learned language and scholarly descriptive techniques in an unscholarly context is enough to create humour. For example, he uses a complex negative construction to make a humorous definition of a common word: *homme* becomes *le sexe auquel je ne dois pas ma mère* (*SG* II 1100).[1]

---

[1] Brichot's pedantry seems even more extreme when we remember that he is here making a literary allusion, adapting the last line of Legouvé's poem *Le Mérite des femmes* (1801): 'Tombe aux pieds de ce sexe auquel tu dois ta mère!'

His only means of varying his humour is to reverse the order of the combination; when he is not referring to the mundane in scholarly terms, he is alluding to the scholarly in casual terms. Both variations show an intense consciousness of the humorous potential of combining the commonplace with the scholarly. Proust often reminds the reader of this consciousness:

Brichot souriait, pour montrer ce qu'il y avait de spirituel à unir des choses aussi disparates et à employer pour des choses communes un langage ironiquement élevé. (*SG* II 937)

But the true irony of Brichot's humour is that the very fact that he employs philology and scholarship for purposes of humour prevents his witticisms from being funny in the way he intends them to be. In the first place, the reader knows that Brichot really takes scholarship seriously and has devoted his life to it. One feels that scholarship forms the basis of his humour simply because he is so imbued with it that he has no other material at his disposal. Unfortunately, this is not the case with his listeners, who remain unaware of the daring impertinence of his treatment of characters like *cette vieille chipie de Blanche de Castille*, since they know very little about her anyway. In fact his use of scholarship for humour, by revealing the limitations of the way he sees things, makes him seem pathetic rather than witty. Besides, the vocabulary of philology and scholarship is shrouded in such an atmosphere of painstaking, detailed research that it is intrinsically unsuitable as a vehicle for spoken humour, which, as has been shown, depends on spontaneity and speed for much of its effect.

At times, characters use humour for a different purpose. They pretend to be amused simply in order to conceal their own violent emotions and find things out about other characters. Both Swann and the Narrator hide their anguish or excitement over women by this means. For example, the Narrator, in love with Mme de Guermantes, tries to persuade Saint-Loup to give him her photograph:

—Oh! Robert! Écoutez, dis-je encore à Saint-Loup pendant le dîner,— oh! c'est d'un comique cette conversation à propos interrompus et du reste je ne sais pas pourquoi—vous savez la dame dont je viens de vous parler? [. . .] vous ne voudriez pas me donner sa photographie? (*CG* II 103)

Significantly, Proust makes no comment on the hysterical form in which this request is couched, no mention of the disparity between the importance the Narrator attaches to his request and the jocular language he uses. Swann, too, speaks in this strained way. For example, he forces M. de Charlus, who has spent his evening with Odette, to tell every detail of where they went:

Mais comment, mon petit Mémé, je ne comprends pas très bien . . . ce n'est pas en sortant de chez elle que vous êtes allés au musée Grévin. Vous étiez allés ailleurs d'abord. Non? Oh! que c'est drôle! Vous ne savez pas comme vous m'amusez, mon petit Mémé. (S I 316)

This hysterical jocularity in a completely serious context makes both Swann and the Narrator seem, perhaps involuntarily on the part of Proust, a little ridiculous.

Elsewhere, Proust combines the serious and the humorous in a completely different way. Several of his characters use humour to wound others. This is a much more serious fault than to belittle others to seem amusing, which is what Mme de Guermantes does when she mocks at the General. One of the most revolting passages in *ALR* is the long speech made by M. de Charlus about Mme de Saint-Euverte, in her hearing, in which, amongst other things, he compares her breath to a cess-pool (*SG* II 700-1). In such passages, the combination of the serious and the humorous is found in the response of the reader as well as in the intentions of the speaker. M. de Charlus presumably means his listeners to admire him for his wit and daring, to laugh at his jokes and to despise his victim, but also to be thoroughly shocked at his daring and brutality. He basically seeks to arouse the audience's admiration and disgust for his contempt both of his victim and his audience. He succeeds completely.

At other times characters may use humour to boost their own self-confidence, if necessary at the expense of others. Again M. de Charlus is the outstanding example. When he feels that he has been insulted, he immediately resorts to his own brand of humour which combines grandiose verbosity with the most mundane or vulgar subject-matter. Phrases such as:

Croyez-vous que la salive envenimée de cinq cents petits bonshommes de vos amis, juchés les uns sur les autres, arriverait à baver seulement jusqu'à mes augustes orteils? (*CG* II 558)

occur only when M. de Charlus is furious. But on these occasions, he is so hysterical that one wonders whether in fact he is trying to be as rude as he can while preserving a jocular front, or whether it is not more probable that he has completely lost all self-control and is giving voice to genuine megalomaniac fantasies. There is a possibility that M. de Charlus is here being ridiculous completely without intending to be amusing.

General Considerations

Despite the welter of material that engulfs any analysis of Proust's chracters, it is possible to distinguish certain clear patterns. Implicit in this chapter has been the evolution of Proust as a portrayer of humorous characters. Early examples show far less subtlety and verisimilitude than their later counterparts. It would be platitudinous to stress the point that a writer's understanding of character is likely to develop as he grows older. But it is interesting to note that the capacity to make general observations was apparent in Proust's writing from the first, and that what seems to have evolved is his gift for reproducing the tiny details that bring a character to life. In *PJ* such humour as is found in character portrayal tends to take the form of whimsical generalizations ('Son snobisme n'était qu'imagination et était d'ailleurs toute son imagination'. *Un dîner en ville, JS* p. 99. 'Les femmes d'esprit ont si peur qu'on puisse les accuser d'aimer le chic qu'elles ne le nomment jamais'. *Fragments de comédie italienne, JS*, p. 43). In his early portraits of specific characters he will concentrate for his humorous effects on salient features in their personalities, rather than on incidental details. If such details are mentioned they take on considerable importance. For example, in the 'Salon de la Princesse Mathilde', 1903 (*CSB* p. 447), he talks of

M. Pichot, dont le monocle a pris une position inébranlable qui témoigne chez celui qui le porte, de la ferme volonté de prendre connaissance d'un article avant que commence la soirée.

It is not until *ALR* that he introduces such details as purely incidental, referring in passing to the moustache of Albertine's governess (*JF* I 829) or to Saint-Loup's fondness for tall *képis* (*CG* II 93), without attempting to make anything of these details. The reader is free to remember them and add them to his store of knowledge about the characters involved, or to smile at them when they occur and then forget them. The implication is that the mature Proust was far more at ease with his material in portraying characters.

Despite the apparent ease with which Proust inserts details about his characters, there is considerable internal evidence that he lavished great care on just such details. For instance, he would revise his writing to include links between small details occurring at different stages throughout the book. Again, he would alter small points to make them more perfect. Baronne Putbus was at first called Mme Picpus (see *Textes retrouvés*, p. 198). The original name is intrinsically less funny:

it is less odd, and it is the name of a real place.

The skill with which Proust combined an easy control in the handling of his characters and a scrupulous attention to detail makes these mature creations a much more satisfactory subject of study than his earlier portrayals. It is for this reason that in this chapter I have concentrated almost exclusively on *ALR*.

Another point that emerges is the universality of humour applied to character. All the characters in *ALR*, including the Narrator as we shall see, are mocked. No one is spared. But I have already pointed out that Proust rarely laughs with his characters; almost always he mocks them. In other words, humour is used to mock and hence belittle all Proust's characters: humour reveals Proust at his most disparaging. There is clearly a close link between humour in character portrayal and satire, which combines mockery with criticism. The examples given in this chapter have shown Proust to be a merciless critic of his fellow-men, picking out and exposing their most secret, subtle faults.

V

AUTHOR AND NARRATOR

When the young Narrator of *ALR* is at last privileged to meet the great writer Bergotte, the *doux chantre aux cheveux blancs* at whose shrine he has long worshipped, he comes face to face, not with the grandiose, priest-like figure he was expecting, but with a little red-faced man with a nose like a snail (*JF* I 547). When he reads in an 'unpublished diary' of an evening spent by Edmond de Goncourt with the Verdurins, he discovers to his amazement that the selfish, grotesque old harridan Mme Verdurin had in her youth been the beloved of Fromentin, and had inspired him to write the romantic novel *Dominique*, with herself as its exquisite, saintly heroine (*TR* III 709). To Proust, in short, the imaginary world of fiction is often completely different from the real-life world from which it is derived, and it may be misleading to try and compare the two.

Proust felt that this was equally true of his own novel, and, in particular, was anxious to stress the difference between himself and the Narrator of *ALR*. ' "Je" (et qui n'est pas moi)': in these words he describes his Narrator.[1] He is warning the reader not to equate his Narrator with himself, not to draw conclusions from the book about the author's personality.

In this chapter it will be shown how Proust's humour pinpoints the differences between the author and his creation. For humour is an excellent vehicle for revealing such differences. Not only Proust's attitude to humour itself, but his whole outlook as a writer and as a man, are illuminated by studying his humour in conjunction with his personality. A man's sense of humour is one of the most fundamental, most important elements in his make-up. To be told that one has no sense of humour is far more shattering than to be told that one is immoral or corrupt. It is moreover impossible to divorce a writer's humour from the rest of his personality.

The relationship between the author and Narrator in connection with humour will be looked at from two points of view. First comes

---

[1] *Textes retrouvés*, interview with Élie-Joseph Bois, p. 219.

the dichotomy between the mature Narrator and the protagonist in his earlier days. Often the Narrator will mock at Marcel's behaviour and reactions, or, conversely, will sympathize with them. This technique unmistakably affects our attitude to Proust, his Narrator, and his protagonist. Secondly, and perhaps most interesting, there is sometimes a telling difference between the sense of humour of the author and that of his protagonist, which suggests a fundamental difference in personality between the two.

Narrator and Protagonist

Before the Narrator begins to write his novel, his active life must be over, for the whole point of *ALR* is that it is about lost, not present time, in accordance with his theory that experiences are more, not less real when we remember them than when we live through them. It is not until the end of *ALR*, paradoxically, that the Narrator begins to write the very novel we have just been reading.

One must bear this point in mind when considering the relationship between the Narrator and his active protagonist in the text. The Narrator has in fact distanced himself from his protagonist. When he looks back on time past, he sees his earlier self as forming part of the picture, to be considered with as much detachment and scientific curiosity as the other characters present at the time. To use his own phrase, he is to be the object of scientific scrutiny.

As a result, one would expect the Narrator to see his own shortcomings with as candid an eye as he does those of Bloch or Legrandin, and to mock at his own ridiculous side as impartially as he does at the absurdities of Mme Verdurin or Mme Bontemps. But this is not in fact what he does. The Narrator is on the whole treated far more gently than almost any of the other characters except his own family. One could suggest several reasons for Proust's leniency towards his protagonist. Apart from the Narrator's natural reluctance to see his own failings, one must remember that he is frequently presented in a tragic, moving light. It might be that too much levity in his portrayal would detract from the effect of the serious passages. Against this it must be pointed out that M. de Charlus is often ridiculous without being in the least prevented from appearing tragic, touching, and pathetic at certain moments in *ALR*.

Another possible reason for neglecting the Narrator's ridiculous side is that he is presented very often as a rather negative character, as though he were simply the instrument through whose lens a scene was projected. If the protagonist's own personality were to interfere with the action of the novel the reader might feel that he was getting a one-sided view of things, and would certainly tend to feel less vividly present during the scenes described. It is certainly true that the parts of *ALR* that are written in the first person strike one as more vivid than the descriptions seen very strongly through Swann's eyes. It is also true that the Narrator is a far more acceptable character than his earlier prototype, Jean Santeuil, who, with his tantrums and his violence, is too obtrusive. Proust is well aware of the extent to which he has made the reader accept the world he presents through his Narrator's eyes as the inevitable, true world. The Goncourt pastiche at the end of *ALR* (*TR* III 709–17) can be regarded as playing on this fact in a piece of self-mockery and of mockery at the expense of the reader. Proust knows that his portrayal of the Verdurin salon, seen through the Narrator's eyes, is so real to the reader by this stage that one cannot imagine any other way of looking at it. By pretending to view the same salon through Goncourt's eyes, he then shows us that a different person could have described it in quite a different light: the implication is that his Narrator has been very narrow-minded and that the reader has docilely allowed himself to be taken in. It is only at this stage that the Narrator tells us:

Certes, je ne m'étais jamais dissimulé que je ne savais pas écouter ni [. . .] regarder. (p. 717)

But unlike the Narrator, the reader has assumed that he was witnessing things through the eyes of an infallible observer; and this tardy confession makes one realize that one has been to a certain extent deceived.

But Proust's Narrator is not simply an instrument for recording or distorting reality. He is also a character in his own right, with distinct personality traits, though these have to be sought for because they tend to be subordinated to the wilfully negative impression produced by this character. In particular, the Narrator has faults or failings which often make him look ridiculous.

The most striking examples occur at the beginning of *ALR*, when the mature Narrator mocks at the naïvety of his youthful self. Here Proust views the situation from two standpoints. The Narrator knows the implications of the situation (and so, incidentally, does the reader). But the child is completely ignorant. This technique often enables

Proust to question something that one normally takes for granted, and to show it up as ridiculous. It is exactly the same technique as Voltaire uses, for instance in his *L'Ingénu*, where a man endowed with common sense but no experience is faced with a variety of sophisticated situations which seem pointless to him. A good example in Proust is the way in which the youthful Narrator fails to realize that a performance of a play has begun:

juste comme je dressais l'oreille avant que commençât la pièce, deux hommes entrèrent sur la scène, bien en colère, puisqu'ils parlaient assez fort pour que dans cette salle où il y avait plus de mille personnes on distinguât toutes leurs paroles [. . .] mais dans le même instant, étonné de voir que le public les entendait sans protester [. . .] je compris que ces insolents étaient les acteurs et que la petite pièce, dite lever de rideau, venait de commencer. (*JF* I 447)

This demonstration of naïvety does not discredit the Narrator in the reader's eyes, but rather makes one take a fresh look at the nature of a stage performance. It does seem rather strange that a thousand people should suddenly sit quiet and listen to two shouting men.

Elsewhere, the Narrator's naïvety is more of a gratuitous piece of humour than a social comment. When he talks of 'des cocottes que je ne distinguais pas nettement des actrices' (*CS* I 75), one simply smiles at his ignorance and excuses it because of his youth.

On other occasions, however, his innocent approach leads him to forget his commonsense, and become rather ridiculous. The quality that Proust seems to criticize most in the young Narrator is his whole-hearted reverence for anything that is connected with the objects of his interest. Proust has already studied this characteristic in the young Jean Santeuil, who goes round with albums full of pictures of his latest craze, the moon, and shows them proudly to all and sundry (*JS* 307). The child Narrator of *ALR* is even more ridiculous when he adores Gilberte. He tries to look like the bald, middle-aged Swann, and longs to embrace the Swanns' old *maître d'hôtel* as a substitute for Gilberte. He adopts the Swanns' pronunciation and vocabulary (he talks of *Christmas*, for instance). He even tries to make Françoise more like Gilberte's governess, with a blue feather in her hat (*NPN* I 395). Later it becomes plain to us how much he had lost his commonsense, since we learn that one of the factors that made him seem acceptable to the Swanns was the good impression made by Françoise.

Worse still, the Narrator's obsessive interests lead him to be dishonest, both with others and with himself. At first this is regarded as

ridiculous rather than serious by Proust. For instance, the Narrator is
so impressed by the beauty of everything surrounding the Swanns that
he pretends, even to himself, that their perfectly ordinary staircase is
an antique specially installed by Swann:

il ne me parut pas certain qu'en avertissant mes parents de la valeur
artistique et de la provenance lointaine de cet escalier, je commisse
un mensonge. Cela ne me parut pas certain; mas cela dut me paraître
probable, car je me sentis devenir très rouge quand mon père m'interrompit en disant: 'Je connais ces maisons-là; j'en ai vu une, elles sont
toutes pareilles [. . .]' (*JF* I 505)

Throughout *ALR*, the Narrator gives instances of his basic dishonesty;
and this is perhaps the greatest fault he suffers from in the book. He
confesses that

le mensonge et la fourberie étaient chez moi [. . .] commandés d'une
façon si immédiate et contingente [. . .] que mon esprit, fixé sur un bel
idéal, laissait mon caractère accomplir dans l'ombre ces besognes
urgentes et chétives et ne se détournait pas pour les apercevoir. (*CG*
II 66)

Instances of this dishonesty occur at serious moments in *ALR* and strike
a note of perhaps not involuntary absurdity. For instance, when the
Narrator is trying to get Albertine back, he sends Saint-Loup to see her
aunt, and to bribe her to make Albertine return. He then writes to
Albertine flatly denying his action in exaggeratedly violent terms:

'P.-S.—Je ne réponds pas à ce que vous me dites de prétendues proposi-
tions que Saint-Loup (que je ne crois d'ailleurs nullement en Touraine)
aurait faites à votre tante. C'est du Sherlock Holmes. Quelle idée vous
faites-vous de moi? ' (*F* III 456)

By protesting violently against something that the reader knows is true,
and by implying that it is ridiculously far-fetched, the Narrator risks
appearing absurd in the eyes of the reader. If he had been content
to tell us that he had lied to Albertine without going into the details,
we could have accepted his statement without demur.

In less painful contexts, Proust is more explicit about the Narrator's
absurdity when being dishonest. He frequently lies for social reasons,
to be polite, and accuses himself later of stupidity. When M. de Charlus
reproaches both himself and the Narrator for their dilettantism,

Par surprise du reproche, manque d'esprit de repartie, déférence envers
mon interlocuteur, et attendrissement pour son amicale bonté, je
répondis comme si, ainsi qu'il m'y invitait, j'avais aussi à me frapper la
poitrine, ce que était parfaitement stupide, car je n'avais pas l'ombre
de dilettantisme à me reprocher. (*TR* III 808)

The Narrator's politeness elsewhere leads him to deprecate his qualities or advantages. For instance, in order to be polite to Brichot, he pretends he never travels by carriage, which leads him into complications when his coachman comes up and asks for instructions:

'Ah! vous étiez en voiture, me dit [Brichot] d'un air grave.—Mon Dieu, par le plus grand des hasards; cela ne m'arrive jamais. Je suis toujours en omnibus ou à pied. (*P* III 201)

Elsewhere, he goes to even more absurd lengths, for instance when he tells the lift-boy at Balbec that he would like his job, simply in order to be polite (*JF* I 665).

In general, then, the Narrator appears as a modest person, so modest that he can become ridiculous. This is not invariably the case. Very occasionally, the Narrator seems ludicrously snobbish. For instance, he tries to impress a country girl by telling her that he is travelling in a carriage owned by a marquise and drawn by two horses (*JF* I 716). But here he has good reason for this ostentation, as he has to impress the girl quickly, at all costs; and this example must be regarded as exceptional.

Not only the Narrator's failings but also his qualities can give Proust scope for humour. When the Narrator has good reason to feel pleased with himself, Proust views his pride with affectionate amusement. When he has produced his first piece of serious writing,

comme si j'avais été [. . .] une poule et si je venais de pondre un œuf, je me mis à chanter à tue-tête. (*CS* I 182)

There is an indulgent note in Proust's mockery of his protagonist here.

The only other fault of the Narrator that is held up to ridicule is his temper. Particularly in his relations with Françoise, he often loses his dignity through anger. He descends to play-acting in order to upset his servant, and to telling stupid lies:

Alors (d'un ton doux et ralenti pour que ma réponse mensongère eût l'air d'être l'expression non de ma colère mais de la vérité [. . .]), j'adressai à Françoise ces paroles cruelles: Vous êtes excellente, lui dis-je mielleusement, vous êtes gentille, vous avez mille qualités, mais vous en êtes au même point que le jour où vous êtes arrivée à Paris, aussi bien pour vous connaître en choses de toilette que pour bien prononcer les mots et ne pas faire de cuirs.' Et ce reproche était particulièrement stupide [. . .] (*SG* II 736)

Here the contrast between the evil intentions of the Narrator and his honeyed tones (conveyed by the exaggeratedly sugary word *mielleusement*) is as ridiculous as his motives are despicable.

Elsewhere, the humour in the portrayal of the Narrator is less a product of his own personality than the result of a confrontation with another person. This sort of humour is the one most frequently used in the case of the Narrator. Occasionally he is himself slightly at fault, for instance when he tries unsuccessfully to deceive Françoise, and is furious because she refuses to be taken in:

je n'ai jamais dans ma vie éprouvé une humiliation sans avoir trouvé d'avance sur le visage de Françoise des condoléances toutes prêtes; et lorsque dans ma colère d'être plaint par elle, je tentais de prétendre avoir au contraire remporté un succès, mes mensonges venaient inutilement se briser à son incrédulité respectueuse mais visible [. . .] (*CG* II 65)

But more often, he is shown to be the helpless victim of others. One laughs at him because the fates conspire against him to reduce him to a state of helpless rage or frustration, just as one laughs at the impotent anger of Shakespeare's Mr. Page, whose every attempt to discover his wife's infidelity (which he has good reasons for suspecting) is foiled. In order to increase the humour of such situations, Proust piles on the effects. For instance, Proust encloses the Narrator and the lift-boy who has whooping-cough in the confined space of the lift:

Le lift me dit ces mots d'une voix absolument cassée et en me toussant et crachant à la figure. 'Quel rhume que je tiens!' ajouta-t-il, comme si je n'étais pas capable de m'en apercevoir tout seul. 'Le docteur dit que c'est la coqueluche', et il recommença à tousser et à cracher sur moi. 'Ne vous fatiguez pas à parler', lui dis-je d'un air de bonté, lequel était feint. Je craignais de prendre la coqueluche qui, avec ma disposition aux étouffements, m'eût été fort pénible. 'Non, ça ne fait rien, dit-il (pour vous, peut-être, pensai-je, mais pas pour moi) [. . .] Nous étions presque arrivés à mon étage quand le lift me fit redescendre jusqu'en bas parce qu'il trouvait que le bouton fonctionnait mal, et en un clin d'œil il l'arrangea. Je lui dis que je préférais monter à pied, ce qui voulait dire et cacher que je préférais ne pas prendre la coqueluche. Mais d'un accès de toux cordial et contagieux, le lift me rejeta dans l'ascenseur. (*SG* II 1025–6)

Here the effect is considerably stressed, almost to farcical lengths. One shares the Narrator's impatience, and can appreciate his feelings of frustration when, just as his ordeal is ending, the lift-boy makes it begin all over again. The Narrator's attempts to save himself from catching whooping-cough are reiterated throughout, and his inner thoughts are thrust on the reader's attention much more crudely than is usual with

Proust, so that the Narrator's comic dilemma cannot but strike the reader forcibly. There are many of these episodes of frustration.

Elsewhere, the Narrator is made to experience such disappointment that he temporarily appears ridiculous. One cannot help but laugh when, having chased a beautiful girl through the dark streets, he finds himself face to face with Mme Verdurin instead (*JF* I 713–14). Here our amusement is at least partly caused by his disappointment. Elsewhere, this disappointment may be combined with the obsessions that we have already seen leading him to lose his sense of proportion. For instance, at one stage the Narrator is suddenly infatuated with a milkmaid who he thinks looked at him insistently as she brought milk to the hotel at Balbec.

Or le lendemain, jour où je m'étais reposé la matinée, quand Françoise vint ouvrir les rideaux vers midi, elle me remit une lettre qui avait été déposée pour moi à l'hôtel. Je ne connaissais personne à Balbec. Je ne doutai pas que la lettre ne fût de la laitière. Hélas, elle n'était que de Bergotte [. . .] (*JF* I 714)

Here the Narrator seems absurd for two reasons: first, his obsession has so blinded him that he is no longer aware of how unlikely it is that a milkmaid to whom he has never spoken should write him a letter. Secondly, his taste is so far in abeyance that he would prefer an illiterate scrawl from the milkmaid to a charming note from a famous writer.

Another quality in the Narrator that is brought out by the situation is his changeable personality. Indecisiveness is frequently used in humorous writing. Alceste in Molière's *Misanthrope* shares this quality with the Narrator of *ALR*. Usually the humour seems to depend on a combination of this indecisiveness and of a series of circumstances designed to emphasize the fundamental insincerity involved. For example, at one stage the Narrator changes his mind completely about an important step, and within a few sentences, owing to intervening circumstances, has changed it back again. When he has just written to Albertine asking her to return,

Le résultat de cette lettre me paraissant certain, je regrettai de l'avoir envoyée. Car, en me représentant le retour en somme si aisé d'Albertine, brusquement toutes les raisons qui rendaient notre mariage une chose mauvaise pour moi, revinrent avec toute leur force. J'espérais qu'elle refuserait de revenir. J'étais en train de calculer que ma liberté, tout l'avenir de ma vie étaient suspendus à son refus: que j'avais fait une folie d'écrire; que j'aurais dû reprendre ma lettre hélas partie, quand Françoise [. . .] me la rapporta. Elle ne savait pas avec combien de timbres elle devait l'affranchir. Mais aussitôt je changeai d'avis; je souhaitais qu'Albertine ne revînt pas, mais je voulais que cette décision vînt d'elle pour mettre fin à mon anxiété, et je voulus rendre la lettre à Françoise. (*F* III 458)

In many ways the indecision of the Narrator here is tragic, not amusing; we know that he really longs for Albertine's return, and that his surface indecision is probably a function of his over-anxious state. Nevertheless, the actual fact of changing one's mind so radically in such a short space of time, and the feebleness of the excuse he thinks up to justify his change of attitude to himself, provoke a smile even in this most serious of moments.

In a less serious context, the humour of such situations is brought out much more plainly. For instance, there is the occasion on which the Narrator, assuming he is going to be introduced to Albertine and her friends, immediately loses interest in them; but when the introduction is not made, he is suddenly obliged to be interested again. This example has already been mentioned in connection with the bathetic effect it produces.

There are some obvious conclusions to be drawn from the examples quoted above. Although there are comparatively few instances of humour at the expense of the Narrator of *ALR*, such as there are fall into distinct places in the novel. Clearly, all the examples of childish naïvety occur at the beginning, where the Narrator is a child still. But it may be of more significance to note that most of the purely light-hearted examples occur fairly early on in the novel, before Albertine has come to live with the Narrator. After this has happened, the same sort of characteristics seem much more painful. Just as one cannot read about M. de Charlus without remembering his vice after the beginning of *SG*, so we cannot divorce the Narrator from his tragic love affair and laugh at him as we did before.

Finally, the complex subject of Proust's intentions must be touched on, though nothing that is said in this connection can be considered as anything but speculation. I have already said that several of the instances quoted as humorous appear perfectly serious and indeed moving if considered in a different light. It is not possible to say what Proust wanted one to feel; but it is feasible that he required a double response from us. Like Balzac in his *Lys dans la vallée*, he seems to evoke in the reader a complete identification with his protagonist and his romantic plight, while at the same time being able to stand back and be aware of the potential absurdities of the situation. But whereas Balzac cost different lights on his basic situation by viewing it through such different eyes as those of the romantic Félix de Vandenesse and the cynical Natalie de Manerville, Proust's technique is more complex. His protagonist is himself aware of the ridiculous element behind some of the most serious moments in the novel, while at the same time participating wholeheartedly on the emotional plane.

At the same time, there are many potentially humorous characteristics in the Narrator which are left completely untouched. The Narrator is over-eager to fall in love. But whereas Proust makes us laugh at the complex results of this tendency, he does not make a point of how basically ridiculous this characteristic is. The Narrator of *ALR* would be somewhat like the traditional comedy womanizer, if only he had more success with the women he pursues. When he does have some success with the object of his affections, he becomes exaggeratedly suspicious. The basic plot of *P* is not unlike that of Molière's *L'École des maris* in which the jealous lover imprisons his beloved, who nevertheless manages to elude his vigilance. In fact, Proust's theme is one that is almost more common in comedy than in tragedy. This jealous intrigue leads the Narrator into situations where he has to pretend he is perfectly at ease, to conceal his violent emotions of love and jealousy (see *P* III 114). This is exactly the same as Molière's George Dandin or Arnolphe, both of whom are obliged to listen with pretended equanimity while the machinations of their ladies are developed to them. With such characters, too, the Narrator shares his abnormal fussiness (he cannot bear the slightest noise when he is asleep, *P* III 11, and is intensely irritated if Françoise comes in at the wrong moment, *P* III 101). It is a common characteristic of most of Molière's comic protagonists that they should be fussy about one thing or another. Alceste cannot bear to say anything complimentary or dishonest. Sganarelle in *L'École des maris* cannot abide fashionable dress. Argan in *Le Malade imaginaire* cannot exist without medicines every few minutes, and so on. Yet though their situations are similar, the Narrator has little in common with Molière's heroes.

On the whole, then, the personality of the Narrator seems to be biased in a different way from most of the others in *ALR*. Hitherto, it has been noticeable that even the mainly serious characters are yet lent humorous qualities. Here we have a character whose humorous potential has partly been suppressed in favour of his more serious qualities.

But this does not amount to suggesting that the Narrator of *ALR* is unsuitable as a tragic hero. Quite the contrary. For the ideal tragic hero suffers through faults within himself as much or more than through the blows dealt him by Fate. Othello is even more insanely jealous than the Narrator; King Lear is as fussy, ready to take offence at a word; Mithridate is far more dishonest. Both the comic protagonist and the tragic hero must have flawed personalities. The difference between them is sometimes simply one of treatment, not of situation or personality. In comedy, the faults are mocked; in tragedy their consequences are felt. In Proust's Narrator we have at once a comic and a tragic figure.

Author and Narrator

Close scrutiny of the Narrator as a comic figure reveals a further interesting point. Occasionally there seems to be a definite divergence between Proust's sense of humour and that of his protagonist. I have already discussed the obvious cases in which Proust is mocking at his own creation. Elsewhere, he makes him respond differently from himself to a joke.

All the examples of this are similar in form. A rather unpleasant joke is made or trick played. The protagonist reacts with horror to the cruelty. But Proust tells of the incident with such gusto that one cannot but feel that an element of enjoyment is involved. For instance:

Un numéro du programme me fut extrêmement pénible. Une jeune femme que détestaient Rachel et plusieurs de ses amies devait y faire dans des chansons anciennes un début sur lequel elle avait fondé toutes ses espérances d'avenir et celles des siens. Cette jeune femme avait une croupe trop proéminente, presque ridicule, et une voix jolie mais trop menue, encore affaiblie par l'émotion et qui contrastait avec cette puissante musculature. (*CG* II 173)

Proust goes on to describe in great detail how Rachel and her friends mock her physique until she is obliged to leave the stage. Proust has himself clearly observed the ridiculousness of the contrast between her figure and her voice (the phrase *puissante musculature* is far too strong to be normally applied to a woman, and he later contrasts it with *note flûtée*, which further points the incongruity of such a voice emerging from such a shape). He does not hesitate to go into the details of the fiasco, where one feels that the Narrator, who afterwards says 'Je m'efforçai de ne pas [. . .] penser à cet incident [. . .] je préférai ne pas parler de cet incident puisque je n'avais eu ni le courage ni la puissance de l'empêcher' (pp. 173–4) would at least have turned away if he felt unable to stop the scandal, and would have refrained from describing with such vividness an incident that he found intolerable.

A similar case is the public wetting of Mme d'Arpajon by a fountain at a ball. Again, the tender-hearted Narrator begins by expressing disapproval:

Un de ces petits accidents [. . .] fut assez désagréable. (*SG* II 657)

But he goes on to describe the incident with such cruel wit that it is plain that he has not the slightest sympathy for the victim or concern for how 'disagreeable' it must indeed have been for her:

un fort coup de chaude brise tordit le jet d'eau et inonda si complètement la belle dame que, l'eau dégoulinant de son décolletage dans l'intérieur de sa robe, elle fut aussi trempée qui si on l'avait plongée dans un bain. Alors [. . .] un grognement scandé retentit [. . .] c'était le grand-duc Wladimir qui riait de tout son cœur en voyant l'immersion de Mme d'Arpajon, une des choses les plus gaies, aimait-il à dire ensuite, à laquelle il eût assisté de toute sa vie. Comme quelques personnes charitables faisaient remarquer au Moscovite qu'un mot de condoléances de lui serait peut-être mérité et ferait plaisir à cette femme qui, malgré sa quarantaine bien sonnée, et tout en s'épongeant avec son écharpe, sans demander le secours de personne, se dégageait malgré l'eau qui mouillait malicieusement la margelle de la vasque, le Grand-Duc, qui avait bon cœur, crut devoir s'exécuter et, les derniers roulements militaires du rire à peine apaisés, on entendit un nouveau grondement plus violent encore que l'autre. 'Bravo, la vieille!' s'écriait-il en battant des mains comme au théâtre. Mme d'Arpajon ne fut pas sensible à ce qu'on vantât sa dextérité aux dépens de sa jeunesse. (pp. 657–8)

It seemed necessary to quote at length there to show to what extent Proust heaps the indignities on poor Mme d'Arpajon's head. He emphasizes the contrast between her previous elegance and her ridiculous appearance when wet by referring to her ironically as *la belle dame*. He impertinently examines the extent of the damage. He will not allow the 'malicious' water to leave her alone, even when she has dried the worst of it off. Worst of all, he gives her a large audience, and he causes her disgrace to be trumpeted abroad by the laugh of the Grand Duke. He emphasizes this element by the references to the imaginary army that hears the laugh, and the imaginary theatre audience that hears the hand-clapping of the Grand-Duke Wladimir. At the height of her disgrace, Proust reveals the age of the victim, in undignified terms. One would say of someone who was trying to appear younger than she was that her forty years were 'bien sonnés', and it would be very impolite to use such a phrase in her presence. A final touch is added by the insult of the Grand-Duke. Proust describes Mme Arpajon's reactions to his *bravo* in deliberately high-falutin terms which provide a ludicrous contrast to the crudeness of Grand-Duke Wladimir's remark, and also to what one must assume was the misery of Mme d'Arpajon's real inward response to it. On the whole then, the incident is disagreeable only in the initial comment; afterwards we settle down for a good and heartless laugh at Mme d'Arpajon's expense. And however disagreeable the Narrator may have found the whole thing, Proust certainly shares in the laughter, even assuming that as author he had not engineered the situation, but was simply reporting a real incident that he had seen.

There are several other incidents that could be adduced here to support the theory that Proust is a much crueller, more mocking person than he would like his Narrator to be.

In effect, by endowing his Narrator with sympathy for others and reluctance to laugh at them, while at the same time preserving his own brand of pitiless mockery at their expense, Proust is getting the best of two worlds. The Narrator's sympathetic attitude enables the reader to appreciate the feelings of his victims; the author's cruel wit brings home the absurdity of the situation with its full force.

VI

CULTURE AND SOCIAL THEMES

Proust's attitude towards culture is an uneasy one. At times he sees cultured people as ridiculous, simply by virtue of being cultured:

La culture est comme les bonnes manières des esprits. Il y a, entre les esprits cultivés, la franc-maçonnerie du monde élégant. On fait allusion vague à un écrivain et chacun sait de qui il s'agit, il n'y a pas besoin de mettre les gens au courant. On est du même monde. Aussi tout cela a sa faiblesse [. . .] (*CSB* 'Joubert' p. 651)

Culture leads to absurd in-group behaviour similar to that of the aristocracy. It is not surprising that the Verdurin circle, who fit this description perfectly, finally work their way up into the Guermantes circle. They have exactly the same patterns of behaviour as the aristocracy, and hence will easily adapt themselves to an elegant salon.

But it is not possible for Proust to reject and mock at culture wholeheartedly. He himself, as is well known, came from an excessively cultured family. His mother and he enlivened their conversation with quotations (*CSB* pp. 126–7, Le Fallois ed.) and his letters to his father tended to conclude gracefully on some choice line from a suitable poet. His mother's dying words were a quotation from *Horace* (*CSB*, Le Fallois ed., p. 125). It is not surprising that, despite his suspicion of culture, Proust's writing is full of allusions to the arts, particularly literature. Indeed, much of it could, if the term were not pejorative, be described as that of an intellectual snob. He frequently draws on his own culture, and appeals to a similar culture in his readers, making no concessions to their possible ignorance. He assumes that his reader is educated enough to share his contempt for Mme de Cambremer-Legrandin when she does not recognize a particular allusion to *Pelléas et Mélisande* (*SG* II 822). He mentions resemblances between portraits and his characters, often without bothering to describe the portrait for the benefit of those who may not know it (for instance, he makes Swann compare Mme Blatin to a portrait of Savonarola in a passage already quoted, *JF* I 535, and his coachman Rémi to Rizzo's Doge Loredano, merely alluding to 'la saillie des pommettes, l'obliquité des sourcils', *S* I 223). In an article on Robert de Montesquiou, Proust

comments on this tendency. Montesquiou takes his scholarliness
jusqu'à dérouter et essouffler parfois son lecteur moins agile, et qu'il
feint, avec une politesse où il entre peut-être un peu d'impertinence,
de croire aussi savant que lui, tandis que l'autre, qui n'en peut mais,
voudrait bien comme M. Jourdain lui dire: 'De grâce, Monsieur, faites
comme si je ne savais pas.' (*Textes retrouvés*, 'Un Professeur de beauté',
p. 155)
Whether or not Proust aimed to dazzle his readers with his culture, he
does adopt a similar standpoint.

Proust has two distinct approaches to the arts as a humorous subject. First, his impatience of intellectual snobbery and ignorance makes
him use the arts to mock at people who are guilty of these faults.
Secondly, his interest in the arts leads him to allude to them frequently,
producing humour either when the allusion is funny in itself, or, more
frequently, where the context casts a humorous light on it.

Attitudes to the Arts

As far as Proust is concerned, it is difficult to have the right attitude
to the arts. Gross ignorance is frequently mocked at, with varying
degrees of disapproval. We share in the author's sneer at the expense of
Mme d'Arpajon and the Prince d'Agrigente, who appear not to know
who wrote *Salammbô* (*CG* II 489–90), though much of the laughter is
at the expense of these two pretentious characters, who attempt to
conceal their ignorance, only to be cruelly exposed by Proust. Where
ignorance is frank and unpretentious, Proust feels kinder towards it.
For instance, he is indulgent in his mockery of the innkeeper at Rive-
belle who admires Elstir because he recognizes a wooden cross in one of
his paintings:
'C'est bien elle, répétait-il avec stupéfaction. Il y a les quatre morceaux!
Ah! aussi, il s'en donne une peine!' (*JF* I 826)
But where naïvety is excusable and indeed charming, philistinism is
despicable. Andrée's mother regards paintings as status symbols, and
thinks that someone is worthwhile if he possesses 'chevaux, voitures,
tableaux'. Albertine comments cynically:
Ce qui m'étonne, c'est qu'elle élève les tableaux à la dignité des chevaux
et des voitures.' (*P* III 17)
But nothing to Proust is as repulsive as a combination of artistic or
literary pretension and lack of real artistic feeling. He is merciless in
exposing this fault. He ridicules the stupidity of people too insensitive

to appreciate real genius. After attending a concert given by Saint-Saëns,

A la sortie, on voyait beaucoup de gens déçus et qui, ne connaissant pas la raison de leur déception, l'attribuaient à des causes diverses: il a joué trop vite, il a joué trop sec, il avait mal choisi son morceau. Or, voici la raison: c'est que c'était vraiment beau. (*CSB*, 'Camille Saint-Saëns, pianiste' p. 382)

If they had been content humbly to admit that they did not understand why they were disappointed, as the Narrator does when he sees La Bérma in *Phèdre* (*JF* I 457), they might have had more indulgence from Proust.

Conversely, he notes extravagant admiration, and points out that it is often insincere. He describes the students who, in his youth, adored Wagner, and 'applaudissaient indéfiniment à tout rompre', even though the piece in question was mediocre (*CSB*, 'A Propos de Baudelaire' p. 623).

In his fiction, Proust uses two principal techniques to expose this combination of ignorance and pretension. First, he draws our attention to the social gaffes caused by the failure of would-be culture. Frequently, people make ludicrous mistakes, the sort of mistakes one rarely comes across in real life. Proust seems to be exaggerating in order to emphasize this point. Mme de Guermantes exclaims 'C'est admirable' in the middle of a poem that is being recited: her lack of literary sensibility made her think it was finished (*TR* III 1001). Mme de Gallardon talks disapprovingly of Aristotle instead of Aristophanes (*CG* II 447). A whole gathering of intellectual snobs cry 'Sublime!' at a piece by Meyerbeer which has been announced as Debussy (*SG* II 954). There are many other examples.

The second technique shows even more malice on Proust's part. He uses his powers of 'radiography' (which he mentions in *TR* III 719) to uncover the ignorance and false pretension underlying seemingly perfectly acceptable appraisals of the arts. Odette cannot sit quietly listening to a recital of La Fontaine; Proust mercilessly scrutinizes and interprets her facial expression:

Mme de Forcheville [. . .] avait pris une mine attentive, tendue, presque carrément désagréable, soit pour montrer qu'elle était connaisseuse et ne venait pas en mondaine, soit par hostilité pour les gens moins versés dans la littérature qui eussent pu lui parler d'autre chose, soit par contention de toute sa personne afin de savoir si elle 'aimait' ou si elle n'aimait pas, ou peut-être parce que, tout en trouvant cela 'intéressant', elle n'"aimait" pas, du moins, la manière de dire certains vers. (*TR* III 1000)

Although Odette's expression is meant to be dictated by her feelings, and not put on in order to demonstrate her attitude to others, the lengthy discussion of her motives makes her look seem false and affected. Again, perfectly acceptable remarks are turned against the speaker by Proust's interpretations of them. For instance:

Un duc, pour montrer qu'il s'y connaissait, déclara: 'C'est très difficile à bien jouer.' (*P* III 258)

Or the damning comment on Mme de Guermantes's opinion of Elstir:

Elstir, ce peintre dont vous avez été regarder quelques tableaux tout à l'heure,—les seuls du reste que j'aime de lui, ajouta-t-elle. En réalité, elle détestait la peinture d'Elstir, mais trouvait d'une qualité unique tout ce qui était chez elle. (*CG* II 500)

In such instances, Proust relies entirely on his scathing asides to demolish the artistic pretensions of his characters. At other times, he has concrete evidence to support his malice. He makes a cruel generalization about M. de Cambremer's poor conversation:

Il [. . .] citait volontiers une fable de La Fontaine et une de Florian qui lui paraissaient [. . .] lui permettre, sous les formes d'une dédaigneuse flatterie, de montrer aux hommes de science qui n'étaient pas du Jockey, qu'on pouvait chasser et avoir lu des fables. La malheur est qu'il n'en connaissaient guère que deux. Aussi revenaient-elles souvent. (*SG* II 916)

Later he substantiates this generalization by means of specific examples (see *SG* II 925–6 and 963–4).

It is usually aristocrats that are stripped of their cultural pretensions in this way. The reason is the one that prompted Proust to compare them to animals. They are twice as arrogant as anyone else, so that destroying their pretensions is at the same time a salutary lesson and wittily bathetic.

Affectation in appreciating the arts can seem ridiculous even if there is genuine culture behind it. Apart from the general point that culture is in itself an affectation, Proust singles out particularly mannered ways of indicating one's response. In an article on Saint-Saëns's sober style of playing, he points out that the popular style involves accompanying one's playing with

ces ondulations de corps du pianiste, [. . .] ces hochements de tête, [. . .] ces frémissements de mèches qui mêlent à la pureté de la musique la sensualité de la danse [. . .] (*CSB*, 'Camille Saint-Saëns, pianiste' p. 383)

He cynically concludes that the audiences prefer this mannered style because it gives them something concrete to tell their friends afterwards.

The same sort of point is made by Proust in a fictional context. He mocks at Morel's 'mèche' (*P* III 287); at Ski, who half closes his eyes in artistic appraisal (*SG* II 887); at Bloch's and Brichot's affected language when they talk of literature. Even the Narrator's grandmother seems a little ridiculous when she desperately tries to cram in 'un degré d'art de plus' (*CS* I 40) to add to her grandson's artistic education. Again, the whole episode in which the Narrator offends the Verdurins by admiring all the wrong things at La Raspelière contains much more criticism of the Verdurins, who are so proud of the banal advantages of their beautiful house, than of the Narrator, whose powers of appreciation make him see beauty in a broken window-pane or the sound of his footsteps on the tiled floor (*SG* II 944).

Proust assumes that the reader is cultured enough to share his mockery at the expense of these attitudes. He also has to assume that the reader shares his tastes. Clearly, if the reader adored Tagliafico's *Pauvre Fou* he would fail to see the joke when Proust makes Odette request that the piece be played at her funeral (*S* I 236). This presents a real difficulty, for there are occasions when at least some of his readers will disagree with his aesthetic judgements. His disparaging references to Ingres and Scarlatti will be quoted later. As a rule, Proust avoids this difficulty. He may provide reasons other than a divergence in taste for laughing at his characters. Cultural pretension is ridiculous even if it takes the form of admiring a great creative artist. We have seen Odette's affectation when listening to La Fontaine, M. de Cambremer's when quoting him. Another technique is to tell the reader what his attitude should be, so that he is obliged to share the author's opinion. In particular, Proust uses his three great imaginary creators, Elstir, Bergotte and Vinteuil, in this way. We are told that their works are magnificent, so we laugh at a character who fails to appreciate them.

Most often, Proust relies on his own taste, and is not afraid to present his opinion. We shall see that in all the arts his preferences and dislikes shine out strongly through his humour.

Literature

Proust's writing abounds in quotations and in references to literature. The most serious, immediate subjects suggest literary parallels to him. When he hears that a friend has murdered his own mother, he immediately thinks of Virgil, Tolstoy, the Oedipus legend, Dostoyevsky, *King Lear*, Michelet, Cervantes and other literary allusions (*CSB, Mélanges,* 'Sentiments filiaux d'un parricide', 155–9). In humorous contexts, his bias can be equally literary. Either he will use an appropriate allusion to a humorous work, or an inappropriate reference to a serious one. These two principal techniques will be examined in turn.

When Proust quotes from or refers to humorous works of literature, it is most often to plays. Not surprisingly, Molière receives the most attention. He is, of course, frequently referred to in his capacity as great writer rather than as humorous writer; he is quoted to relieve the tension in an unbearably sad moment by the mother in *CSB*, (Le Fallois ed. p. 125) and by the Narrator's grandmother (*CG* II 312). But where the allusions are to Molière as a writer of comedy, the bias is rather an unexpected one. Proust tends to mention the more extravagant elements in Molière's plots, or, even more frequently, to allude to the physical action of his characters on stage.[1] For instance, M. de Charlus's insolent assessment of Mme de Surgis's sons, made in her presence, which he gets away with by pretending he does not know that they are related to her, is likened to *Les Fourberies de Scapin*, III 2. Here Scapin tricks his master into hiding in a sack and pretends to be someone else in order to beat him (*SG* II 696). Elsewhere the jealousy of homosexuals is compared to Harpagon's jealous guarding of his treasure in *L'Avare*:

L'inverti [. . .] est obligé, comme Harpagon, de veiller sur son trésor et se relève la nuit pour voir si on ne le lui prend pas. (*SG* II 921)

Stage action is reproduced when Mme de Villeparisis and the Narrator's grandmother run into each other at Balbec: they behave like characters

dans certaines scènes de Molière où deux acteurs monologuant depuis longtemps chacun de son côté à quelques pas l'un de l'autre, sont censés ne pas s'être vus encore, et tout à coup s'aperçoivent, [. . .] (*JF* I 694)

---

[1] There are, of course, quotations from Molière, but mostly made by the characters. For example, Saint-Loup deliberately quotes from *Les Femmes savantes*, (*SG* II 697), while the *mauvais prêtre* unwittingly reproduces almost word for word a line from *Tartuffe* (*TR* III 829).

Again, M. de Charlus and M. de Sidonia converse by each talking un-interruptedly:

Cela avait réalisé ce bruit confus, produit dans les comédies de Molière par plusieurs personnes qui disent ensemble des choses différentes. (*SG* II 639)

And when M. de Charlus is about to fight a duel:

M. de Charlus, ne se tenant pas de joie, se mit à faire des contre-de-quarte qui rappelaient Molière, nous firent rapprocher prudemment de nous nos bocks, et craindre que les premiers croisements de fer blessassent les adversaires, le médecin et les témoins. (*SG* II 1070)

These examples are particularly interesting. Proust has relegated Molière to a level of comedy that is far more artificial than his own. The effect of this artificiality is to abolish any participation on the part of the reader, who observes the antics of the characters as though they were a piece of witty choreography. It can also provide an implied comment on the situation. One has hitherto participated in the feelings of the pro-tagonists, sympathized with the grandmother's desire for privacy on her holiday. Now we are shown the impression an outsider might have. A final point to be noted is that the Molière references tend on the whole to be applied to the more elegant of Proust's characters. A con-trast is established between their pretensions and their artificiality. Moreover, many of them occur at roughly the same point in *ALR* (*CG* and *SG*). Proust's literary allusions do in general go together in groups, providing *leitmotive* which make the various parts of his novel hang together.

Humorous literature other than drama lends itself to a different technique. And Proust in all his literary allusions tends to use a parti-cular method: he will associate the writer concerned with a specific characteristic and concentrate chiefly on it, thereby giving the sum of his allusions a coherence of their own. We have seen that with Molière this involves concentrating on the artificial effects. He scarcely goes into other equally important aspects. Similarly, with La Fontaine he tends to quote the plots of the *Fables* as instances of showing-off on the part of the characters (see *CG* II 538, *P* III 235, *TR* III 710). Very rarely does he quote the language of La Fontaine, although it can often be very witty. Again, Voltaire is never quoted (except by Bloch, who is in fact quoting from Corneille though he thinks it is Voltaire, *JF* I 880), although Proust uses many tricks of style similar to Voltaire's. What does seem to happen is that Voltaire's name is distorted through affectation by various characters. Bloch calls him 'le sieur Arouet'

(*JF* I 880); Brichot 'M. de Voltaire' (*SG* II 877). Rabelais, another humorous writer that has been compared to Proust, seems to be associated in *ALR* with pedantry. Apart from Cottard's eagerness to master and reproduce the idiomatic phrase 'le quart d'heure de Rabelais' (*S* I 200, *SG* II 1051), the only people who mention him are the pompous, artificial speakers, M. de Norpois and Brichot. M. de Norpois refers to Panurge's sheep (*CG* II 246), while Brichot says:

pour parler comme Maître François Rabelais, vous voulez dire que je suis moult sorbonagre, sorbonicole et sorboniforme. (*SG* II 1051)

The same basic technique applies to the serious writers that Proust mentions. The humour usually consists in a combination of aptness and inaptness between the reference and the context. But the type of combination tends to vary according to the authors quoted. Racine is the serious author that Proust uses most often. Almost always where Racine is used in a humorous context, Proust actually quotes, in order to contrast the intense emotion and noble poetry of the classical writer with an appropriate but at the same time incongruous situation. For example, Proust quotes from the end of *Andromaque* (V, 5) to illustrate the rage of Mme de Villebon when Mme de Guermantes receives a member of the lesser nobility, while excluding her:

'Ce n'est vraiment pas la peine que ma cousine soit si difficile sur ses relations, c'est à se moquer du monde', concluait Mme de Villebon avec une autre expression de visage, celle-là souriante et narquoise dans le désespoir, sur laquelle un petit jeu de devinettes eût plutôt mis un [. . .] vers, que la comtesse ne connaissait naturellement pas [. . .]:
    Grâces aux dieux! Mon malheur passe mon espérance. (*CG* II 443)

To appreciate the humour here we must remember that the quotation is from Oreste's most tragic speech. He has just lost his honour and his mistress, and this line constitutes his response to the news of Hermione's death. The actual words are appropriate to Mme de Villebon's feelings; but they degrade those feelings by unspoken comparison with Oreste's far nobler, more tragic despair. Elsewhere, with more inappropriateness, Proust makes his mother adapt a quotation from *Esther*. He says to her

—Peut-être ferais-tu bien de laisser un petit mot à Robert dans la crainte [. . .] qu'il n'entre directement chez moi.
— Entrer directement chez toi!
    Peut-il donc ignorer quelle sévère loi
    Aux timides mortels cache ici notre roi,

Que la mort est le prix de tout audacieux
Qui sans être appelé se présente à ses yeux?
(*CSB*, Le Fallois ed. p. 127)

Here there is a deliberate fancifulness in the use of the quotation. Proust himself has been elevated to the rank of king, so as to inflate his desire not to be woken during the day into a matter of life and death.

The basic technique is further enhanced by a recurrent series of comparisons involving Racine. The chorus of young Israelite girls in *Esther* and *Athalie* is repeatedly compared to young men, and the comparison reinforced by quotations (*SG* II 665, 774, 843, 978). Quotations from Racine applied to the Narrator's desire to be left alone in his room occur not only in *CSB* but also in *ALR* (where Albertine uses the same quotation as the one cited here, *P* III 18, and different ones from *Esther*, *P* III 120 and *P* III 412, or exaggerates the Narrator's anger with a quotation also from *Esther*, *P* III 395). The desire of Assuérus to please Esther is several times applied to social situations. The *bâtonnier* at Balbec offers to present the Cambremers to his fellow-guests as though he were Assuérus offering half his kingdom to Esther (*JF* I 687); Mme de Guermantes, loading the Narrator with gifts 'tel Assuérus', invites him to dinner (*CG* II 378). By building up a cumulative impression, Proust emphasizes the specific character of his humorous references to Racine.

References to other writers are equally specific. Balzac, despite the fact that Proust saw his ridiculous side, does not tend to be the subject of humour in Proust's fiction, except for the title 'Le cousin Bête' applied to Swann by his cousins (*JF* I 518). Virgil represents the distant past, so that the humour tends to take the form of links between the ordinary present and the misty fabulous world of antiquity. Swann's frequentation of the most elegant salons

eût paru aussi extraordinaire à ma tante qu'aurait pu l'être pour une dame plus lettrée la pensée d'être personnellement liée avec Aristée dont elle aurait compris qu'il allait, après avoir causé avec elle, plonger au sein des royaumes de Thétis, dans un empire soustrait aux yeux des mortels, et où Virgile nous le montre reçu à bras ouverts. (*CS* I 17–18)

George Sand is essentially the author of the *romans berrichons* that the Narrator read in his childhood; he smiles at her naïvety and at his own response to her books (*CS* I 41–2; *TR* III 883–6). Stendhal is repeatedly spoken of as the socialite whom none of his contemporaries except Balzac admires. This element is almost invariably present if he is spoken of on a humorous note. Mme de Villeparisis says:

Beyle (c'était son nom) était d'une vulgarité affreuse, mais spirituel dans un dîner. (*JF* I 710)

The Narrator compares Mosca in *La Chartreuse de Parme* to M. de Norpois, emphasizing the *mondain* element in Stendhal (*CG* II 106, note).

It seems that Proust's humorous references to literature have the same effect as much of his humorous imagery: they provide a thread which runs through *ALR* and help to give coherence to the novel by linking the various parts together.

But Proust is too deeply imbued with literature to confine his use of other writers to this sort of example. There are other references to literature at all sorts of moments, that have their own individual humorous impact. Literature is brought in to the text of Proust's writing repeatedly. M. de Charlus talks of Mme Molé as

cette petite grenouille bourgeoise voulant s'enfler pour égaler ces deux grandes dames [. . .] (*P* III 234)

Saint-Loup misquotes Hamlet to refer to the Narrator's position in the *petit clan*, and so on.

Opinions on literature can be extremely amusing. Proust quotes Mallarmé's impertinent assessment:

'Un critique est une personne qui se mêle de ce qui ne la regarde pas' (*CSB* p. 501)

and cites Sainte-Beuve's literary opinions with malicious enjoyment and sarcasm. The list of faults that Proust finds with Sainte-Beuve is too long to be included here. Suffice it to say that after producing a vast number, he remarks:

Les autres critiques de Sainte-Beuve ne sont pas moins absurdes. (*CSB* p. 275)

In his fiction, too, Proust reproduces absurd pieces of literary criticism. The most far-fetched are Bloch's assessments of 'le nommé Racine', the 'sinistre brute' Musset and 'le père Leconte, agréable aux Dieux immortels' (*CS* I 90). But there are numerous other literary judgements, such as Mme de Guermantes's on Zola:

Mais Zola n'est pas un réaliste, Madame! c'est un poète! [. . .] il a le fumier épique! C'est l'Homère de la vidange! Il n'a pas assez de majuscules pour écrire le mot de Cambronne. (*CG* II 499)

or Brichot's judgement of 'cette vieille peste de Saint-Simon' (*P* III 303) or 'cette bonne rosse d'Ovide' (*SG* II 1052). Again, there is Cottard's low opinion of Socrates (*SG* II 1051).

In all these examples, the humour rests on the assumption that the cultured reader knows what he ought to think about those writers, and so will share the author's amused contempt for the less cultured or (in the case of Brichot) sensitive characters.

It is worth pointing out that Proust's imaginary writer, Bergotte, is treated in precisely the same way as real writers where humour is concerned. This is one of the things that bring him to life. The different characters have their opinions of him, often derogatory ones. M. de Norpois says

Jamais on ne trouve dans ses ouvrages sans muscles ce qu'on pourrait nommer la charpente [. . .] l'œuvre [. . .] de Bergotte est parfois assez séduisante, je n'en disconviens pas, mais au total tout cela est bien mièvre, bien mince, et bien peu viril. (*JF* I 473)

and Bloch *père* comments:

Ce Bergotte est devenu illisible. Ce que cet animal-là peut être embêtant. C'est à se désabonner. (*JF* I 771)

Proust tells amusing anecdotes about Bergotte, commenting that his way of speaking was characteristic of all members of his family, but that when Bergotte began to write in this style, he ceased to use it in speech (*JF* I 554). Proust also quotes anecdotes about real writers. He mentions many amusing episodes in the life of Sainte-Beuve, such as his excessive rage when attacked by a literary opponent (*CSB* p. 230), or his comment on the Académie française to his new secretary: 'Le jeudi je vais à l'Académie, mes collègues sont des gens insignifiants' (p. 230). Literary anedotes also appear in Proust's fiction. Mme de Villeparisis, in particular, talks at great length of the literary figures she knew in her youth (*JF* I 710).

Finally, a more tenuous point must be mentioned. Proust's humour occasionally seems reminiscent of the styles of other writers, although there is no mention of the prototype's name. This is a lesser type of pastiche, in which the reader may feel that there is some slight element of another writer, but which is not sustained or explicit enough to convince one. For instance, he lapses into language very reminiscent of Stendhal's when describing the past diplomatic triumphs of M. de Norpois, whom he compares to Mosca (see *F* III 634–7). He imitates Balzac in giving some of his characters speech defects and foreign accents. He often lapses into Latinate language, for instance in this passage, highly reminiscent of Virgil, where the humour rests in the contrast between the dignity of the language and the triviality of the newspaper that forms the subject:

Il dit, et la divinité sembla avoir entendu sa prière. La flamme nourrie un instant par le malheureux journal qui lui était jeté comme une offrande agréable et une victime expiatoire brilla d'un éclat plus fort et tordit un instant comme des serpents les signes éclatants de la céleste colère, puis épuisée retomba [. . .] (*JS* p. 404)

But this degree of similarity is enough to make the passage into a pastiche.[1]

Music

There are relatively few obvious links between music and people, and this limits Proust's scope for creating humour out of music; for as we have seen, it is chiefly by juxtaposing the arts to characters that Proust creates humorous effects connected with this subject. With music, it is not surprising that Proust relies mostly on mocking tastes, whereas the majority of his humorous references to literature concern parallels with his characters. We shall see later that the same restriction applies to painting, which with one important exception is funny in respect of what people think of it.

There is, however, one respect in which music links up with character. Both music and people make sounds. Proust puts this fact to humorous use. I have described elsewhere his comparisons between the music of Bach and the human voice.[2] Other composers are treated in the same way, often with subtle effect. M. de Norpois spaces his utterances with as great an art as Mozart's in ordering his instruments; when he makes a remark,

l'immobilité qui l'avait précédée la faisait se détacher avec la netteté cristalline, l'imprévu quasi malicieux de ces phrases par lesquelles le piano, silencieux jusque-là, réplique, au moment voulu, au violoncelle qu'on vient d'entendre, dans un concerto de Mozart. (*JF* I 456)

But such examples are exceptions. Usually, humorous references to music are used by Proust to reveal his likes and dislikes in music, and his awareness of which composers are in fashion. Occasionally, he expresses his personal preferences without any intermediary. Mme de Cambremer-Legrandin hysterically shrieks her admiration of a piece by the newly fashionable Scarlatti; and Proust wryly comments:

---

[1] Unfortunately there is not the space here for a sustained discussion of the humour in Proust's pastiches, which I hope to discuss elsewhere.

[2] 'Some Recurrent Comparisons in *ALR*', *Modern Language Review*, Oct. 1967, vol. 64 no. 4. pp. 629–30.

c'était un de ces morceaux maudits qui vous ont si souvent empêché de dormir et qu'une élève sans pitié recommence indéfiniment à l'étage contigu au vôtre. (*SG* II 955)

Proust's irritation implies an element of dislike of the music.

Elsewhere his attack is aimed more directly at attitudes to music than at the music itself. He describes the absurdity of people who are too scrupulous about allowing themselves to enjoy good music:

Je n'avais, à admirer le maître de Bayreuth, aucun des scrupules de ceux à qui, comme à Nietzsche, le devoir dicte de fuir, dans l'art comme dans la vie, la beauté qui les tente, qui s'arrachent à Tristan comme ils renient *Parsifal* et, par ascétisme spirituel, de mortification en mortification parviennent, en suivant le plus sanglant des chemins de croix, à s'élever jusqu'à la pure connaissance et à l'adoration parfaite du *Postillon de Longjumeau*. (*P* III 159)

He points out the stupidity of contemporary music criticism ('on recommandait de ne pas fatiguer l'attention de l'auditeur, comme si nous ne disposions pas d'attentions différentes dont il dépend précisément de l'artiste d'éveiller les plus hautes'). He exposes the ephemeral nature of musical tastes:

D'ailleurs le jour devait venir où, pour un temps, Debussy serait déclaré aussi fragile que Massenet et les tressautements de Mélisande abaissés au rang de Manon. (*SG* II 815)

In these examples, though the tone is ironic, one can detect the conviction behind Proust's comments. When he is content to show up the musical tastes of his characters, his humour has less seriousness behind it. One can laugh wholeheartedly at M. de Chevregny:

Nous sommes allés une fois à l'Opéra-Comique, mais le spectacle n'est pas fameux. Cela s'appelle *Pelléas et Mélisande*. C'est insignifiant. (*SG* II 1086)

or at M. de Guermantes, whose taste in music lacks discrimination:

Fra Diavolo, et la *Flûte enchantée*, et le *Chalet*, et *les Noces de Figaro*, et *Les Diamants de la Couronne*, voilà de la musique! (*CG* II 491).

Conversely, he laughs at musical snobs who invariably express admiration for *Pelléas et Mélisande*. The worst offender is Mme de Cambremer-Legrandin, whose pretension is unfortunately accompanied by ignorance (*SG* II 822). Mme Verdurin's response to music is as great a subject of mockery as her laugh (*S* I 189, *SG* II 906).

Although music is used less often to provide humour, the reason is certainly not that Proust was less interested in it than in the other arts. It lies in the difficulty of expressing music in words, a difficulty of which, despite his own brilliant reconstruction of Vinteuil's music, Proust was well aware (see *JF* I 533 for example).

The Visual Arts

Proust's most striking humorous use of the visual arts is to point out the resemblance between the artists' models and his own characters. This technique enables the cultured reader to appreciate the appearance of a character without Proust's having to indulge in long descriptions. He simply tells us, with a minimum of explanation, that Odette is like Zephora, the daughter of Jethro, in Botticelli's fresco (*S* I 222), or Bloch like Bellini's *Portrait of Mahomet II* (*CS* I 97). At the same time, it can be extremely amusing. For the character who is the subject of such a comparison is automatically imbued with the characteristics of the original in the painting. It is highly inappropriate to compare a coachman to a portrait of a Doge, as Swann does (*S* I 223), for the coachman is a vulgar, uneducated fellow, the Doge a dignified ruler. But the visual appropriateness of such comparisons makes them acceptable as well as absurd.

Proust's taste seems to have been chiefly for Italian and Flemish painters. The Italians tend to be used in comparisons with his characters, as in these examples. The Flemish, represented chiefly by Vermeer, seem much more obscure and *recherché* and tend to be unknown to all except the cultural *élite*. Proust assumes that the reader is as knowledgeable as he when he makes him share in laughter at the expense of Odette and Albertine, who think that Vermeer is still alive. M. de Guermantes, too, is mocked when, despite his professed admiration for the museum at the Hague, he appears not to remember Vermeer's *View of Delft* ('si c'est à voir, je l'ai vu!' *CG* II 523–4).

With other artists, he uses a technique already discussed with regard to literature: he singles out a salient feature and repeatedly refers to it, drawing basically the same humorous inference each time. Rembrandt is essentially the creator of rich interiors, in which the use of light and dark transforms everything into magic. Proust draws several incongruous parallels. Swann's dining-room, the table laid for the children's tea, is like 'l'intérieur d'un Temple asiatique peint par Rembrandt', and later the chocolate cake ('gâteau architectural', 'pâtisserie ninivite') seems to have become the temple itself (*JF* I 506). The corridors of the hotel at Balbec, seen through the lift doors, are illuminated like

Rembrandts (*JF* I 800). A squalid junk shop changes by candlelight from a 'taudis où il n'y avait que du toc et des croûtes' to 'un inestimable Rembrandt' (*CG* II 97). In each case, there is an element of humour combined with a favourite aesthetic point of Proust's, that beauty is in the eye of the beholder, so that a perfectly ordinary object can appear as exotic as an old master if only one can strip it of its banal associations.

Elsewhere, Proust examines this aesthetic point seriously and in detail, though not without a fleeting touch of humour. In his essay on Chardin, he tells us

une poire est aussi vivante qu'une femme, [. . .] une poterie vulgaire est aussi belle qu'une pierre précieuse. (*CSB* p. 380)

The first reaction to something banal may be a half-humorous sneer of disgust; but this can be replaced by admiration. For example, a table after a meal seems ridiculously trivial:

Sur le buffet un peu de soleil, en touchant gaîment le verre d'eau que des lèvres désaltérées ont laissé presque plein, accentue cruellement, comme un rire ironique, la banalité traditionnelle de ce spectacle inésthétique. (*CSB* p. 372)

But Chardin, and later Proust himself in his beautiful after-dinner *Tableaux* (*JF* I 694, 869), have managed to transform this unromantic scene into an exquisite vision.

Proust insistently reminds us of the grandeur of art, only to contrast it with our banal, everyday world. The monumental sculptor Michelangelo is contrasted with the sculptor of beef jelly, Françoise. The classical perfection of Poussin's gods is compared to children playing in the park (see *JF* I 445, 458, *NPN* I 395). Proust can laugh at what he holds most dear in art.

He can also mock with gusto his artistic dislikes. He objects most strongly to the exaggeratedly detailed, sentimental nineteenth-century Romantics and their followers of the next generation. He mocks them by making M. de Guermantes express admiration for them while denigrating Elstir. As we know Elstir is meant to be admirable, we assume that Proust is condemning his rivals:

Du reste, il n'y a pas lieu de se mettre autant martel en tête pour creuser la peinture de M. Elstir que s'il s'agissait de *la Source* d'Ingres ou des *Enfants d'Édouard* de Paul Delaroche [. . .] je préfère mille fois [aux tableaux d'Elstir] la petite étude de M. Vilbert que nous avons vue à l'Exposition des aquarellistes. Ce n'est rien si vous voulez, cela tiendrait dans le creux de la main, mais il y a de l'esprit jusqu'au bout des ongles: ce missionnaire décharné, sale, devant ce prélat douillet qui fait jouer son petit chien, c'est tout un petit poème de finesse et même de profondeur.' (*CG* II 501)

To some extent, Proust is here relying on the reader's sharing the opinion of the contemporary cultural élite. Nowadays, we would not find M. de Guermantes quite so ridiculous, since it is fashionable to recognize the charm of the nineteenth-century Romantics, and since Ingres is certainly thought of as one of the great painters of the period. Indeed, Proust's scathing attitude to Ingres seems peculiar unless one remembers that contemporary art-lovers had to fight reactionaries whose admiration for the older painter led them to consider Manet shocking (see *CG* II 420, 522). In Proust, Philistines who fail to appreciate the Impressionists are objects of scorn. In particular, people fail to appreciate Elstir, and their reasons give scope for humour. The Cottards are bewildered by the paintings:

Quand [. . .] ils pouvaient reconnaître une forme, ils la trouvaient alourdie et vulgarisée [. . .] et sans vérité, comme si M. Biche n'eût pas su comment était construite une épaule et que les femmes n'ont pas les cheveux mauves. (*S* I 213)

Proust points out that this lack of verisimilitude is an essential attribute of the more recent schools of painting (*JF* I 861-2). However, it is scarcely surprising that laymen cannot take the work of even great artists seriously, since artists at times can appear utterly ridiculous. Proust repeatedly stresses the narrow margin separating the sublime from the ridiculous in painting. For instance, he mentions the self-portraits of great artists in their old age, in which the very insistence on the absurdities of their faces has a beauty of its own (see his description of Chardin's self-portrait *CSB* pp. 581-2, or of the face of Rembrandt, 'de qui tout le monde se moquait' *TR* III 906).

Proust is less indulgent in his attitude to the artists he has invented. He uses them to illustrate the tendency of the painter, sculptor, or visual aesthete to invent what nowadays we would call 'happenings', combining artistic manifestations of all the senses in an elaborate and artificial form. The most outrageous instance is the sunset banquet imagined by Ski:

—Qu'est-ce que c'est que cette chose si jolie de ton que nous mangeons? demanda Ski.—Cela s'appelle de la mousse à la fraise, dit Mme Verdurin. —Mais c'est ra-vis-sant. Il faudrait faire déboucher des bouteilles de château-margaux, de château-lafite, de porto.—Je ne peux pas vous dire comme il m'amuse, il ne boit que de l'eau, dit Mme Verdurin pour dissimuler sous l'agrément qu'elle trouvait à cette fantaisie l'effroi que lui causait cette prodigalité.—Mais ce n'est pas pour boire, reprit Ski, vous en remplirez tous nos verres, on apportera de merveilleuses pêches, d'énormes brugnons: là, en face du soleil couché, ça sera luxuriant comme un beau Véronèse.—Ca coûtera presque aussi cher, murmura M. Verdurin.—Mais enlevez ces fromages si vilains de ton, dit-il en essayant de retirer l'assiette du Patron, qui défendit son gruyère de toutes ses forces. (*SG* II 939)

Proust consistently makes such fantasies seem absurd by contrasting them with a sensible approach. In another example, 'M. Tiche' forgets about common tact when he is carried away by the aesthetic possibilities of a moonlight picnic: he inadvertently reveals to Swann that an outing is being planned from which he will be excluded (*S* I 284).

Architecture can be as much victim of Philistinism as painting. M. de Cambremer pretends judiciously to admire 'le buffet d'orgue, la chaire et les œuvres de miséricorde' in any church he visits (*SG* II 945). The Curé at Combray longs for his beautiful old church to be restored to garish modernity (*CS* I 103).

Other offshoots of the visual arts are frequently drawn on for humour: these are interior decorating, dress and furniture. But in these cases, Proust takes a different standpoint: for these things have ephemeral, not lasting appeal. They are in fashion for a while, then are rejected in favour of something new. This aspect of aestheticism is so important that it deserves a general discussion on its own.

Fashion

Fashions in general lend themselves to ridicule, since basically they are motivated by the desire to imitate and outdo others. This may involve professing to like, and even liking, something simply because others do. Sometimes the favoured objects are beautiful. Mme de Cambremer-Legrandin follows the fashion in adoring Debussy; the Swanns have elegant grey damask napkins 'exigées par l'etiquette' (*JF* I 506). Proust reserves his greatest contempt for fashions for worthless objects. Commenting on a recent aesthetic fad, he says:

Pendant deux ans les hommes intelligents, les artistes trouvèrent Sienne, Venise, Grenade, une scie, et disaient du moindre omnibus, de tous les wagons: 'Voilà qui est beau.' Puis ce goût passa comme les autres. (*P* III 136)

Apart from the question of whether it is a worthy object that is in fashion or the reverse, Proust is interested in the progress of fashions in general. We move from the mid-nineteenth century, when houses are cluttered with picturesque but useless objects, and women uncomfortably squeezed into awkward clothes, to the self-conscious stylization of *art nouveau* and the simple clothes of the First World War.

The scope of *ALR* in particular allows Proust to expand on the development of fashions through the years, and to extract from them a variety of humorous effects. We have seen how he refers to Mme de Guermantes's taste in painting and how she is led to contradict her previous opinion when a new attitude becomes fashionable. We have also seen her rejection of Empire furniture which she calls 'cet affreux style', and which she later professes to adore. In both cases she foolishly gives away her best specimens to her cousins, who later exhibit marvellous examples of the fashionable style, much to her rage. In both cases, the effect is built up over a long period of time.

Elsewhere, Proust shows us the precise moment at which a follower of fashion changes his opinion. The most obvious example is the change in Mme de Cambremer-Legrandin when she is told that Chopin, whom she detests, is now in vogue:

Je me fis un plaisir de lui apprendre [. . .] que Chopin, bien loin d'être démodé, était le musicien préféré de Debussy. 'Tiens, c'est amusant', me dit en souriant finement la belle-fille [Mme de Cambremer-Legrandin], comme si ce n'avait été là qu'un paradoxe lancé par l'auteur de *Pelléas*. Néanmoins il était bien certain maintenant qu'elle n'écouterait plus Chopin qu'avec respect et même avec plaisir. (*SG* II 817)

More often, however, Proust explains or generalizes about changing fashions, rather than allowing his examples to speak for themselves. He tells us baldly that Odette is a slave of fashion:

Mme Swann manquait rarement d'adopter les usages qui passent pour élégants pendant une saison et, ne parvenant pas à se maintenir, sont bientôt abandonnés [. . .] (*JF* I 546)

Elsewhere, he reminds the reader of other fashions to emphasize the ephemeral nature of the one at present in question:

Les théories de William Morris, qui ont été si constamment appliquées par Maple et les décorateurs anglais, édictent qu'une chambre n'est belle qu'à la condition de contenir seulement des choses qui nous soient utiles et que toute chose utile, fût-ce un simple clou, soit non pas dissimulée, mais apparente [. . .] A la juger d'après les principes de cette esthétique, ma chambre n'était nullement belle, car elle était pleine de choses qui ne pouvaient servir à rien et qui dissimulaient pudiquement, jusqu'à en rendre l'usage extrêmement difficile, celles qui servaient à quelque chose. (*CSB*, 'Journées de lecture' p. 164)

It is with interior decoration that Proust most frequently makes this point. Another good example is the changing tastes of the Verdurins, who,

par le progrès fatal de l'esthétisme, qui finit par se manger la queue, disaient ne pas pouvoir supporter le modern style [. . .] ni les appartements blancs et n'aimaient plus que les vieux meubles français dans un décor sombre. (*TR* III 731)

Since we have seen exactly the reverse process earlier in the novel (*NPN* I 426-7), we cannot but think that this professed admiration for one style and dislike for another is on the whole artificial. In general, although Proust admires beautiful rooms, he implies that there is something artificial about caring so much for them. For instance, Odette pretends that she cares little for her beautiful room, rue La Pérouse; but although she flings cushions about as though she were 'prodigue de ces richesses et insouciante de leur valeur', she is feverishly anxious when the servant brings in the lamps: they will ruin the effect unless they are put in exactly the right place (*CS* I 220-1).

Despite his contempt for the fashion-conscious and his basic assumption that the concept of fashion is intrinsically worthless, which makes all the instances given here contain an element of scornful mockery, Proust himself often reveals an acute awareness of the latest fashions. Apart from his admiration of women's clothes, or of leaders of fashion such as M. de Charlus (see *JF* I 753, *SG* II 652), there are examples of humour which depend on our adopting a fashion-conscious standpoint. The historian at Mme de Villeparisis's *matinée* is ridiculed because he does not know the latest fashion:

Suivant une habitude qui était à la mode à ce moment-là, ils posèrent leurs hauts de forme par terre, près d'eux. L'historien de la Fronde pensa qu'ils étaient gênés comme un paysan entrant à la mairie et ne sachant que faire de son chapeau. Croyant devoir venir charitablement en aide à la gaucherie et à la timidité qu'il leur supposait:

—Non, non, leur dit-il, ne les posez pas par terre, vous allez les abîmer.

Un regard du baron de Guermantes [. . .] glaça le bienveillant historien. (*CG* II 212-13)

One could argue here that there is an element of laughter at the expense of the followers of the fashion, who think themselves elegant but look like peasants to the uninitiate. Elsewhere this double humorous standpoint is more clearly apparent. An example is the elegant lunch party given by the Swanns in honour of Bergotte. The elaborate rigmarole enacted by the guests is no less riduculous than the naïvety of the Narrator, who does not know any of the fashionable rituals he is expected to observe. For instance, a servant hands him a sealed envelope, and, not wishing to appear rude in front of the guests, he refrains from opening it in their presence. When he gets home, he finds it in his pocket:

J'étais seul maintenant. Je l'ouvris, à l'intérieur était une carte sur laquelle on m'indiquait la dame à qui je devais offrir le bras pour aller à table. (*JF* I 575)

On the whole, however, Proust respects the leaders of fashion, since despite the triviality of their preoccupations, they have *panache*. He is merciless about those whose desire to be fashionable is not accompanied by any elegance or skill. Mme de Cambremer-Legrandin is despicable because her imitation of Mme de Guermantes's way of dressing is uninspired, and because her love of Debussy is uninformed. Saint-Loup is ridiculous in his love of *art nouveau* furniture and current literary movements because here he lacks the aristocratic grace that once made his father's love of the then acceptable Offenbach delightful (*JF* I 733). Odette is absurd because her professed love of antiques is accompanied by such ignorance that when she uses the word *moyenâgeux* 'elle entendait par là qu'il y avait des boiseries' (*S* I 244).

Proust's attitude to fashion suggests a dual standpoint similar to his view of snobbery. He despises snobs and followers of fashion; but he admires leaders of fashion and aristocrats. It is not surprising that he disclaims any interest in fashion, just as he insists that he is not a snob. But without a doubt, it is his keen awareness of the latest fashions that enables him to mock at them so convincingly.

Social Themes

Finally, there are numerous subjects that preoccupy both author and characters, the sort of subjects that would interest most reasonably cultured people: history, geography, science, medicine, education, and politics.

History and geography are particularly interesting from the point of view of humour, for they enlarge its scope, even beyond the already wide limits of a monumental work such as *ALR*. Proust can extend his wit to include distant lands when he compares Mme de Cambremer-

Legrandin to a female savage (*SG* II 814), or bring Africa and England into France when he compares an English spinster to a giraffe (*JS* p. 677). Even more striking is the way he links past and present, giving his work roots in the past, making it extend backwards even further than his own memories can reach. A good example is the mistake of Mme d'Arpajon already mentioned in this chapter: she thinks the Narrator has said that Paul Bert or Fulbert are the authors of *Salammbô*, instead of Flaubert (*CG* II 489–90). Proust has wittily linked these three incompatible names, simply because they sound similar: thus we find a medieval archbishop, a nineteenth-century novelist and a left-wing contemporary of Proust's juxtaposed.

Another important potential of this technique involves the implicit grandeur of references to the past. To begin with, the historical events that the reader is likely to recognize are important ones, so these are the ones that tend to be used. Any allusion to some important past event is likely to seem incongruous unless the contemporary situation is of comparable significance. It seems ridiculous to compare the life of Tante Léonie to that of Louis XIV (*CS* I 118).

Proust several times makes the point that for him the past is so imbued with magic and mystery that the present, however splendid, is bound to be a disappointment by comparison, simply because it really exists, and cannot be transformed by the imagination. This helps to explain why he prefers to recall time past, rather than living in time present. Usually, the disappointment is so great that the anticlimax provided by the present does not seem funny. One does not on the whole feel inclined to laugh when the descendant of the great medieval duke, Gilbert le Mauvais, turns out to be an ordinary woman with a red face and a pimple on her nose, because of the serious reflections engendered by this discovery (*CS* I 174–5). But Proust can exploit the humour in such a situation. It does seem slightly ridiculous that Prince von Faffenheim, with his noble Germanic title, should, by his banal present-day life, play his poetic origins so false:

les revenus qu'il tirait de la forêt et de la rivière peuplées de gnomes et d'ondines, de la montagne enchantée ou s'élève le vieux Burg qui garde le souvenir de Luther et de Louis le Germanique, il en usait pour avoir cinq automobiles Charron, un hôtel à Paris et un à Londres, une loge le lundi à l'Opera et une aux 'mardis' des 'Français'. (*CG* II 257)

Other characters remain true to their heritage, but this makes them seem out of touch with the present. Françoise has retained many of the characteristics of the medieval peasant, which seem unreasonable and inappropriate in the modern world; but in her case the incongruity between past and present is no less apparent for being reversed (see *CS* I 28–9). Other characters exhibit the same lack of contact with the present. The Prince de Guermantes and M. de Charlus live in a dream world of grandeur and chivalry, which contrasts with their instinctive desire for cheap vice.

The historical references themselves are rarely intrinsically amusing. There is the contemporary macaronic verse about the Prince de Condé and La Moussaye that Brichot tells M. de Charlus (*P* III 303). There are Brichot's heavy historical witticisms. But more often, historical allusions are perfectly serious, and the humour lies exclusively in the contrast between past and present. One smiles at the mention of Joan of Arc's page because he is compared to Mme Verdurin, and Joan of Arc is by implication equated with M. de Charlus (*P* III 275). Primitive man is not intrinsically ridiculous, but it seems absurd to compare him to Françoise (*CS* I 29).

Science and, in particular, medicine are also frequently used in humour, chiefly in the form of comparisons which again serve to enlarge or explain the basic material. We have seen that optics and optical illusions play an important part in the humour in *ALR*: Proust frequently juggles with size, or uses vague physical resemblances as the basis of a humorous comparison. Another technique is to observe the characters as though they were specimens under a microscope, tiny and helpless. This Proust frequently does. Again, we have seen repeated comparisons between the behaviour patterns of his characters and insects, plants, water or minerals. The science of mechanics is invoked in comparisons involving the characters' movements (*CS* I 125).

But by far the most important class of scientific humorous references is that of medicine. Curiously enough, for one whose father and brother were both doctors, Proust seems to have had the most sceptical attitude towards medicine and doctors in general. *JS* opens with an absurd conversation between Mme Santeuil and an important doctor, Professeur Surlande. The Professor is given to pompous technical language:

–C'est [. . .] un nerveux, dit le docteur, en souriant comme après un bon mot. Son facies l'indique assez d'ailleurs. (*JS* p. 202)

and immediately demonstrates the fallibility of medical treatment:

–M. Marfeu le traite certainement par l'eau froide.–Par l'eau froide? dit avec étonnement Mme Santeuil. Mais non, M. Marfeu nous a bien recommandé de nous servir seulement d'eau chaude.–De l'eau chaude?

dit en riant M. Surlande. Ah! Vraiment, de l'eau chaude, cela est assez curieux. D'ailleurs, M. Marfeu est un savant remarquable, et vous ne pouviez choisir un meilleur médecin pour votre fils.

In *ALR*, the doctors tend to be more reliable, but equally pompous. Cottard insists on using technical terms when addressing laymen (*SG* II 961). Equally, most of the doctors in *ALR* are rude and coarse. Cottard rudely interrogates M. de Cambremer:

Vous parlez de trional, savez-vous seulement ce que c'est?—Mais . . . j'ai entendu dire que c'était un médicament pour dormir.—Vous ne répondez pas à ma question, reprit doctoralement le professeur [. . .] Je ne vous demande pas si ça fait dormir ou non, mais ce que c'est. (*SG* II 961)

Another, more unpleasant, characteristic of Proust's doctors is their callousness. They are so used to people dying that they scarcely bother to show concern. There is an element of humour in the way Cottard refuses to attend to his maidservant, although she is critically ill, because he has a social engagement (*SG* II 880), or Professor E. being more upset by the fact that his *Légion d'Honneur* cannot be fitted on to his evening dress than by the fact that he has just pronounced the death-sentence of the Narrator's grandmother (*CG* II 318). Even the most sophisticated of doctors, Professeur Dieulafoy, owes his perfect tact to his skill as an actor (*CG* II 342–3).

The attitude of the public towards medicine is as funny as the behaviour of the doctors. People glory in the money they spend on cures, even if they are ruined at the end, like Françoise's cousins (*CG* II 331–2). They each feel that their own doctor is the only one who can cure people, like M. de Guermantes (*CG* II 337). Patients can be figures of fun, like the poet who claims that he is not mentally unbalanced simply because he is not obsessed with his weight like the other patients in his mental home (*CG* II 305). On the whole, this burlesque attitude to medicine predominates over the serious references.

Education is mentioned far less in *ALR* than in *JS*. In the earlier work, Proust goes into Jean's education, the eccentricities of boys such as Buffeteur and the mannerisms of masters such as Clodius Xelnor. In *ALR* there are repeated comparisons between social situations and examinations. When the Narrator cannot negotiate the swing-door into a restaurant, he incurs the wrath of the proprietor:

Cette marque flagrante d'ignorance lui fit froncer le sourcil comme à un examinateur qui a bonne envie de ne pas prononcer le *dignus est intrare*. (*CG* II 401)

Again, when the Narrator doesn't recognize the middle-aged Gilberte, he stares at her:

Tel un candidat au baccalauréat attache ses regards sur la figure de l'examinateur et espère vainement y trouver la réponse qu'il ferait mieux de chercher dans sa propre mémoire, tel, tout en lui souriant, j'attachais mes regards sur les traits de la grosse dame. (*TR* III 980)

In conclusion, it seems that there are several basic types of humour that arise from culture. First, deviation from a standard accepted both by the reader and by the author can seem amusing, for instance when M. de Guermantes expresses admiration for 'les enfants d'Édouard'. Secondly, rigid adherence to the accepted view can seem just as ridiculous, should the reasons for it be inadequate. Finally, the author and reader may disagree with the accepted opinion of the cultured characters: witness Proust's sarcasm at the expense of aesthetes who prefer railway carriages to St. Mark's.

A characteristic quality of the examples in this chapter has been the complicity that the author demands from his reader. We are meant to feel that we share Proust's tastes, and expected to participate in his scorn for those who fail to live up to his high standards. Thus his humorous treatment of culture is a skilful tool for getting the reader on his side: the reader has the satisfaction of being able to mock at the characters from a highly cultured standpoint. It is by subtle techniques such as this (almost more than by obvious tricks such as associating the reader with common experiences by talking of 'nous') that Proust makes the link between author and reader so strong.

As well as this, the references in this chapter all have a considerable effect on their context: they expand the implications of the situation, giving us glimpses of distant islands or the even more distant past. The technique of referring widely to all sorts of subjects has helped Proust to make his universe grow: his world reaches out to other things just as ours does. As a result, Proust's world strikes one as highly lifelike, despite the preponderance of caricatures and the obvious lacunae (one gets to know few tradesmen, one sees no serious business done, and so on). These references and allusions, humorous in themselves, have a very serious part to play in Proust.

VII
THE HUMAN SITUATION

There is no satisfactory term which includes the subjects discussed in this chapter. The material is drawn from the sort of subjects people generally think important, and which Proust mentions, at least in *ALR*. These subjects are: time and memory, love and friendship, war and the army, youth, age and death, money, and religion. They are all serious subjects; but just for this reason, it is important to include them here, for the full extent of Proust's humour cannot be appreciated until one sees that even such subjects are not spared. It is particularly necessary to point this out, since one does not generally remember the humour in the treatment of such subjects. Perhaps because the serious element is so powerful, perhaps because one's response to subjects like love, war and death tends to be conventionally serious, one remembers an episode like the death of the grandmother or the imprisonment of Albertine as unmitigatedly sad. It will be seen that this is not the case.

Time and Memory

Proust's most famous technique, that of recreating the past through involuntary memory, is taken very seriously both by critics and by the author himself. Yet even the most serious treatment of memory has its funny side. Take for instance the long key passage in *TR* in which the Narrator discovers that 'le but de ma vie et peut-être de l'art' is the reconstruction of the lost past through memory. Even here there are passing references that will arouse a fleeting smile, as when the Narrator inappropriately remembers his father saying 'tiens-toi droit' even as he recalls the anguish of his love for Gilberte (*TR* III 887). Such humorous touches contribute to the impression of richness and variety that Proust associates with memory, and help him to convey his feeling that memory consists in 'des sensations multiples et différentes' (*TR* III 889).

Proust also juxtaposes the present with the past to create larger-scale humorous effects. We have seen that comparison between two things is potentially a humorous device since it enables one to point out the incongruities as well as the similarities between them. In the last great scene of *ALR*, much of the humour depends on the fact that the aged characters are seen in terms of what they were like when young. A similar effect is achieved when the Narrator compares the modern people at the Bois de Boulogne with the grace and elegance of their predecessors a generation earlier (*NPN* I 425-6).

As a variation of this technique, Proust may contrast his preconceived idea of something he has not seen with the thing itself when he finally sees it. There is often an element of humour in these anticlimaxes, such as his first sight of the church at Balbec, which he had imagined on a grandiose cliff with the waves crashing at its mighty base, and which turns out to be on an ordinary village square (*JF* I 658).

In Proust's own opinion, his aim of viewing reality through the perspective of time contains an element of the absurd. This is clearly implied in the final pages of *TR*. Proust's view is that his characters will become 'des êtres monstrueux' because they drag their past with them, and that his confrontation of the reality of the past with that of the present will lead to ridiculous contradictions, a shower of rain in a bedroom, a *tisane* bubbling in a courtyard. Nevertheless, Proust feels it is vital to preserve these incongruities. He refuses to allow his intelligence to step in and make things seem more rational (*TR* III 1045-8). At the heart of his theory of the novel, we find the absurd.

Love and Friendship

Although love is the subject that affords the most distress to Proust's characters, he is well aware that even this most moving experience has its ridiculous side. He frequently contrasts the protagonist's standpoint with an outsider's, to show how unrealistic this preoccupation with one person seems to others. We have seen M. Verdurin's crude comment 'Je crois que ça chauffe' on the progress of Swann's love. The actual process of infatuation is equally ridiculous. Swann pretends to be fascinated by the explorer La Pérouse simply in order to mention the rue la Pérouse where Odette lives, and is in general indifferent to anything that is not connected with her (*S* I 343). He even prefers the squalid staircase of a friend of hers to the noble entrance of Mme de Saint-Euverte. Proust makes the contradiction clear when he talks of the former as 'l'escalier pestilentiel et désiré' (*S* I 325). We have seen that the Narrator does the same, particularly with regard to Gilberte. As well as this, Swann loses his sense of logic, and can persuade himself that what it suits him to believe is true. He admires the Verdurins excessively when they further his relationship with Odette, but when they stand in his way, he is equally unreasonable in his expressions of dislike (*S* I 286). However intense the infatuated lover may be, Proust is ready to laugh at him.

The beloved, too, can be ridiculous, even to the lover. Odette's lack of taste is seen through Swann's eyes (*S* I 244), and he occasionally makes comments like:

elle est si vulgaire et surtout, la pauvre petite, elle est tellement bête!!! (*S* I 286)

The Narrator is aware of Albertine's lack of logic and tendency to tell lies, which sometimes leads her into ludicrously overcomplicated situations (see, for example, *P* III 332-6). The absurdities of the Narrator's family, whom he loves tenderly, are also pointed out, though without the malice that otherwise tends to characterize such remarks. The eccentricities of the grandmother, the father with his passion for meteorology, Oncle Adolphe and the great-aunts have been mentioned. On the whole, the attitude to the people the Narrator loves is considered from a dual standpoint: the protagonist may be deeply, even tragically involved, but the Narrator stands back and makes humorous comments which presuppose a certain degree of detachment.

Friendship is characterized by less indulgence on the part of Proust. He said himself that he was a bad friend (in a letter to Antoine Bibesco he calls friendship 'une chose sans réalité', and equates it with insincerity—Princesse Bibesco, *Au Bal avec Marcel Proust*, p. 19). At one stage he outlines the typical defects of friends, with telling examples. One type is too hypocritical to tell you the things you should know, while another

a plus de sincérité, mais la pousse jusqu'à tenir à ce que vous sachiez, quand vous vous êtes excusé sur votre état de santé de ne pas être allé le voir, que vous avez été vu vous rendant au théâtre et qu'on vous a trouvé bonne mine [. . .] (*JF* I 741)

Where specific friends are concerned, the Narrator often shows a remarkable lack of tenderness for those that he professes to hold dear. It seems incredible that he can tell us 'j'aimais Bloch' (*CS* I 93), when he points out his grotesque faults with so little compunction, and allows him to be so rude to him. For instance, Bloch impertinently inquires:

'Est-ce par goût de t'élever vers la noblesse—une noblesse très à-côté du reste, mais tu es demeuré naïf—que tu fréquentes de Saint-Loup-en-Bray? Tu dois être en train de traverser une jolie crise de snobisme. Dis-moi, es-tu snob? Oui, n'est-ce pas?' (*JF* I 740)

But shortly afterwards, the Narrator can say:

Ce n'était du reste pas absolument un mauvais garçon que Bloch, il pouvait avoir de grandes gentillesses. (p. 746)

However, examples of *gentillesse* on his part seem as absurd as his malevolence. He bursts into loud sobs when told that the Narrator's grandmother is slightly unwell (*CS* I 92) and when he mentions his fondness for the Narrator (*JF* I 744). In fact, the Narrator's professions of affection are incompatible with his presentation of Bloch, who is a caricature.

Indeed, at their worst, relationships between friends in Proust can be imbued with extreme malevolence, and frequently there is an absurd contrast between the way friends behave to each other and their remarks behind each other's backs. Albertine and her *petite bande* are constantly maligning each other through jealousy. The Narrator assumes from their outward behaviour that they are fond of each other, only to be put right in private later. People delight in causing trouble between their mutual friends. Bloch maligns the Narrator to Saint-Loup and Saint-Loup to the Narrator (*JF* I 745). Even Saint-Loup is capable of similar behaviour:

'Tu sais, j'ai raconté à Bloch, me dit Saint-Loup, que tu ne l'aimais pas du tout tant que ça, que tu lui trouvais des vulgarités. Voilà comme je suis, j'aime les situations tranchées', conclut-il d'un air satisfait et sur un ton qui n'admettait pas de réplique. (*CG* II 399)

The humour in such cases often lies in the reasoning whereby such behaviour is justified by the culprit.

Finally, even the most serious, tragic or moving instances of love or friendship may have sudden humorous touches, which momentarily make one look at the situation from a more detached point of view. For instance, the first time the Narrator kisses Albertine, he keeps us in suspense for some time: the moment is so important to him that he cannot bear to hurry it. Several pages of exalted description culminate as follows:

—tout d'un coup, mes yeux cessèrent de voir, à son tour mon nez, s'écrasant, ne perçut plus aucune odeur, et [. . .] j'appris, à ces détestables signes, qu'enfin j'étais en train d'embrasser la joue d'Albertine. (*CG* II 365)

As well as providing an effect of humorous bathos, this conclusion is a further instance of Proust's belief that the imagination is a better vehicle for appreciating an experience than living through it. Just as he prefers to relive rather than to live his life, so his idea of what the kiss is going to be like is better than the kiss itself. And in general, the humour in Proust's treatment of love and friendship can be considered as the expression of a profound disillusionment in the Narrator. He cannot throw himself into a relationship; he is too aware of its absurdities. Just as he retired from active life, he withdrew from close relationships the better to observe them. Talking of his relationship with Saint-Loup, the Narrator makes this point plainly:

je n'éprouvais à me trouver, à causer avec lui—et sans doute c'eût été de même avec tout autre—rien de ce bonheur qu'il m'était au contraire possible de ressentir quand j'étais sans compagnon. (*JF* I 735–6)

The Narrator's cynical mockery of those he believes he likes can be funny in itself: but it also brings home to the reader his solitary nature, which devalues both friendship and love.

War and the Army

It is not surprising that *ALR*, much of which was written during and after the First World War, should contain numerous references to the army and to war. These subjects are taken seriously by most of the characters, however ridiculous their opinions may seem.

War, in particular, is discussed eagerly by all classes of people during the wartime years. Proust ridicules them for inventing implausible theories to explain the progress of the war. The *Maître d'hôtel* claims that the French have been depriving King Constantine of Greece of his food in order to make him abdicate (*TR* III 845). M. de Charlus attributes the alliance between Bulgaria and Germany to a homosexual relationship between their rulers (*TR* III 788). Equally ridiculous is the expression of a perfectly plausible opinion, if recited parrot-fashion. Odette produces authoritative statements about the war:

il fallait voir les moments de silence et d'hésitation qu'avait Mme de Forcheville, pareils à ceux qui sont nécessaires, non pas même seulement à l'énonciation, mais à la formation d'une opinion personnelle, avant de dire, sur le ton d'un sentiment intime: 'Non, je ne crois pas qu'ils prendront Varsovie'; 'je n'ai pas l'impression qu'on puisse passer un second hiver'; 'ce que je ne voudrais pas, c'est une paix boiteuse'—'ce qui me fait peur, si vous voulez que je vous le dise, c'est la

Chambre'; 'si, j'estime tout de même qu'on pourra percer'. (p. 788)
We know Odette too well for Proust to have to tell us that she is not
likely to have thought out these opinions for herself.

Another fault that is criticized, even in the intelligent, is the
tendency to adopt one side or another as one's own. The familiarity
with which Mme Verdurin says 'nous' when talking of France is as
absurd as the Maître d'hôtel's habit of referring to kings by their nick-
names (p. 729).

All the examples so far are perfectly compatible with loyalty and
real concern about the progress of the war. Any deviation from perfect
patriotism is mercilessly ridiculed by Proust. The cowardice of various
people who attempt to evade participation in the war is cruelly brought
to light. We are told that

Si Bloch nous avait fait des professions de foi méchamment antimilitar-
istes une fois qu'il avait été reconnu 'bon', il avait eu préalablement les
déclarations les plus chauvines quand il se croyait réformé pour myopie.
(pp. 741–2)

and that

Cottard mourut bientôt 'face à l'ennemi', dirent les journaux, bien qu'il
n'eût pas quitté Paris [. . .] (p. 769)

Others enjoy the war because it enables them to indulge in some satis-
fying pursuit. The most far-fetched example is that of the *Maître
d'hôtel*:

La victoire des Alliés semblait, sinon rapprochée, du moins à peu près
certaine, et il faut malheureusement avouer que le maître d'hôtel en
était désolé. Car, ayant réduit la guerre 'mondiale', comme tout le
reste, à celle qu'il menait sourdement contre Françoise [. . .] la Victoire
se réalisait à ses yeux sous les espèces de la première conversation où
il aurait la souffrance d'entendre Françoise lui dire: 'Enfin c'est fini . . .'
(p. 843)

M. de Charlus enjoys hearing about all the hardships suffered by young
men at the front (p. 825). Mme Verdurin and Mme Bontemps enjoy
the war because it has turned them into fashionable leaders of society
(pp. 726–9).

But perhaps the most despicable yet inevitable aspect of the war is
the way that life goes on in spite of it. Mme Verdurin manages
somehow to get her favourite morning croissants despite rationing:

Mme Verdurin [. . .] avait fini par obtenir de Cottard une ordonnance
qui lui permit de s'en faire faire dans certain restaurant dont nous avons
parlé. Cela avait été presque aussi difficile à obtenir des pouvoirs publics
que la nomination d'un général. (p. 772)

Fashion journalists adapt their dicta to suit the situation: the wartime episode in *TR* begins with a *pastiche* of a fashion article which reveals an underlying callousness and triviality. Playing on the courage and pride of the war-widows, the fashion magazines advocate white satin, and even pearls, for mourning—'tout en observant le tact et la correction qu'il est inutile de rappeler à des Françaises' (p. 724). They even go so far as to claim that the new style of dressing 'sera même une des plus heureuses conséquences de cette guerre' (p. 725). This twisting of normal patriotic sentiments to express a completely trivial preoccupation is both amusing and cynically destructive.

One of the most curious features of Proust's treatment of war is its lack of seriousness. There is the odd mention of destruction or political manœuvring, but the vast majority of allusions make cynical points about character like those mentioned here. Clearly, war gives the student of character a unique opportunity to examine the effect of total upheaval on the personality. Proust cynically implies that the personality will remain immutable however the situation changes. The best one can hope for is that characters will reveal bad sides which might otherwise have passed unnoticed: Bloch and Saint-Loup both turn out to be cowards. Proust's war, then, simply furthers his derogatory view of people.

The army is frequently mentioned by Proust. The most striking humorous passage is the indictment of the 'stiff upper lip' during the war. Proust baldly points out the absurdity of this convention, which depends on a tacit agreement between the audience and the protagonists: the latter pretend to be unmoved in such a way that the audience are in no doubt as to their inner emotion. Proust illustrates this bluff dishonesty by gloriously plausible examples. The gruff soldier hides his feelings behind words like these:
'Allons, tonnerre de Dieu! bougre d'idiot, embrasse-moi donc et prends donc cette bourse qui me gêne, espèce d'imbécile.' (*TR* III 744)
Elsewhere life during military service also provides a certain amount of humour, mostly connected with army protocol. In *JS*, there is a lieutenant who is so reluctant to salute an inferior soldier that he pretends that when he lifted his hand to his head, it was really to scratch (*JS* p. 563). In *ALR* we have the military jargon, which is intrinsically coarse, but essential if one is to make a good impression on one's fellow-soldiers. This fact is given added pungency by the presence of a novice learning the language:
—Comment que tu le sais, vieux, par notre sacré cabot? demandait le

jeune licencié avec pédantisme, étalant les nouvelles formes grammati-
cales qu'il n'avait apprises que de fraîche date et dont il était fier de
parer sa conversation (*CG* II 94)

As well as the whole episode at Doncières, there are isolated references to soldiering, which often take the form of comparisons. There is
humorous potential in comparing military life to social life, since military life is regimented and tough, while social life is meant to be casual
and graceful. Proust repeatedly draws on this fact. When the Narrator
and his grandmother are shown into the dining-room at Balbec by the
Directeur of the hotel, they are compared to privates in the army: he
leads them in

comme un gradé qui mène des bleus chez le caporal tailleur pour les
faire habiller. (*JF* I 679)

The comparison indicates his contempt of the new guests, and their
docility. Again, the Narrator is invited to meet Bergotte

comme on invite un engagé volontaire avec son colonel. (*JF* I 581)

These parallels serve to indicate the uncompromising rules that
govern society, no less rigid for being unspoken. In society, one is not
meant to assume that hotel dining-rooms and elegant dinner-parties are
as regimented as military life; but the truth is that they are. Proust's
parallels are unexpected but not inappropriate. The humour is increased by the fact that few socialites would be prepared to recognize
the truths that Proust's parallels imply.

We must, however, bear in mind the enthusiastic descriptions of
other aspects of the army than the rigid military protocol. The
Doncières episode is imbued with an atmosphere of enchantment. The
long analyses of military strategy betray Proust's fascination with the
subject. The overall impression of army life is admiring, with little more
than the one aspect mentioned here singled out for mockery.

Youth, Age, and Death

The progress from youth to old age and death is a major theme in
ALR. It preoccupied Proust in his earliest writings: 'Violante ou la
mondanité' is the story of the loss of youth's illusions and ideals;
JS seems to have ended on the subject of the old age of M. and Mme
Santeuil. In *ALR*, however, Proust has made much more of the theme:
the whole question of ageing is linked to that of time past. Not until
one has completed a stage in one's life can one begin to relive it.

In addition, the subject has its own interest: Proust studies the responses of his characters to their own or others' youth, age, and, in particular, death; he also describes the process of ageing in characters without any ulterior motive relating to the theme of *le temps perdu*. This aspect of the subject lends itself to humour, since Proust is not attempting to illustrate a serious theme.

One can distinguish between two techniques here. First, Proust gives us isolated instances of humour. Secondly, he makes a particular aspect or attitude to youth, age, or death recur throughout an episode, giving a feeling of continuity. These two techniques will be discussed in turn for each of the three subjects.

Individual instances of mockery at children occur occasionally. They seem to be motivated by two main elements. The child is not hampered by the conventions that govern the thinking processes of adults; so his logic is all his own. There are several examples: that of the little girl learning her lessons in *JS* (p. 196) and that in which the Narrator and Gilberte laugh at a child in a shop, who

les larmes aux yeux, refusait une prune que voulait lui acheter sa bonne, parce que, finit-il par dire d'une voix passionnée: 'J'aime mieux l'autre prune, parce qu'elle a un ver!' (*NPN* I 402)

This example also illustrates another facet of childhood used by Proust: the preoccupations of the child are almost always trivial, but his emotions can be very powerful, so that an incongruous contrast is established between subject and emotions. Other isolated examples, included purely for their humorous effect, are the description of Proust's brother's passionate farewell to his pet goat (already mentioned, *CSB*, Le Fallois ed., pp. 293–5) and little Alexis, resolving with his friends to renounce the vanities of this world, is a further instance (*PJ*, 'Mort de Baldassare Sylvande', *JS* p. 14)

These two characteristics are combined in the child Narrator of *ALR*. Instances of his *naïvety* and of his passionate nature have already been quoted in the discussion of the differences between the author and his protagonist in *ALR*. Often they are contrasted with the standpoints of adults. The Narrator's eagerness to behave politely and respectfully to 'la dame en rose' is contrasted with his uncle's reluctance for him to meet this undesirable person (*CS* I 76). His nervousness when he has to give a tip to Françoise is set against her formal way of receiving it (*CS* I 53). His passionate excitement when he visits Gilberte is contrasted with his mother's damping comments on his health (*JF* I 507). In short, youth is used as a means of getting outside the adult world, and of examining the things it takes for granted from a fresh standpoint. In such cases, one often laughs both at the Narrator and at the adults.

Teenagers are treated differently from children. Their affectation of casual elegance and superiority is a frequent source of humour. Octave, for instance, indulges in futile activities, 'pâle, impassible, un sourire d'indifférence aux lèvres' (*JF* I 677), in a patent imitation of the typical Romantic hero. Others, amongst them the Jeunes Filles, adopt a tough, dissolute manner, which seems equally affected (*JF* I 877, for example). Those not fortunate enough to have style spend their time in ludicrous envy of the others. The Narrator himself is miserable at his dearth of slang terms for the little train:

Je sentais sa maîtrise [celle d'Albertine] dans un mode de désignations où j'avais peur qu'elle ne constatât et ne méprisât mon infériorité. (*JF* I 877)

He envies the socially inferior boys who go riding every day (*JF* I 683). Gilberte affects childish charm (*JF* I 511), Andrée sophisticated maturity (*JF* I 914), Bloch other-worldly serious preoccupations (*CS* I 92). But all these characters are motivated by a childish eagerness to impress, which has a certain charm and is certainly less criticized than similar behaviour in more mature characters.

The child that a character was occasionally interferes with his mature personality. The Narrator's great-aunt cannot see Swann as anything but the child he once was (*CS* I 34). Of the embarrassingly affected Ski it is said:

Ses mouvements de tête, de cou, de jambes, eussent été gracieux s'il eût eu encore neuf ans, des boucles blondes, un grand col de dentelles et de petites bottes de cuir rouge. (*SG* II 874)

Again, there are direct confrontations with youth and old age, the most striking being Andrée's leap over the old man's head on the sea-front at Balbec (*JF* I 792). On this occasion, the humour rests largely in the blithe indifference of the Jeunes Filles to the horrified old man. Their sympathy for him is confined to the perfunctory and ironic comment of Gisèle: 'C'pauvre vieux, i m'fait d'la peine, il a l'air à moitié crevé'.

A much more important sustained confrontation between relative youth and age is the last scene of *TR*. The way in which the old people are described in terms of what they were like in their prime has already been discussed in an earlier chapter, although it has been impossible to go into more than a few examples illustrating the diversity of means Proust uses to illustrate the phenomenon of ageing. In this scene we also have examples of the thought processes of the old. An old lady spitefully remarks about her friends:

ils sont vieux: à cet âge-là on ne sort plus. (*TR* III 978)

showing a malice that is equalled by her complete blindness as to her own situation. The same old lady is delighted when any of her friends die, as if she had beaten them in a competition (p. 978).

Such lack of feeling is paralleled by the cruelty of others to the aged. Proust himself does not spare them, comparing M. d'Argencourt for instance to an old beggar (p. 921) or a snowman (p. 922). The younger characters are even more hard-hearted towards their elders. Guests at a *soirée* given by Gilberte comment on the aged Odette within her hearing:

On la laisse dans son coin. Du reste, elle est un peu gaga. (*TR* III 952)

But though ailing, Odette understands what they say, and suffers. Mme de Guermantes comments extremely rudely about an older woman:

Tenez, regardez la mère Rampillon, trouvez-vous une très grande différence entre ça et un squelette en robe ouverte? Il est vrai qu'elle a tous les droits, car elle a au moins cent ans. Elle était déjà un des monstres sacrés devant lesquels je refusais de m'incliner quand j'ai fait mes débuts dans le monde. Je la croyais morte depuis très longtemps; ce qui serait d'ailleurs la seule explication du spectacle qu'elle nous offre. (*SG* II 685)

The humour of such cruelty is enhanced by the fact that the aged themselves are, one assumes, anxious to deceive themselves into imagining that they are still reasonable in appearance, and able to hold their own in society.

Death lends itself to a different sort of humour. The assumption is that it is an awesome subject, and this is contrasted with flippant or disrespectful treatment. There are isolated references to the subject. Mme de Guermantes wittily comments:

on va à leur enterrement, ce qu'on ne fait jamais pour les vivants! (*CG* II 507)

An old maid indulges in pleasant fantasies on the subject of how her mother's death will be described (*TR* III 978). A cruel anecdote about the Queen of Naples's callous attitude to her sister's death goes the rounds (*CG* II 511).

More important are the series of humorous situations surrounding particular deaths. The basic tragedy is intertwined with humour to produce different effects. In the case of the most lengthily described death, that of the Narrator's grandmother, the humour helps to alleviate the situation, making it stand out by contrast. The humour takes the form of several different threads running through the episode. First, there are people from different walks of life, who appear in the flat and demonstrate their lack of real concern. The aristocracy is represented by M. de Guermantes, who cannot understand that his patronizing expressions of sympathy should seem inappropriate when the grandmother is literally breathing her last (*CG* II 336). The family seem amusing when, through hours of anxious waiting, they have become so exhausted as to seem indifferent:

l'interminable oisiveté autour de cette agonie leur faisait tenir ces mêmes propos qui sont inséparables d'un séjour prolongé dans un wagon de chemin de fer. (p. 341)

The doctor is like a Molière character, and plays to perfection the part of seeing others die, 'un rôle aussi original que le raisonneur, le scaramouche ou le père noble' (p. 342). The servant class is represented by Françoise's daughter, with her contention that the grandmother should have been treated *radicalement* (p. 331). The clergy appears in the shape of a distant relative who, despite his pious sorrow, peers at the Narrator from between his fingers (p. 339). As well as these incidental references, there is the whole theme of Françoise's response to the grandmother's illness and death, which progresses alongside the illness itself, and is repeatedly brought in. Françoise's rigorous protocol clashes with the illness to no less an extent than that of M. de Guermantes. She prefers to gossip with an electrician, whom it would be rude to send away, than to sit by the invalid's bedside (pp. 330-1). She leaves the grandmother when it is time for Mass or for lunch (p. 321). She also has preconceived ideas about illness, deciding that it is good for the dying woman to have her hair combed (pp. 333-4), disappointed because she is not stuffed with more expensive medicines (p. 331). But at the same time, Françoise is in a way more sensible than the family, for since she is sure that the grandmother is going to die, she does not think it worthwhile ruining her own comfort to make the grandmother's last moments less painful (pp. 319-20). These references to Françoise occur throughout the description of the grandmother's death, ending with her ghoulish fears of spooks as they wake over the dead body (p. 343). As well as lightening the gloom of the episode, this insistence on the constant presence of Françoise helps to place the death of the grandmother within the framework of the Narrator's normal life. It is clearly not true that just because a tragedy has occurred, the surrounding people are all ennobled and taken out of

their ordinary existence. Proust has in this case used humour to incor-
porate death into the novel, rather than grafting a tragic scene on the
rest of the text.

Another technique is to present the same characters with the deaths
of various acquaintances, and observe their reactions each time. Both
the Guermantes and the Verdurins are treated in this way. The Guermantes have a rigid code of manners which falls flat when death is in
question. When Swann tells them he is going to die, Mme de Guermantes is at such a loss that all she can think of to say is 'Vous voulez
plaisanter?', and Proust explains that

Placée pour la première fois entre deux devoirs aussi différents que
monter en voiture pour aller dîner en ville, et témoigner de la pitié
pour un homme qui va mourir, elle ne voyait rien dans le code des convenances qui lui indiquât la jurisprudence à suivre [. . .] (*CG* II 595)

This quotation illustrates another of their characteristics: they are so
selfish that they do not care about the deaths of others. All they want
is a polite formula with which to dismiss the problem. M. de
Guermantes has a solution, but it is invariably inadequate. He pretends
that things are not as bad as they seem. This makes him produce the
ludicrous assessment of the news of his cousin's death: 'on exagère'
(*SG* II 725), and also to say to Swann, with callous bonhomie: 'Vous
vous portez comme le Pont-Neuf. Vous nous enterrerez tous!' (*CG*
II 597). In the case of the Narrator's grandmother, he makes believe
that if only his own doctor is called, she will perhaps recover.

The Verdurins adopt a more subtle attitude. The assumption, as
usual, is that Mme Verdurin is deeply sensitive. M. Verdurin sets himself
up as her intermediary, and prevents anyone from mentioning the
death, so that she is not obliged to put on a convincing act of sorrow.
This elaborate pretence is accompanied by utter callousness on the
part of M. Verdurin. There are several occasions on which the technique is brought into play. When the pianist Dechambre dies, M. Verdurin stresses his wife's sorrow, and makes sure that the subject will not
be brought up:

Vous savez qu'elle cache beaucoup ce qu'elle ressent, mais elle a une
véritable maladie de la sensibilité [. . .] Si vous lui en parlez, elle va
encore se rendre malade. (*SG* II 901)

Having provided Dechambre with a suitable mourner, and ensured that
his evening will not be spoilt, M. Verdurin appears to consider that he
has done his duty, for he himself makes no attempt to appear sorry,
saying callously:

Vous ne voulez tout de même pas nous faire crever tous parce que
Dechambre est mort et quand, depuis un an, il était obligé de faire des
gammes avant de donner un concert [. . .] (p. 901)

Proust insists on this callousness by his own comments, as in this conversation with Brichot:

'Hé bien! ce pauvre Dechambre! . . . —C'est affreux, répondit allégre-
ment M. Verdurin.—Si jeune', reprit Brichot. Agacé de s'attarder à
ces inutilités, M. Verdurin répliqua d'un ton pressé et avec un gémisse-
ment suraigu, non de chagrin, mais d'impatience irritée: 'Hé bien oui
[. . .]' (p. 899)

His reluctance to put off a dinner because the Princesse Sherbatoff is
dead later leads him to make the same comment as M. de Guermantes:

—[. . .] elle est morte à six heures, s'écria Saniette.—Vous, vous exagérez
toujours', dit brutalement à Saniette M. Verdurin, qui, la soirée n'étant
pas décommandée, préférait l'hypothèse de la maladie, imitant ainsi
sans le savoir le duc de Guermantes. (P III 228)

But although the words are the same as M. de Guermantes's, the atmosphere is different. M. Verdurin is brutally callous, while M. de Guermantes attempts to hide his callousness beneath a sophisticated veneer.

It is curious that the characters who are most often confronted with
death, in order to reveal their selfish lack of sorrow and sympathy,
are the two main focal points of the social world in *ALR*: the
Guermantes are the hub of high society, the Verdurins that of the intellectual bourgeoisie. One might deduce from this that these attitudes to
death provide a further instance of the selfishness and artificiality of
social life in general, since this life is organized by such callous specimens. It is typical of Proust that he should not shrink from mocking
when confronted with this most sacred and tragic of human
experiences.

On the whole, Proust's mockery at the different ages of man is
subtly revealing of his attitude to these ages. The examples given here
show him regarding children as creatures from another planet. Their
passionate feelings seem totally incomprehensible. The elderly, on the
other hand, are only too easy to understand: selfish, competitive
towards others, preoccupied with trivia. The only age that seems to
arouse the Narrator's admiration is adolescence. Teenagers, however
ludicrous, always have charm. This underlying admiration suggests that
the Narrator identifies himself with this age-group, a fact which is
wittily brought home in the final scene of *TR*, with his absurd amazement at suddenly realizing that he is elderly, and not, as he had hitherto

believed, the eternal 'jeune homme de Combray' (*TR* III 927). This underlying assumption of eternal youth by the protagonist is ridiculous in a way, but also very important in the novel's structure. It is not until the Narrator has painfully and suddenly grown to accept that he is elderly that he can begin to write. And he emphasizes the enormous mental leap he has had to make, not from maturity but from adolescence to old age, in an absurd but poignant comment:

C'est avec des adolescents qui durent un assez grand nombre d'années que la vie fait des vieillards. (*TR* III 929)

Money

Proust's society, composed mainly of the very rich, must of necessity be interested in money. Proust mocks their attitudes in various ways, most of which are standard ones. We have the rich person who pretends to be poor in Mme de Guermantes:

Les mots 'trop chers', 'dépasser mes moyens' revenaient tout le temps dans la conversation de la duchesse, ainsi que ceux: 'je suis trop pauvre' [. . .] (*P* III 31, see also *S* I 341)

The rich miser is represented by Mme Verdurin when she has become the Princesse de Guermantes. With a cunning worthy of le père Grandet, she acclaims Rachel's recital in order that her praise should replace financial remuneration (*TR* III 1000). Interest in others' finances appears vulgar in Bloch, whose pretence that his interest is purely academic does not deceive the reader:

Mais dis-moi, reprit Bloch en me parlant tout bas, quelle fortune peut avoir Saint-Loup? Tu comprends bien que, si je te demande cela, en soi je m'en fiche comme de l'an quarante, mais c'est au point de vue balzacien, tu comprends. (*CG* II 219)

M. de Norpois, on the other hand, is more tactful, and one laughs not at what he says, but at his smug assumption of moneyed superiority:

comme il était lui-même colossalement riche, il trouvait de bon goût d'avoir l'air de juger considérables les revenus moindres d'autrui, avec pourtant un retour joyeux et confortable sur la supériorité des siens. (*JF* I 454)

The servant class is very money-conscious, and has its own financial rituals. Eulalie pretends every week that she is not going to accept the money Tante Léonie offers her, and finally accepts it with visible displeasure (*CS* I 106). Françoise's acceptance of the Narrator's tip is a ceremonial occasion (*CS* I 53). But despite their formal approach, the servants have passionate feelings towards money. Françoise feels it deeply if ever her masters give a tip to anyone else. Proust points out the illogicality of her reasoning:

Françoise [. . .] avait une tendance à considérer comme de la menue monnaie tout ce que lui donnait ma tante pour elle ou pour ses enfants, et comme des trésors follement gaspillés pour une ingrate des piécettes mises chaque dimanche dans la main d'Eulalie. (*CS* I 107)

The lift-boy, too, is deely upset because he has not been given his usual tip, and Proust mocks at him by depicting his despair in exaggerated terms: he is

prêt, dans son désespoir, à se jeter des cinq étages [. . .] (*SG* II 826)

The most original humorous references to money take the form of comparisons. Proust several times indicates that a character is physically changed by being rich. The curious comparison between M. de Guermantes and the mass of his riches, which literally seem contained within his body, has already been discussed. Elsewhere, there is a comparison between an ageing banker's daughter and her father's gold:

Chez une [. . .] fille de banquier, le teint, d'une fraîcheur de jardinière, se roussissait, se cuivrait, et prenait comme le reflet de l'or qu'avait tant manié le père. (*TR* III 951)

Almost everyone in *ALR* is very rich, and poverty is almost always a pretence, and hence funny (the most striking example is the Narrator's grandfather who was so mean he tried to avoid paying his bus fare). If poverty is real (as in the case of Brichot, who lives with a washerwoman on the fifth floor) its funny side is stressed. The novel as a whole is written with a cheerful assumption that most of the characters can enjoy everything that money can buy.

Religion

Whether or not Proust really meant it when he wrote to Mme Straus:

Au nom du ciel . . . auquel nous ne croyons hélas ni l'un ni l'autre. (*Corr. gén.* VI 94)

it is certainly the case that he frequently uses religion for humorous effect. As one would expect, humorous references to religion tend to have an atmosphere of daring and of impertinent irreverence. Usually, these references take the form of comparisons. The basic assumption is that people are desperately earnest about religion. Proust compares attitudes to religion and to more trivial subjects and hints that the feeling is the same in each case. This can often be extremely funny. We have already seen Françoise's lunch-time observances compared to the religious solemnities of the early Christians (*CG* II 17), and how the *petit clan* band together like a religious sect. Other examples produce more unexpected parallels. Etiquette demands that the Princesse de Parme be the first to leave the Guermantes's dinner-party:

Dès que Mme de Parme fut levée, ce fut comme une délivrance. Toutes les dames ayant fait une génuflexion devant la princesse, qui les releva, reçurent d'elle dans un baiser, et comme une bénédiction qu'elles eussent demandée à genoux, la permission de demander leur manteau et leurs gens. (*CG* II 544)

The dignity of the Directeur at Balbec cutting turkeys with his own hands produces a whole series of religious parallels, all having the self-importance of the protagonist as their basic justification for existing:

J'étais sorti, mais j'ai su qu'il l'avait fait avec une majesté sacerdotale, [. . .] (plongeant d'un geste lent dans le flanc des victimes et n'en détachant pas plus ses yeux pénétrés de sa haute fonction que s'il avait dû y lire quelque augure) [. . .] Le sacrificateur ne s'aperçut même pas de mon absence. [. . .] Depuis ce jour-là le calendrier fut changé, on compta ainsi: 'C'est le lendemain du jour où j'ai découpé moi-même les dindonneaux.' [. . .] Ainsi cette prosectomie donna-t-elle, comme la naissance du Christ ou l'Hégire, le point de départ d'un calendrier différent des autres [. . .] (*SG* II 1084)

Apart from these comparisons, there are other humorous references to religion. Religious observance is mocked at in *JS*, when the behaviour of churchgoers is described: people hypocritically refrain from acknowledging a friend's presence, although they know he has arrived. Jean equally hypocritically receives the Host

comme on reçoit d'un air triste un héritage dont on sait déjà pourtant qu'il se transformera dès que les convenances le permettront en une belle paire de chevaux ou une loge à l'Opéra. (*JS* p. 338)

We have seen Tante Léonie's preoccupation with religion juxtaposed with her interest in her health (*CS* I 52), and Mme Sazerat's packet of *petits fours* described in the same breath as the stained glass windows at Combray (*CS* I 59–60). In *JS* we have Félicie

qui tout en tenant au salut de l'âme de ses maîtres tient encore plus à ce que son gigot soit mangé à point. (p. 337)

Proust does not use humour to criticize the Catholic Church; the observances he mocks at he also admires and thinks beautiful. The churches themselves often seem mildly amusing as well as beautiful, simply because they have so much character. The church at Combray is like a *brioche* (*CS* I 65), or like a 'simple citoyenne' (p. 62). The one at Guermantes is round-shouldered (*CSB*, Le Fallois ed. p. 285); the one at Saint-Jean-de-la-Haise placidly ignores visitors (*SG* II 1013). These parallels are affectionate ones.

Proust's attitude to Judaism is far less indulgent. Some of the most painful mockery in *ALR* relates to the Jewishness of Bloch. Bloch and the other Jews in the novel are ashamed of their race, while sticking together and enjoying it in private. M. Bloch *père*, for instance, prefers to talk Yiddish with his family, but considers it *vulgaire et déplacé* when Gentiles are present (*JF* I 773). Proust is particularly cruel about analysing the attempts of Jews to rise above their origins, either by changing their names and becoming typically French, like Bloch or Gilberte, or by frankly confessing them. He mercilessly interprets an attempt at honesty on the part of Bloch:

'[. . .] Au fond, c'est un côté assez juif chez moi', ajouta-t-il ironiquement en rétrécissant sa prunelle comme s'il s'agissait de doser au microscope une quantité infinitésimale de 'sang juif'. [. . .
. . .] Le genre de fraude qui consiste à avoir le courage de proclamer la vérité, mais en y mêlant pour une bonne part des mensonges qui la falsifient, est plus répandu qu'on ne pense [. . .] (*JF* I 746–7)

One gets the feeling that none of the Jews' attempts will be given a chance of succeeding.

Moreover, the other characters in *ALR* are allowed to ridicule and revile the Jewish characters with impunity. The Narrator himself comments on the Jewish holiday-makers at Balbec with distaste thinly disguised by a veil of ironic detachment:

cette colonie juive était plus pittoresque qu'agréable. (*JF* I 738)

Elsewhere, the aristocrats humiliate Bloch in public by referring to his Jewish origins. On these occasions one has no sympathy for Bloch because he has earned these snubs by his own impudent remarks. In his humiliation he becomes incoherent, and Proust maliciously builds up to his pathetic discomfiture:

Tout le monde sourit, excepté Bloch, non qu'il n'eût l'habitude de prononcer des phrases ironiques sur ses origines juives [. . .] Mais au lieu d'une de ces phrases, lesquelles sans doute n'étaient pas prêtes, le déclic de la machine intérieure en fit monter une autre à la bouche de Bloch. Et on ne put recueillir que ceci: 'Mais comment avez-vous pu savoir? qui vous a dit?' comme s'il avait été le fils d'un forçat.

D'autre part, étant donné son nom, qui ne passe pas précisément pour chrétien, et son visage, son étonnement montrait quelque naïveté. (*CG* II 247–8)

The aristocrats are allowed to make outrageous remarks, like the Prince de Guermantes, who, according to his cousin the Duchess,

a toujours soutenu qu'il fallait renvoyer tous les juifs à Jérusalem [. . .] (*CG* II 235)

or various insolent comments about Dreyfus. Proust does not reveal his own Dreyfusard sympathies, but allows the anti-Dreyfusards to state their views unimpeded. In this respect, his attitude has changed since *JS*, in which Proust seriously attributes to Jean the enthusiasm for the case of Dreyfus that he later ridicules in Bloch.

A curious sideline is Proust's reference to corrupt members of the Church. His *mauvais prêtre* in the male brothel is a grotesque caricature whose religious background emerges at this most inappropriate of moments. He lifts 'un doigt de docteur en théologie' to explain his evil morals, and is asked to pay his room 'pour les frais du culte' (*TR* III 829). The promiscuous nun in *JS* is taken more seriously, apart from her vulgar smile (*JS* p. 852). But there is an opposite situation which is exploited for humour when the prostitutes at Jean's first brothel make hats for nuns (*JS* p. 242).

Humorous treatment of religion in Proust varies largely according to the religion under discussion. Where Catholicism is concerned, he writes with affection tempered by a more or less thinly disguised irreverence. With Judaism, he is biting and cruel.

In examining how Proust finds laughter in the very serious subjects treated here, we touch on a central issue in any discussion on humour. Does seeing the funny side of death, war or anti-Semitism imply serene detachment on the author's part? It would seem at first sight that it must. If Proust were identifying with the Narrator, could he even smile as his protagonist's beloved grandmother died? But if we accept that Proust is detached in his treatment of these subjects, how can we account for the bitterness of his mockery of the Jews, or the wistfulness of his smile when describing adolescents? We must, I feel, recognize that Proust is at once a precision instrument, an X-Ray camera as he puts it, pitilessly recording the unvarnished truth, and a very human writer whose feelings shine through the superficially impartial attitude.

This double standpoint on the author's part leads to a similar duality on the part of the reader. Initially, the impression of authorial detachment leads to a lightening of the tension for the reader as well. But this feeling of release may prove to be a spurious one. Ostensibly, the remarks about Albertine's lies or the grandmother's death are detached; but the Narrator's underlying pain still stings. Proust has pointed out similar dual standpoints in his characters: Legrandin outwardly smiles but inwardly winces when the Guermantes are mentioned (*CS* I 128-9). It may not be over-subtle to suggest that here the humour is sad: Legrandin's smile shows his wry awareness of his own absurdity, but does not alleviate his predicament. Proust repeated a remark that Molière should have played his own Alceste as a tragic figure (*TR* III 981). And Proust's own tendency to ridicule serious subjects does nothing to diminish our final impression that his is a deeply serious work.

VIII
CONCLUSION

It now remains to consider Proust's humour in relation to his work as a whole. It must be immediately stressed that, in this respect as in others, he evolved. In his earliest works, the humour is superimposed, not closely bound up with the ideas behind his writing, largely because these ideas were not fully worked out. He was not yet in complete control of his material, not yet confident enough to combine the serious and the humorous as he was to do later in *ALR*. It is not surprising that an early story like 'La Fin de la jalousie' contains none of the humour that appears in passages of mature writing dealing with the same subject, such as those in which the Narrator analyses his relationship with Albertine.

Two other factors might help to explain Proust's development as a humorist. First, humour presupposes authorial detachment. In his early works, especially in *JS*, he identifies far too strongly with his hero for the humour to achieve the requisite atmosphere of detachment. Secondly, the humorist must know where to stop. The mature Proust, despite his general tendency to elaborate on his subject-matter, is on the whole admirable in this respect. His shortcomings are few enough to be singled out: the endless *cuirs* of the Directeur, the persistent attacks on Bloch's dignity in public. Usually, he will take his mockery just far enough, and stop when the humour is at its zenith. In this respect he is more skilful than the heavy-handed Balzac, and, writing in a more flexible *genre*, he is inevitably more subtle than Molière. In his earlier works, however, he has not achieved this sureness of touch. He protests too much about the absurdity of Mme Marmet or Rustinlor; or, conversely, he fails to take his humour far enough (the later version of the 'article dans *Le Figaro*' episode is infinitely superior in this respect to that in *CSB*, Le Fallois ed. p. 95). Furthermore, in *ALR*, his use of humour extends far wider than in the earlier works. As his philosophical horizons broadened, so his humour developed.

Proust himself clearly felt that he had evolved a great deal since he first started writing. Indeed, in *ALR* he actually seems to parody his earlier self, putting into the mouth of the absurd Legrandin the

selfsame fulsome lyrical effusions about clouds that he had produced
in all seriousness in *PJ*. Even more amazing, if we read Proust's own
early letters to his mother, we find a foretaste of the neo-Parnassian
bombast of none other than Bloch.

Looking back over *ALR*, we can see two distinct approaches to
humour. It is used as a technical device, an integral part of the narrative
technique; but it is also a philosophical tool, a vehicle for some of
Proust's own thoughts. These two aspects often exist concurrently, but
will be considered roughly in turn, although I have not attempted to
separate them stringently.

As a technical device, humour is pervaded by Proust's sharp eye for
minute detail. I say 'sharp' advisedly, for Proust's humorous details are
as pointed as pinpricks. He pins down the tell-tale gesture that reveals
the pederast, the imperceptible curve of a well-camouflaged Jewish
nose. His gimlet eye mercilessly exposes what his victim is hoping to
conceal. We have seen this sharp attention to detail in his style, his
character portrayal and his imagery. His ear is equally acute,
particularly with regard to character. He reproduces the spoken word
with unbelievable exactness. Here the overall impression is different.
We are amazed at his control over his dialogue, we laugh partly through
admiration at his skill.

His ability to capture fine details also produces an impression of
delicacy, for it presupposes an indirect approach, one that excludes
obvious, crude observations. He tells us that a homosexual calls a good-
looking young man 'une personne'. He does not elaborate on the fact
that this use of the feminine gender to describe a male illustrates the
light in which the homosexual views the person in question. He favours
insinuation, not bald statement. On the rare occasions when he gives
us a straightforward explanation, like his elucidation of the Directeur's
malapropisms, he seems unusually unsubtle and over-explicit. This
delicacy is characteristic of the frequent humorous touches in the body
of the text. They do not detract from the overall impression of realism
because they are not so far-fetched as to be unrealistic.

If Proust wants to go to the opposite extreme, and be farcically
crude, grossly vulgar, he will often create a separate farcical scene which
stands apart from the surrounding text. He treats M. de Charlus's duel in
this way, heaping on ludicrous touches, like Cottard repeatedly needing
to urinate through over-excitement. Between these two extremes, the
fleeting, declicate touch and the sustained farcical episode, there is a
wide range of intermediate effects. The commonest is the amusing aside

which is yet elaborate enough for its humorous potential to be appreciated to the full. Proust usually dwells, however briefly, on his humorous passages; it is characteristic of him to examine the implications of his ideas, to delve deep, rather than allowing them to slip in unanalysed. But even so there is an immense difference between a sustained humorous scene like the Princesse de Guermantes's *baignoire* and a brief mention like the glimpse of the grandmother in the guise of an army scout.

This variety in scope and tone is given a feeling of unity by one feature that is almost always present: malice. Whether he is pricking his characters with the delicate point of a pin, or stamping on them with a hobnailed boot, we always get the impression of spiteful glee. He implicitly degrades his own characters: he laughs not with but at them.

Often his baiting of his characters seems venomous; but at times he can seem more interested in the techniques for creating the humour than in malice. This is particularly true of passages that have been carefully worked over before achieving their final form. It is impossible to detect any spontaneous malice in the child Narrator's farewell to the hawthorn. In itself, the passage is carefully, almost laboriously constructed, full of elaborate parallels with Racine. Furthermore, it is a careful reworking and perfecting of an earlier passage (*CSB*, Le Fallois ed. p. 293). This scrupulous attention to craftsmanship is one of Proust's most striking features, and sometimes softens the rancour of his observation.

Proust uses another technique to temper his malice, or make it more subtly witty. He creates a spurious atmosphere of authorial detachment. In particular, he uses dialogue to give his characters an illusory independence. Many of them consistently lay themselves open to mockery, condemning themselves out of their own mouths. This is a sly, underhand way of criticizing them, since he preserves the illusion that they are autonomous, although of course it is he who has been making them talk all along. He varies his role of puppeteer considerably. At times there is no doubt that he is pulling the strings, although often he feigns ignorance, or leaves the characters to act 'independently'. The effect on both characters and humour will vary according to which of these two techniques is in operation. If he makes it clear that he is in control, the characters really are reduced to the role of puppets; but if he gives them their heads, he creates a feeling of realism.

Realism is important in *ALR*. The overall impression is of a lifelike world, where the characters are people we might have met. This impression is so powerful that if Proust varies it with a strongly artificial episode we are surprised. We cannot believe that M. de Charlus can summon up distant music with a snap of his fingers, because such things do not happen in real life, and we believe in M. de Charlus as we do in a real man, despite his extravagances. Not surprisingly, Proust contributes to this realistic impression by playing down unnatural elements in his humour. Surrealism occurs in dreams or in imagery, not in direct narrative. Coincidence is not impossibly far-fetched. And he makes frequent use of a favourite technique, surprise. Humorous shocks abound in *ALR,* and even as they jolt us into laughter, they contribute to the impression that we are reading about actual people, who are just as likely to be unpredictable as their real-life counterparts. A cheap prostitute reappears as a famous actress, a tailor's niece as a great noblewoman, a womanizer as a homosexual. To Proust, this element of surprise is more than a technique, it is the expression of his view of reality, which is not static, not even palpable, because what is real at one moment may later prove to be false.

How does caricature fit in with this view of his characters as 'real'? In the first place, caricature often creates an impression that is less artificial than it ought to be. Readers are so attuned to the existence of caricatures that they readily suspend disbelief and give credence to extravaganzas like the portrayal of Mme Blatin. Furthermore, Proust rarely leaves his caricatures alone. They are not predictable and static; they too have the ability to surprise and shock. Octave, the languid, impassive young man whose energies are exclusively spent on frivolity, amazes us by becoming a writer of genius. Again, Proust uses both the predictability of caricature and the humorous shock in character portrayal to make an ultimate criticism of social life and its shallowness. Caricatures are puppets, whose preoccupation with their superficial, predictable existence is ridiculous. They are despicable because they have so little independence that their next move can be foreseen. Surprise devalues social structures in a different way, based on the initial assumption that the *status quo* is of paramount importance to almost all the characters. When Proust repeatedly turns the social structure upside down, he is showing how unstable and shallow their world really is.

Proust's humour is not only an important technique in his portrayal of character. It is an essential narrative tool, an integral part of the book. One of the ways in which he fixes humour firmly in the novel is by the use of repetition. The fact that he thinks of certain subjects in terms of a particular type of humour creates a series of threads that run through the novel, stringing the different episodes together. There are conscious *leitmotive*, which have been discussed in the chapters on imagery and character. There are also irresistible parallels that well up from his subconscious. The repeated comparisons between aristocrats and trees form a conscious link between the different aristocrats throughout the book; and his attitude to servants in livery is perhaps an unconscious variation on this sort of treatment. Servants always suggest something frail, delicate, vaguely effeminate, and though there is a great variety of images describing them, these tend to contain an element of fragility or girlishness. They are angels, carefully swaddled babies, hothouse plants, Israelite girls. Each individual humorous image is enhanced by the vague memory of the other similar parallels. Proust can vary this technique to suit his subject-matter. With the group of young girls at Balbec, he makes a point of using a widely disparate selection of humorous parallels. At one stage the images emphasize their composite character, at another their separate personalities; now their toughness, now their ladylike elegance; now again their childish-ness, now their veneer of sophistication. He is using his humorous imagery as an illustration of the fact that the young girls have reached a crucial point in their lives when they change from childhood to adult-hood; the variety of humorous parallels echoes this metamorphosis.

This example shows Proust using humour to make a serious point. He repeatedly does this, even when considering the most painful subjects. His treatment of jealousy, for instance, is almost entirely serious. Yet even here there can be a humorous element which shows up the solemn emotion in a new light. There are situations that seem to parody the main theme of the Narrator's jealousy of Albertine. The child Narrator's somewhat naïve jealousy and anguish over Gilberte is a case in point, as are the more ludicrous sufferings inflicted on M. de Charlus by Morel. These humorous parallels make the point that however serious something may be to oneself, the same thing may be ridiculous when viewed in retrospect or when applied to others.

Most often the serious and the humorous will be interspersed, for a variety of reasons. The material is likely to seem more interesting if seen from more than one point of view, just as an architect's model is more interesting than a mere blueprint. Furthermore, the fact that the same thing can appear both serious and humorous is very important to Proust, and relates to his conviction that there is no absolute reality.

Proust frequently regards this flux between serious and humorous as funny in itself. The changes and surprises in *ALR* tend to be viewed in a humorous light: the reader is jolted out of his complacency: just as he thinks he has the situation under control, Proust turns everything upside down, and he has to start from the beginning again. It is not for nothing that the final manifestation of this change, the great last scene, is a comic one. Moreover, just as the novel ends with a humorous scene, so its elements are introduced on the same note. The majority of the characters seem funny when they first appear, however serious they are to become later. Mme de Guermantes is introduced as the possessor of a large red nose, Françoise with her hand outstretched, hypocritically eager for a tip, Odette as an ex-tart who thinks she is too good for the great ladies of the Faubourg Saint-Germain. However seriously we may later come to take the characters, we should not forget how absurd they seemed at a first glance.

On the whole, the humorous aspect of *ALR* will be incomprehensible without an understanding of its serious side. We have seen how both moods colour each other: Odette's absurd salon is given a serious introduction and thereafter seems far less ridiculous than the more aesthetic, intellectual salon of Mme Verdurin, which has been mocked at from the first.

Proust seems to be combining humour with its direct opposite in relating it to the serious. But perhaps the true opposite of humour is tragedy. Being opposites lends a certain affinity to the two *genres*. The very funny can readily seem tragic and vice versa. As a result, as La Bruyère says, comedy and tragedy are very closely related. Proust seems to bear out this view, and frequently shifts from one mood to the other, or combines the two in a passage. The searing death of the grandmother gives him scope for sustained humour, as does the most tragic moment in M. de Charlus's life, that of his public humiliation by Morel. Excessive grief is generally laughed at, either overtly (witness Bloch's lamentations when the Narrator is indisposed) or implicitly (when the Narrator's tears at losing Mme de Stermaria are juxtaposed with the rolled-up carpets and dusty furniture of his dining-room). Laughter does not always accompany grief (there is no humour in the Narrator's sorrow at Albertine's death). But most often the two do go together, and juxtaposing these two emotional extremes makes both stand out by mutual contrast.

Another subject closely associated with humour is beauty. One reason for this close association may be the subjective nature of one's response to beauty. One has to be honest, to lay bare one's emotions. In such a situation the individual is vulnerable and open to mockery. He becomes even more ridiculous if he tries to protect himself by responding insincerely to beauty. Mockery of the many permutations and aberrations in one's response to beauty is frequent in Proust's writing. It reveals the same preoccupation as his introspective fascination with his own response to beauty, which finds its expression in his most poetic writing.

So there is an essential link between humour and poetry. We have seen that poetic imagery and humour are trying to do the same thing, to establish unexpected relations between things. It has become clear that humour is related to many of Proust's most important preoccupations, and that in a sense the exercise of viewing the humour in isolation from the other elements in his work has been a highly unrealistic one.

This is particularly true of *ALR*. Unlike *JS*, it always seems close to laughter. Proust chooses to combine lyrical descriptions of Nature with the naïvety of childhood and country life; to set an emotional love-affair in an absurd salon full of affected caricatures; to juxtapose the torments of the invert with his ludicrous style of life; to introduce comic characters into a tragic death scene. The greater part of the novel comprises this sort of juxtaposition between humour and other elements. It is because the captivity of Albertine contains no essential humour (though there is much of an incidental kind) that it stands out, together with her death, as the most painful part of the novel. One need not conclude from this that the humour detracts from the essential seriousness of other episodes: it simply makes them bearable. How else could we endure the flagellation of M. de Charlus, the refusal of Mme de Guermantes to acknowledge Swann's daughter and grant his dying wish, or Mme Verdurin's selfishness in pointlessly separating Brichot from the only person he loves, the prop and stay of his old age?

This brings us to another problem: despite the integral part played by the humour, *ALR* is first and foremost a serious novel. It seems reasonable to suggest that humour has several serious functions in it. First, like Voltaire, Proust may sugar a pill that would otherwise be too bitter to swallow. By the time we finish the novel, we have been subjected to a full-scale indictment of society, an utterly disillusioned exposure of love and human relationships, and a horrifying demonstration of the ephemeral nature of man and his ultimate defeat by Time. Yet we are able to accept, and perhaps share, the Narrator's final standpoint, which is one of serenity and hope.

Another, and very different, function of humour is as a weapon of criticism. It is by laughing at society that Proust criticizes it. We can see, by comparing this method with *JS* (where Proust allowed his resentment of society serious expression), how effective this weapon is. On the whole, he uses humour in this way when he stands aside as a dispassionate and amused observer before the self-important posturing of his characters: his mockery is particularly powerful as it is the last thing that the characters themselves could tolerate.

Further, humour is occasionally used to condone or attenuate. It is through humour that we can sympathize with the predicament of homosexuals or social climbers. It is not simply that Proust is using humour to enable us to stomach strong meat like scenes of sexual sadism; he is asking us to sympathize through laughter. When we are confronted with eccentrics like Tante Léonie, we are made to smile, and not allowed to remain detached and aloof.

I have said that Proust uses humour not only as an element of narrative technique, but also as a vehicle for his own philosophy. What, then, does he reveal in this way? First, there is a theory behind his readiness to shift from the humorous to other moods. Not only will he treat the same subjects both seriously and humorously, but he will shift from one mood to the other and back again without any warning. Why does he feel so free to do so? The answer, I think, lies in his conception of the writer's duty to his subject-matter. He reiterates the belief that the important thing is for the writer to be absolutely honest. The subject-matter is virtually irrelevant: anything is worth writing about if one can really render genuine perceptions, since

Ce travail de l'artiste, de chercher à apercevoir sous de la matière, sous de l'expérience, sous des mots quelque chose de différent, c'est [. . .] justement le seul art vivant. (*TR* III 896)

If what matters is the way one penetrates the subject, not the subject itself, then there is no reason to assume that the most trivial or ridiculous subject, provided it be plumbed to its depths, is unworthy to stand beside the most noble and grandiose theme. He expressed scorn for contemporary writers who were unaware of this essential fact (*TR* III 881).

As for the reader, Proust remains very much in control of him, choosing when to give us the illusion of independence and when to step in, criticizing or establishing 'correct' value judgements with which we must agree (so Vinteuil and Bergotte are geniuses, and people who disparage them are ridiculous).

The varied approach suggested here and elsewhere represents one of Proust's most fundamental beliefs concerning the attitude to the perception of reality. He shows us in *ALR* a protagonist searching for truth, continually attempting to distinguish between illusion and reality. This attempt is doomed from the start, because there is no objective reality, no absolute truth. So M. de Charlus can be at the same time deeply moving and a figure of fun. One cannot say which is the real M. de Charlus: both are equally real, equally illusory. Innumerable permutations of serious and humorous illustrate this point in Proust.

He sees reality as not only bewilderingly varied but even as self-contradictory. He constantly shows us two facets of an object that are irreconcilable opposites. He presents a confusing world which he makes no attempt to render consistent. This approach pervades the book, and makes for endless humour as he fluctuates between moods and standpoints and even between terseness and verbosity of style. He can make us laugh at this very fluctuation, and also make us mock at opposites: at bad and good taste, at naïvety and sophistication. An awareness of the universality of the ridiculous is central to his approach. A desire to be consistent is irrelevant.

The humour in Proust also reveals his attitude to the human condition. We have already seen how devastatingly critical he can be. He seems chiefly perturbed by the selfishness of man, which he attacks consistently and viciously, revealing almost every apparent act of altruism as just another instance of egoism. He can often seem bitter when he makes this point, which suggests a fundamental pessimism in his view of humanity. To him, man is a lonely, self-centred being who never enjoys the genuine support and co-operation of his fellows, and very rarely deserves it.

But at times he goes beyond the individual and reaches a more abstract attitude. Here one of his chief preoccupations is time: what changes it can effect, how to recapture it and so on. He often expresses this interest through the paradoxical type of humour: the truth at one time may contradict the truth at another.

Paradox is also used to express his wonderment. One of the strangest features of humanity to him is the way people sail blithely through life taking things for granted, competently disporting themselves on a sea of clichés and accepted attitudes. He takes nothing for granted, but sees everything through fresh eyes. If that makes it ridiculous, no matter.

In viewing Proust the craftsman together with Proust the philosopher, we are faced with a bewildering dichotomy. On the one hand we have the dazzling wit, the rapier-sharp mind; on the other the profound cynicism and pessimism of a totally disillusioned man. To reconcile the two, one must view the craftsman as a completely different person from the philosopher; one who put all the vigour and enthusiasm withdrawn from living into the construction of his masterpiece.

BIBLIOGRAPHY

The subject of the humour in Proust has been treated several times, with varying amounts of detail. It seemed helpful to supplement my bibliography by briefly describing the approach of other writers to this subject, as it often complements my own.

To begin with one of the earlier writers on Proust, Léon Pierre-Quint has a section on 'Le Comique de Proust' in his book *Marcel Proust, sa vie, son œuvre* (1928 edition onwards). His study was written at a time when, as he seems to have felt, readers were unaware of this element in Proust. This is no longer the case. A professed disciple of Bergson, Pierre-Quint devotes some space to 'le contraste entre le mécanisme et la vie' (p. 273). He briefly covers characters, style (word-plays, parodies, imagery), mentions Proust's use of anecdotes, reversals of situation, and misunderstandings.

André Maurois also devotes some twenty pages of his book *A la Recherche de Marcel Proust* to *l'humour*. After a brief definition, in which he claims as the object of humour 'de dégonfler certaines formes du sérieux qui nous oppriment' (a variation on the degradation theory), he discusses a selection of elements: the use of humour in three subjects (death, medicine, and snobbery), close observation of personalities, the use of mechanism and of contrast. He concludes with a section on some of the more extreme characters, or *monstres*. Despite the limited scope of a single chapter, this study is very interesting, and pinpoints some of the main tendencies in Proust's humour.

Germaine Brée, in her book *Du Temps perdu au temps retrouvé*, also has an interesting chapter on 'La Comédie humaine', though lack of space compels her to limit her study to comedy of character. She maintains that 'l'humour proustien repose presque toujours [. . .] sur l'incongruité entre deux aspects d'une situation' (p. 118). There are also two articles on the subject, both published in the *Bulletin de la Société des amis de Marcel Proust et des amis de Combray*. Michihiko Suzuki's article 'Le Comique chez Marcel Proust' (Nos. 11 and 12) is, however, more closely concerned with the process of composition of *ALR* than with humour. Mme Moulines's article, 'L'Humour et l'esprit dans l'œuvre de Marcel Proust' (No. 15) is extremely interesting. In only twenty-two pages, she defines humour, gives a lightning survey of Proust's development as a humorist, and distinguishes between 'l'humour' and 'l'esprit' in *ALR*. However, she is obliged to limit her study to the characters.

The subject has been treated at more length in two books, Lester Mansfield's *Le Comique de Proust* (1953) and Roland Donzé's *Le Comique dans l'œuvre de Marcel Proust* (1955).

Mr. Mansfield's book is short and very much biased towards character study. He rightly spends much time analysing social situations, snobbery and so on, but his treatment of style, imagery, and structure is correspondingly weak. Moreover, he is too anxious to stress the importance of 'le comique' and to prove that 'Marcel Proust fut avant tout un créateur comique' (p. 11), an exaggerated assertion which does not enable one to see Proust's humour in balanced relation to the rest of his work. Most important, the book fails to consider Proust's development as a humorist, since it was written before either *CSB* or *JS* were published.

Roland Donzé's book was published in 1955, and he refers to both *CSB* and *JS*, though he makes very little mention of the former. Nevertheless, Donzé's short book can by no means be considered to be the last word on Proust's humour. Much of it is concerned with the theory of humour in general, rather than with Proust. When he comes to examine Proust in detail, Donzé divides his study into the types of *comique* that he has found in Proust's work: *humour*, caricature, techniques of style, and imagery. He is interested in a wide, general approach, which is inevitable in such a short book, and which produces some interesting, some dubious results.

Finally, it is worth drawing attention to the many interesting works on pastiche that have been appearing recently, most of which are not specific studies of humour in pastiche, but which touch on this subject. These will be found amongst the works listed below.

I   Chief Works by Proust

For a full bibliography in chronological order of publication, see Philip Kolb and Larkin B. Price, *Textes retrouvés*, pp. 263–90.

Les Plaisirs et les jours, and *Jean Santeuil*, published together, Gallimard, Paris, 1971.

Contre Sainte-Beuve, and *Pastiches et mélanges*, published together with Proust's main journalistic articles and essays on the arts, Gallimard, Paris, 1971.

A la Recherche du temps perdu, Gallimard, Paris, 1954.
Correspondance générale, Plon, Paris, 1930-6.
Correspondance de Marcel Proust, ed. Philip Kolb, Plon, Paris 1970.

For other letters not yet republished in the Kolb edition, see the bibliography mentioned above.

II Books and Articles on Proust

For a full bibliography, see Victor E. Graham, *Bibliographie des études sur Marcel Proust et son œuvre*, Droz, Geneva, 1976. The following works have been particularly relevant to this book:

Adam, A., 'Le Roman de Proust et le problème des clefs', *Revue des sciences humaines*, 1952, 359-65.

Alden, Douglas W., 'Proust and the Flaubert controversy', *Romanic Review*, vol. 28 (1937), 230-40.

Bailey, Ninette, 'Symbolisme et composition dans l'œuvre de Proust: essai de "lecture colorée" de la *Recherche du temps perdu*', *French Studies*, vol. 20 (1966), 253-66.

Barnes, Annie, 'Le Retour des thèmes dans la *Recherche du Temps perdu* et l'art de Proust', *Australian Journal of French Studies*, vol. 6 (1969), 26-54.

Beckett, Samuel, *Proust* (*in Proust and Three Dialogues with Georges Duthuit*), J. Calder, London, 1965 (*Proust* first published 1931).

Bersani, Leo, *Marcel Proust: The Fictions of Life and of Art*, Oxford University Press, New York, 1965.

Bonnet, Henri J. R., *Le Monde, l'amour et l'amitié. Le progrès spirituel dans l'œuvre de Marcel Proust*, Belles Lettres, Paris, 1950 (Etudes françaises 44).

Brée, Germaine, 'New Trends in Proust Criticism', *Symposium*, vol. 5 (1950), 62-71.

——, 'Marcel Proust: changing perspectives', *Australian Journal of French Studies*, vol. 1 (1964), 104-13.

——, 'Le "Moi œuvrant" de Proust', *Modern Language Review*, vol. 61 (1966), 610-18.

Brombert, Victor, 'Le Comique dans le roman de Proust' *Littérature Moderne* 2, 6 (Nov.-Dec. 1951).

Bulletin de la Société des amis de Marcel Proust et des amis de Combray, Illiers, 1950.

Butor, Michel, *Les Œuvres d'art imaginaires chez Proust*, University of London, Athlone Press, London, 1964.

Cahiers Marcel Proust, Les vols. 1–7, Gallimard, Paris, 1927–35.

Cahiers Marcel Proust: Nouvelle Série vols. 1–6, Gallimard, Paris, 1970–3.

Cattaui, Georges, *Marcel Proust*, Éditions Universitaires, 'Classiques du XXᵉ siècle', Paris, 1958.

Clarac, Pierre, and Ferré, André, *Album Proust*, Gallimard, Paris, 1964.

Cocking, John M., *Proust*, Bowes and Bowes (Studies in Modern European Literature and Thought), London, 1956.

Cordle, T. H., 'The Role of Dreams in *A la Recherche*', *Romanic Review*, vol. 42 (1951), 261–73.

Delattre, F., 'Bergson et Proust. Accords et dissonances', *Les Études bergsoniennes*, vol. i, Paris, 1948, 7–127.

Donzé, R. A., *Le Comique dans l'œuvre de Marcel Proust*, Attinger, Neuchâtel and Paris, 1955.

Duncan, J. Ann, 'Imaginary Artists in *A la Recherche du temps perdu*', *Modern Language Review*, vol. 64 (1969), 555–64.

Feuillerat, A., *Comment Marcel Proust a composé son roman*, Yale University Press (Yale Romain studies no. 7), New Haven, 1934.

Fowlie, Wallace, *A Reading of Proust*, Anchor Books, New York, 1964.

Galey, Matthieu, 'Une véritable comédie humaine' in *Proust* (Coll. 'Génies et Réalités'), Hachette, Paris, 1965.

Goodell, Margaret Moore, *The Snob in Literature*, Part I, 'Three Satirists of Snobbery: Thackeray, Meredith, Proust', Friedrichsen de Gruyter, Hamburg, 1939.

Graham, Victor E., *The Imagery of Proust*, Blackwell, Oxford, 1966.

Green, Frederick C., *The Mind of Proust. A detailed interpretation of "A la Recherche du temps perdu"*, Cambridge University Press, Cambridge, 1949.

——, 'Le Rire dans l'œuvre de Proust', *Cahiers de l'Association internationale des études françaises*, 12 (1960), 243–58.

Gutwirth, M. M., 'Le Portrait de Charlus dans l'œuvre de Proust', *Romanic Review*, vol. 40 (1949), 180–5.

Hicks, E. C., 'Swann's dream and the world of sleep', *Yale French Studies*, no. 34 (1965), 106–16.

Hier, Florence, *La Musique dans l'œuvre de Marcel Proust*, Institute of French Studies, Columbia University Press, New York, 1933.

Hindus, Milton, *The Proustian Vision*, Columbia University Press, New York, 1954.

Howard, R. G., 'The Construction of an episode in *A la Recherche du temps perdu*', *Australian Journal of French Studies*, vol. 4 (1967), 74–85.

Jefferson, L. M., 'Proust and Racine', *Yale French Studies*, no. 34 (1965), 99–105.

King, Clifford, 'The Laughter of Marcel Proust', *Adam International Review*, no. 260 (1957), 126–9.

Kolb, Philip, 'Inadvertent Repetitions of Material in *A la Recherche du temps perdu*', *Publications of the Modern Language Association of America*, vol. 51 (1936), 248–62.

—, *La Correspondance de Marcel Proust; Chronologie et commentaire critique*, University of Illinois Press, Illinois Studies in Language and Literature 33, 1–2, Urbana, 1949.

—, 'An Enigmatic Proustian metaphor', *Romanic Review*, vol. 54 (1963), 187–97.

—, 'Proust's Protagonist as a "Beacon" ', *Esprit créateur*, vol. 5 (1965), 38–47.

Kostis, Nicholas, 'Albertine: Characterization through Image and Symbol', *Publications of the Modern Language Association of America*, vol. 84, no. 1 (Jan. 1969), 125–35.

Le Sage, Laurence, *Marcel Proust and his Literary Friends*, University of Illinois Press, Illinois Studies in Language and Literature, no. 45, Urbana, 1958.

Linn, John Gaywood, 'Proust's Theatre Metaphors', *Romanic Review*, vol. 49 (1958), 179–90.

—, 'Notes on Proust's manipulation of chronology', *Romanic Review*, vol. 52 (1961), 210–25.

—, *The Theatre in the Fiction of Marcel Proust*, University of Ohio Press, Columbus, 1966.

Louria, Yvette, *La Convergence stylistique chez Proust*, Droz, Geneva, 1957.

—, 'Recent studies of Proust's stylistic and narrative techniques', *Romanic Review*, vol. 58 (1967), 120–6.

Mansfield, Lester, *Le Comique de Marcel Proust*, Nizet, Paris, 1953.

March, Harold, *The Two Worlds of Marcel Proust*, University of Pennsylvania Press, Philadelphia, 1948.

Maurois, André, *A la Recherche de Marcel Proust*, Hachette, Paris, 1949.

May, Gita, 'Chardin, vu par Diderot et par Proust', *Publications of the Modern Language Association of America*, vol. 72 (1957), 403–18.

Mein, Margaret, *A Foretaste of Proust: a Study of Proust and his*

Precursors, Saxon House, London, 1974.

Milly, Jean, 'Le pastiche Goncourt dans *Le Temps retrouvé*', *Revue d'histoire littéraire de la France*, 71, no. 5–6 (1971), 815–35.

——, *La Phrase de Proust*, Larousse, Paris, 1975.

Minogue, Valerie, *Proust: 'Du côté de chez Swann'*, Studies in French Literature no. 25, Edward Arnold, London, 1973.

Monnin-Hornung, Juliette, *Proust et la peinture*, Droz, Geneva, 1951.

Morrow, John H., 'The Comic Element in *A la Recherche*', *French Review* 27 (Dec. 1953) 114–21.

Moss, Howard, *The Magic Lantern of Marcel Proust*, Macmillan, New York, 1962.

Moulines, Madame, 'L'humour et l'esprit dans l'œuvre de Proust', *Bulletin* no. 15 (1965), 266–88.

Mouton, Jean, *Le Style de Marcel Proust*, Corrêa, Paris, 1948.

Muller, Marcel, *Les Voix narratives dans la 'Recherche du temps perdu'*, Droz, Geneva, 1965.

Nathan, Jacques, *Citations, références et allusions de Proust dans 'A la Recherche du temps perdu'*, Nizet, Paris, 1969.

——, 'Dickens et Proust: les Wittiterley et les Verdurin', *Bulletin* no. 14 (1964), 170–82.

O'Brien, Justin, 'An Aspect of Proust's Baron de Charlus', *Romanic Review*, vol. 55 (1964), 38–41.

——, 'Proust and "le joli langage" ', *Publications of the Modern Language Association of America*, 80 (1965), 259–65.

Philip, M., 'The Hidden Onlooker', *Yale French Studies*, no. 34 (1965), 37–42.

Pierre-Quint, Léon, *Marcel Proust: sa vie, son œuvre*, Paris (the edition quoted is the 1946 one, which contains the section on 'Le Comique et le mystère chez Proust', first included in 1928; the earliest edition appeared in 1925).

Pommier, J., 'Marcel Proust et Sainte-Beuve', *Revue d'Histoire littéraire de la France*, vol. 54 (1954), 536–42.

Poulet, Georges, *l'Espace proustien*, Gallimard, Paris, 1963.

Proust Research Association Newsletter, Lawrence, Kansas, 1969.

Remacle, Madeleine, *L'Élément poétique dans "A la recherche du temps perdu" de Marcel Proust*, Académie de Langue et de Littérature françaises de Belgique, Palais des Académies, Brussels, 1954.

Revel, Jean-François, *Sur Proust: remarques sur A la recherche du temps perdu*, Denoël, Paris, 1970.

Rogers, Brian G., 'The Rôle of Journalism in the Development of

Proust's Narrative Techniques', *French Studies*, vol. 18 (1964), 136–44.

—, *Proust's Narrative Techniques*, Droz, Geneva, 1964.

Rousset, Jean, 'Notes sur la structure d'*A la Recherche du temps perdu*', *Revue des sciences humaines*, 1955, 387–99.

Sayce, R. A., 'The Goncourt Pastiche in *Le Temps retrouvé*' in *Marcel Proust: A Critical Panorama*, ed. Larkin B. Price, University of Illinois Press, Urbana, 1973.

Seznec, Jean, *Marcel Proust et les dieux*, Clarendon Press, Oxford, 1962.

Shattuck, Roger, *Proust's Binoculars. A Study of Memory, Time and Recognition in 'A la Recherche du temps perdu'*, Random House, New York, 1963.

Slater, Maya, 'Some Recurrent Comparisons in *A la Recherche du temps perdu*', *Modern Language Review*, vol. 62 (1967) 629–32.

Spagnoli, John J., *The Social Attitude of Marcel Proust*, Publications of the Institute of French Studies, Columbia University, New York, 1936.

Sticca, Sandro, 'Anticipation as a Literary Technique in Proust's *A la Recherche du temps perdu*', *Symposium*, vol. 20 (1966), 254–61.

Strauss, Walter A., *Proust and Literature: The Novelist as Critic*, Harvard University Press, Cambridge, 1957.

Sullivan, Dennis G., 'On Vision in Proust: the Icon and the "Voyeur" '. *Modern Language Notes*, 84 (1969) 646–61.

Suzuki, Michihiko, 'Le Comique chez Marcel Proust', *Bulletin de la Société des Amis de Marcel Proust et des Amis de Combray*, Nos. 11 and 12, 1961, 377–89, 1962, 572–86.

Tadié, Jean-Yves, *Proust et le roman: essai sur les formes et techniques du roman dans 'A la Recherche'*, Gallimard, Paris, 1971.

Ullmann, Stephen, 'Transposition of Sensations in Proust's Imagery', *French Studies*, vol. 8 (1954), 28–43.

—, *Style in the French Novel*, Cambridge University Press, 1957.

—, *The Image in the Modern French Novel*, Cambridge University Press, 1960.

Vigneron, R., 'Structure de "Swann": prétentions et défaillances', *Modern Philology*, vol. 44 (1946-7), 102–28.

—, 'Structure de "Swann": Combray ou le cercle parfait', *Modern Philology*, vol. 45 (1947), 185–207.

Virtanen, Reino, 'Proust's Metaphors from the Natural and the Exact Sciences', *Publications of the Modern Language Association of*

America, vol. 69 (1954), 1038–59.

Winton, Alison, *Proust's Additions. The Making of 'A la Recherche du temps perdu'*, Cambridge University Press, Cambridge, 1977.

SUBJECT INDEX

INDEX OF NAMES